AMERICAN
EXODUS

To Sam + Copie ...
whose friendship
treasure !

E) Fight

AMERICAN EXODUS

A HISTORICAL NOVEL ABOUT INDIAN REMOVAL

_____

LE TRIPLETT

iUniverse, Inc.

New York Lincoln Shanghai

AMERICAN EXODUS
A HISTORICAL NOVEL ABOUT INDIAN REMOVAL

iUniverse books may be ordered through booksellers or by contacting:

iUniverse
2021 Pine Lake Road, Suite 100
Lincoln, NE 68512
www.iuniverse.com
1-800-Authors (1-800-288-4677)

The cover painting, *The Trail of Tears*, was painted by Robert Lindneux and was provided courtesy of Woolaroc Museum in Bartlesville, OK.

This is a work of fiction. All of the characters, names, incidents, organizations and dialogue in this novel are either the products of the author's imagination or are used fictitiously.

ISBN-13: 978-0-595-39588-0 (pbk)
ISBN-13: 978-0-595-83993-3 (cloth)
ISBN-13: 978-0-595-83991-9 (ebk)
ISBN-10: 0-595-39588-0 (pbk)
ISBN-10: 0-595-83993-2 (cloth)
ISBN-10: 0-595-83991-6 (ebk)

Printed in the United States of America

DEDICATED TO
NANCY ANN HODGE TRIPLETT

WHO INSISTED THAT OUR THREE SONS
ARN, LON, AND TIM KNOW SOMETHING
ABOUT THEIR HERITAGE

AND TO MY CHEROKEE GRANDMOTHER,
LILLIE MAE LAWRENCE RENFROW,
WHOSE REAL LIFE EXPERIENCES PLANTED SEEDS
FOR THIS NOVEL

ACKNOWLEDGEMENTS

I am awed by librarians and their stubborn refusal to quit before they locate the correct answer or the right book. I have benefited from the suggestions and assistance from the following: Jack Haley and Emily M. Myers, Western History Collections at the University of Oklahoma; Dr. Kenneth Coleman, Professor of History, University of Georgia; The Georgia Department of Archives and History, Atlanta, Georgia; Pat Edwards, Gilcrease Institute, Tulsa, Oklahoma; Harold F. Worthley, Congregational Christian Historical Society, Boston, Massachusetts; Dr. T. L. Ballenger, Professor of History, Northeastern Oklahoma State University, Tahlequah, Oklahoma; Helen Wheat and Dolores Sumner, Special Collection Librarians, John Vaughn Library, Northeastern Oklahoma State University, Tahlequah, Oklahoma; Paul H. Chamberlain and Marion A. Blake, Cornwall Historical Society, Cornwall, Connecticut; Sharon Johnson, Superintendent, Dahlonega Gold Museum, Dahlonega, Georgia; Susan M. Eltscher, Director of Library, American Baptist Historical Society, Valley Forge, Pennsylvania; Suzette Raney, Chattanooga Public Library, Chattanooga, Tennessee; Denver Public Library, Western History Collection, Denver, Colorado; The Oklahoma Historical Society; Barbara Fagen, Cleveland Public Library, Cleveland, Tennessee; Shirley Pettingill, Site Manager, George M. Murrell Home, Tahlequah, Oklahoma, James Sweaney, Library of Congress, and the staff at Michener Library, University of Northern Colorado, Greeley, Colorado.

Special thanks to Jane Simpson, Head Librarian, Sibley Cone Library, Milledgeville, Georgia for her unwavering assistance in searching for documents and to Dr. Gary Moulton, Thomas C. Sorensen, Professor of American History, University of Nebraska, Lincoln, Nebraska whose monumental work on John Ross papers kept this novel true to the chronology and thoughts of Ross.

Finally, my appreciation to June Petersen, copy editor, for her mastery of computer technology.

CHAPTER 1

TOHOPEKA—27 MARCH 1814

A pain in the gut roused him from a troubled sleep. He moaned and tried to control his bowels. His stomach squeezed and twisted as the dysentery clawed at his entrails. Flushed and feverish he mopped beads of sweat from his brow. No use trying calomel or laudanum. A sip of gin and water would have to do. As the general stretched for his canteen, a sharp pain flashed in his left shoulder. With his fingers he lightly brushed the festering wound. Another needle-sharp fragment of bone was working through his skin. "Damn that Jessie Benton," he muttered. Slowly, he withdrew the sliver. Five months had passed since the Nashville shootout and his shoulder was inflamed where the ball from Jessie's gun was embedded.

As he struggled to his feet, a wave of nausea swept over him. In the predawn light he made for a nearby live oak tree. Pressing his body hard against a low-lying limb secured a measure of relief. Why it worked, he didn't know. Though the pressure gave temporary respite from the spasms, it aggravated an old pain in his chest. He had lived with that pain for eight years. Charles Dickinson's gun had lodged a bullet in his chest too near the heart to be removed. "By the eternal," he grunted, "that sonuvabitch Dickinson will fight no more duels."

Looking to the east he watched the rising orb bronze the horizon and fade the stars overhead. Not a breath of air moved. For many days, a dome of stagnant, hot air had covered the southland. Today would be another scorcher. He took another sip of gin and gently booted his companion.

"Alright, John. Get your ass outta th' sack. Its fighting time."

Coffee stirred in his blanket. He had been awake for some time, listening to Jackson's restless movements. Casting aside his covers, he grumbled. "General, for god's sake, just once, ease up. You know damn well you ain't fit to set your saddle much less fight."

The general grinned. "Wellington figured Napoleon's presence on the battle-field was worth forty thousand men. Surely, I'm worth at least as much. Shurer'n hell, if I'm not there, my men will call me a pussy willow instead of Old Hick-ory." Jackson's visage turned stern. "Too much is riding on what happens today, John. I've got a score to settle with that sunovabitch, Weatherford."

Coffee shrugged. He knew the two recent defeats he had suffered at the hands of the Creeks had left Jackson seething for revenge.

"How many mounted troops we got, John?"

"Counting the five hundred Cherokees and about a hundred friendly Creeks, I'd guess something around thirteen or fourteen hundred."

"Good. Let's ride."

Shelocta, his Creek guide and interpreter, brought Jackson's horse. With effort, the general mounted and nudged his horse forward. Coffee followed alongside as Jackson rode through the troop encampment.

Over six feet tall, dressed in a uniform of coarse, blue cloth, yellow buckskin, and battered, high dragoon boots, Jackson looked every inch the commander. Barely forty-seven years of age, his once dark, red hair was iron gray. His sallow complexion and gaunt frame revealed the ravages of dysentery and long months of campaigning in the field. His erect carriage and penetrating blue eyes, eyes that mirrored both defiance and deeply-seated pain, bespoke of something else; a spirit that willed mastery over his body...and those about him. It was that spirit, Coffee knew, that not only held Jackson together but the army as well.

Jackson eyed his soldiers as he rode across the clearing. On the alert since long before dawn, the men were finishing a breakfast of fried mush and sow belly laced with liberal swigs of whiskey. It was a motley, rag-tag army at best, over two thousand Tennessee men dressed mostly in nut-brown homespun and buckskin hunting shirts and leggings. They were crude, dirty, and unlettered but skilled in the art of survival on an unforgiving frontier. Jackson knew these unruly men, not accustomed to imposed discipline, were as likely to vote to go home as they were to volunteer to fight. It all depended upon the availability of food, whiskey, and the status of their enlistment period.

Smoke from the cooking fires rose lazily in the calm, morning air. Below its steady rise the men went about their business, coughing, swearing, packing bed-rolls, relieving themselves in the pines, seeing to their horses, and inspecting rifles—age old rituals for an awakening army.

On the other side of the clearing, more orderly action was taking place. Another body of men was readying itself for relocation but its actions were exe-cuted in a defined, systematic, fashion. The 39th Regiment of the United States Infantry, 360 in number, was striking its tents and preparing to march. Only their white crossbelts and tall shakos distinguished them as regulars. That regulars were the only ones issued tents was just one of the factors that riled the volunteers whose lot it was to unroll blankets under the trees. Knowing the feelings that existed between volunteers and regulars, Jackson had wisely camped them sepa-rately.

The 39th had been recruited and trained by Thomas Hart Benton, who had high hopes of seeing action. Because the shootout in Nashville between Jackson and the Bentons was so recent, feelings were still raw and Benton had been returned to recruiting.

Jackson observed, "These are good men, Coffee. Well trained, disci-plined…they will not only serve as a model for the volunteers but discourage them from mutiny or desertion."

"Mornin', Gen'rul Jackson."

A blue-eyed, young giant with wavy chestnut hair from the 39th grinned up at Jackson.

A smile of pleasure cracked Jackson' grim features. "Mornin', Lieutenant Houston. I trust you are ready for the day's festivities."

"General, I'm as ready as a bitch in heat."

"I'd never throw water on a bitch in heat. Spoils all the fun." The general sobered. "Take care today, Sam. Weatherford's Creeks are tough as mulehide and mean as hell."

"I know," Houston responded, "but I think we're ready for them."

"Ready is what we ain't. Summon all the officers to meet with me and we'll get ready in a helluva hurry."

Houston grinned and threw a casual salute. "Consider it done, Gen'rul."

"Good man, that Sam Houston," Coffee ventured.

"We'll soon know," Jackson murmured. "We'll soon know."

*   *   *   *

Jackson watched through a cloud of powdery, red dust as a thousand mounted Cherokees, led by the halfbreed Gideon Morgan, departed to take positions south of the horseshoe bend in the river. In the clearing dust he noted a solitary figure standing beside his horse. Nudging his mount closer, Jackson could see the figure was no more than a mere youth. In one hand the lad held the reins of a magnificent sorrel; in the other he held a long Tennessee rifle.

"Seems to me, you're gonna get left behind if you don't get on that nag and high-tail it," ventured Jackson.

"She ain't no nag."

Bemused at the note of defiance in the boy's voice, the general looked down at two belligerent eyes set in a face smudged with dust and smoke. Too young for a razor, the face showed no recent acquaintance with soap and water. A picture flickered through Jackson's mind of another boy, about this age, in another war, defying a British officer.

"Well, nag or no nag, you'd better mount and catch up with your company."

"Can't do that. She threw a shoe coming into camp last night."

"And you wait until now to do something about it? Why-n-hell didn't you have the farrier take care of it? Or is this just your way of missing the fight?"

The youngster clenched his fists and stepped toward the general.

"Ginrul, this boy ain't no coward. Nosiree! In fact, he rode all night just to get here in time for the fight. Rode into camp just before sunup, he did. He lost kin-folk at Ft. Mims, he did, and he's here after scalps. Watch em general; yours may be the first." With that, gunnery Sgt. "Boots" Brill doubled up wheezing and coughing over his own humor.

"Brill, you've had too much of that bust-head."

"Never too much, general. I hope to tell ya'" Brill cackled. "Besides, I made this myself."

Jackson turned back to the boy. "What's your name, son? Where ya from?"

The lad drew himself up to his full height. "Hanks, sir. Thomas Jefferson Hanks. Folks just call me Tom."

"How old you be, Tom?"

"Fourteen...goin' on fifteen." Noting the skeptical look on Jackson's face, he hurried to add, "I'm old enough to fight, general."

"Well, son" replied Jackson in a gentle tone, "You can't fight on a lame horse. Sgt. Brill, get this boy another horse." He threw a glance at the sun, then looked at his watch to confirm his appraisal. "It's time to get moving."

Although Jackson did not expect an ambush, a detail of soldiers was sent out in advance of the column. A work detail, equipped with axes to clear the trail of any fallen timbers, followed close behind. As the army uncoiled, it stretched into a ragged, mile-long column.

For Houston the march was becoming agony, a torment of heat, dust, and thirst. The sun's rays pressed down with the blast of a furnace. Thousands of boots kicked up a choking dust that fogged the listless air and masked his face with reddish powder. Rivulets of salty sweat coursed downward through the grime, eroding the geography of Houston's features. Under the stiff shako his sun-baked mind pulsated in and out of reality.

What had brought him to this suffocating wilderness? Why was a young man, just past his twenty-first birthday, placing himself in a place of such danger and fear? What motivated a pretense of bravery when this could be his last day on earth? Was it the pride of a slighted son that had caused him to run away from home to live with the Cherokee? And his years with the Cherokee…was it their carefree, unhurried way of life that he admired so much? Was it the easy ways of the Cherokee maidens that lingered so strongly in his memory? When the war with the English came, was it some strange, inner drive to prove himself that compelled him to step forward on the 24th of March last year to pick up a silver dollar from the drumhead of the army recruiter? And what perverse sense of pride caused him to utter the boast, "Maryville will hear of me before I return"?

Awareness of a shadow falling across his path brought Houston back to the present. Jackson reined in alongside, his horse stained red with dust and foam.

"How ya' like eatin' this dust, Houston?"

"At least we ain't walking in horse shit, general."

Jackson grinned. "Well, it won't be long now. The Tallapoosa is just ahead." He rode in silence for a moment.

"Tell me, Houston, ever kill a man?"

"No, sir. I've done my share of fightin' and hell-raisin' but can't say as I've ever had cause to kill anybody."

"Ever kill a redskin?"

"I just told ya', general, I've never killed any man."

"Killing a white man is one thing, Houston. Killing an injun is another matter altogether. Let me tell you, it's not dishonest to cheat an injun, it's not criminal to rob him, and it ain't murder to kill the scum. You're doing your country a favor any time you kill one."

Houston shot a puzzled glance at Jackson but said nothing.

"Understand you spent a lot of time with them Cherokee. What th' hell fer?"

Houston wiped his brow with a sleeve. "Well, I dunno, general. No particular reason. Just like them, I guess. They seem to know how to live. There ain't a dog-eat-dog way with them."

Jackson shifted in his saddle. "Look, Houston, I can understand a young man with fire in his prick enjoying some easy nookie with those Cherokee girls. Hell, yes! They are damn, fine-looking women. But where is that gonna get you in the long run? What future is there for you with those pitiful aborigines...a dying race?"

Again, Houston did not respond.

"What ya planning to do with yourself once this campaign is over?"

"Beats the hell out of me, general. Right now I'm more concerned about being alive when that sun goes down...if it ever does."

Jackson refused to be diverted. "Look at this land, Houston. The soil is ready for the plow. It will produce thousands of bales of cotton. Just look at the timber, just waiting for the axe. And there is gold in this country. Soon this very land we are marching on will be a state, not just a wilderness inhabited by savages in Georgia territory. And with Jefferson buying Louisiana from the French, our country now stretches from the Atlantic to the Pacific. Like a beautiful, virgin, this land is wild and fertile just waiting for men with the balls to take it. Wake up, my boy, wake up. Destiny is an impatient lady."

Before Houston could respond, Jackson spurred his horse to the head of the column.

*   *   *   *

By ten o'clock they had reached Horseshoe Bend, so called because the river formed a shape like a horseshoe. In short order Jackson had some two thousand troops deployed across the neck of the peninsula. The 39th Infantry was to lead the attack. From a small, tree-covered hill on its west side, Jackson surveyed the ground before him through his glass. The Horseshoe enclosed about a hundred acres, furrowed with gullies and covered with timber and thick brush. At the southern end of the stronghold he could see smoke lazily ascending from the fires in the Tohopeka village. He reckoned that the Creeks had wintered there. Now he swung his glass to an object of much greater concern. Across the neck of the peninsula the Creeks had erected a breastwork of green logs. Jackson estimated the wall to be about 350 yards wide and from five to eight logs high. Two rows of loopholes were strategically located. The jagged bulwark was shaped like a shallow crescent so that an attacking force would be exposed to crossfire while the defenders could not be enfiladed. His scouts had reported accurately; the cleared ground in front of the breastwork was so stump infested that it precluded use of cavalry.

"Those bloody, British bastards," the general swore audibly.

"You must be seein' things, general. There ain't a redcoat in sight."

"You're right, Brill. But there's every sign they've had a hand in this. No Creek savage is smart enough to erect defenses like these." Jackson lowered his glass and turned to Brill. "Alright, sergeant, you see what has to be done. Train your cannon on the center of that wall and be ready to blow it to hell when I give the order." With that he spurred his horse down the hill toward the 39th Infantry.

"Alright, boys," wheezed Brill. "You heard the general." Overweight and booze induced stupor seemed to count for naught as Brill and his sons, Virgil and Junior, turned into an efficient team of action. The two-wheeled vehicle, to which the gun trail was attached for transport, was quickly uncoupled from the gun carriage. Mules and limber were dispatched to the rear. With muscle on the wheels and ropes on the twin-tail, the cannon was wrestled into place with its muzzle pointing directly toward the center of the breastwork. Bullets whined and knocked bark from the trees overhead as Creek snipers detected activity on the hill.

"You two," shouted Brill, "off yer asses and hep unload that cart." To Virgil and Junior fell the task of unloading and stacking cannon balls near the muzzle of the gun. As they piled the six-pound iron shot, a safe and simple assignment for an untrained soldier, another smaller cannon was being readied alongside by another crew.

"I figure the range about 250 yards," Brill grunted. He sighted down the barrel and fiddled with the elevating screw mechanism. "Let's load 'er up."

Though lacking in formality, the Brills functioned smoothly enough to reflect credit on regular army procedures. The tampion was removed from the muzzle and the dust cover from the vent hole. The sponge, a wooden cylinder about a foot long and covered with lambskin, was dampened with water. Mounted on a long staff, the sponge was thrust into the bore of the cannon to clear it, a necessary precaution after each firing thereafter to make sure no sparks remained in the barrel. A charge of powder, followed by wadding, was thrust home with a rammer. The rammer, attached to the opposite end of the shaft holding the sponge, was a wooden cylinder about the same diameter as the shot. A cannon ball, after being carefully brushed for sand and mud, was next rammed home. Brill put the primer in the vent then turned and reached for his jug.

"That's it, boys, 'til the general gits back. Better tend to your drinkin' and pissin' cause it's gonna get a damn-site hotter in a few minutes." With that, Brill slumped against a tree trunk to catch his breath.

*　　*　　*　　*

On the field Houston stood at the head of his platoon, the fiery sun beating down relentlessly. He wiped the sweat from his forehead and shifted the grip on his musket. He flinched as the hot metal burned his hand. What was it his mother had said before he left home, when she had given the musket to him as a going-away gift? He tried to remember…tried not to think of the heat…tried not to think of what waited beyond the ominous log wall just a rifle shot ahead.

"My son, take this musket and never disgrace it; for remember, I had rather all my sons should fill one honorable grave than that one of them should turn his back to save his life. Go, and remember too, that while the door of my cabin is always open to brave men, it is eternally shut against cowards." In spite of the heat, a cold tremor rippled down his spine.

*　　*　　*　　*

John Ross hunkered under the shady willows that bordered the river. The smell and the coolness of the water beckoned.

"How come you didn't argue with Jackson when he sent us here? We'll miss out on all the fighting and he will get all the glory."

"John, you don't argue with Jackson," Morgan replied. "Remember, I'm married to his wife's niece and I know that man's temper."

"That cannon's been boomin' for the last two hours. Something must have gone wrong with his plans."

"Nothing ever goes wrong with Jackson's plans, Ross, you should know that. He's never had a day's training in military affairs but he thinks he's Napoleon. I'm gonna move ahead and see what's up."

Left alone, Ross looked around. The Cherokee were spread out, concealed in the thick growth along the riverbank. Jackson had sent them here to prevent any Creek reinforcements from the south, and any escapes from the peninsula. The muddy river, about 120 yards wide at this point, flowed deep and sluggish around the bend. Its ocher color reminded Ross of coffee...coffee loaded with rich cream which Quatie served him at home. What was Quatie doing now? He had left in such a hurry. Dear God, he should be home what with her being pregnant and having the care of six year old Susan and his elderly father. He should be home tending to business. Since the second war with England had begun in June of 1812, business at Ross' Trading Post on the Tennessee River had been good. Blankets, lead, powder, canvass, and foodstuffs were in high demand for the soldiers and militia on the western frontier. Through the United States Indian Agent to the Cherokee, Return J. Meigs, he had contracts with the United States Government to supply them. He also had a brisk trade going with some of the Cherokee who were outfitting themselves before emigrating west of the Mississippi.

To his left Ross could see Sequoyah, bent over, tracing lines in the sand, oblivious to activity around him. Fascinated at an early age by the magic of the white man's "talking leaves", Sequoyah had, for the past half-dozen years, been attempting to develop a set of characters that would express the sense and sound of the Cherokee language. Now, in his early fifties, and slowed by a limp, Ross questioned the wisdom of his being on this campaign. Yet, Ross knew, when it came to loyalty, there were none more faithful than Sequoyah.

Near the water's edge Ross could see Major Ridge, Charles Reese, The Whale, Tobacco Juice, and Junaluska engaged in animated conversation. Bony of body, grayed by time, and scarred by battle, Junaluska was not to be denied what might be his last battle.

Major Ridge, so named because of the rank bestowed upon him by Jackson at the outset of this campaign, was indisputably responsible for recruiting the six to eight hundred Cherokees who were assisting Jackson in putting down the rebel Creeks. Although only in his early 40s, his commanding countenance was already thatched with gray. Ross, even though twenty years younger, felt a close kinship with Ridge.

Someone slipped quietly into place beside Ross. "Had any bucks making eyes at you lately?"

Ross grinned at his brother's reference to the white deer tail each Cherokee had attached to his hair as a means of identification. "Not so's you'd notice, little brother. Who's this with you?"

"Name's Hanks," replied the boy. "I'm hungry."

"What's going on down there with Reese and Ridge?"

"I have a pretty good idea," said Lewis. "Look across the river." On the opposite bank the Creeks had several canoes drawn up on the gravel beach. They would serve as a means of escape if the battle went against them.

"You're right," responded Ross. "Those guys intend to steal those canoes. Come on. Let's get in on this."

Before he and Lewis could slip through the willows, Reese, The Whale, and Tobacco Juice stripped to the waist and quietly slid into the river. As Ross peered through the pale, green leafage of the willows, he noticed movement in the Creek village.

From one of the huts a strikingly, beautiful Creek maiden emerged. Intent on securing water, she approached the river just as Reese and his companions crawled onto the beach.

"Damn poor timing," whispered Lewis. Ross nodded silently. With held breath they watched the maiden near the water. She hesitated. Sensing the danger, she wheeled and ran toward the village screaming an alarm. Drawing his knife, The Whale scrambled to his feet in pursuit. A Creek warrior appeared at the door of the hut, leveled his rifle and fired. The Whale crumbled.

"Give 'em cover, boys," Ross yelled. Immediately, the Cherokees laid down a withering, covering fire as Reese and Tobacco Juice frantically paddled canoes on a return crossing. Soon as they reached shore, the canoes were filled with armed men. Led by Major Ridge, they pushed hard for the opposite shore. A frenzied shuttle across the stream was soon underway. John, Lewis, and Hanks crowded into a canoe.

Across the river they found resistance to be light. They moved quickly toward the Creek village. Forcing the women and children from the lodges, the Cherokees fired the village and moved northward where the Creek Red Sticks were concentrated at the barricade. Upon hitting the shore, Ross dashed to the side of The Whale who was conscious but bleeding profusely. Ross set about to stanch the flow.

"This ought to teach me not to chase women," The Whale joked. Then he passed out.

From inside one of the burning lodges, Hanks heard a cry. Rushing into the smoke, he scooped up a child and ran out just as the lodge collapsed. At a safe distance from the fires, he placed the youngster in the shade of a tree. As he stood to leave, the toddler grasped an amulet hanging around Hank's neck. Anxious to join the battle, Hanks thought, "What the hell, let him have it."

*   *   *   *

With ill-concealed anger, Jackson watched as the cannon balls buried themselves in the green timbers or bounced harmlessly against them. "Keep firing, Brill. Blow the hell outta that wall…get my infantry through," his shrill voice alternating with the cannon roar.

The sun rose higher and hotter as the minutes ticked into hours. A rage built within Jackson as he watched the ineffectual pounding of the six pounder. The jeering and taunting of the Red Sticks added to his fury. With shouted challenges and obscene gestures, the Creeks tormented his men. Jackson stewed in his helplessness. He swore under his breath. Damn! This could not be happening. After all these months of struggle to secure troops in strength, then having to tyrannize them to keep them from desertion; after kissing the collective ass of Washington bureaucracy for necessary food and supplies, he could not fail. He had courted dismissal, or worse, for his open contempt for the ways his superiors, including President Madison, were conducting "Madison's gentlemen's war." Now! This moment! He had the troops in strength. He had the enemy outnumbered and cornered. But he could not come to grips with them. If he ordered his infantry to attack the barricades, he would be exposing them to certain slaughter. Damned if he would have that on his record! No, bygod, he would not be another in the long string of military debacles that had beset American troops since the war began.

"Look, general!"

Jackson's gaze followed the direction Brill was pointing. His despair, frustration, and indecision vanished at the sight. Pillars of smoke were rising over the pines at the south end of the peninsula. Coffee must have crossed over and fired the village! The Red Sticks were now caught between his forces. Glancing down at the barricade, Jackson saw groups of Creeks slipping back into the brush to meet the new threat. They, too, had seen the smoke. Now! Now, bygod, was the time to commit his troops!

*   *   *   *

After more than two hours waiting in the blistering sun, the signal to attack was almost welcomed by Houston. As they moved forward with disciplined tread, he measured by eye the distance to the log barricade. The Creeks were firing madly but Houston knew that their British supplied Brown Bess muskets were not accurate beyond fifty yards. It was small consolation to know that the Harper's Ferry musket carried by the 39th Infantry was only slightly more effective. He would have preferred the Kentucky rifle which the Tennessee militia had brought. Those volunteers, who provided their own weapons, were deadly up to 300 yards with the rifle.

As they approached the barricade, the regulars unconsciously quickened their pace. The longer they were exposed in the open, the more vulnerable. Better to close with the enemy at the wall.

A zing of an arrow and a soldier to his right moaned and slumped to the ground. As if on signal, the troops voiced a throaty roar and charged the wall. Houston was sure he was yelling but his words were lost amidst the firing. In the dust and smoke, filtering a reddened sun, swearing and screaming men locked in mortal combat. In the bedlam, shouts of meaningless obscenities filled the air. Directed to no one in particular, the hoarse shouts were essential and primitive elements of battle…to screen off the panic…to block the mind to paralyzing fear…fear of the unthinkable!

Suddenly, the wall loomed. Men flailed in hand to hand conflict at the portholes while others struggled to scale the logs with their thirteen-pound muskets. Ahead of him Houston saw Major Montgomery assail the rampart and topple backward. A warrior raised both arms in exultation as the major fell. Taking quick aim, Houston shot the warrior dead. No time to reload the musket in this melee. He threw it to the ground, drew his sword and mounted the wall. A flash of pain hit his thigh. He leaped down into a maelstrom of smoke, dust, and blood. Desperately fending off assailants with his blade, he felt himself going down, unable to stay on his feet. Through eyes blurred with pain, Houston saw the shadow of a huge warrior loom over him. He saw the gleam of the raised tomahawk. Too weak to defend himself, he waited for the end. The blow never came. As he crumpled to the ground, his ears rang from the blast of a musket at close range. His hands groped for the leg which was afire. Now he could feel it…an arrow deeply embedded in his thigh. With hands wet and slippery with blood, he grasped the shaft and pulled. Agony racked his body.

"Y'all alright, lieutenant?"

A face spun in his misty vision. "Hell no, you stupid bastard, I ain't alright. Help me get this damned thing out," he panted.

"I dunno, lieutenant. That looks purty deep."

"Pull it out, I tell you!"

The soldier pulled. Blood spurted but the arrow stuck.

"Lieutenant, you'd better have the surgeon tend to this…"

Maddened with pain, Houston brandished his sword. "Pull it out, godammit, or I'll run you through."

The soldier planted his feet and grasped the arrow with both hands. "Better brace yourself, sir. This is gonna hurt like hell."

He pulled. Houston screamed. The barbed arrow came free, festooned with chunks of flesh, along with a gush of blood. His head swimming with nausea, Houston leaned against the wall and vomited. Around him carnage covered the blood-soaked ground. Sounds of the continuing battle now emanated from the timber south of him. His jaw set tightly, he stumbled off to find a surgeon. Behind him, a giant warrior moaned then lapsed into unconsciousness.

From his vantage on the hill Jackson watched his men overrun the barricade then drop into a cauldron of smoke, dust, and slaughter. Outnumbered three to one, the Creeks fought savagely with guns, knives, tomahawks, and naked courage. Pushed back from the wall, they retreated into the undergrowth and fought on in small groups. Several battles raged at once. No quarter was given. Band after band of warriors were encircled by the troops and slain to a man.

By mid-afternoon Jackson ordered a cease-fire. He sent his interpreter, Selocta, to explain to the Creeks that all who surrendered now would be spared. Selocta's voice was gentle and persuasive. The Red Sticks hesitated, uncertain. Menawa, their leader, was no where to be seen and there was no one else to speak for them.

During this lull, this fleeting moment pregnant with peace, a lone, white cloud appeared in the western sky. The Red Stick's prophets broke the spell. With shouts and bursts of fervent incantations, the prophets, with red-dyed cowtails in each hand, urged resumption of hostilities. This was a sign! The Great Spirit was with them. He would grant them victory. The trance was broken. Creek warriors renewed their fighting with fanatic frenzy. Selocta spurred his horse toward safety in a hail of bullets.

As the afternoon wore on, greatly outnumbered, uncoordinated in battle, and running low on ammunition, the Creeks were systematically slaughtered. Even with bayonet at throat, not one warrior offered to surrender. Some attempted to escape down the river in canoes, on logs, or by swimming. Anticipating this, Lieutenant Jesse Bean, with about forty men, had taken a fifteen-acre island, which lay in the river directly opposite the western end of the breastwork. The Creeks were picked off like squirrels as they attempted to flee down the river. Some hid in caves and brush along the riverbanks. Jackson promptly ordered the brush to be torched. In the tortured terrain south of the barricade, some Creeks held on. Several holed up in a ravine, well covered with fallen timbers. In this natural bunker they were able to inflict maximum casualties while suffering little themselves. Peering through his glasses, Jackson could see only one solution.

"I need some volunteers to burn those bastards out."

The soldiers, exhausted, wounded, and fearful, looked intently at the grass between their feet or gazed vacantly into the distance. A feverish lieutenant struggled to his feet.

"Gimme a musket. I'll go."

"You're crazy as hell, Houston. Sit down. You ain't in no shape to even walk."

Houston seized a musket from one of the soldiers. "You asked for volunteers, general. Bygod I'm volunteering."

Jackson hesitated. "Alright, Houston. Take some men with you...and be careful."

The grassy slope down the hill to the Creek fortress offered little in the way of cover except scattered stumps. Calling his men to follow, Houston pressed forward. A volley of bullets and arrows from the bunker made his men dive for cover. Houston remained on his feet.

"They can't shoot for shit. Git off your asses, men. Our only chance is to rush them."

Only Houston plunged ahead. Five yards from the redoubt he stopped and leveled his musket. Before he could fire a blast from a porthole knocked him to his knees. He waved and shouted to rally his men but when he dropped his musket and collapsed, they fled.

From the hilltop Jackson, Brill, Ross and others watched as a Red Stick, tomahawk in hand, crawled out of the hole and move toward the inert Houston.

"My god...my god!" Hanks sobbed. Feverishly, he loaded his Kentucky rifle, rested it on a stump, and sighted down its long barrel. It was a good two hundred yards to Houston.

"God, don't let me miss." He took a deep breath and held it. Feeling himself safely out of range, the Creek warrior gleefully gave the finger to Jackson. Then, bending over, he seized a fistful of Houston's hair with his left hand, the tomahawk raised high with his right. The report of Hank's rifle reverberated across the peninsula. The warrior slumped forward over Houston's body.

A collective whoop went up from the hill. "Bygod, you got the sunuvabitch," shouted Jackson. He quickly sobered. "Houston's been hit...god knows how bad and we can't get to him."

"I'll get 'em, general." Looking around, Hanks picked up a bow and a couple of spent arrows. He took a piece of wadding, smeared it with axle grease from the gun carriage, then crushed gun powder into the greasy wadding. In the lengthening shadows and drifting sheets of smoke, Hanks slithered down the slope between rocks and tree stumps. An occasional shot rang out from the bunker. The gathering twilight was working in his favor. Now he was close enough. Curling up behind a stump, he poured some powder into the flash pan of his empty rifle. Holding the powder-soaked wadding near the pan, he pulled the trigger. The wadding flickered and, after a moment, flared. Bullets ricocheted off the stump as the Creeks in the bunker reacted to the threat. Lying on his back, Hanks fitted the arrow to the bowstring and pulled. Rolling left, he came quickly to his knees and fired. The arrow lodged in the dry leaves and brush on top of the bunker. Within minutes, the tinder-dry oak leaves and pine needles became a roaring mass of flames. Twigs, branches, and limbs ignited turning the bunker beneath into a death trap. One or two Red Sticks tried to escape out the south end of the bunker before the fiery timbers collapsed upon the remaining warriors.

Hearing a sound behind him, Hanks rolled quickly to one side, knife drawn.

"It's me, Hanks. It's me, Virgil."

"God, you scared me. Come on. Let's see what we can do for Houston."

They crawled forward to where Houston lay motionless. As they rolled the big buck off Houston, Brill saw a hole in the Creek's right temple, still coursing dark blood.

"Hanks, you sonuvabitch," he said admiringly. "A head shot at two hundred yards."

"If'n I hadn't been hurried, I'da hit him in the left eye," replied Hanks. As they rolled Houston over, his right arm fell uselessly to one side.

"He's still breathin', Virg, but barely. If'n he ain't bled to death, he's shore close to it."

Struggling and panting the two youngsters dragged Houston away from the raging fire. Out of the smoke a party of soldiers appeared, led by Ross. They carried Houston up the hill where a surgeon was summoned. Almost unnoticed in the smoke and gathering dusk, a cold drizzle of rain set in.

As Houston struggled with consciousness, a canteen of whiskey was held to his lips. By the flickering light of brush fires, Dr. Amos Spettles and his son went to work. One bullet had shattered Houston's right arm. Another was lodged deep within his right shoulder. Spettles splintered the right arm but, after repeated efforts to fish the ball out of the shoulder, he gave up. Wiping his bloody hands on his trouser legs, he turned to Jackson.

"Sorry, general. If I probe anymore he'll sure to god bleed to death."

"What's his chances?" asked Jackson.

Spettles didn't look up but continued to rub his hands absently against his pants.

"I said, what are his chances?" Jackson repeated testily.

"Next to none," Spettles mumbled. "He's bled too much. I doubt if he will make it through the night. Sorry."

"Sorry!" Jackson snorted in disgust. "Damn sorry doctoring, I'd say. Useless as tits on a boar!"

"I'm no miracle worker. I didn't graduate from the Royal College of Surgeons," retorted Spettles.

Jackson let out a weary sigh. "Alright, men. Cover him. Make him as comfortable as possible." He knelt beside Houston. "Damned shame. He was a good man...damned fine soldier. Would've gone far."

CHAPTER 2

A ROAD IS CHOSEN

Concerned about Houston, Jackson did not detect movement among the bodies strewn about the ground. Hanks and Junaluska reacted simultaneously to the cocking sound of a rifle. Hanks threw his body into Jackson, knocking him sprawling just as the gunshot exploded. Junaluska, with his tomahawk, was swift and lethal. The wounded Red Stick was dispatched once and for all.

"What the hell…?" Jackson stormed to his feet.

"I'm…I'm very sorry, sir." Hanks scrambled to his feet flustered and scared.

Jackson picked up his hat, slapped it against his leg and looked around, taking in what had just happened. The rifle was still smoking. Junaluska grinned and pried a dripping tomahawk from the skull of the dead Creek.

Jackson looked at Hanks. "Sorry? Son, you just saved my ass from an early grave. Don't be sorry for that. You and Junaluska…I'm beholden' to both of you." He extended his hand to the wrinkled, old warrior. He clamped a hand on Hanks shoulder. "You are one helluva fighter, son. I'd be damned proud to have you soldier with me anytime." He cleared his throat. Praise did not come easily from Old Hickory.

*　　*　　*　　*

Houston lay on the cold, wet ground throughout the night. His fitful sleep, with consciousness coming and going, was an amalgam of fever, chills, and nightmares. Frequently, the great warrior came at him, a gleaming tomahawk held high. Houston was too weak to fend off the attack but the deadly blow never fell. Now he was happy and safe splashing in the warm waters with Diana on Hiwassee Island. She reached to caress him but it was his mother's hand stroking his hair and crooning softly to him. A feeling of peace spread through his body, warming it like good whiskey coursing throughout his blood. Yes, he had come home now. He had done enough for the folks at home to hear about. Houston awoke, aware of ghostly bodies encircling him. He brushed his hand across his eyes, trying to wipe away the cobwebs.

"Damned if I know how he made it through the night. By all rights, he should be dead."

A stab of pain in Houston's right shoulder honed his awareness. A face came into focus. He recognized it as belonging to the doctor.

"Decided to stay with us, did ya', Houston?" The doctor probed the mass of torn, swollen flesh now streaked with red and purple. Houston flinched.

Finishing his ministration, the doctor took Jackson aside. "Nothin' I can do for him here in the field. Put him on a litter and pack him off to Ft. Williams. As weak as he is, I doubt he'll make it more than a day or two at best."

Hanks, Ross, and others lifted Houston on to a litter made of green saplings and blankets and started him on a journey he was not expected to survive. It was a hot, wet, green wilderness to Fort Williams, some sixty miles away.

As the procession disappeared around a bend in the trail, Jackson turned to his men. "There's a few Red Sticks still holed up in caves along the river banks. Flush 'em out and kill 'em. If you find Weatherford or Menawa, I want them taken alive."

Later Ross and Hanks found themselves alone moving cautiously through the wet weeds and mist along the east edge of the peninsula. Soft ground cushioned their steps. Quiet lay like a blanket over what had been a resounding battlefield the previous day. Occasionally, they halted as thick patches of fog engulfed and isolated them even though they were only a couple paces apart.

"Mr. Ross…Mr. Ross!" Hanks choked.

Ross turned to see the boy trembling and gasping for breath. "What is it, lad, what's wrong?"

"My god…my god…look there!" Hanks pointed.

The parting fog revealed a tall pole standing in the center of the burned village. On the pole, fluttering in the wisps of mist, hung human scalps: scalps of black hair, long, golden tresses, white hair, children's hair. Some of the scalps were fresh and bloody.

Ross silently took it in. He counted. "Must be close to 300 scalps there. I suspect many of them came from Ft. Mims."

Hanks swallowed. "I've seen fistfights, eye gouging, knifings...but I've never seen anything like this before." Now his brow furrowed with puzzlement. "If these scalps are from Ft. Mims, how come there's no nigger scalps here. Lotsa niggers was at the fort."

"Probably the Creeks took them as slaves. The Creeks wouldn't take a nigger scalp...they place no value on it. Come on, let's get out of here."

Turning north they had not proceeded far when they heard a noise to their left. Rifles at ready, Ross challenged the mist. "Who goes there?"

"Hold yer fire, Ross. It's just me." Virgil Brill and his brother, Junior, emerged from the mist each carrying an armful of potatoes.

"Want somethin' good?" offered Virg. "Have some of these taters."

Brill thrust into their hands hot, buttery, baked potatoes. A famished Hanks was quick to accept. "Man, I haven't had a bite since yesterday. Where'n the world did you stumble onto these taters?"

"Found 'em in the ashes of one of them burned out houses. Figured the former owners didn't have use for them anymore," Brill laughed. "Cooked to perfection, don't ya think?"

"Never tasted none better," responded Hanks who was just starting to peel his second. "But where did you find butter for 'em?"

"Well, as a matter of fact, that ain't real butter," Brill admitted. "That's really Creek butter. Some of the fat cooked outta them dead Red Sticks and soaked the taters."

Hanks had difficulty swallowing. He dropped his remaining potato discreetly into the weeds. "Guess maybe I've had enough," he said weakly.

∗   ∗   ∗   ∗

Men gathered around the general as they returned from their search of the peninsula. A few pockets of resistance had been wiped out but there was no trace of Weatherford or Menawa.

"Where are those sunsabitches?" a frustrated Jackson muttered. He surveyed the carnage-littered battlefield. Fog, mixed with smoke from still smoldering fires, drifted across the ground, first revealing grotesque corpses, then mercifully covering them. He turned back to his men.

"Prepare the wounded for travel. For my official report to Governor Blount, I'll need a count of the dead and wounded. Sgt. Brill, form a detail to count our dead. After they are identified, weight their bodies well and sink them in the middle of the Tallapoosa. I'll not bury them here and have some filthy savage dig them up and desecrate their bones. As for the Creeks, after you've counted them, leave 'em lie. Their squaws will take care of them after we're gone."

"That might be alright for your soldiers, general, but not for the Cherokee."

In irritation at the countermand of his orders, Jackson turned. "What is it now, Ross?"

"Meaning no disrespect, general, but it is an age-old custom that when a Cherokee dies, he will lie alongside the bones of his father, and his father's father. He will lie where his grave can be watered by the tears of his mother. He will return to the earth that gave him life. He will not be buried here nor will he be consigned to a watery grave to be eaten by fish."

Jackson's mouth twitched. These uppity breeds were a pain in the ass. "Alright, Ross. Do with them as you wish. Sgt. Brill, get on with it. Any Cherokee you find, turn them over to Ross."

Brill turned to his ever-present sons. "You heered whut the gen'rul sed, Virgil. You and Junior git some detail and git to countin'."

"Come on, Junior. Let's get on with it."

"Dammit, Virg, you know I h'aint no good at countin'." He cast a fearful eye at the dead now lying in grotesque formations. "Besides, once them sonsabitches are kilt, they're kilt. Why th' hell should we count 'em? It don't matter no more."

"Just do it, Junior. Just do it! I ain't of no mind to mess with them flea-bit devils neither but I'm damned site more shore that I don't wanna be shot by Jackson."

Head down, Junior set himself to the distasteful task. At times it was necessary to unstack bodies, pull them apart, untangle limbs now stiff where they had died hand-on-throat, knife in belly, thumbs hooked in eyesockets. Open eyes fixed on Junior seemed to question his presence. Huge, blue-green flies walked across the glassy stares, exploring the cavities of nostrils and bloody, open mouths. He choked down the bitter bile rising in his stomach.

"Junior, what 'n hell do ya think y'er doin?"

Junior stood up, thankful for the interruption. "Whaddya mean, what am I doin? I'm countin', Virg, just like you tole me to."

"Ya dumb bastard, can't you see I've already counted those?"

"How the shit would I know, Virg. They all look the same to me."

Virg scratched his head. "Y'er right, Junior. This means we gotta start all over. Tell ya what, though. This time let's mark these bastards so's we can tell whose been counted."

"Just how ya gonna mark 'em, Virg?"

"Use y'er head, Junior. Watch this." Virgil slipped his hunting knife from its sheath, bent over, lifted a head by the hair and, with a deft stroke, whacked off the tip end of the nose.

"There, bygod, do that and you'll know th' bastard is counted."

With a working solution at hand, the whacking and counting was carried out across the peninsula.

Trying to keep his thoughts focused elsewhere, Hanks watched the Brills carry out the sickening process along the wall where the bodies were concentrated. He saw Junior stop the delivery of another chopping blow, his knife frozen in mid-swing.

"Virg", he called in a hoarse voice. "Come here."

"What is it, boy? Whadja find? Weatherford?"

"Look here," Junior whispered.

"Well, I'll be double-damned," Virgil breathed. "Wonder where she came from and how come she's naked?"

At their feet lay a beautiful Indian woman, totally nude. Eyes closed, her cheek resting on one hand as if in sleep. Awe struck, they drank in her beauty from the firm rounded breasts to the dark nest of pubic hairs.

"Didja ever in yer whole borned life see anything as purty as that?" Junior whispered softly. "I shore wanted to find me a purty pussy like this…now I find it and she's dead."

"Can't be helped, little brother. She's as dead as the rest of 'em. Mark her and let's get this stinkin' job done."

"Don't you dare cut her, Virg." Junior pushed his brother away.

"I'll swear the rain has soaked yer pea-pickin' brain. You can stand lookin' at that purty pussy all day and it ain't gonna change a thing. She's dead and that's all there is to it. To hell with ya, I'm gonna git myself some bridle reins." With that he turned and strode away.

Hanks watched in puzzlement as Virg walked over to a slain warrior. Rolling the corpse over on its belly, Virg grunted with satisfaction. "Looks like a good 'un. Skin ain't all shot to hell."

Stripping a few shreds of clothing from the body, Virg drew his hunting knife. Starting at the heel of the right foot, he made an incision which ran up the leg, across the buttocks, up the back to the top of the right shoulder, then across to the left shoulder. From there, in one continuous cut, the incision was extended down the left side of the body to the heel. Another incision was then made, about two inches from the first, and parallel to it. This done, Virg ripped out a bloody strip of skin two inches wide and about ten feet long.

"This ought to make a damn fine bridle rein," he chortled.

Furtively glancing around to make sure no one was watching, Junior drew his knife and felt between the woman's legs. In a moment or two, the deed was done. Straightening up, he poked his fingers into the black, fuzzy mass, stretching the hole in the now stiffening skin. With a grunt of satisfaction, he slipped the grizzly mess over the barrel of his rifle. He smiled as he smoothed the glistening pubic hair with his fingers, then hurried off to catch up with the detail.

*   *   *   *

Jackson sat under a tarp, leaning against the wheel of a supply wagon. He was warmed by the flickering fire before him, a cup of Tennessee whiskey in one hand and his pipe in the other. Yet, the chill and damp of the night seemed to penetrate every aching joint and rib cage.

"Bygod, John, we finally done it. Andrew Jackson can't help but get some attention when word gets back to Washington City. Those gutless wonders back there will have to sit up and take notice."

Coffee lifted his cup. "Let's drink to the Napoleon of the West," he jested.

Jackson chuckled. His admiration for Napoleon was no secret. "Yes, bygod, I'll drink to that." He sipped his whiskey. "Ya know, I don't think Bonaparte could have come up with a better plan for lickin' those damn Red Sticks than we did here at The Horseshoe."

"Agreed, general. But you gotta admit…if them Cherokee hadn't crossed the river and hit the Creeks in the rear, our collective asses might still be hanging out."

Jackson scowled and squirmed uncomfortably. "John, the Cherokee will go the way of the Creeks. It's just a matter of time…"

Before he could finish Sergeant Brill and Lieutenant Ross entered the circle of firelight.

"What is it, sergeant?"

"We have the final count on casualties you asked fer, gen'rul." Brill held a smugged piece of paper to the firelight. "Best I can tell, we killed about 587 of them devils. At least, that's how many we could find and count before dark. Don't know how many was killed tryin' to escape down the river."

"From the reports I got, we must have killed around 300 at the river," Coffee volunteered.

"How many prisoners?" Jackson probed.

"We're holdin' about 300, gen'rul. All of them kids and womenfolk, cep't for 4 men…all shot to hell."

Jackson leaned forward. "Anyone of them Weatherford?"

"No, gen'rul. The prisoners say Menawa was here but we can't find his body. They also say Weatherford wasn't even here. He's s'posed to be somewhere down south at a place called Hickory Ground."

"Damn," Jackson swore. "I'll get that sunuvabitch if I have to chase him to the gates of hell. He's got to pay for what he did at Fort Mims." Jackson caught himself. He turned to Brill. "Anything more, sergeant?"

"Uh…yes, sir." Brill knew Jackson's aversion to bad news. "We lost 47 of our own men and we have 159 wounded…some real bad."

Jackson grunted. "What about your men, Ross? How did they fare?"

"We had eighteen killed and thirty-six wounded, sir. I've already dispatched a detail with a pack train to take the bodies home."

"Yeah…well, you can't waste any time gettin' them underground," Jackson added dispassionately. "Brill, release the prisoners in the morning. They can take care of their own dead."

Brill turned to leave. "One more thing, sergeant. Be sure you let them know that I'll be after Weatherford and every other breathing Red Stick. If they don't want to die, tell them to surrender."

*   *   *   *

Ross slowed his horse and fell behind the Cherokee column moving north from Fort Williams. He needed to be alone with his thoughts, to purge his mind of the scenes on the corpse-strewn peninsula where blood, offal, and mud had mixed so freely and where, even now, buzzards wheeled silently overhead, establishing their waiting vigil. The smell of sweat, wood smoke, and gun powder permeated his clothing. In the gentle, now warm, rain he removed his shirt, twisted it into a roll, squeezing out the water and stench.

Looking ahead Ross saw that Major Ridge had pulled up his horse, waiting. As he came alongside, Ridge clucked to his horse and kneed in beside Ross. For a time they rode in silence broken only by the plop and sucking noise of horses' feet in mud. Finally, Ross cleared his throat.

"Major, we lost eighteen good men back there. Whose cause was served by their deaths? Certainly not their families. For the mothers, fathers, wives, children, or sweet-hearts, the pain of loss will last forever. To the mighty British, who are behind every bit of the Red Stick's skullduggery, this will only be an insignificant skirmish. And the Americans...?" he snorted.

The Ridge nodded. "I understand your feelings, Little John. It's hard to see any advantage for our people. During the Revolutionary War it was to our advantage to side with the British. Had they won, Whitehall would have exercised some restraint on the westward movement of their colonist. At least they would have tried. But, they didn't win. Since then the Americans have spread across our lands like starving locusts. Their government promised them land for fighting the British, as if this land belonged to them."

"Maybe we should still be fighting alongside the British like my grandfather," Ross ventured with irony.

The Ridge chuckled. "The British would like that. John McDonald was their strongest agent in these parts."

"Tell me, Major, why did you plead so strongly in Council for the Cherokee to fight alongside Jackson. Most of the chiefs felt neutral about it. So why didn't we just stay out of it?"

"I see it this way," Ridge replied. "After the Red Sticks wiped out the garrison at Ft. Mims, and all the white settlers who had taken refuge there, Cherokee neutrality became impossible. The outrage of the frontier whites over the massacre would lead them to interpret Cherokee neutrality as sympathy for the Red Sticks. We really had no choice." After a moment's silence, he added. "Besides, those of us who lead the Cherokee volunteers believe that by demonstrating loyalty to the United States, and fighting side by side with the whites, we can obtain gratitude toward our people and a better relationship with the whites. So, maybe we have bought ourselves some good will and maybe some time."

Deep furrows formed on Ross's brow as he quietly replied, "I'm not sure that I share your expectations, Major. Certainly, not where Jackson is concerned."

The Ridge breathed a sigh of impatience. "Little John, I've been in the fighting business all my life. I took my first Unaka scalp in '88. I was big for my age...I was strong...and the lure of the warpath was more than I could resist. I must have seen all of seventeen summers when I got into my first fight with some of Sevier's men at old Setico. That was the year some crazy Tennessee settler killed our chief, Old Tassel, in cold blood, under a flag of truce. I'll tell you, we took bloody vengeance on those Tennesseans. We won that fight, and the next, and the next. But as the years have passed I have come to realize that our numbers were no match for the Americans. Our losses could not be replaced. But for them, new settlers kept pouring in every day through Charleston, Boston, and Philadelphia and every one of them were on fire to possess land, our land. And still they come. There is no stopping them now. What we witnessed back there at the Horseshoe is strong proof of that."

Ross shifted uncomfortably on his horse. "What are you trying to say, Major? That we should have joined forces with Tecumseh?"

The Ridge shook his head. "No. It's too late for that. It was too late three years ago but Tecumseh could not see that." He straightened in his saddle and looked directly at Ross. "John, if we are to survive as a people, we must forget the war-path. We must buy time, time to educate our children in the ways of the whites, time to teach our people to farm instead of pursuing the deer, time to learn to govern ourselves in the way of the whites. Only if we are accepted as civilized people will the whites endure our existence."

"But we already have written laws. And so far as schools, just look at our school at Spring Place that the Moravians run."

"Agent Meigs feels we must move faster. It was his idea, you know, that we raise a few companies of Cherokees to help Jackson in this campaign."

"Good thing we did," Ross grunted, "else Jackson would still be back there banging away at the Creek barricade." He pulled his horse to a halt. "Major, do you realize the full implications of what you are proposing? You are talking about changing an entire culture, an age-old way of life."

The Ridge nodded. "I have thought on this long days and night. Our culture changes or we die as a people. I do not wish that to happen to my children. From the full bloods in the hills, who cling to the old ways, we will receive strong resistance. And, that is to be expected. No man freely surrenders all that he holds dear. From the mixed bloods, who have already chosen many ways of the whites, it will be an easy transition.

"Take yourself, John, as a prime example. You know the ways of both the Unaka and the Cherokee. Your father provided you with books and schooling. You read and speak the English tongue with great skill. You know how the white man thinks. It's people like you who must lead. You must if our people are to survive."

*   *   *   *

Shinbone Ridge was casting long shadows across the Coosa River as the wet and weary group approached Chief Pathkiller's ferry at Turkey Town. After three days of riding in constant rain, Ross was anticipating a hot meal and the luxury of a dry bed beside the huge fireplace. There were other feelings animating Ross. In 1788 his father, Daniel, and his mother, Mollie, daughter of John McDonald, had established a trading post here among the Cherokee. Two years later they were blessed with a son who they named John, after Mollie's father. They had moved away when John was a small boy and he had never returned to the place of his birth.

In small groups they were hauled across the river on a flat bottom ferry pulled across with a rope made of plaited hide. The old chief solemnly greeted each of them as they embarked. It was then that Ross was struck by the eerie silence of the place. Looking around he could see that the corral was vacant, the pig pens were torn down and empty. Not a single cluck of a chicken could be heard. On the empty corncrib a door hung uselessly on a single leather hinge. Ross turned to Pathkiller, his eyes full of questions.

"It was the militia...the Tennessee volunteers," Pathkiller explained. "Never have these old eyes seen a more disorderly and destructive pack of men." He waved his hand toward the north. "Their trail is marked by looted homes, slaughtered hogs and cattle, stolen corn and horses, ruined fields and fences...and these were our supposed friends and allies."

"Those were Jackson's men." Ross's lips tightened in anger. "They have never been too concerned about who is friend or foe where Indians are concerned." He laid his hand gently on the old man's shoulder. "Send me a list of everything destroyed or stolen. I will do all in my power, with the help of Agent Meigs, to see that everything you have lost is replaced. I have confidence that the government of the United States will right these wrongs."

The old chief smiled his appreciation. "I'm sorry...I have no food to offer but you are welcome to the warmth of this house."

"And that we will gladly accept," replied Ross.

*   *   *   *

Next morning, about six miles north of Turkey Town, the mounted party came to a halt. Here Major Ridge and his companions would follow the Coosa River east to the Major's home at Oothcaloga.

The Ridge extended his hand to Ross. "Remember to think on what I have said to you, Little John. Your people are going to need you, maybe sooner than you think."

Ross smiled and with a wave of his hand turned his horse up Yellow Creek. "If you want to see me," he called, "look for me at Lookout Mountain."

Big Wills Valley ran for eighty miles on a northeast-southwest course. The path wound upstream through groves of white oak, scrubby, mountain pine, and

maple, emerging from time to time into small meadows covered with pink spi-
derwort. Curious children and barking dogs greeted the weary Ross party as they
entered Wills Town about sundown. Set against the west base of Lookout Mountain, some distance back from Wills Creek, Wills Town was little more than a
few dozen cabins. Trampled gardens of corn, beans, and pumpkins were scattered
around the houses where Cherokee women struggled to squeeze sustenance out
of the chert and flinty soil. Glancing around as he unsaddled his horse, Ross
could see the same pattern of looting and waste that he had seen at Turkey Town.

A gray and bent figure hobbled from one of the huts. A welcoming smile that
wreathed his face revealed broken and missing teeth.

"Little John, my friend. Welcome! Welcome!" he said embracing Ross. "Come
in, come in."

"How have you been Will Webber?"

"You can see for yourself, John," he replied with a note of tired resignation.
"Bring your saddle and blanket inside out of the damp"

Webber led the way into a modest cabin made of hewn logs. At one end of the
one-room cabin stood a dilapidated bed; at the other a smokey fire burned in the
stone fireplace. Ross stacked his saddle in a corner and spread his saddle blanket
on the rough-hewn floor. As there were no chairs, Ross seated himself on the
blanket near the fire.

Webber seated himself on the floor across from Ross. Be crumbled some dried
leaves of home-grown tobacco, carefully packed his clay pipe and lit it with a
glowing coal from the hearth.

"Tell me, Little John, how is your grandfather?"

"He's fine, Will. He and grandmother are still living on Chichamaugah
Creek."

Webber grunted. "We had ourselves some hellish good times when we were
young sprouts. My hair was red then instead of the color of snow. I well remember their wedding here in '69. We gave John McDonald and Anne Shorey one
helluva shivaree on their wedding night. Don't think they had a chance to
sleep...or anything else." The old man gave a soft cackle at the memory, coughed
in the pipe's smoke, and spat into the fire. At that moment a young, attractive
woman entered the door with a kettle of steaming stew. As she bent to serve
them, the old man whispered in her ear. She nodded and left the cabin without
speaking. In a few moments she returned accompanied by a tall, swarthy, young
man. Smiling, he extended his hand to Ross.

"Benito Ramirez at your service, Señor." Ross struggled to his feet to shake
hands.

"Señor Ramirez represents the interests of Panton, Leslie, and Company out of Pensacola," Webber offered by way of introduction. "But, I think he has other interests here as well," glancing pointedly at the woman.

"Grandfather!" she exclaimed. The embarrassed girl quickly left the room.

"Yes," said Ramirez, ignoring the latter part of the old man's remark. "I am one of their agents for trade. I believe your grandfather was in their employment some years ago."

"That's true. For many years. But in those days the old Chickamauga trader had things of value to trade. Now, as you very well know, the fur trade has moved far to the west."

Ramirez nodded, recognizing the implied question. "So…why am I here?" He turned his backside to the warmth of the fire. "I am well aware of your changing economic conditions. Your hunting grounds are depleted and the pressure of the Americans for your lands is untenable. Frankly, I see no reason why your people would want to continue living here among these circumstances>"

"What choices do we have, Señor Ramirez?"

Old man Webber roused himself. "Señor Ramirez is here to offer us land across the great water. At my age, I fear the offer comes too late…."

"I see," said Ross, raising his eyebrows. "Then you are an agent of Spain, señor?"

Ramirez shrugged. "This near to the Americans, it would be unwise to admit any such suggestion. Officially, I am what I said; a trade representative of Panton-Leslie. Unofficially, I am authorized by my government to extend certain invitations to you and to others who can no longer accede to the injustice of the Americans. You are aware, of course, that Chief Bowl and many Cherokees have already taken up residence along the Red River."

"Yes, of that I am aware," responded Ross, "but Spain is not known for its altruism."

"Your wariness is understandable, Señor Ross. But Spain has much land across the Mississippi that is sparsely settled. Your own bitter experience has shown you that the Americans look upon land with few occupants as an invitation to move in. We want to settle the land. We would welcome any of your people who wish to move. The land is good, game is plentiful, and you would be beyond the reach and control of the Americans."

"For now, yes," Ross answered, "but how long will that condition exist? Do not deceive yourself, señor. Having the Cherokee as a buffer between your land and the Americans will not stop them for long. If we cannot retain our lands here and now, where our people have ancient roots, how strong would be our claims as transplants in a foreign soil? I thank you, Señor Ramirez, for your generous offer, but no."

*   *   *   *

Just north of Wills Town the trail left the valley and abruptly ascended the west side of Lookout Mountain. As the Ross party plodded up the steep and stony trail, they gradually emerged from the fog-shrouded valley into blue skies and bright morning sun. At a switchback on the zig zag trail they paused to rest the horses.

"You were a bit rough on Ramirez last night, weren't you?" Lewis ventured to his brother.

"As I said," replied John, "Spain isn't making an offer out of the goodness of her heart. Spain fears the encroachment of the Americans as much as we. Back in '84 they tried to choke off expansion by closing the Mississippi to American trade and Jackson hates them for that. Now Spain is looking for someone they can use as a buffer. The Cherokee don't need to be the grain between grindstones."

Lewis sat quietly for a moment. "John, tell me...honestly. What are the chances the Cherokee can survive as a nation?"

"It depends on whether the United States honors its treaties with us."

Lewis snorted. "Not a very reassuring thought, considering their past record."

"And it might hinge on whether Major Ridge is correct in his thinking."

"Godallmighty, John. Does he really think we can unify seven clans spread all over these hills. Does he believe some eighty Cherokee towns will give up their independence to a central type government? I just don't see it happening."

"The thirteen colonies did it. Not because they wanted to but it was either unify or be gobbled up one by one...by England, Spain, or France. We are facing the same...we unify or cease to exist."

CHAPTER 3

A POLITICAL NOVITIATE

Jackson put aside his pen and pushed back from the crude, wooden table. He flexed his cramped fingers and reread the papers he had just completed. One was a report to General Thomas Pinckney, commander of the regular army for the department of the South; another copy went to Willie Blount, Governor of Tennessee. The contents of the third paper he would share with no one. This paper listed his demands from the defeated Creek chiefs with whom he would soon meet. Guidelines for treaty-making with the Creeks, which he had received from General Pinckney, were deliberately disregarded. Pinckney was too soft and knew little about how to deal with Indians. Sure, there would be some protests by some fat-assed bureaucrats in Washington over the amount of land he was demanding from the Creeks, but Jackson knew they wanted the land. Once he pushed the treaty through, Washington would be overjoyed.

Jackson folded the dispatches and dripped some hot wax on the folds to seal them. As he was finishing, a shadow fell across the doorway. Looking up, he saw a tall, hand-some warrior.

"Who the hell are you?" Jackson growled, "and how the hell did you get past the guards?"

"I'm William Weatherford, "the man calmly responded. "I've heard you were looking for me."

Jackson slowly rose to his feet. "Well, I'll be damned! So you are Red Eagle?"

"To save my people from more suffering and shame, I have come to give myself up, to make peace and seek the protection you have offered the other chiefs."

Astonished at the Indian's quiet composure, Jackson was at a loss for words. Recovering quickly, he stepped threateningly toward Weatherford. "You murdering bastard. How can you come in here with the blood of Fort Mims on your hands and ask me for protection?" The nasal pitch of his voice rose higher. "You slaughter innocent people by the hundreds and you ask me for peace? You rip open the bellies of pregnant women, you bash the skulls of children...blood and brains and guts were splattered all over the grounds and...you, you...and you ask me for mercy?

Where do you get such balls, Weatherford?"

"I tried to stop it, general. When I did, my own warriors turned on me and I left to save my skin." Meeting Jackson's fierce glare without blinking, Weatherford quietly continued. "I am in your power, general. Do with me as you please. I too am a soldier. I have defended my home and my people. In doing so, I have done to the white people all the harm I could. If I had an army, I would yet fight and contend to the last. But I have none. My people are all gone. I can now do no more than weep over the misfortune of my nation."

Breathing hard, Jackson stared at Weatherford then turned away to regain control of his emotions.

"You are a half-breed?" asked Jackson.

"My father was a Scot. My mother was a Creek."

"With good Scot blood in your veins, why did you choose the path of a savage?"

"A savage? Did you see the work of your soldiers at Tohopeka?" The strength and evenness of his voice belied no fear.

Evading the question, Jackson pressed his attack. "Would you prefer a continuation of the war? If so, I can damn well accommodate you."

"General, you know I have no choice. There was a time when I had a choice and could have answered you. I have none now—even hope is ended. Once I could animate my soldiers to battle, but one cannot animate the dead. My warriors can no longer hear my voice. Their bones lie at Talladega, Tallushatchee, Emuckfaw, and Tohopeka."

Jackson peered with wonder at Weatherford. He could not deny an admiration he felt for the courage of this man. In spite of himself, a smile flickered across his face. He quickly suppressed it. After all, he was the conqueror.

"What is it you would have me do for you, Weatherford?"

"I have not surrendered myself without thought, general. While there was a chance for success, I never left my post nor sought peace. But my people are gone and now I ask it for my nation—and for myself. On the miseries and misfortunes brought upon my country, I look back with deepest sorrow…and I wish to avert greater calamities. You are a brave man. I rely upon your generosity. You will exact no terms of a conquered people but such as they should accede to. You have told us where we might go and be safe. This is a good talk and my nation will listen to it."

A stir at the door caused Jackson to turn. Hanks and Brill stood with pistols trained on the back of Weatherford. Jackson waved his hand. "It's alright, boys. Leave us." He turned and looked in silence at Weatherford, groping for words. After a moment he spoke.

"Weatherford, I'm not sure what I should do with you. There was a time I'd hanged you on sight. Maybe I still should. But you are a man of courage. Few would have had the guts to walk into my camp unarmed knowing that I was after their head. You have stature among your people. You could help bring an end to this needless bloodshed. I may be crazy for doing this, but I'm going to let you go…but with one unalterable condition…that you promise to make it clear to your people that their only hope for peace and safety is to submit to my authority. Else I will hunt them down one by one and kill them like dogs."

*   *   *   *

Moses refilled the coffee cups. After adding some split oak to the crackling fire, he quietly left the room.

"John, if you ever decide to sell that nigger, let me know. I'd like to have him."

"Major, I don't plan to sell him. He came here on his own; he can stay or leave on his own."

"Not many run-away slaves are as lucky." The Major shifted comfortably in his chair and stretched his booted feet toward the open hearth. The flickering firelight illum-inated a strong, round face crowned with a thatch of gray hair. Vestiges of his Scottish grandfather reflected in his features. For a time, only the popping and hissing of the flames broke the silence. Ross respectfully waited for the Major to disclose the purpose of his visit.

"Pears like General Jackson's become quite a hero since whipping the Brits down in New Orleans."

"Yes," Ross responded. "Understand there's even some talk around Nashville about running him for president. You should be very happy to have such a powerful friend."

"Powerful? Yes. Friend?…well, I'm not too sure about that right now. After all the help we Cherokee gave him fighting the Red Sticks, I thought we could count on his favor…but now, I don't know."

"Could be he is just sore because we didn't help him more last September when he tangled with the British at Mobile."

"Maybe," said Ridge, "and maybe it's more than that. Agent Meigs tells me Jackson is fighting tooth and toenail against our efforts to regain our land and get compensation for our losses in crops and livestock suffered in the Creek War."

"Agent Meigs is such a respected man in Washington. How can they doubt the claims?"

"They don't doubt the claims; they fear trying to bring a national hero to heel just to please us Indians. And it's more than the damage claims; it's something more serious than that." The Ridge set his coffee mug on the table and turned to Ross. "Little John, I don't have to tell you…I didn't ride all this way from Oothcaloga on a social call. How soon can you be ready to go with me to Washington City?"

"Washington City?" Ross sat upright. "Why, that's a month's ride from here."

"I know how far it is, John. I've been there. The question is, how soon can you be ready to go?"

Somewhat stunned, Ross responded. "I can't say, right off hand, Major. With my partner, Tim Meigs, dying and Quatie having a new baby, I hadn't thought of going anywhere."

The Ridge edged forward in his chair. "After the fight at Tohopeka, General Jackson made a treaty with the Creeks at Fort Jackson. Made it," he snorted. "He literally forced it…and he forced it on his friends, the Creeks who fought for him at Tohopeka." He sprang to his feet and paced back and forth before the fireplace. "As reparations, the Creeks ceded a great amount of land to Jackson. Problem is, much of the land they gave up in the treaty is not their land. It is Cherokee land…and it belongs to the Cherokee people. That's why we must go to Washington City to straighten things out…and that's why we need you with us…you savvy the white man's thinking."

Ross sat silently, taking it in. After a time he responded. "I'm honored with your confidence, Major. Of course, I'll accompany you. Just give me a little time to set things in order around here.

*   *   *   *

Hoary frost covering the brown grass sparkled like diamonds in the early morning sun. A soft blanket of fog hung over the waters of the Tennessee River. Seven mounted men, bundled against the December cold, headed up the Tennessee Valley on Christmas morning, 1815, bound for Washington City. Ross turned in his saddle to wave one last time to Quatie, then a bend in the trail and she was lost from view. It would be three months before he saw her again.

From Ross's home at the foot of Lookout Mountain, they followed the Great War Trace, a trail followed by marauding tribes on the war path since ancient times. As they rode, Ross let his gaze dwell on Agent Meigs. Colonel Return J. Meigs had served as United States agent to the Cherokee for the past 14 years, since May of 1801. A yankee from Middletown, Connecticut, and a Revolutionary War veteran, Meigs had just reached his seventy-fifty birthday on the 17th day of the month. It was a day not celebrated. His son, Tim, had been a business partner of Ross until his death earlier that month. Age, plus the loss of a loved one, made Ross wonder if the agent was up to the rigors of the trail. It was a certainty that they would not be able to travel as rapidly with Meigs in the delegation.

As they moved up the valley of the Tennessee, Ross could see to his left the heights of Walden's Ridge rising above the layer of fog. Whites had named the ridge after Elisha Walden, one of the restless hunters who had penetrated into the Tennessee country in the 1760s. His arrival portended what was to come. Thirty-six years later the state of Tennessee took on its first form. It bulged now with settlers who were not too concerned about expanding beyond the state boundaries.

"Damn! It's cold! My feet feel like they are frozen in my boots! Let's walk awhile."

Occupied with thought, Ross had not noticed as Major Ridge reined up alongside.

Ross lowered the muffler covering his nose. "You're gonna miss that feather bed and Sehoya tonight," he grinned.

"You're damned right I will," Ridge retorted. "We should be able to make it to a farm up ahead. Belongs to a fellow by the name of Bushyhead, son of Captain James Stuart. He was a Scot stationed over at Ft. Loudon."

Darkness came early in December. Orion was rising in the east as they halted for the night on Candies Creek, just south of the Hiwassee River. Aching from the cold, and hours in the saddle, Ross stiffly dismounted.

"Name's Bushyhead. This is my boy, Jesse." With handshakes all around, Bushyhead led the way into his corral and tossed hay in for the horses. "It's a mighty frosty night. Come on in and warm your back sides."

Though cramped in their two room log cabin, Bushyhead and his wife, Nannie, made the party welcome. Nannie, small and lithe with gleaming black hair, was half Cherokee. She busied herself around the fireplace serving up bread, pork, potatoes, and dried peaches. Bushyhead, hungry for news, plied the party with questions.

"When will the pressure let up? Since 1721 the Cherokee have made no fewer than twenty treaties with the whites, each treaty yielding land, moving the boundaries ever deeper into Cherokee country. Where will it end?"

Agent Meigs stirred. "You've got to understand something about boundaries; to the English they are sacred. It might go against their conscience to take land forcibly from others but if they can legally, and when I say legally, I mean according to British law…if they can extinguish your title and rights to land by treaty, no matter what kind of chicaneries are involved in securing the treaty, then their ethical and moral principles remain unsullied. And, I'm afraid, the Americans have adopted the same attitudes."

"I find it strange", Bushyhead countered, "that the English place such stock in boundaries. With the French or Spanish settlers, there is never any boundary. They build their homes side by side the Cherokee, hunt the same woods together, and often intermarry on terms of equality."

"True," Meigs admitted, "but for the Englishman it is otherwise. It has never occurred to him that anyone could be his neighbor who was not of his own language and color."

$$*\qquad*\qquad*\qquad*$$

Across the Hiwassee River, and across the Holston, they intersected the road that ran between Southwest Point and Knoxville. Narrowed by dense forest, muddy and rutted in the rainy season, the road provided little comfort to travelers.

Almost a week had passed since they had left Ross's home. Their clothing reeked with sourness. Soon, the sour smell became overpowering. Ross longed for a hot bath.

"From these tracks, and all the pig shit on the road, it's a fair guess that we're following some drovers heading to Knoxville," Ridge observed.

"So that's what I'm smelling!" Ross replied with obvious relief.

Shortly afterward they overtook a drove of hundreds of hogs that had come to a standstill. Drovers to the rear and on both sides were working back and forth, cussing and yelling, to keep the hogs from wandering off into the woods. Across the way, Ross could see three wagons also at a standstill. Hemmed in by the thick growth of timber, there was no room for the wagons to turn aside and let the hogs pass. The lead wagon was piled high with chests of furniture, headboards, plows, boxes, and sacks of seeds. Tousled heads of children poked out here and there among the clutter. A pinch-faced mother, holding a newborn, sat in front of the wagon. Beside her an animated driver faced the head drover in a heated exchange over the right of way. Seeing no progress being made, The Ridge started to move forward. "Dark is gonna catch up with us if we don't get this settled," he muttered.

"No, let me," grinned Agent Meigs. "This calls for the skills of a Yankee negotiator and the full weight of an agent of the United States. No offense, Major, but these red necks wouldn't take kindly to an Indian butting in."

Meigs nudged his horse slowly through the pack of hogs until he was alongside the wagon. Ross, unable to hear what was being said, noted that the driver and drover both simmered down. After a bit, the driver got down, took a sack from the wagon, and gave it to Meigs. Meigs rode slowly alongside the wagons, dropping nubbins of corn as he went. Hogs immediately started trailing after him, eating corn in his wake. In a matter of minutes, the hogs had bypassed the wagons.

I'm beholdin' to ya fer gittin' us outta that snarl," spoke the driver. "Name's Riggs...Josiah Riggs...bound for Chickasaw Bluffs."

"Well, you've got a good ways to go," said Meigs. "We won't be holding you up. Oh, bye the way, did you pass any settlements along the way?"

"Sure did. "Bout a mile back down the road there's a place. Feller by the name of Brill lives there. S'pect that's whur thu hog drovers will bed down for the night."

"A man could ask for better company but we've got to spend the night somewhere. Let's get moving," sighed Meigs.

*   *   *   *

A cold, January breeze rustled through the branches of the oak tree under which Ross had bedded down. He had courteously declined Brill's invitation to unroll his blankets on the cabin floor. Instead, he went upwind from the drove of grunting and squealing hogs that surrounded the house. In a grove of oaks he found a deep pile of dry leaves. He burrowed into the leaves and pulled his blanket up under his chin. A sigh of contentment escaped his lips. There was no question that a night under the stars was preferable to sleeping on the tobacco-stained, dirt floor of Brill's cabin. Ross was quite convinced that with the passel of cats and mangy dogs that overran the cabin, the presence of fleas had to be considered.

With a cud of tobacco in his cheek and a jug of corn near at hand, Brill had spent the evening recounting his exploits at Horseshoe Bend. Ross assumed his accounts of the events were no more accurate than his frequent spurts of tobacco juice into the fireplace.

Brill's wife sat beside the fireplace, smoking her pipe, saying not a word. With several children of various ages sitting around, the absence of Virgil and Junior Brill was not even mentioned.

A rustle in the leaves roused Ross. Standing over him was one of Brill's daughters. A light breeze teased her blonde hair and a cold light from the moon illuminated her full breasts.

"Mr. Ross, my name is Kate. I want to go with you to Washington City. I'll do anything you say if you just take me."

Ross sat up, surprised by the bluntness of the request. He ignored her obvious offer. "Kate, you shouldn't be out here. What will your father think?"

"Pa won't miss me. It's Mollie's turn tonight."

"I don't understand, Miss Kate…"

"Ma is old and dried up. Pa takes turns sleeping with me and Mollie."

Stunned by this revelation, Ross sat in silent thought. Could he, with a clear conscience, possibly leave this young girl in such a predicament?

"Kate, do you know anyone in Washington City?"

"No, but that don't matter. I can get along."

After more thought, Ross replied. "Alright. In the morning meet us a mile down the trail. I'll get you to Washington, but I can't promise more than that."

*   *   *   *

By the tenth of January they were in Knoxville. This settlement, established in 1791 where the French Broad and Holston Rivers came together, now boasted a log-cabin executive mansion and the State Bank of Tennessee. Here Ross luxuriated in a hot bath and a change of clothing.

Leaving Knoxville, the party plodded on to Rogersville, Tennessee where they joined up with a postal route to Richmond, Virginia. Established in 1792, the route now allowed mail from the east to arrive every two weeks.

Late afternoon, February 8, 1816 found the road-weary party crossing the bridge over Rock Creek and entering the outskirts of Washington City. As they proceeded along a wide, dirt street named Pennsylvania Avenue, a mild southern breeze wafting off the Potomak River brought smells of garbage and sewage. They rode silently past the President's House, now in a state of restoration following its burning by the British. Off to the right Ross took note of a cluster of shacks which housed saloons and the obvious poor. Ladies of pleasure waved as the party passed. Beyond these slums Ross saw cattle and sheep grazing on a large, grassy swamp. Children were now sorting out the cows and driving them homeward for milking. As they neared the capitol, buildings along the left side of the avenue became more numerous: banks, shops, hotels, and boarding houses. Dirty urchins playing in the streets paused momentarily, struck with curiosity. A long line of slaves, chained together, crossed in front of them. After a long day of laboring to restore the capitol building, they were being returned to the jail for the night.

Ross stiffly dismounted under a sign board which depicted a comely Indian lass, Pocahontas. This was the Indian Queen hotel which was, as Ross was to learn, the most popular of Washington's hotels and a favorite stopping place for Indian delegations to the City.

Jesse Brown, owner of the hotel, effusively greeted each guest, saw to their luggage, and escorted them to the front door. Black lackeys took the horses to the rear of the hotel for corn and hay and a much needed rest.

A hot bath, a change of clothing, and a good night's sleep refreshed Ross. He stood now at the third-floor window, a copy of a newspaper in hand, overlooking Pennsy-lvania Avenue. Beneath him carriages were arriving in numbers depositing their clients at the door of the Indian Queen. He was feeling a tingle of excitement and anticipation at being in Washington City when he heard a knock on his door. Expecting Major Ridge and other members of his party ready to go below to eat, he opened it. Instead, he was greeted by a tall, distinguished-looking gentleman whose hawklike nose separated piercing blue eyes. A shock of red hair, showing some gray, crowned his features.

"Welcome to Washington City," the man said, extending his hand. "Name's McKenney…Thomas McKenney. I've been expecting you for some days. I'm here to show you around…introduce you to people."

Ross shook hands. "I've heard of you, Mr. McKenney. Aren't you the one President Madison is planning to nominate as the new head of the office of Indian Trade?"

"Well, yes! That's true. But how did you know?"

"It's no mystery," laughed Ross holding up a copy of the National Intelligencer. "I read your newspaper. And I do appreciate your offer to show me Washington."

"Is there anyone in particular that you'd like to meet?" asked McKenney.

"I'd like to meet your most powerful, influential men in Congress."

"That would include Calhoun, Clay, and Webster, at the very least," replied McKenney. "Come, let's get started."

As they headed up Pennsylvania Avenue toward the capitol, Ross raised the matter of Kate Brill. Finding the girl living in such degrading conditions, he explained, as best he could, why he had aided her flight.

McKenney nodded in understanding. "It will be no problem to place her as a housemaid in one of the boarding houses here in the city."

Somewhat relieved, Ross asked, "Just what is it you plan to do as the new Superintendent of Indian Trade?"

"How familiar are you, Mr. Ross, with the present state of trade with the natives of this land?"

"Quite familiar. You see, I own a small trading post on the Tennessee River. My father was a trader among the Cherokee as was his father before him."

"Then you are aware of how Astor's American Fur Company conducts business, as well as that scoundrel Chouteau. Unlike those operations, my conduct will be, without question, one of protection and justice for the Indians. Astor and Chouteau's Missouri Fur Company cannot compete in quality in blankets, calicoes, beaver traps, or prices. They compete in whiskey. Whoever can ply the poor Indian with the most whiskey wins the business. Not a drop of brandy, rum, or whiskey will be permitted to pass through our factories. For reasons unknown, Indians have no tolerance for whiskey."

"Your convictions in these matters appear to be quite strong," observed Ross.

McKenney chuckled. "Yes, I suppose they do. It's my Quaker upbringing."

"I greatly admire your sentiments, Mr. McKenney, but I hope you realize that if you follow through with your plans, you will not be very popular with either Astor or Chouteau. They are powerful men who can bring a lot of pressure on you through your government."

"What you say is true. Astor is a personal friend of Madison. He funded the war against England to the tune of two million dollars. But it's a risk I'm willing to assume."

"Astor isn't the only source of trouble you will encounter," Ross continued. "You can expect the farmers of the back country to object as well. You see, there is no way they can get their corn to market except in liquid form. So, they convert their corn to whiskey and sell it to the American Fur Company, who in turn trades the whiskey to Indians for furs. Anyone who disrupts this operation won't be a very popular fellow."

"I hear what you are saying, Mr. Ross." He came to an abrupt halt in front of a tailor's shop. "Ah! Here we are."

Noting the puzzled expression on Ross's face, McKenney laughed. "Don't look so dismayed, my friend. It's the custom of my government to equip each Indian delegate with a new suit before an audience with the President. Just chalk it up to good will."

*   *   *   *

On February 22, 1816 Ross and the Cherokee delegation met with President Madison. Since the president's official residence still lay in ruins, they were received in the Octagon House. Located at the muddy intersection of 18th Street and New York Avenue, just a block southwest of the president's official home, the Octagon House was an imposing structure. It had been designed by William Thornton, who was the architect for the capitol. The owner, Col. John Tayloe, had made the residence available to President Madison while the executive mansion was under repair. Entering the circular marble hall on the ground floor, Ross was immediately impressed with the surrounding opulence; curtains of blue embossed cambric, trimmed with red silk fringe, hung at the windows. They were seated on couches covered with blue patch and French chairs covered with striped blue silk.

Dressed in a brown coat, knee breeches, stockings and buckled shoes, the President greeted the delegates. Now sixty-five, his wizened features were dominated by clear, blue eyes peering from under bushy eyebrows. A good-natured smile wreathed his face as he greeted Ross. Here was a man who shared something in common with the President; his height!

As clerk of the delegation, Ross seated himself as Col. John Lowrey, their official speaker, formally addressed the President. In the discussion following, the Cherokees laid out their concerns: equal pensions for those Cherokee wounded in the fighting against the Creeks, payment for destruction of Cherokee property during the war, cession of more land to South Carolina, and settlement of boundaries.

The President listened carefully to their presentation and assured them that their requests would be given sympathetic consideration. Detailed resolution of the matters would, of course, be referred to Secretary of War, William Crawford. As Ross closed his ledger he surmised that the President was not anxious to be caught in a direct line of fire from the hero of New Orleans who was also in Washington City actively opposing any concessions to the Cherokee.

During the days following the audience with the president Ross availed himself of the opportunity to explore Washington City with Thomas McKenney as guide. On March 9 they left the hotel and walked up Pennsylvania Avenue toward the gutted capitol building. On the south side stood Center Market where, Col. McKenney explained, most of the 12,000 residents of the city did their shopping for food. "Also," he added, "stay away from Marble Avenue. That's where ladies of ill repute ply their trade."

Between 7th and 3rd Streets nearly every building on the north and south sides of Pensylvania Avenue was a boarding house. "They call this Hash Row," McKenney wryly commented. "This is where many of our legislators abide while Congress is in session. Housing is a severe problem here, along with the weather in summer. Congressmen don't like to bring their families here."

Between 3rd and 2nd Streets they crossed the bridge over Tiber Creek. Once a beautiful stream, the Tiber was now an open sewer. Waste from many of the hotels on Pennsylvania Avenue, as well as the capitol building, was piped into this stream.

Still under construction when the building was fired by the British in August of 1814, the capitol now presented two scorched wings, the House and the Senate.

Ross and McKenney made their way toward a newly erected three-storied brick building that stood just east of the ravaged capitol.

"Congress seriously considered abandoning Washington City after the British burned it," McKenney explained, "but a group of private citizens had this building erected as an inducement to keep the government here. This is where Congress now meets. This morning they are debating a bill that deals with establishing a national bank. You may find it interesting." The room they entered was so packed they were barely able to shoulder their way in. As Ross maneuvered for standing room he stepped on something that produced a loud yelp. A man seated nearby glanced upward with a scowl. Ross then noticed several hunting hounds lying at the man's feet. "That's John Randolph of Virginia," McKenney said quietly. "He's something of a gadfly in Congress. Some refer to him as Mad Jack."

Even before becoming aware of the topic under discussion, Ross was captured by the melodious tone of the speaker's voice. It had a majestic richness and a persuasive harmony that held him spellbound.

"That's Speaker of the House, Henry Clay, from Kentucky," McKenney explained. "He's advocating a national bank and national currency."

"Will the speaker yield?" The words seemed to reverberate in the chamber.

"The speaker will gladly yield to Congressman Webster."

"That's Daniel Webster from New Hampshire," McKenney whispered.

As Ross looked on the young congressman rose deliberately, almost theatrically, from his chair. He was dressed in a long-tailed black coat with gold buttons and a buff colored vest. Blue pantaloons girthed a midrift that exhibited acquaintance with good food and drink. Though only of average height, Webster gave the impression of a giant. Black eyes burned beneath the shadow of heavy brows. When he spoke his words seemed to rumble from his massive chest.

"Our forefathers," said Webster, "resisted to the death the concept of centralized power. Would we so soon depart from their paths of wisdom. And, may I ask my learned friends, where in the venerable constitution of limited powers is the authority necessary for this Congress to regulate state banks?"

Before Webster could continue, a screech of chairs, a yelping of dogs, and a shrill voice erupted. It was John Randolph. Standing with a glass of bourbon in his hand, he shouted at Clay, "Thou hypocrite!! Why does the honorable speaker of the house now repudiate the very ideas he espoused earlier in opposing the renewal of the bank charter? Perhaps the Western Star now smells political roses!" Turning to Webster, he pointed a bony finger. "And has this second-term congressman, this Black Dan of New Hampshire, had an overnight conversion to strict interpretation of the constitution...or is it that his wallet is being fattened by the Yankee banks that have profited during the recent war?"

Instantly, the house was in an uproar. As Clay vigorously pounded his gavel and called "Order! Order!" Randolph raised a finger to the House members and went snarling out the door with his dogs.

Clay mopped his brow with a linen handkerchief as the House members resumed their seats. "Congressman Webster still has the floor. I apologize for the unseemly interruption."

Before Webster could speak, a high, flat voice cut in. "Would the Congressman from New Hampshire yield?"

Webster turned his leonine head and bowed. "It is with pleasure that I yield to my friend from South Carolina."

Ross watched as this new player in the drama rose to his feet. Standing a full six feet two inches tall, stiff, brown hair that stood straight up on his angular head, gave the appearance of even greater height. Deep-set, hazel green eyes calmly surveyed the House. Square-jawed and handsome, the young congressman confidently addressed the members.

"That's Calhoun," McKenney whispered.

Calhoun spoke at length regarding the need for a national bank. His eyes swept the entire assembly as he concluded. "May I remind my esteemed colleagues of this Fourteenth Congress, that liberty and sound morals are served by a sound currency and a nation free of debt. Disordered, depreciated currency, and empty treasury, and general economic depression are the breeding grounds of tyranny and anarchy."

"It is now approaching three o'clock," Clay announced. "The House will adjourn for the day and reassemble tomorrow morning at our regular time, nine o'clock." He banged his gavel and the House adjourned.

As Ross and McKenney made their way out of the building, they followed the crowd. Located at 3rd Street, on the south side of Pennsylvania Avenue, Mades was the nearest hotel to the capitol…and it was also the closest bar.

"Congressmen usually eat between three and four in the afternoon. We might as well join them." McKenney led the way into a dim, noisy, and smoky room.

"Ah, Colonel. Come and join us for a drink."

McKenney recognized the voice. "Thank you, Mr. Clay. I respectfully decline the drink but I would like to introduce to you a new-found admirer of yours. Gentlemen, meet John Ross, a delegate from the Cherokee nation."

"Welcome to Washington City, Mr. Ross." Clay stood and extended his hand. "Cherokee, you say? Looks more like a Scotsman to me."

"You're more right than wrong," Ross grinned. "I'm only one-eighth Cherokee. My father is Daniel Ross, originally from Southlandshire, Scotland."

"You're in good company, Ross. Let me introduce you to another Scot, John C. Calhoun from South Carolina."

Calhoun stood to shake hands. "Welcome, Mr. Ross. Please, join us for supper."

Ross seated himself and looked around. "Where is the gentleman from New Hampshire, the one opposing the bank bill?"

"Ah," said Clay. "You mean Mr. Webster. It's like this, Mr. Ross. The Yankees and gentlemen from the south don't socialize much. Of course, we have to work together in Congress, but, after their Hartford Convention, some of us see them as traitors. We see them as a cold-blooded lot and they see us as a bunch of immoral sots, what with our slaves and bourbon." He laughed and stirred some brown sugar into his glass of whiskey. "They're really not much fun."

"And what manner of business brings you to Washington City, Mr. Ross?" inquired Calhoun.

"The Cherokee rendered invaluable service to our side during the recent war," McKenney volunteered. "In fact, without their help, Jackson would have lost it all in the back country fight with the Creeks. Now, we need to reimburse the Cherokee for property losses they incurred, due to some of our undisciplined soldiers. And, there is some boundary questions that need to be ironed out."

"I see," Calhoun said quietly. "The Calhouns have had some experience with Cherokee and boundary problems."

"Oh? How is that?" asked Ross.

"It was back in the '60s, down along Long Canes Creek. The Cherokee killed dozens of settlers, including several Calhouns."

Ross met Calhoun's level gaze. "I see. Did the killings happen on your land or Cherokee land?"

Calhoun flushed slightly. "What is the nature of the boundary problem, Mr. Ross?"

"It seems that the Creek nation ceded some land to General Jackson that didn't belong to them. It belongs to the Cherokee. We want your government to restore that land to us."

"Come, come, Mr. Ross. The land in question, in truth, belongs to neither the Creek or the Cherokee. It belongs to the state of Georgia, according to the agreement worked out between the U.S. government and the state of Georgia back in 1802."

"I'm familiar with the circumstances, Mr. Calhoun, but I must differ with you. The Cherokee were not a party to that agreement. The land has long been home to the Cherokee and we have never ceded it to anyone. I'm sure that you will recall the Treaty of Ghent which your country signed with the British government. Article nine of that treaty provides that the United States will restore to such tribes all possessions which they enjoyed in 1811 prior to hostilities."

Calhoun's jawline stiffened. He rose and bowed stiffly. "You gentlemen will excuse me. I have other affairs to attend."

"Nothing rankles Calhoun more than meeting someone who is superior to his intellect," Clay laughed after Calhoun's departure.

A buxom barmaid bent over and whispered in Clay's ear. He smiled. "You gentlemen will also excuse me. I have been challenged to a game of poker…I have always paid homage to the fickle goddess of luck." With that, he stood, wrapped his arm low around the waist of the maiden, and left the room.

"Women, whiskey, and cards…nothing means more to Clay except political power," observed McKenney. "Calhoun on the other hand is something of a puritan, consumed singularly with political ambition. In him I think you will face a powerful enemy."

CHAPTER 4

BUSINESS
IN THE EAST

Ross and his party were permitted no further audiences with President Madison or Secretary of War, William Crawford. For a time they were apprehensive that Jackson had sabotaged their efforts. It was rumored that he had departed for his home in Tennessee and was smiling when he left Washington City. Finally, on March 22, 1816, they signed a treaty which had been concluded with Special Commissioner, George Graham. They regained the boundary line desired and were authorized a payment of $25,000 for war damages. In return the Cherokee agreed to permit the United States to open and have free use of all roads in Cherokee country.

Homeward bound, they traveled by way of Baltimore. From there they took a coach to Knoxville, arriving April 12. Here they discovered that their elation with the newly signed treaty was not shared by the whites. Tennessee had erupted with outrage. Speedy and violent protests, including those from Andrew Jackson, flooded Congress, the President, and Secretary of War, Crawford. Initially, Crawford refused to be intimidated and returned four million acres to the Cherokee.

Jackson raged and ranted. In his letters to Crawford he claimed that "the real Indians, the natives of the forest, had little quarrel with his treaty." It was the "designing half-breeds and the renegade white men who were at fault." "An

Indian," he lectured Crawford, "will claim anything and everything. Give them a single acre and they will demand the whole territory. It is high time the government of the United States stop worrying about rapacious Indians and start earning the confidence of its own citizens."

Threats of political retaliation took their toll and Crawford yielded. His intense, and long-term, political ambitions would not be served by siding with the Indians. They didn't vote!

Ross was at his home at Lookout Mountain when he received a letter from President Madison stating that three commissioners had been named to re-examine territorial claims. One of the commissioners was Andrew Jackson!

"Your cynicism regarding the Americans honoring treaties is justified," said Ross as he passed the letter to his brother, Lewis.

Lewis scanned the letter. "I see that Jackson wants to include Creeks, Choctaws, Chickasaws, and us in a meeting at the Chickasaw Council House. He knows we and the Chickasaws don't see eye to eye. It's another one of his attempts to divide and conquer."

Ross nodded. "Agent Meigs has just given me several large contracts. According to him, the United States government has decided to station troops here in the west. Ostensibly, the purpose is to keep an eye on the Spanish. Our contracts say we will be responsible for supplying them. That means I have to leave for Baltimore right away to make purchases. I can't make the meeting. You will be in charge of the business here so you can't go. So...who do we send?"

"Well, laddie, have you thought about your brother, Andrew?"

Ross slowly shook his head. "Yes, father, I have thought about Andrew. We have tried working together before. He seems to resent everything I tell him to do. He just isn't cut out for this line of work."

Dan Ross sighed. "I know...I just wish you boys could...well, get along with Andrew."

Ross looked at the aging Scot, now stooped and slow in his late fifties. "Father, we try. It would help if Andrew would also try."

$$* \qquad * \qquad * \qquad *$$

On the 12th of April, having been home less than thirty days, Ross packed his saddle bags and, with his servant, Moses, was off for Baltimore and business with the trading firm of Talbot Jones. When the Council met at Willstown on August 20, it would name someone to meet with Jackson. Meanwhile, his brother, Lewis, and his father would be overseeing construction on a new, larger warehouse and establishing a ferry across the Tennessee. The Federal Road, running from Savannah, thorough Augusta to Nashville, would require a ferry. It only made sense that Ross own the ferry.

Unlike the primitive conditions at Washington City, Baltimore was a beautiful and flourishing city. Virginia tobacco flowed out of the busy port as part of the growing trade with Europe. At the huge warehouses of Talbot Jones, Ross placed his orders. Blankets, traps, lead, bullet molds, ladles for melting lead, gun powder, salt, bolts of cloth, Barnett muskets, blacksmithing equipment, kettles, beads, knives, axes, saws, wedges…an endless list of goods to meet the needs not only of soldiers but the Cherokee as well.

"You might want to try out some of the gunpowder being made over in Delaware," offered Mr. Jones. "A young feller by the name of Du Pont set up business a few years back near Wilmington and he's been selling quite a bit of it to the government. And," he continued, "I'll stand behind these Gonter rifles made up in Lancaster. At ten-fifty apiece, you can't beat 'em."

"Not that I doubt your word, Mr. Jones," Ross responded, "but where I come from people insist that blankets, cloth, muskets, and gun powder be of English make. In the back country American made goods have a reputation for being shoddy. But I can use some advice on where to get some horses and wagons for hauling these goods to Tennessee."

"It's pretty well agreed that the best wagons are made by the Germans up around York and Hanover. C'mon, there's a dealer down the street."

Ross whistled in admiration as he examined the quality of the hand-crafted vehicles. They were smaller, lighter relatives of the Pennsylvania made Conestogas. With a blue-painted bed, ten feet long and three and a half feet wide, they could haul up to one and a half tons. Big red wheels, with broad, iron-bound rims, these wagons were more suitable for the primitive western roads. Ross purchased six wagons at eighty-five dollars each, including brakes. He then had a frame of hickory bows installed on each wagon which was then covered with heavy-duty canvas made of hemp. Waterproofed with linseed oil, the canvas offered protection to the goods as well as the drivers.

"I can recommend some drivers for you," Talbot volunteered. "A rough bunch…temperate in neither tongue nor drink…but they know how to drive."

During the days it took to load the wagons, Ross discussed with Mr. Jones the road options to Tennessee.

Talbot tapped the crude map with his pipe stem. "You could take the National Road. It starts up here at Cumberland…it ends up in Wheeling. Only it ain't done yet. Been workin' on it since 1808 but politics keeps holding up its funding. Or, you could head north and catch the road to Pittsburg at Lancaster. It carries a helluva lot of traffic between Philadelphia and Pittsburg. From Pittsburg, you can take the steamboat or flat boat all the way to Louisville."

With some time on his hands, Ross walked the streets of Baltimore. He was tired and he was lonely for Quatie. He had seen so little of her these last few months. Even though his father was around to watch over her, Ross knew she carried a heavy load of work in caring for the children and managing the house. Then the idea came to him. He would secure some assistance for Quatie. He turned down the street toward the slave market.

At this time of day there was little activity but under the shade of a magnolia tree Ross saw two forlorn blacks squatting, anchored to the tree with chains around their ankles. One of the blacks was a muscular man of magnificent build. He glowered as Ross approached. The other was a young girl, around age sixteen, Ross guessed. A voice called out from a shady doorway.

"Yo're in luck, mah frien. Yo're timin' is impeccable. Possibly th' best buy of the year and ya'll just walked right into it."

From the doorway a short, obese man emerged, fanning his florid face with a beat-up straw hat and carrying a cane. "Tucker's the name…Horace Tucker. Ah deal only in th' best of merchandise. Now, ya take these two. Just got 'em in yesterday. Seems the massa died and they hafta be sold to settle th' estate. Why, they're such perfect specimens that I'd keep 'em for m'self if I wuz a man of means."

"Well, I was just sorta looking around," Ross stammered. "Just thought I'd see what was available."

"Hmmm. Sounds to me lak yer new to th' tradin' business. Ever buy a slave afore?"

"No, I haven't, to be honest with you."

"Well, it makes no never mind. If you've dealt with horses and mules it's the same thing with niggers. Just don't buy one that's winded or has bad teeth," he wheezed. "Now, you take this big buck. Isn't he somethin'?"

Tucker prodded the black with his cane. "Stand up, boy. Let's have a look atcha. Now, see what I mean? With a cock like his, you could put him to stud with all the darkie gals you own and he'd keep 'em all happy. And you would improve your stock considerably. Lotsa owners are doing just that. Gals can screw around all they like but only after the plantation stud has gottem pregnant."

Ross rubbed his chin. "I was really thinking more about buying a female."

"Well, why'd ya say so? Here, stand up, girl."

The girl stood, her eyes downcast. Ross noted a tremor in her body.

Tucker took his cane and lifted her thin, cotton skirt to display her thighs. "Now tell me, friend, where have you ever seen anything prettier than that?"

Embarrassed, Ross turned his head. "Alright, I'll take her. How much?"

"Considerin' the amount of pleasure she's gonna bring ya, I should ask a premium price. But, since I'm a man of sentiment, I'm willin' to sacrifice her for four hundred dollars."

"Sounds like no sacrifice to me. Besides, I'm not buying her for myself."

"Well, of course not," Tucker leered. "We never do. But, friend, since this is your first buy, I'm gonna outfit her with a new dress and new shoes…just for the sake of friendship…and any future business you might bring my way."

"Alright, done," said Ross, "See that she's delivered to me at Talbot Jone's warehouse this afternoon. While you're at it, get her a good mule to ride. There's enough profit in your price that you can afford a thirty-dollar mule."

He started to leave, then turned. "Bye the way, girl, what do they call you?"

"Zipporah," she said softly.

*   *   *   *

John looked at the small caravan with a feeling of pride. The wagons were heavily, but carefully, loaded. The horses, feisty from inactivity, snorted and kicked in their harness. A few miles on the road would take the sass out of them.

He turned to Moses. "Are you sure you can handle this?"

Moses laughed. "Comes the day I can't herd six wagons…" He pointed to the girl with Ross. "Who is she and what is she doing here?"

"This is Zipporah," said Ross. "I put her in your care until we get home. She will be of help to Quatie around the house."

Moses frowned.

They had decided that John would take the stage to Pittsburg. Moses would follow with the wagons. During the three weeks or so that it would take for the wagons to get to Pittsburg, John would be arranging for boats to float their gear down the Ohio.

The cluster of teamsters who had been engaged in animated conversation, now broke and moved toward them.

"Time to go, men," Ross announced. "We're wasting daylight."

"Sorry, Mr. Ross. Don't think we're going with you."

"What?" Ross blurted out in astonishment. A vision of being stranded before the journey even began chilled him. "What's the problem?"

The speaker cleared his throat nervously. "Tha' problem is, we'uns are free men…and it ain't to our likin' to be workin' aginst slave labor." The other teamsters grunted assent.

"For heaven's sake! Do you mean Moses?"

"If that's tha' name of your slave, that's exactly what we mean. Honest men can't stand up to slave labor."

John paused for a moment. "Your name is Kruger?"

"Yes, Uriah Kruger. I'm a proud man, Mr. Ross. Been a teamster all my life. Made a good living at it…but I won't work alongside slave labor…none of us will."

"Well, Mr. Kruger, Moses is no slave. He's a free nigger. He gets paid driving for me same as anyone else."

The teamsters looked at each other in surprise. "Well, that sorta throws a different light on the matter," said Kruger. "But what about the gal?"

"Zipporah? Yes, I did buy her. But she won't be competing with you men. In fact, she will be doing the cooking for you the next few weeks."

"Well…," Kruger dropped his head and cleared his throat. "Come on, men. Get them broomtails movin'."

Ross paid his fifty dollars for a ticket from Baltimore to Pittsburg. The stage ride from Baltimore to Lancaster proved uneventful. Surrounded by fertile wheat farms, fat cattle, and sleek horses, Lancaster was the breadbasket of the coastal region. It was the meeting place for roads from south and west. It was also the end of the journey for teamsters making their way over the mountains from Pittsburg.

At Lancaster the road divided. To the east the pike ran sixty-three miles to Philadelphia. To the west a stump-studded road cut a raw slash through unbroken, timbered wilderness some 240 miles to Pittsburg. By stagecoach the journey would consume the better part of a week, depending upon road conditions and weather. For Moses and the loaded wagons, plodding along at a rate of one to two miles an hour, the trip would consume at least three weeks of very long days.

From Harrisburgh to Carlisle the road wound southwest through dense forests of pine and oak following the valley between South Mountain and Tuscarora Mountain. From time to time the stage passed bands of laborers digging stumps and cutting trees to widen the road. If it wasn't road conditions that impeded their progress, it was the heavy commerce. Day after day the stage squeezed past heavily laden Conestoga wagons filled with corn and wheat moving east to Philadelphia and New York. Others were moving west with manufactured goods. Weathered teamsters, with stogies clamped grimly between their teeth, making no attempt to hide their disdain for the stagecoach drivers, walked alongside their wagons, skillfully guiding their six-horse teams along the narrow, rutted roads.

Jostling the Conestogas for room were endless numbers of emigrant wagons. The wagons, most often pulled by one horse, contained the worldly goods of the family. Father and mother trudged alongside, encouraging the horse. The good woman would be carrying, or leading by hand, some weary little traveler. Other children, of whom there were many, trailed behind the wagon. Rich or poor, the speed of travel was tied to the abilities of the horse. To Ross it seemed that the whole country was on the move.

At a wagon stand at Greensburgh wilted spirits started to revive. From here it was only forty miles of finished turnpike on to Pittsburg. In the wide, open yard surrounding the inn at Greensburgh, drivers of the Concord coaches, teamsters of the Conestogas, and emigrant families unharnessed and fed their teams. Those who could afford it took their meals inside the inn. Others cooked their meals around communal fires. It was time for sharing information about road conditions, telling yarns, and smoking stogies. Those who had the energy danced to the innkeeper's fiddle. But soon the night echoed with a cacophony of snoring as, with feet to the fire, the drivers slept on the barroom floor. At dawn, a quick breakfast, a harnessing and hitching up of braying mules, a crack of whips, and the long train of wagons was again in motion. The crush of humanity, moving west, caused Ross to ponder the future of his people.

*   *   *   *

As Ross stepped out of the City Hotel, the smoke and bustle of Pittsburg immediately assaulted his senses. Over breakfast the enthusiastic hotel proprietor referred to the city as the Thermopylae of the west. Flowing from the northeast, the Allegheny River met the Monongahela to form the Ohio River. Situated on the point of land where the two rivers met, Pittsburg was the funnel through which flowed thousands of immigrants making their way west.

From his hotel on Liberty Street, Ross walked south through the narrow, grubby streets lined with brick houses. Along the banks of the Monongahela were boatyards and warehouses, small inns, and grog shops. The shores of the river were lined with boats of every description: steamboats, barges, keels, and arks, or flats. Sounds of hammer, saw and hewing ax rose from the many projects under construction. Ross noted that some were being loaded with finished iron products, barrels of flour, beer, glass, and pottery.

In Baltimore Talbot Jones had recommended that Ross seek out a seasoned Pittsburg riverman by the name of Murdock Rook. A few inquiries led him to the person he sought.

In his mid-forties, Murdock Rook was a man of medium height with a powerful build. A chesty man with burly biceps, Rook boldly looked at the world through bright, blue eyes. A ruddy, weathered face was framed with white chin whiskers and tufts of white hair encircled his bald head. Ross had barely begun to explain his need to transport loaded wagons down river to Tennessee when Rook raised his hand to indicate that he had heard enough.

"It's Orleans boats ye need," said Rook. Seeing the puzzlement on Ross's face, he hurried on. "Thems flatboats. We call 'em Orleans boats because they are one-way boats. Once ye gettum to Orleans, ye break 'em up and sellum for lumber. They are worth their weight in salt anywhere they ain't got sawmills. Then agin', I could put ye in keel boats, but they take a lot more time to build and they cost you more money. Back in 1803 we built a keel boat for Lewis and Clark right here on this spot."

Noting that Ross seemed impressed, Rook went on. "Nother thing…we built the first steamboat on the Ohio right here in Pittsburg. Back in 1810 it was. Built by a feller named Roosevelt…Nicholas J. Roosevelt. So we ain't no johnny-come-lately to the boat business here in Pittsburg."

"Guess that's why Talbot Jones recommended you."

"Umm, well, yes. Now about that flatboat. We can make 'em any size ye want…up to twenty-five feet wide and ninety feet long…cost ye a dollar a foot in length."

"You know what we need. I'll leave the specifications up to you. How long will it take to construct four of them?" asked Ross. "I'll need them in about two weeks."

Rook frowned and pulled on his whiskers. "Well, can't rightly say. Gotta awful lot of work piled up ahead of ye."

"It will be hard cash up front."

Rook brightened immediately. "Well, I'll tell ye. Let me juggle some of my men around. Wouldn't be surprised if we couldn't get 'em done in, oh, I'd say about two weeks."

Ross laughed, "Done. Shake on it."

As Ross turned to go, Rook called after him. "Ever floated the Ohio afore?"

"No, I haven't."

Rook rubbed his chin with the back of his hand. "Uh huh! Well, yer gonna need four men for each boat. Come 'er. Let me show ye."

Rook led the way to a flatboat nearing completion. "Look", he pointed to the rectangular raft. "Thar's a oar on each side of the boat. Them's what we call sweeps. That long oar in the back is yer rudder. Ya got another shorter oar up front called the gouger. Yer gonna need all of 'em to keep that goddamned thing in the current and off the sandbars. That Ohio is damn near a thousand miles of reefs, snags, and shifting sandbars."

Ross grinned. "You can tell I'm green as grass about these things. I do thank you for your help."

Rook grinned in turn. "Nother thing. Ye better stop over at Cramer's Place and pick up a copy of The Navigator."

"What's The Navigator?"

"It's a pilot's manual for the Ohio. A feller named Zodak Cramer prints it and updates it every year. If'n I wuz you, wouldn't try to float that damn Ohio without it."

During the days Ross spent waiting the arrival of Moses and the wagons, he studied the pilot's manual and took in the sights. He climbed the five-hundred foot Grant's Hill that overlooked the city. Here he saw the miners extracting coal from a horizontal bed six feet in depth. He visited the Bakewell glass works where the beautiful white and friable sandstone, so prevalent in the area, was being converted into exquisite flint glass. At this first glass factory west of the Alleghenies, he purchased a set of elegantly cut goblets as a gift for Quatie. To fill up the days, he even made a call at Porter's Brewery and sampled the wares. Much of Porter's beer was shipped down the Ohio and Mississippi to New Orleans.

From some unknown sense of urgency, Ross settled up with Rook, who agreed to pass along the pilot's manual and further advice to Moses. He then purchased passage on a steamboat to Louisville, Kentucky.

*   *   *   *

For days they had floated down the Ohio, past growing settlements with names like Wheeling, Marietta, Maysville, and a thriving town called Cincinnati. During the daylight hours they steered carefully against the rain-swollen river currents and southwesterly winds that were constantly blowing upriver creating white caps on the water. Miami Indians had given the Ohio its name; Ohiopeekhanne, meaning the foaming white river, or the river of white caps.

They were constantly on the lookout for keelboats being rowed or hauled upriver. Another danger was that of being overtaken by craft being floated by men totally ignorant of the river. Once across the Appalachian Range there was but one river that would take settlers to the heartland and that was the Ohio. To Ross it seemed that settlers were streaming down the river by the thousands.

Here and there they passed isolated cabins where farmers were struggling mightily to upturn the native grasses and plant a crop of corn. Ross found himself pondering over these people, always restless, always pushing, always searching for some better country which always seemed to lie to the west.

At length they arrived at the flourishing town of Louisville with a growing population of almost four thousand people. Here they encountered the Falls of the Ohio. Freight and passengers were unloaded and transferred to Shipping-sport, a town directly below the falls. Here steamboats of up to 500 tons made their turnaround to New Orleans. Some, handsomely fitted, could move their passengers to New Orleans within eight or ten days.

Ross set out to explore the steamboats. Finding one that suited his tastes, he walked up the gangplank of The Washington where he found the captain in the wheelhouse.

"Does this craft make a stop at Nashville on the way south?" inquired Ross.

"The Washington stays with the Mississippi all the way to New Orleans," replied the captain. "Would you be needing passage?"

"Yes, I would. Oh, I apologize for not introducing myself, captain. Name's Ross. John Ross."

The captain extended his hand. "Shreve to you. Captain Henry M. Shreve."

Ross glanced around. "I've never been on a steamboat before, Captain Shreve. How long does it take you to get to New Orleans?"

Captain Shreve smiled and laid a loving hand on the wheel. "This beauty will take you to New Orleans and back in forty-one days. Come, let me show you around. I sired this lady. Supervised ever lick of work done on her. Her hull was built at Wheeling. Used seasoned timbers out of old Fort Henry. These double high pressure engines were built on the Monongahela. Placed them on deck instead of down in the hold. She's a double decker. The first of its kind." Shreve turned to Ross. "You asked me if we made a stop in Nashville. You got business there?"

Ross nodded in the affirmative.

"You'll have to make a transfer at Paducah. There's smaller boats there that will get you up the Cumberland to Nashville. We cast off at daylight tomorrow morning, soon as we get all this Kentucky tobacco stowed."

Dusk was falling as Ross stiffly got out of the boat that had rowed him from Eddyville to Johnson's Landing on the riverfront at Nashville. Wearily, he started climbing up steep, muddy streets past the rock-faced bluff, past warehouses and shabby cabins. The path soon led him onto Market Street which terminated at the town square. As he emerged on Market, a voice called out. "Mr. Ross? Is that you, Mr. Ross?"

Ross turned to see a black man approaching. "Yes, I'm John Ross."

"Ah'm Robert Rentfro, Mr. Ross. Would you come with me please? Ross, too tired to argue, followed Rentfro across the street into a tavern. A sign over the entrance read "Black Bobb's".

"Sit, Mr. Ross. Let me fetch you a cold drink."

Ross took a long drink of the liquid set before him. "Why, that's lemonade," he exclaimed.

"Made from lemons shipped all the way upriver from New Orleans," boasted Rentfro with a toothy smile.

Ross took another swig than placed his glass on the table. "Now, tell me, Mr. Rentfro, how did you know I was John Ross?"

"Yore pappy wuz here t'other day. Sed you would be coming along and would I keep an eye out for you. Ah sez glad to do it. He sez to tell you there wuz a mighty serious meetin' comin' up on June 20 at a place called Calhoun. Sez its important that you be there. Sez for you to git a horse and git on home. Sed somethin' about a Gin'rl Jackson bein' there."

"Ah, so that's it. Wonder what Sharp Knife is up to now." Ross finished his drink and reached to pay his bill.

"Never you mind, Mr. Ross. The drink's on me. Ah owns this place."

"You own this place?" Ross asked in surprise.

"Yessuh. Ah'm a free black. Ah owns this place for the lass fo'teen years."

"Well, I think that's just fine. I thank you for the drink…and for passing along the information. Now, could you direct me to someplace where I can get a good night's sleep. I haven't slept in a bed that wasn't moving for the past few days."

"You'd be welcome to stay here but ah feels you would be more comfer'ble in the Talbot House."

Ross thanked Rentfro again and walked on up Market Street to the public square. Here was the stone courthouse, a whipping post and stocks, and a shed where farmers marketed their produce. Facing the square were Talbot's Hotel, Winn's Tavern, and the Nashville Inn. Now, for a hot bath and sleep in a real bed. Whatever Sharp Knife had in mind would have to wait.

CHAPTER 5

WE ARE DISTRESSED

The slanting rays of a setting sun beat down upon Ross and Ridge as they rode into the Cherokee Agency at Calhoun on June 20, 1817. The tiny settlement, nestled in the wooded hills on the north side of the Hiwassee River, had been laid out by a prominent Cherokee, Major John Walker, who had distinguished himself at the Battle of Horseshoe Bend. He named the hamlet after the secretary of war. The agency, which was located at Southwest Point from 1801, had been moved to Calhoun in 1807.

"Seems that Jackson beat us here," observed The Ridge as he dismounted under the shade of a large cedar tree. "Gives him a little extra time to line some pockets."

"And he doesn't seem too particular who he consorts with," added Ross. "Isn't that John D. Chisholm from the Arkansas Cherokee with him?"

Ridge peered at the group lounging on the porch of the agency. "Yes, it is. I should have killed him when I sunk a tomahawk into Doublehead." Noting the quizzical look on Ross's face, he added, "He married Doublehead's daughter…was in on his father-in-law's plan to sell Cherokee land. For the sake of his health, he fled to Arkansas country."

"We'll find out soon enough why he is here. Right now, let's get some supper," said Ross. Later, as the glowing embers died in the campfire, Ross and Ridge sat pondering the upcoming meeting with Jackson.

"This will be your first meeting as a negotiator with Jackson," said Ridge. "You can expect trickery and fits of temper. He is a master at terrorizing his enemies. That's how he browbeat the Creeks into signing the Treaty of Ft. Jackson when the war ended. He lied to them, threatened them, bribed them, and ignored the Treaty of Ghent…treated the friendlies same as his foes. And, his government let him get away with it. Not too surprising, seeing as how they want us all removed so they can take over our lands. John Coffee and a lot of Jackson's Tennessee speculators have already swarmed into the Creek cession."

"Not likely the federal government would try to bring a national hero to heel just to please the Indians and England," Ross concurred. "With the Treaty of Fort Jackson, he has accomplished two things: he has set a precedent for removal of all Indians and he has thrown the fear of God into the Spanish."

By the end of June enough chiefs and headsmen from the eastern and Arkansas Cherokees had assembled. Jackson, flanked by Governor Joseph McMinn of Tennessee and General David Meriwether of Georgia, opened the meeting in his usual intimidating manner.

"I have," he explained, "been appointed by your Father, the President, to secure compensation to the United States. My country is willing to exchange land in the west, now occupied by your Cherokee brothers, for the remaining Cherokee land east of the Mississippi. Let me read to you President Jefferson's message to the Cherokee, dated January 9, 1809."

Concluding his reading, he removed his glasses and fixed the assembly with cold, blue eyes. "This," he stated, "constitutes a firm, binding agreement between the Cherokee people and the Great Father for an exchange of lands and your removal west of the Mississippi. It has been years and you still have not lived up to your part of the bargain. You have not acted in good faith. Too long you have neglected your sacred promise to the Great Father."

Charles Hicks rapidly translated Jackson's remarks. For a moment there was nothing but stunned silence. Then a rumble of dissent rolled across the assembly. It subsided as The Ridge rose to his feet and crossed his arms across his chest.

"All who hear my voice know of my great admiration for General Jackson. But I must respectfully dispute his interpretation of President Jefferson's letter. I had the honor to be one of the six Cherokees who met with the Great Father in Washington City in December of 1808. We went to thank him for his benevolence to his red children and to say goodbye as he departed office. We had a talk with the president, nothing more. There was no treaty."

Caught flat-footed with this exposure, Jackson responded furiously. "Does Major Ridge take me for a fool? Was there not a more compelling reason for your visit to President Jefferson? Do you deny that many of your people at that time wanted to remove beyond the Mississippi and that President Jefferson pledged his support to them?"

Ridge refused to be intimidated. "It is no secret that there have long been differences between the Cherokees of the upper and lower towns. Some refused to give up the hunt and then there were those of us who wish for education, for government, and other blessings of civilization. The hunters would abandon our homeland in exchange for a pittance. I resist it here in my place as a man, as a chief, as a Cherokee. I scorn the movement of a few men to unsettle the nation and trifle with our attachment to the land of our forefathers. Look abroad over the face of this country—along the rivers, the creeks, and their branches, and you behold the dwellings of people who repose in content and security. Why is this grand scheme projected to lead away to another country the people who are happy here? Do I speak without the response of any heart in this assembly, or do I speak as a free man to men who are free and know their rights? I pause to hear. A-wani-ski."

The sounds of approval that rose from the Cherokee fed Jackson's rage. "Words! Words! What you hear are words that serve the selfish interests of a few. Words that do not honor a treaty with the Great Father."

"I repeat, General Jackson, there was no treaty. The delegation that visited President Jefferson was not authorized to divide the Cherokee lands." Ridge swung to fix his gaze upon Chisholm. "As for those Cherokee in Arkansas, they went as individuals without the blessing of the Council. If they have encountered difficulties, they have no one to blame but themselves. If they are not happy with their plight, they have but to come home."

Jackson struggled to regain the initiative. "Do you take me for a fool? Major Ridge, you were only one of the six in the delegation to meet with the president. There were others in attendance whose version differs from yours. Will Chief Toochalar step forward?"

Toochalar rose, looked nervously from side to side, and placed himself alongside Jackson. In a voice hardly audible, he stated, "I declare to you that the other chiefs and I had full powers from the lower towns to treat with President Jefferson. What General Jackson is telling you is true."

The chiefs and headsmen stared with obvious disbelief, appalled at Toochalar's treachery. That night as the chiefs met around a council fire, The Ridge rose to speak. "It is with shame that I call Toochalar kinsman. The shame he brought on by his betrayal of our trust last September at the Chickasaw Council House, by his disobedience to the only instructions we gave him before the meeting…sell no land! And now, in his greed and weakness he is willing to sell out his people for a few cheap presents offered by General Jackson. We are in a struggle for our very survival. We cannot tolerate traitors among us. Doublehead met his reward, Tahlonteskee, for his own good health, imigrated to Arkansas, and Black Fox was deposed. I now call on this council of chiefs to remove Toochalar from office and to require of him a signed statement repudiating Jackson's claims."

Despite Toochalar's weak protest that he was only following the advice of Agent Meigs, the council quickly removed him from a position of authority.

For eight days the dispute continued, to no avail, over the meaning of Jefferson's "talk" in 1808 to the Cherokee. On July 2 John Ross stood to read a memorial which he and Elijah Hicks had prepared.

"It has always been our desire to meet and promote the views of the General Government, so far as it is consistent with justice and reason. In 1809 the upper towns had no knowledge of the intentions of the lower towns but we absolutely deny that any commitment was made to exchange lands."

As Ross continued to read, a glance at Jackson told him that old Sharp Knife was indifferent and unmoved. "We feel assured that our father, the President, will not compel us into measures so diametrically against the will and interests of a large majority of our nation. True, there might be some chiefs and families who are ready to emigrate, but as a nation, we wish to remain on our land and hold it fast. We appeal to our father, the President, to do us justice. We are now distressed with the alternative proposal to remove from this country to the Arkansas or stay and become citizens of the United States. We oppose both proposals. We are not yet civilized enough to become citizens of the United States nor do we wish to be compelled to move to a country so much against our inclination and will. To go west would mean a return to the same savage state of life that we were before." Ross paused and looked directly at Jackson. "You tell us to speak freely and make our choice. We believe there is a third choice; a choice we want and feel we are entitled to. Our choice is to remain on our lands and follow the pursuits of agriculture and civilization. Suffer us to remain in peaceable possession of this our country. We appeal to our father, the President of the United States, to do us justice. We look to him in our hour of distress."

Ross handed the document to Jackson. "This memorial is signed by sixty-seven chiefs here attending."

Jackson snatched the paper his face twitching with anger. "Do you realize what you have signed? Do you realize that this paper labels your father, the President, a liar? Do you understand that? How many of you are prepared to call the President a liar?" He turned to Toochalar. "I see your name affixed to this document. This contradicts what you said previously. Where th' hell do you stand, Toochalar? And you, Old Glass? I see your name here too." One by one Jackson called on the chiefs and one by one they denied knowing what they had signed.

Jackson looked up in triumph. "Well, Mr. Ross, I think we have completely exposed this base attempt of fraud and deception. Before you indulge in more such deception, I would have you look around and recollect what has happened to your brothers, the Creeks. Do you want similar treatment?" He wadded up Ross's paper and threw it on the ground. "By the eternal, I shall prepare a treaty for you to sign that keeps your agreement with President Jefferson. This meeting is adjourned."

Ross turned to The Ridge, his face taut with anger. "Never have I seen such arrogance...such blatant intimidation. What happened to our people? Why did they cave in so shamelessly?"

"Not all of them caved in. The general knew who to call on...those who owed him favors but mostly those he had bribed. Most of them were friends of Double-head."

Six days later Ross sat reading the treaty Jackson had prepared for their signatures. "Jackson is always consistent with his priorities; the first two articles take away more of our lands. The rest deal with dust and feathers. I will not sign."

As the chiefs and headsmen lined up to affix their signature, or X, to the treaty, Jackson noted several of them hanging back. "If you do not choose to sign this treaty," he threatened, "the government might cease to protect you from intruders. Your annuities and assistance from the government might be cut off. If you do not sign, it will certainly be deemed unfriendly by your father, the President. And...maybe I'll deal solely with the Cherokee of Arkansas."

Ross nervously awaited the results of the voting. In spite of Jackson's threats only thirty-one of the sixty-seven chiefs signed. That was less than half, not enough to secure a valid treaty. Angered and embarrassed, Jackson sent for Chisholm.

"I don't see you signature on this treaty. Mind telling me why?"

Chisholm grinned and tugged at his scraggly beard. "This treaty...it must be powerfully important to you to git it signed."

"Of course it's important," Jackson testily replied. "What the hell kind of game are you playing?"

"Seems to me you would 'preciate havin' fifteen more names on that treaty, gin'rul. I can give you that."

"What the hell are you talking about?" growled Jackson.

"I hold the proxy of the thirteen Cherokee that have already gone back to Arkansas. That, plus mine and Roger's names, would put you over the hump."

Jackson's breath quickened. "Just how much appreciation are you looking for, Chisholm?"

"Oh, I'd leave that up to the ginerosity of the gin'rul."

"Deliver that proxy and you'll have a thousand dollar's worth of appreciation."

*   *   *   *

Ross scanned the treaty. "I don't think you have a valid treaty, General. Less than half the chiefs have signed."

Jackson shrugged. "Sorry to disappoint you, Ross, but Chisholm and John Rogers have yet to sign."

"Chisholm?" snorted Ross. "You would deal with a man of such low character?"

"He can read and write. He understands the treaty. That's all I need to know about him."

"That still leaves you with less than half the needed signatures."

"Not if I count the other thirteen Arkansas delegates."

"But they can't sign. They've already gone home."

"Yes, but they gave their proxy to Chisholm. Thirty-one plus fifteen makes forty-six. The way I count, that makes a majority any way you slice it."

"That's plain fraud, general. Your congress won't approve such a fraudulent treaty."

"You overestimate our congressmen, Ross. As always, they will do what's in their best interest."

"Are you saying there is no honor among your congressmen?"

Jackson chuckled. "Ross, if you intend to become a political leader among your people, there are a few things you need to learn. If it comes down to honor or a chance to profit from a deal, you can damn well bet that profit will win."

*   *   *   *

He had failed! On his first attempt at negotiating with Jackson, he had been defeated. Now it was time to report the failure to the Council. Ross gently guided Old Pathkiller through the east entrance of the seven-sided council house. After seventy-three winters white hair crowned the weathered, walnut visage.

Ross seated Pathkiller on a mat at the center of the room and braced the old man's back with a roll of blankets. No breeze lessened the August heat. On each side of the council house, the Cherokee seated themselves by clan. In a semi-circle facing Old Pathkiller sat the seven prime counselors representing the seven clans of the Cherokee: Ani-waya, the Wolf People; Ani-Kawi, the Deer People; Ani-Tsiskwa, the Bird People; Ani-Wadi, the Paint People; Ani-Sahini, the Blue People; Ani-Gatu-ge-u-e, the Kituwah People, and Ani-Gilahi, the Long Hair People. A distinctive headdress indicated clan membership. Each clan was the descendant of one family.

With the clan counselors sat the council of elders, the chief speaker, Major Ridge, messengers, and ceremonial officers. Behind these stood a mix of young warriors and women. The matriarchal stage of government among the Cherokee was passed.

Through rheumy eyes, Old Pathkiller peered at the assembly before him. Though their images were not clear, he knew these were the Ani-Yunwiya, "The Real People", once so great and formidable. From the time the Great Buzzard had formed the Great Smokies, the Cherokee had dominated them. Once greatly feared by their enemies, they were now becoming a splintered and divided people. Pathkiller knew he could no longer hold them together. The pressure of the whites and the complexity of events were coming too fast for him. Born in another world, Pathkiller brooded over the destiny of his people. He pulled the blanket tighter over his thin shoulders. In his heart he knew that he would be the last of the full-blooded Cherokee chiefs.

"Di-ginay' li." He spoke the language of the Cherokee. He had never seen the need to learn the words of the whites. "Friends," he began. "We had hoped that the white man would never travel to our side of the mountains. That hope is gone. They have crossed over the mountains and settled upon our lands. There are many good white men, I know, but I am afraid of them as a race. I can shake their hand, a custom pleasing to the white man, but I cannot trust them. The Great White Father in Washington City will speak kindly to the Cherokee but his promises are soon broken by his people. They ask for treaties and their treaties always ask for more land. After every treaty comes another president and another demand for our land. Now the Cherokee have set their faces forever against further cessions."

His high-pitched voice quavered. He struggled to project his words to the assembly. "We must make it most difficult for anyone to go west. Any Cherokee who would enroll is no longer a Cherokee. He will no longer be a citizen of our nation. He will be guilty of…" Pathkiller's words trailed off. Outside the council house rose a cacophony of yelps and shouts. All heads turned as a solitary rider, soiled and stained with travel, stumbled toward the center of the room, followed closely by a rabble of excited young warriors.

Hicks blocked the intruders. "What is the meaning of this? Can't you see the Council is in session?"

"I am Tsisqua-ya, Red Bird," said the rider. "I am sent by Tahlonteskee, principal chief of the western Cherokee. Our enemies, the Osage, are at our throats. They steal our horses, they plunder our crops, they kill our people. We need your help. I have ridden night and day to bring this request to you."

"Your plight is no concern of ours," said the Ridge. "Your troubles are of your own making. You chose to move west."

A rumble of dissent rose from the ranks of the young warriors.

"But we are your kin," pleaded Red Bird. "We are of the same blood, the same clans." He turned to the young warriors. "The moment of great danger grows near. Which of you would count it as nothing for the Osage to kill your brother?"

Shouts of support rose from the warrior ranks. Older members of the Council sat quietly, casting side glances at one another.

Old Pathkiller raised his hand for silence. "There is truth in what has been spoken here, on both sides. Those who chose to listen to the white man and moved toward the setting sun did make their own beds and we should let them lie in them. But, it is also true that many in the west are friends and kinsmen. In time of distress, we cannot turn our backs on our people. So that we do not tear the seam that ties us together, let those who would fight the Osage depart peacefully from our midst...if you can find a leader."

"I will lead these warriors to the aid of our western brothers."

Old Pathkiller peered into the gloom. "Will the one who just spoke step forward?"

A young man emerged from the crowd. "I am John McLamore. I served as a captain under General Jackson during the war against the Red Sticks."

Pathkiller studied the face of McLamore for a moment. "You will do just fine. These hot-blooded young men will profit with a man of your experience to lead them. May the Great Spirit, Asgaya-Galun-lati', the Man Above, watch over all of you."

✳ ✳ ✳ ✳

"You sent for me, General?"

"Yes, I did, Houston. Come on in." With his gnarled thumb Jackson firmly tamped the tobacco into his corncob pipe. "You know, Houston, there's nothing like a good smoke, a good whiskey, and a good woman."

"Yessir." Houston knew that the general had not requested his presence to discuss any of these topics.

The puff of smoke Jackson blew into the air drifted lazily across a beam of late October sun. Suddenly, he was racked with a spell of coughing. He spit into a handkerchief already tinged with red. Regaining his composure he continued. "Houston, I'm sitting here on my ass waiting for orders to Florida. Those goddamned Seminoles need just what we gave the Creeks. Out west the Osage are raising hell with the Cherokee. None of this helps in moving the rest of the Cherokee."

"Yessir." This wasn't the point of the meeting either.

"I'm ordering Major Stephen Long to build a new fort on the Arkansas near the Osage border. Now, you've done a fine job in the office of the adjutant general here in Nashville, but I think you are as bored sitting on your ass as I am." Jackson turned to his desk and picked up an official looking paper. "I have secured for you from the War Department an assignment as sub-agent to the Cherokee. I need someone to counteract the intimidation that Ross, Ridge, and others of their ilk, are spreading. I need someone to encourage the Cherokees to enroll to move west. I think you are just the man for the job."

"Will I have to resign from the army?"

"Not at all. You will retain your rank. I seem to recall a certain Cherokee squaw you were fond of. This, what we will call a special assignment, will get you a little closer to her. Make the most of it."

✳   ✳   ✳   ✳

Houston drained his tankard and reached for a refill. He mopped up a spill on the bar with his index finger and licked it. "I swear, Rogers, this is the best whiskey in Knoxville."

"Whiskey's whiskey, Sam. Right now you wouldn't know good whiskey from horse piss."

Houston steadied himself against the bar. "John Rogers, you're some sunuvabitch of a buddy. Why'nd you not tell me Tiana was married 'stead of lettin' me make an ass outta myself?"

"Fer god's sake, Sam. The last we heard about you was when you were wounded at Horseshoe Bend. That's almost four years ago. Did you expect my sister to wait forever?"

Houston studied the tankard between his palms. "Little Tiana Rogers...now Mrs. David Gentry...wife of David Gentry, blacksmith. Not just any ole blacksmith, mind you, but a wealthy blacksmith." With the back of his hand he mopped the dribble of whiskey off his chin. "Without a doubt, she's much better off. What th' hell...I couldn't afford her on a soldier's pay. Just look at me, John. Four years I've been wearing this monkey suit and what has it brought me? I'm a goddam lieutenant...that's all I am. And now, by the grace of General Jackson, I'm a sub-agent to the Cherokee."

"That's an appointment not to be taken lightly, Sam."

"Yeah, but it's only temporary, John. Most likely, it's a position not even needed. Hell Fire Jack lit out for Arkansas without a bit of my persuasion."

"You gotta remember, Sam, my father is one unrepentant Tory. He couldn't wait to put distance between himself and these Americans."

"I hope he realizes what danger he is putting Tiana in...them damn Osages are not a pretty bunch."

"There's not a helluvalot you can do about that, Sam. To get your mind off her, why don't you come with my uncle and me? Chief Tahlonteskee is leading an Arkansas delegation to Washington City to straighten out a treaty problem. We can always use a good translator. Why don't you ride along with us?"

Houston thought for a moment. "What the hell...why not? I can use a change of scenery."

*   *   *   *

Outside a cold November rain slashed across a colorless land, flooding the creeks and making the roads a quagmire. Ross handed a hot toddy to his guest. "Here, Hanks, this will take the chill off. Now, sit back and tell me what happened and how you got in on that awful campaign."

Hanks cupped the drink in his hands and sipped, letting the warmth sink into his body. "It was stupid. I had some furlough time and nothing special to do with it so I thought it might be fun to go west with McLamore. I wanted to see the country and maybe get in on some action with the Osage. I got more than I bargained for."

"Go on," urged Ross.

Hanks shook his head in disbelief. "Never before have I been ashamed to have Cherokee blood."

"Why now?"

"During the Deer-Mating Moon, October, the Osage warriors are always on the plains hunting buffalo. But McLamore wanted to be double sure they were away from their village. We stopped our warriors on the Neosho River at a saline spring called the Lick and sent a letter to the village of the Grand Hunkah inviting him to send representatives to the Lick to talk about peace. An old man, who had been left in charge of the village, came out and told us the Grand Hunkah and all the able-bodied Osage had gone to the Salt Fork to hunt buffalo. Apparently, this was the information that McLamore had been waiting for. Someone brained the old man with a war club and the warriors attacked the village. McLamore had picked up a ragtag bunch of Choctaws, Chickasaws, Delawares, and Miamis…all of them crazy drunk. There were only old men, women, and children in the village. What took place was a slaughter…older boys were emasculated…the girls were raped. I was sick with shame."

"You had no part in the killing?"

"No, but I was there. I don't want to be associated with the great victory at Claremore Mound. Next day I left for home." Hanks paused to sip his toddy. "Ever hear of a Rev. Elias Cornelius?"

"Yes, I met him last September. The mission folk up north sent him. They want to establish some schools among our people."

"On the way home I camped with him on Caney Creek. A party of Cherokee warriors swam the Caney and camped nearby. Cornelius noted they had a small girl with them and he went over for a visit. Come to find out, the little girl was a prisoner they had taken at Claremore. They intended to sell her. Cornelius asked where her parents were and one of the Cherokee pulled two scalps out of a sack. Cornelius offered to buy the girl and promised to send her to school at Brainerd…but he didn't have the hundred dollar asking price."

"My god, what must Cornelius think of our people…a bunch of renegades. If word of this gets around we will lose our support in the north and Jackson will make hay with news like this. We must do whatever is necessary to find and redeem the girl."

*   *   *   *

On Christmas Day, 1817 Major William Bradford's keelboat was hauled to shore from the Arkansas River by two men left behind my Stephen Long. Bradford's troops would occupy the new Fort Smith, built and named by Long. Unknown to Bradford, he had arrived too late...the Osage War had already started.

CHAPTER 6

POLITICS ON THE POTOMAC

Because of the aging Tahlontusky, the party moved slowly toward Washington City. Houston, reveling in his freedom from military discipline, had donned his breech clout and blanket. It was good to be back among the Cherokees.

The weary group reached the capitol on February 5, 1818. Sam had not been in Washington City since August of 1814 when he had journeyed there in search of medical treatment for the wounds suffered at Horseshoe Bend. As they rode down Pennsylvania Avenue, Sam noticed that the president's home had been painted a gleaming white. The house was now occupied by President Monroe and his family.

The sights and sounds of busy taverns poured out into the street. Flouncing skirts and coquettish glances cast his way convinced Sam that all his hard miles of riding would have its reward. He gave particular attention to a buxom blonde who waved to him as she turned down Marble Avenue.

Houston was awakened next morning by a pounding on his door. Tahlontusky's group had been summoned to meet with the Secretary of war, John C. Calhoun. With bleary eyes and an aching head, he quickly donned his breech clout, blanket, and turban. There was no time for shaving.

At a four-story, red, brick building located next to the president's home, the group was ushered into a cramped office in the southeast corner of the first floor.

Here Calhoun greeted them with warm, South Carolinian hospitality. Seating himself he said, "I have here a letter from Governor McMinn informing me that you were coming to Washington and advising me of some of your concerns. Please, tell me what my government can do to alleviate your distress."

Since Tahlontusky spoke no English, Houston spoke for him. "My revered uncle, the great Cherokee chief, Tahlontusky, is feeble and ancient in days. Out of concern for his people he has traveled far, at great risk to his health, to speak to the Great Father about matters close to his heart. After the treaty of 1808, he led a band of more than one thousand Cherokees west of the Mississippi to the Arkansas Territory. Although the treaty was made with all the Cherokee people, all of the payments of annuities have gone to the Cherokees in Georgia. The Cherokees of the west have received very little of the proceeds promised for giving up their homes and making the long trek westward. In light of these conditions, Chief Tahlontusky would like to secede from the Cherokee nation in Georgia and set up his own nation in the west. He will do so if Washington will recognize his government and pay the promised annuities to him.

"His second complaint concerns the Osage. Apparently, it had occurred to no one in Washington that the lands assigned the Cherokee in Arkansas Territory was already occupied by other Indians. The Osage, in particular, have viciously attacked the Cherokee. It would be appropriate, and deeply appreciated, if the government could provide some protection from Osage attacks."

Calhoun listened courteously to the presentation by Houston. With a smile, he rose from his chair. "I fully comprehend your concerns and the seriousness of these matters. I will discuss them at length with President Monroe at the proper time. But right now, the president himself is waiting down the hall to receive you."

As the group was leaving, Calhoun said, "Mr. Houston, would you remain for just a moment?"

When the door closed, Calhoun in rage turned on Houston. "Lieutenant Houston, what do you think you are doing appearing before the Secretary of War out of military uniform? When did it become the dress of the day for an officer of the United States Army to appear in public in the garb of a savage? Look at you! You are an embarrassment and a disgrace to your race and your country. Is it your practice to go unshaven? Well, what do you have to say for yourself?"

Surprised and shaken by Calhoun's hostility, Houston stammered in response. "Mr. Secretary, I did not choose this dress in order to show disrespect for you. I did it to show respect for the Cherokees. After all, I am a sub-agent to these people. I thought I would be more effective with them if I wore their clothing."

"I am not in the least impressed with your reasoning, Lieutenant. Hereafter, you will not appear in public without regulation dress. Do you understand me? Now, go get a shave. You are dismissed."

Flushed with anger and humiliation, Houston departed.

∗   ∗   ∗   ∗

Lying abed in a state of arousal, Houston watched as the woman brushed her long, blonde hair. The morning sun, streaming through the window, warmed her full, bare breasts. A short, flimsy robe revealed smooth, rounded buttocks.

"Like what you see, Sam?" she asked, catching his stare in the mirror.

"I like Kate Brill…all of her. Come here."

"Not now, Sam. I'm expecting a caller."

"How the hell did you end up in this line of work, Kate?" Sam sat up on the bed and started pulling on his pants.

"It beats washing dishes and scrubbing floors in boarding houses. I'm treated like a lady, I meet only refined gentlemen, and the money is good. What more could I ask for?"

"You could be a real lady, Kate."

She turned on him defensively. "I have no plans to continue here forever, Sam. When I make my stake, you won't find me in Washington City."

A knock on the door ended their sparring. Houston opened it to a young, embarrassed chap. "Lieutenant Houston?" he asked.

"I'm Sam Houston. What can I do for you, sonny?"

"I have a message from Secretary Calhoun. You are to report to his office immediately."

∗   ∗   ∗   ∗

As Houston was ushered into Calhoun's office, the secretary remained seated. He did not ask Sam to sit.

Calhoun looked coldly across his desk. "Being out of uniform is one thing, Lieutenant. Misconduct as an officer is a more serious matter."

"I have no idea what you are talking about, Mr. Calhoun."

"Individuals have reported to me that last November you did engage in the act of transporting black slaves from Georgia to Florida. You well know that such activities are a crime. If these charges are proven true, things will go especially harsh against anyone who committed such crimes while in uniform."

Houston's jaws tightened and his eyes narrowed. "Sir, these accusations are scurrilous and damnably false. Plumb the depths of this matter and you will find that it was I who broke the ring of white smugglers. Obviously, this is an act of revenge. I am innocent and, if necessary, I will insist that this complete matter be laid before President Monroe."

Calhoun eyed Houston and drummed the desk with his fingers. The straight-forward response gave him pause. "Alright, Lieutenant, I will investigate. In the meantime make no plans to leave Washington."

Houston leveled his gaze at the secretary. "Mr. Calhoun, you can damned well rest assured that I will go no place until the name of Sam Houston is exonerated."

*   *   *   *

"Let it be, Sam. You were found innocent. What more do you want?"

"What do I want? Let me tell you what I want, John Rogers. I want justice. I bust my ass helping to expose slave smugglers and do they get punished? Hell no! They don't even get charged. I don't even get an apology from Calhoun. The whole affair is swept under the rug."

"What you say is true but there's not one damn thing you can do about it."

Houston ceased his ranting and stared out the hotel window. Lost in thought, his words came quietly as if speaking to himself.

"I've been shot all to hell for my country and what thanks do I get for it? Insulting, false charges that could have ruined my career as an army officer. Perhaps they already have. I'll never get a promotion as long as Calhoun has anything to say about it."

Suddenly he seated himself at a small table. Taking paper and quill in hand he hastily scribbled a note, addressing it to Calhoun and dating it March 1, 1818, Washington City. "Sir, you will please accept this as my resignation to take effect from this date. I have the honor to be Your most Obt Servt, Sam Houston, lst Lieut. 1st Infy."

*   *   *   *

Houston stiffly dismounted and draped bridle reins over the hitching rail. "Hello, Ross," he said in a tired voice.

"Hello yourself, Sam. Supper's about ready. Wash up. You look like you could use a good meal."

"Been eating on the trail for the past month. One of Quatie's home-cooked meals sounds just great to me."

"I see you're out of uniform. Which hat are you wearing today, the army lieutenant's or the Cherokee agent's?"

"Truth is, Little John, neither one. I resigned from the army a month ago. 'Bout an hour ago I gave Agent Meigs my resignation as sub-agent to the Cherokee."

Ross looked closely at Houston but contained his curiosity. "Let's get some food in you. We can talk later."

As he watched Houston wolf down his food, Ross sensed a change in the man. Later they sat on the east porch listening to the gurgling of Chattanooga Creek. Ross reached to pour Houston a drink.

"This is something new you might like."

Houston took a sip. "Man, this is smooth. Whatcha call it?"

"Bourbon. Some Presbyterian preacher up in Kentuck made it from a mix of rye and corn."

They sat in silence as the purple shadows of dusk softened the landscape. Somewhere a mocking bird sang.

"What results did you get in Washington City, Sam?"

"Not a damn thing. Tahlontusky rode two thousand miles for nothing. It will probably be his last ride." Houston took another sip of bourbon, hesitated, then continued. "From Calhoun I got shit." He then proceeded to relate all that had transpired leading up to his resignation.

Ross nodded his understanding. "Don't you see, Sam. Washington is playing a game as old as time...divide and conquer. As sub-agent to the Cherokee you were party to their game. They were using you to cause splits among our people. Who would have been the winner if Tahlontusky's wish had been granted?"

Ross paused to let his question sink in. "Last month, while you were in Washington City, I said goodbye to Oolooteeskee. He and three hundred thirty one Cherokees left the mouth of the Hiwassee in fifteen boats heading for Arkansas country. He was a good man, a peaceful man, and a good farmer. The whites called him John Jolly but we called him Beloved Father. He was the first to call me Tsan-Usdi, Little John."

He glanced at Houston. "He befriended you, Sam. He adopted you and gave you the name of Colonah, The Raven. The old man left his home, his friends, his farm. And what did he get out of it? A new rifle and provisions for seventy days. Do you really want to be a part of deals like that, Sam. Oolooteeskee made you a Cherokee; when did you forget to think like one?"

Stung my Ross's remarks, Houston struggled to find a defense. "And you…you John are mostly white but you don't think like a white man. Can't you see what is happening in this country? Don't you see that the whites out number you…that they are gobbling up this land like a plague of locusts? John, the whites are going to roll over you like a wagon wheel over a horse turd. It's only a matter of time before they squeeze you out. I'm trying to help the Cherokee see that and get out while they can save something."

Ross smiled. "What you say may be true, Sam, but I still believe that the whites live by their law. I don't think they will stand for such injustice as Jackson advocates."

Houston shook his head. "John, you are so damn Scotch stubborn…so naïve. It's not just Jackson…all the whites think exactly the way Jackson thinks…get rid of the Indians. It if becomes a question of justice or gaining land, which do you think the whites will choose? I just hope the Cherokee don't suffer from your pig-headedness."

"Only time will tell. Now, tell me…what lies ahead for Sam Houston?"

Houston stood and stretched. "What do you see standing before you, Tsan-Usdi? Nothing but a twenty-five year old man who is broke, out of a job, and in debt. But in Washington City, I saw how things really operate. If you get in trouble, you hire a lawyer to get you out of it. If you want to buy a piece of land, you get a lawyer to draw up a deed. If you want to become a successful politician, become a slick-tongued lawyer. So, tomorrow morning I'm heading to Nashville to read law with Judge James Trimble!"

✳   ✳   ✳   ✳

The muggy heat of July 15, 1818 clamping down relentlessly on Washington City did nothing to improve Calhoun's mood. He had just returned from a nine-day visit to his home in the highlands of Bath. For the second year in a row he found his crops withered and drought stricken. Through the hurried sale of some land, he raised enough money to see his family through another year. Now, back in Washington, he was plowing through official dispatches from General Jackson in Florida. Newspapers had reported that Jackson had hanged captured Indians, that he had summarily executed two British citizens, and that he had taken the main Spanish base in Pensacola. Reading Jackson's dispatches only confirmed Calhoun's fears. Such actions were sure to lead to war with Spain and England.

*   *   *   *

Calhoun seated himself in one of the French chairs with which President Monroe had ordered for the oval saloon. He watched as the rest of the president's cabinet assembled. It was a cabinet that held little regard for the president and for each other.

First to enter was Attorney General William Wirt, fanning himself with the latest edition of the National Intelligencer. A genial lawyer from Maryland, Wirt was noted in Washington City for his bevy of beautiful daughters. It was rumored that Wirt would soon resign as the salary for attorney general was insufficient to maintain his large family.

Next came the towering Secretary of Treasurer, William Crawford. Standing six foot three, the blond, flamboyant Georgian had assumed the office of treasurer in October of 1816 under Madison. Like Calhoun, as a boy he had attended the rigorous Academy of Moses Waddel in Columbia County, Georgia. A favorite with the congressmen, he had been nominated for president by those who were tired of the Virginia dynasty. He had lost the last election to Monroe by eleven votes.

Last to enter was the fat, short, bald, weepy-eyed, prim-lipped Secretary of State, John Quincy Adams from Massachusetts. His arrogant intellect set him apart from other members of the cabinet. Not only that, his intense dislike for Crawford was well known, a man whose success, he had said, was far beyond his services or his talents.

Wirt thumped the first page of the Intelligencer. "Boys, the fat's in the fire and that's for sure. Says here that Congress is launching its own investigation of Jackson's latest outrage."

"It's no outrage, Mr. Wirt. General Jackson was merely following orders," Adams commented dourly. Wirt, in Adam's mind, was a man who cared more about bread and meat for his children than service to his country.

"Whose orders, Mr. Adams? The president says he gave no such orders. Did you authorize General Jackson to attack the Spanish, Mr. Calhoun?"

Before Calhoun could respond President Monroe entered the room. Dressed in a suit of rusty black, his neckcloth wrinkled and carelessly tied, his face clearly showing the strain, the tall Virginian seated himself. In a quiet, dignified manner he addressed his cabinet.

"Gentlemen, we are facing a serious matter. We could soon be at war with England, with Spain, or both. Now, Mr. Calhoun, if you would, please bring everyone up to date by summarizing dispatches from General Jackson."

Calhoun picked up a sheet of paper on which he had made notes. "On March 10 General Jackson, with 3000 troops, plus about 2000 Indian allies, mostly Creeks, left Fort Scott. On April 6 they reached St. Marks. The Spanish commandant, who lacked a force to contest Jackson, capitulated. The Spanish flag was lowered and the Stars and Stripes raised. General Jackson found no Seminoles in the fort but he did find Alexander Arbuthnot, a 70 year old Scotch trader.

"On April 16 General Jackson attacked Bowleg's town. Again, the Seminoles, warned of his approach, had escaped. While Jackson was there a former British marine, Robert Ambrister, blundered into the town and was captured. After burning some 300 houses at Bowlegs, Jackson marched his troops back to St. Marks where he declared the war over.

"Jackson turned Arbuthnot and Ambrister over to a courtmartial where they were found guilty. On April 29 Arbuthnot was hanged from the end of a yardarm on his own ship. Ambrister was shot.

"On May 24, 1818 Jackson and his army arrived at Pensacola. Thinking that Seminoles were hiding in the town, he was determined to seize the town and execute the hostiles. After a slight puff of resistance, Colonel Masot, the Spanish governor, surrendered and marched his troops out of the fort.

"On June 2 General Jackson sent his last dispatch saying that St. Marks, Fort Gadsen, and the Barrancas were in American hands and that he was departing for his home in Nashville to rest and recuperate.

"And that's where it stands, Mr. President. We have had an invasion of Spanish Florida without a declaration of war, we have the unlawful execution of two British citizens, and the seizure of Pensacola. We are at risk of war with England and with Spain…and we have an angry Congress now mounting an independent investigation on the conduct of the entire Seminole War. I don't need to tell you, gentlemen, that with the economy is such distress, we are in no position to go to war."

"Thank you, Mr. Calhoun. Since these matters fall primarily under your authority in the War Department, what course of action do you recommend?"

"Quite clearly, Mr. President, the insubordination of General Jackson cannot be tolerated. He may be the most popular military hero in the country, but he absolutely exceeded his authority and instructions. It appears to me that General Jackson wants to provoke a war so that he can lead an expedition against Mexico.

If his actions are permitted to stand, civilian control of the military is lost. It is my recommendation that he be court-martialed."

"Have you ever met General Jackson?" asked Adams.

"No, I haven't," replied Calhoun, "but I fail to see what that has to do with anything."

Monroe turned to his Secretary of the Treasury. "Mr. Crawford?"

Crawford smiled affably. Unlike Calhoun, he knew when to be cautious. Although he could speak with frankness, he now had no intention of repeating the mistake that had cost him the presidency in 1816. "My past experiences with General Jackson's insubordination are well known. In this case, by engaging in hostilities, he has violated the constitution and he has usurped the power of Congress to declare war. If the administration does not act promptly and restore Pensacola, it will be held responsible for Jackson's deeds. In the event of war, the people will not support it. I concur with Mr. Calhoun; we have no choice but to censure General Jackson. On the other hand the arguments of Mr. Adams merit consideration."

Monroe moved on to Wirt. "May we hear from the Attorney General?"

Wirt mopped the sweat from his broad forehead and ran a hand through his crisp curls. "England and Spain will demand more satisfaction than the censuring of Jackson. They will, at the very least, insist upon his being punished. We need to move quickly through diplomatic channels to defuse this matter with both countries."

"Diplomacy is the domain of Mr. Adams." Monroe turned to face his Secretary of State.

The grim Puritan from New England was quick to go on the attack. "Mr. President, there is a slowness, a want of decision, and a spirit of procrastination regarding these matters. It appears that you, and all the members of this cabinet, except myself, are of the opinion that General Jackson went not only without, but against, his instructions, and that he has committed war with Spain. My opinion is that there was no real violation of his instructions.

"The dilemma we face is an impossible one. If you avow and approve of Jackson's conduct, you will incur the double responsibility of having commenced a war against Spain and of warring in violation of the constitution without the authority of Congress. On the other hand, if you disavow Jackson you will give offence to all his friends, encounter the shock of his popularity, and have the appearance of truckling to Spain." Adams paused, his face reddened, his hands trembling.

Calhoun angrily fired back. "Mr. Adams, capturing Pensacola hardly comes within the province of self-defense. By his own arbitrary will, General Jackson set all authority at defiance. Have you no sense of the consequences involved in letting the military set aside and ignore the constitution?"

"In my view," snapped Adams, "everything that General Jackson did was of a defensive nature and, as such, it was neither war against Spain nor violation of the constitution." He paused briefly, then added, "Besides, Mr. Calhoun, you should appreciate the fact that General Jackson's accomplishments will make your work easier."

"I fail to follow your thinking, Mr. Adams."

"You are engaged in the resettlement of Indians, Mr. Calhoun. General Jackson's efforts will encourage the Indians to relocate, which in turn, opens the southwest to white emigration. White immigrants on the frontier will seal off the Spanish. If we hold our course and retain control of St. Marks and Pensacola, we can eliminate trouble with both the Spanish and the Indians."

For the next three days the cabinet met at noon and continued in session until five, exhausted from the heat of their discussions and the weather. In effect, the cabinet gave Monroe two alternatives: return Florida and censure Jackson or retain Florida and defend Jackson. Monroe mulled the options. Censuring Jackson might appease Spain. On the other hand, it might encourage Spain to refuse the surrender of Florida. Weakening Jackson would also play into the hands of Calhoun and Crawford. Monroe was fully aware of their presidential aspirations.

At the meeting on July 18 Monroe announced his decision: there would be no punishment or censure of Jackson. The president himself would deal with the general. Attorney General Wirt would prepare an article, to appear in the National Intelligencer, explaining to the American people just what had happened and defending the administration. Secondly, he would write an explanation to the English. Thirdly, he would frame a reply to the Spanish minister, surrender the captured forts, but, at the same time, justify the conduct of the United States. The Secretary of State, Mr. Adams, would continue to negotiate with the Spanish minister, Mr. Onis.

"That takes care of everyone," said Monroe, "except an irate Congress and that hothead from Kentucky, Speaker Clay!"

CHAPTER 7

A FESTERING SORE

The sun was slipping low in the west as Ross rode past the brick mansion of Joe Vann. A half mile beyond, he turned his horse off the Federal Road into the lane that was the entrance to Spring Place. Just outside the fenced area of the mission school he dismounted and let his horse drink from the large spring that flowed out of the limestone ledges. Ross stretched and looked around. To the east Fort Mountain boldly reflected the setting sun in the blue October sky. Hardwood trees flashed red and gold on the mountain side where early frost had left its mark. Nearby the mission graveyard was surrounded by a peach and apple orchard. Inside the gate a large building stood that served as a school and church in which the Moravians had educated Cherokee children since 1801. South of this building were smaller ones that provided housing for the mission staff and students, a workshop for boys, a garden plot, a kiln, and a kitchen. Across the lane from the school-church building were a stable and barn. Fields of corn and grain took up the ground south and west of the buildings. The Cherokee differed with the Moravians when it came to teaching versus preaching, but Ross conceded that they had never killed an Indian, tried to enslave them, or broken a treaty.

Ross turned at the sound of voices. Coming out of the school building were The Ridge, his son, John, the venerable Reverend John Gambold who ran the mission, and the Reverend Ard Hoyt, superintendent of the mission station at Brainerd. With them was a man Ross had never seen before.

"About time you showed up," The Ridge growled good naturedly.

"The message was that you had urgent matters to discuss, so I high-tailed it down here. So, what's the urgency?"

"We can discuss that later. Right now I'd like you to meet Dr. Dempsey from New York."

Ross shook hands with the stranger. Seeing the question in Ross's eye, The Ridge hurried to explain. "We are sending John north to school, to Connecticut in fact. Dr. Dempsey has agreed to be his escort."

Ross turned to the young Ridge. "Congratulations, John. This is great news."

"Yes, I suppose so," John replied haughtily.

"Cornwall," Father Gambold explained in his heavy German accent, "is a school of higher education for promising youths from the Indian nations. It is provided by the American Board of Commissioners for Foreign Missions, a commission set up by the Congregational Church in Boston. The school is located in the mountains of western Connecticut in a lovely and healthful setting."

Ross quietly studied John Ridge. The lad, now fifteen, was slim and delicate and walked with a slight limp. His complexion was so light that he might have passed as a white. In school he had been quick to learn but he pained his religious teachers because he took little on faith and was skeptical about the gospels.

"Connecticut is a long way off." Ross looked at The Ridge. "Can you and Susanna stand the loss of a daughter and a son?"

The Ridge bowed his head and swallowed hard a few times. "In the natural order of things, a father never expects to bury his children. Our Nancy died out of time in childbirth. It has not been easy for my wife and me to come to terms with our loss." He reached and placed his arm around his son's shoulders. "It will not be easy for us to be without John, but we cannot hold back the living because of the dead. What John is doing is a good thing...for him and for his people."

*   *   *   *

On the morning of October 3 Dr. Dempsey, John Ridge, and two of his friends, John Vann and Darcheechee, mounted their horses and set off down the Georgia Pike. They would ride south of the Blue Ridge Mountains, then turn north into South Carolina and ride through the piedmont to Salem, North Carolina, into Virginia and the nation's capitol, on to Philadelphia, and finally to Cornwall near the end of November.

The Ridge bustled about, eager to get his mind on something other than his son's departure. "Now, Ross, you asked about urgency. I hope you are up to taking on more responsibilities. The Council is set to name you as president of the National Committee." He chuckled. "You are being relegated into purgatory. McMinn has asked for another meeting with the council on the thirteenth of next month. That boozer will try again to get an agreement from us to move west. He's tried bribery, whiskey, threats, and cajoling but I don't think he has convinced many."

"Be that as it may," responded Ross, "we need to meet with him and see what is holding up the tribal census they promised to conduct. They are refusing to pay our annuities until the census is done and the longer they delay our annuities, the deeper in debt we go."

Rev. Hoyt cleared his throat. "You know very well that we missionaries are not supposed to get involved in politics. But you also know where our sympathies lie. The American Board in Boston has powerful friends in congress. I have already taken the liberty of writing Dr. Samuel Worcester, explaining the situation as I see it."

"We recognize the delicate position you occupy with the federal government," Ross replied, "and since we have no power base in Washington City, any advocates for our cause are appreciated."

✳   ✳   ✳   ✳

A chilly, November wind blew down Walden's Ridge, whipping up spray across the broad Tennessee River and up the Hiwasee. As Ross and the delegation of some seventy Cherokees rode into the Hiwasee Agency on the thirteenth of November, a number of United States soldiers were quite visible.

"Nothing subtle about McMinn," groused Charles Hicks.

Ross snorted. "This is their idea of intimidation. I suppose we dumb savages are to quake in fear."

Chief Path Killer turned to Ross and Hicks. "My sons, let not your youth and temper unseat your wisdom and respect. Much rides on your shoulders."

On the morning of the fifteenth McMinn was ready. "I found myself inclined, this morning, to renew, on behalf of your father the President of the United States, and to place on paper what I spoke to you yesterday evening when we held each other by the hand. I feel bound to say at the outset that nothing short of such agreement as provided by our last treaty will be sufficient to attain the desired harmony."

McMinn extolled at length the fertility of land west of the Mississippi and the abundance of game. He concluded his initial remarks, saying, "As soon as your council resolves to enter into the proposed arrangement I will, without a moment's loss of time, present you with the annuities as I have been directed by the Secretary of War."

Flushed with anger at the blatant attempt at blackmail, Ross calmly replied. "We thank your excellency for these shared sentiments. The council will retire for a time of reflection."

Next morning, November 17th, the Cherokee Council, speaking through its secretary, Charles Hicks, replied. "The Cherokees, after the late war, in which they fought by the side of their white brethren, and lost much blood in the cause, had hoped to have been indulged in the possession of their lands. Therefore, taking all the circumstances together, we feel ourselves constrained to object to your excellency's propositions. We consider ourselves a free and distinct nation. Why should we consider a reserve of 640 acres in a vast land which we have owned from time immemorial?"

McMinn was clearly losing patience. "As to you nationhood, examine the Treaty of Hopewell which you signed. You will find that the United States possess the sole right of governing your nation upon all matters. Having gone thus far, little more need be said to prove to you that, as the demand has been made of your country, you are bound to make a surrender of it as good citizens."

Anger coursed through Ross. "Governor McMinn, we are not here to discuss selling our lands or removal. We are here because the treaty we signed with the United States on July 8 of last year has not been honored. Article Six of that treaty specified that annuities shall be distributed in the proportion of two-thirds to those Cherokees east to one-third to those west of the Mississippi. A census was to be taken last June of both portions of the nation to adjust the matter. To our great annoyance and dissatisfaction, as of this date, no census has been taken and neither party has received any annuity payment."

For the next two days the Cherokee remained in council debating the issues late into the night. When they gathered again with McMinn on the morning of the 21st Hicks rose to speak.

"Brother, with deliberation, candor, and good nature, we again inform your excellency that we have decisively rejected your propositions for an entire extinguishment of all our claims east of the Mississippi. We must again solicit your excellency to cause the late treaty to be carried into full effect as early as practicable."

Stunned by their unanimous rejection and their request for the termination of negotiations, McMinn, fortified with courage from a jug, faced the assembled Cherokees the morning of November 23. "Your actions are an insult. You speak of being an independent nation but it is only on paper. Were it not for the protecting arm of the United States, your nation would long ago have succumbed to fraud and violence. What is your purpose in keeping your people here? Is it not to keep them in their present savage state? You oppose the only road for your people to become religious, moral, and industrious."

Seeing no point in holding discussion with a man half in his cups, the Cherokee excused themselves. As the Cherokee rode south to their homes, Chief Path Killer spoke to Ross and Hicks. "I regret tearing you away so soon from the warmth of your hearth and family, but it is imperative that we send a delegation to Washington City as soon as possible. Understanding must be reached as to the meaning of the Treaty of 1817."

*   *   *   *

"Resolved, that the House of Representatives of the United States disapproves the proceedings in the trial and execution of Alexander Arbuthnot and Robert C. Armbrister." The report of the Committee on Military Affairs was the order of the day, January 12, 1819, as Mr. Timothy Pitkin of Connecticut gaveled the House to order.

Representative Thomas W. Cobb of Georgia led off the debate with a resolution that would prohibit the execution of any captive taken by the Army of the United States without the approbation of the President.

Henry Clay leaned back in his chair and relaxed. As Cobb's remarks droned on, Clay basked in self-congratulations. It was all falling into place now—Monroe would get his comeuppance. There was no way the president could publicly defend the actions of his military chieftain, Andrew Jackson. When the House hearings were concluded, not only would Monroe be denied a second term but the political ambitions of Jackson would be destroyed. The nation would gladly turn to him, Henry Clay, for their next president!

It needn't have ended this way. Had Monroe enough brains to hold his hat on, he would have appointed him Secretary of State instead of that dried prune, Adams. Sure, he knew it was Monroe's way of placating the New England states who resented the continuing dominance of Virginia in the federal government. From 1801 till now, every president of the nation had been a Virginian. But everyone knew that being Secretary of State was the royal road to the presidency—and no one deserved, or was better prepared for, the presidency than he, Henry Clay. Bygod, he would show the President who had control over the machinery of government.

The remarks of Cobb consumed most of the day. Tuesday, January 19, Representative John Holmes of Massachusetts rose to defend Jackson.

"It is not, sir, because General Jackson has acquired so much glory in defense of his country's rights that I defend him—I would not compromise the rights and liberties of my country to screen any man, however respectable. If General Jackson has been ambitious, I would restrain him; if he is proud, I would humble him; if he is tyrannical, I would disarm him. And yet, I confess, it would require pretty strong proof to produce conviction that he has intentionally done wrong. At his age in life, crowned with his honors, and loaded with the gratitude of his country, what adequate motive could induce him to tarnish his glory by acts of cruelty and revenge?"

On the morning of January 20, the twelfth day of the debate, Tom Hanks squeezed into a seat in the gallery. The galleries were packed with ladies and gentlemen of the city. Not since the trial of Aaron Burr had the country's interest been so intensely captured. Even the Senate had adjourned to hear the speech. All of Washington knew that this was the day Henry Clay would launch his attack on President Monroe and Jackson for their handling of the Seminole War in Florida.

Smiling mischievously, the tall and lean Speaker of the House exuded total confidence. He waved to friends seated in the gallery. As he stepped into the well, a hush fell over the House.

Clay began in a disarming manner. "In rising to address you on the very interesting subject, which now engages the attention of Congress, I must be allowed to say, that all inferences drawn from the course which it may be my painful duty to take in this discussion, of unfriendliness to either the Chief Magistrate of the country, or to the illustrious military chieftain, whose operations are now under investigation, will be wholly unfounded.

"Toward that distinguished Captain, who has shed so much glory on our country, whose renown constitutes so great a portion of its moral property, I never had, I never can have, any other feelings than those of the most profound respect and of the utmost kindness. I have no interest, other than that of seeing the concerns of my country well and happily administered.

"In noticing the painful incidents of this war, it is impossible not to inquire into its origin. I fear the origins will be found in the infamous Treaty of Fort Jackson, concluded in August of 1814 between the military chieftain, Andrew Jackson, and the Creek Indians. To refresh your memory, I now ask the indulgence of the Chairman that the Clerk might read certain parts of that treaty."

After the Clerk of the House had concluded the reading as requested, Clay proceeded with his remarks.

"I must admit that I had not perused this instrument until a few days past. And I must further admit, that I then read it with the deepest mortification and regret. A more dictatorial spirit I have never seen displayed in any instrument. I challenge honorable members of this House to examine all the records of diplomacy, even those of haughty and imperious Rome, and I do not believe a solitary instance can be found of such an inexorable spirit of domination pervading a compact purporting to be a treaty of PEACE." Here Clay's voice dripped with the acid of sarcasm.

Point by point, Clay moved relentlessly on. "As to the trial and execution of Ambrister and Arbuthnot, what can I say? Where in what code of law or system of ethics can one find any sanction for a principle so monstrous? Let me read to you General Jackson's own letter to the Secretary of War. 'These individuals were tried under my orders, <u>legally</u> convicted as exciters of this savage and negro war, <u>legally</u> condemned, and most justly punished for their inequities.'" Clay looked up from the paper and slowly surveyed his audience. With contempt he quietly added, "The Lord deliver us from such <u>legal</u> convictions and such <u>legal</u> condemnations. These men should never have been tried and executed without the proper authority of the law. No man should be executed in this free country without two things being shown: First, the <u>law</u> condemns him to death; and secondly, his death is pronounced by that <u>tribunal which is authorized by the law to try him.</u>"

After nearly two hours of speaking, Clay wrapped up his comments. Slowly sweeping the House members with his gaze, he spoke in the most solemn tones. "Beware how you give a fatal sanction, in this infant period of our republic, scarcely yet two score years old, to military insubordination. You may bear down all opposition; you may even vote the general the public thanks; you may carry him triumphantly through this house. But, if you do, in my humble judgement, it will be a triumph of the principle of insubordination—a triumph of the military over civil authority—a triumph over the powers of this House,—a triumph over the constitution of the land. And, I pray most devoutly to heaven, that it will not prove, in its ultimate effects and consequences, a triumph over the liberties of the people."

When Clay concluded, bedlam broke out in the House. Cheers, shouts, and applause rose from his supporters; groans, boos, and hisses from the followers of Monroe and Jackson.

Clay stepped out into the lobby to get a breath of air. There he met his good friend, Margaret Bayard Smith, wife of the publisher of the National Intelligencer.

"You were most eloquent, Mr. Clay, but I was disappointed that you spoke only for two hours."

"I'm truly sorry, Mrs. Smith, but I began speaking too loudly and I soon exhausted myself. There will be other opportunities to be heard on this matter."

"It's unfortunate that Mr. Calhoun could not have heard you. As the Calhouns will be dinner guests tonight, it will be my pleasure to inform him on what he missed."

Late the next day, Friday, James Tallmadge, a Democrat representing New York, took up the argument on Jackson's behalf. A man of handsome features and great ability, Tallmadge was known as a man whose grace was exceeded only by that of Henry Clay.

"Sir, it is now denied that the power of retaliation belongs to the commanding general. The honorable Speaker, Mr. Clay, has declared it to be an attribute of sovereignty, and that it belongs to this House, as one of its war-making powers.

"Gentlemen, I question the authority of the House of Representatives to deal with the matter. The President has not arrested Andrew Jackson. In fact, he has approved of his actions. Need I remind you, that the officers of the army are responsible to the Executive alone, not to Congress. We have, in effect, wasted a month's time arguing over an issue that is none of our business. I ask that the proposed resolutions be rejected."

On Saturday morning of January 23 an angry and exhausted Jackson rode across the Long Bridge that spanned the Potomac. After checking in at the Strater Hotel, he set out for the office of Adams, his trusted ally. Finding the Secretary of State absent, he headed for the home of the President. There he met up with Secretary Adams. Shocked at Jackson's haggard appearance, President Monroe urged him inside.

News of Jackson's presence in Washington quickly reached the capitol. Pro-Jackson forces took heart. Each day thereafter, Jackson met with his friends and supporters, making plans for defeating the censure motions. So absorbed was Jackson in his defense that he refused invitations to all social affairs.

For the remainder of January and into the first week of February the debaters clashed. Throughout the country the debates were followed eagerly by legions of Jackson followers. It was the longest debate ever devoted to a single issue by the House.

＊　　＊　　＊　　＊

On Monday, February 1, the Cherokee delegation rode into Washington. From all appearances Ross thought Washington City had changed little since he first arrived three years ago. Tree stumps stood where streets were planned. Piles of brush rotted here and there. Cows grazed on the commons and bullfrogs chorused from the swamps. Hogs were everywhere rooting through refuse. The President's home, now gleaming from a fresh coat of white paint, was still surrounded by workman's shanties, privies, and pools of stagnant water in basins where mortar had been mixed. Old brick kilns still stood amidst piles of shattered rock from stone cutters. The saddle-sore group was thankful to dismount before the Indian Queen Hotel.

Next morning Ross was awakened by Thomas McKenney. "Mr. Calhoun won't be able to meet with you before Friday. There's one helluva fight going on up on the hill and you might as well enjoy it."

"What kind of fight are you talking about?"

"Sorry, I forgot you just got into town. Clay and some of Crawford's cronies have been trying to crucify the president over the way Andy Jackson conducted the Seminole War. The economy of the country is in crisis, people are about to panic, and Congress gives all its attention to events that are history! That's politics for you but that's the only thing this town runs on."

On Monday, February 8, the House of Representatives, after twenty-seven days, without interruption, and to the exclusion of all other business, finally terminated its debate. Nerves were raw and tensions high as the weary House resolved itself into a committee of the whole and prepared to vote on each of the four resolutions that had been introduced by Representative Cobb. With the voting concluded, Jackson was vindicated on all counts. His executions of Arbuthnot and Ambrister, his seizure of Pensacola were approved by substantial numbers. He had gained his greatest victory since New Orleans…and Clay had earned an undying enemy!

On Saturday, February 13, the House attempted to get back to routine matters. It resolved itself into a Committee of the Whole on the bills to allow the people in the territories of Alabama and Misssouri to form state governments. The Missouri bill was taken up first. Representative Tallmadge rose to move two amendments. With features gray and haggard, Tallmadge had returned this very day from New York where he had attended the funeral of his son. The first amendment he introduced would ban the further introduction of slavery; the second declared that children born to slaves, after the admission of Missouri, to be free at the age of 25. For a moment the House sat in stunned silence, then, like a breaking dam, it erupted with speakers clamoring to be recognized. Sensing the explosiveness of the issue, and since it was half-past four, the Speaker declared the House adjourned.

*   *   *   *

"Hmmmm...seems Monroe is caught between a rock and a hard place," mused McKenney. He and Ross were dawdling over Sunday morning coffee and newspapers at the Indian Queen Hotel. Nearby, Clay, seemingly impervious to his recent defeat, leaned against the bar thoughtfully stirring brown sugar into a glass of bourbon.

"Alright, Mr. Insider," Ross replied, "enlighten me on Washington politics."

McKenney put the Richmond Inquirer aside. "It's like this, Ross. Monroe is standing for reelection as president. As a Virginian, his sympathies lie with the south which wants Missouri admitted as a slave state. But, if he comes out in support of the south, he loses the northern votes, which he cannot afford. It goes without saying, if he supported Tallmadge's amendments, he would be a dead duck in the south."

"So, how does Monroe come out of his predicament a winner?"

"He can't," Clay injected. Easing his lanky frame into a chair, he continued. "Ross, there's more here than meets your untrained eye...more than the election of a president. The 'predicament', as you call it, is a problem that can tear the United States apart. The specter of disunion has already appeared. I hear the words 'civil war' and 'disunion' uttered too frequently. It's really a matter of power and control. It involves beliefs in religion, economics, and government. This is a festering sore that the creators of our constitution created."

"A festering sore?" Ross asked.

Clay silently sipped his whiskey, collecting his thoughts. "Putting this nation together was not an easy task. I guess our weakness and fear of other nations were the major inducements that brought about any union at all. A lot of compromises were involved. The biggest, and the hardest for the northern states to swallow, was the three-fifths rule."

"The three-fifths rule?"

"As you already know, Mr. Ross, each state, regardless of population, has two senators. The northern states wanted to apportion seats in the House of Representatives solely on the percentage of each state's population. Naturally, in the less populated south we rejected this idea. We wanted to allocate seats by counting both white citizens and its black non-citizens.

"The real pay-off would come in the electoral college where each state would receive one presidential elector for each senator and each representative. The north could see that by giving the south the extra power in the House of Representatives, the south could elect the president who, in turn, appointed members of the Supreme Court. In effect, the south would control all three branches of government. You can see, this was a very crucial decision for the north. At long length, a compromise was reached on allotting seats in the House by counting each white as one soul and each slave as three-fifths of a human. As I said, it was a hard pill for the north to swallow but it was compromise or no union."

Ross sat silently for a moment. "Which makes this Missouri question a very hot potato."

"Yes indeed. Sway over the entire government is at stake. For thirty-two of the last thirty-six years the nation's highest office has been held by Virginia elite. The north has built up a full head of frustration during that time. My guess is they are not about to cede more power to the south by admitting Missouri as a slave state…which will lead to a crisis of great dimensions. So, somehow I've got to convince gentlemen from the north that the south simply must have additional space in which to disperse the slave population. Confining black masses within ever blacker black belts will encourage slave insurrections. The north does not comprehend how much fear exists in certain southern states of a slave revolt."

McKenney, who had been listening intently, now spoke up. "Mr. Clay, for a slaveholder, you have given Mr. Ross a fair, lucid, and dispassionate picture of the dilemma facing Congress. But it is still unclear to me how, for congressional representation, you can claim slaves as persons then in the next breath claim them as property."

Clay drained his glass before answering. "Obviously, the whole construct is built upon contradictions. I struggle with those contradictions…legislatively and personally. I deplore the very concept of slavery, yet I must defend it…as a representative of my state and as a planter. The south has probably invested three hundred million dollars in slaves. Destroy slavery and you destroy the south. If you took away my dozen slaves, I would be in financial straits, even greater than I am already."

*   *   *   *

On Monday morning, February 15, 1819 Ross and McKenney elbowed their way through throngs of Negroes who had gathered at the House to hear the debate on Missouri. As they found seats, Representative John W. Taylor of New York, proceeded to the heart of the matter.

"First, Mr. Chairman, has Congress the power to require of Missouri a constitutional prohibition against the further introduction of slavery, as a condition of her admission to the union?

"Second, if the power exist, is it wise to express it? Congress has no power unless it be expressly granted by the constitution, or necessary to the execution of some power clearly delegated. The third section of the fourth article of the constitution declares that 'the Congress shall have power to dispose of and make all needful rules and regulations respecting the territory, or other property, belonging to the United States'. It would be difficult to devise a more comprehensive grant of power.

"Having proved our right to legislate in the manner proposed, I proceed to illustrate the propriety of exercising it. And here I might rest satisfied with reminding my opponents of their own declarations on the subject of slavery. How often, and how eloquently, have they deplored its existence among them. How often have they wept over the unfortunate policy that first introduced slaves into this country. How they have disclaimed the guilt and shame of that original sin and thrown it back upon their ancestors. Gentlemen, you now have an opportunity to put your principles into practice. History will record the decision of this day as exerting its influence for centuries to come."

At the conclusion of Taylor's extensive remarks, John Scott, Territorial delegate from Missouri, gained the floor.

"Mr. Chairman, when a question, such as the amendments proposed by the gentleman from New York, are presented for consideration, which infringe upon the constitutional rights of the people I represent, I should consider it a dereliction of my duty if I did not raise my voice in protest. You are sowing seeds of discord in this union by attempting to admit states with unequal privileges and unequal rights. The people of Missouri will, if admitted, come into this union on equal footing with the original states…or not come at all."

From under heavy eyebrows, Tallmadge looked down his long, patrician nose at the House members. "I am not a man who enjoys conflict; neither am I one to shrink from duty. It has been my desire, and my intention, to avoid any debate on the present painful and unpleasant subject. My amendment now under consideration, confines itself to newly acquired territory across the Mississippi. In no way does it meddle with the affairs of the original states in the union. Willingly, therefore, will I submit to an evil which we cannot safely remedy. But, sir, all these reasons cease when we cross the banks of the Mississippi. A newly acquired territory, never contemplated in the formation of our government, must justly be subject to our common legislation."

At this point an outbreak on the floor interrupted Tallmadge. Shaking his fists in great agitation, Representative Cobb of Georgia stood and shouted, "If you persist the union will be dissolved. You have kindled a fire which all the waters of the ocean cannot put out, which seas of blood can only extinguish."

With a cold glance in Cobb's direction, Tallmadge continued. "Sir, language of this sort has no effect on me; my purpose is fixed, it is interwoven with my existence, it is a great and glorious cause…setting bounds to a slavery the most cruel and debasing the world has ever witnessed. Sir, if a dissolution of the union must take place, let it be so! If civil war, which gentlemen so much threaten, must come, I can only say, let it come! My hold on life is probably as frail as that of any man who now hears me, but while that hold lasts, it shall be devoted to the service of my country—to the freedom of man!

"Sir, has it already come to this; that in the Congress of the United States, that in the legislative councils of republican America, the subject of slavery has become a subject of so much feeling, of such delicacy, of such danger that it cannot be safely discussed? The extension of evil must now be met and prevented or the occasion is irrecoverably lost."

As an exhausted Tallmadge retired to his seat, rumbles of approbation and apprehension passed among the members. Weary of debate the question was taken on the following words: "That the further introduction of slavery and involuntary servitude be prohibited, except for the punishment of crimes, whereof the party shall have been duly convicted." By a vote of 87 yeas and 76 nays the amendment was passed.

As they made their way out of the House chambers, Ross said to McKenney, "My god, I'm totally wrung out and I wasn't even involved in the debate."

"Thank your god that you are not involved, Ross. The tiger that has been caged for the last thirty years is now on the loose."

"Then it is a tiger I will have to face because that tiger has a great appetite for land."

CHAPTER 8

GOD HAS HEARD
YOUR PRAYERS

As the cabinet meeting broke up, Adams gathered up his papers and followed Calhoun out the door.

"The Missouri matter weighs heavily upon the president. As a man of independent thinking, and sound judgement, how will you respond to his question regarding the constitutional power of Congress to prohibit slavery in a territory?"

"Mr. Adams, this is just another example of Monroe's reluctance to make an independent decision," Calhoun responded.

"How can you say that, Mr. Calhoun? Are you not aware of the anti-slavery mood that is congealing in the north? Legislature after legislature are passing resolutions condemning slavery."

"Yes, I am aware of those actions but I can conceive of no cause sufficient to divide the nation".

"Then how will you advise the president?"

Calhoun stopped and faced Adams. "You flatter me, sir, in seeking my opinion. In answering you, may I speak confidentially?"

"By all means, Mr. Calhoun."

"Personally, I believe that Congress has the authority to prohibit slavery in a territory but if I make my views public at this time it will only provide Crawford more reason to savage the War Department."

"I gather the ambitious Mr. Crawford is not one of your favorites."

Calhoun snorted. "There has not been in the history of this Union another man with abilities so ordinary, with service so slender, and so thoroughly corrupt, who has continued to make himself a candidate for the presidency. He and his minions in Congress are bent on cutting army pay, cutting expenses for army food, and cutting the army itself to six thousand men. I realize the nation's economy is in dire straits but I tell you, sir, soldiers cannot serve their country for honor alone. I have warned Congress that we are liable to be involved in war. Perpetual peace is a dream no nation has had the good fortune to enjoy. I am determined, in spite of Crawford, to keep our country strong."

"I suspect there are multiple motives behind Crawford's maneuvering."

"Such as, Mr. Adams?"

"If Crawford succeeds in reducing the army to six thousand there will no longer be a need for three top generals. General Jackson, being junior in grade, will be reduced in rank or terminated. Either way, he will not be a rival to Mr. Crawford for the presidency."

"Very perceptive, Mr. Adams. And I, being Secretary of War, will have the duty of axing Jackson. Such news will be ill received by the worshiping populous."

"Mr. Crawford has deftly set a trap for both you and General Jackson."

"So it would seem Mr. Adams. So it would seem. Now, if you will excuse me, I have some work awaiting in my office."

✳   ✳   ✳   ✳

Tuesday morning, February 16, following social amenities and seating of the Cherokee delegation, Calhoun got down to business.

"I have carefully considered your petition of February 8 and I find that several of my proposals have thus far been rejected. Since Congress will shortly adjourn, it is with some degree of urgency that I ask you to reconsider."

"Mr. Secretary," Ross injected, "under article one of your proposal you would have us cede land which, according to your map, is under the jurisdiction of Alabama, Georgia, North Carolina, and Tennessee...some four million acres I'm guessing. I have yet to see it proved that the engraver of a map has the power of disinheriting a whole people and delivering their property into the hands of others."

Calhoun, struggling to control his temper, responded. "Keep in mind, Mr. Ross, that my government is not taking your land. We are only asking an exchange of land in proportion to the number of your people who have already moved to Arkansas. Since a third of your people have already moved to Arkansas, it is only fitting that you compensate my government with land you hold east of the Mississippi."

"That is another point of disagreement, Mr. Calhoun. You claim a third of our people have moved west; we are convinced that no more than 3000, or a fifth of our number, have relocated."

"We could quibble all day over numbers, Mr. Ross, and since we have no census of Cherokees, I must rely upon data supplied by our agents."

"If a cession of land is made, in the size that you are proposing, will your government guarantee us that there will be no more such requests?"

Calhoun shifted uncomfortably. "Let me answer this way, Mr. Ross. So long as the Cherokee retain more land than is necessary, I cannot make such a promise."

"And who is to determine how much is necessary?"

Calhoun evaded the question. "For your continued protection by the United States, I urge you to act now, without delay, before Congress adjourns."

"Protection? If your government cannot protect us now in our present lands, how would it protect us in land far beyond the Mississippi?" asked Ross.

Weary and discouraged with the fruitless negotiations, the Cherokee returned to the Indian Queen for continued discussion among themselves.

*   *   *   *

Thursday morning Ross sat by the south-facing windows overlooking Pennsylvania Avenue, copying a message to Secretary Calhoun. He could not shake feelings of despair, humiliation, and rage. It appeared that the Cherokee enjoyed no rights which the United States government was bound to respect. With no place to turn, the Cherokee delegation was considering capitulating to Calhoun's demands. A knock interrupted his writing. Opening the door he faced a distinguished, elderly gentleman dressed in black.

Extending his hand, the gentleman smiled. "Mr. Ross, I presume. God has heard the prayers of the poor, afflicted Cherokee. I am Dr. Samuel Worcester from Boston. I represent the American Board of Commissioners for Foreign Missions. I have just arrived in town. May I come in?"

"To be sure, Dr. Worcester. My good friend, Rev. Ard Hoyt at Brainerd Mission, told me he was writing to you about our problems."

"And that's why I'm here, my boy. We are not without influence in Washington City. We have friends in Congress, people who are sympathetic to the cause of righteousness."

Worcester hung up his long coat and sat down facing Ross. "Time is short, my son, so let's get to it. How goes your negotiations with Calhoun?"

"They are not going well at all. With all the concern over censuring Jackson and the Missouri question, I feel that Cherokee problems are considered small potatoes here in Washington. Here is a copy of the specifics Calhoun wants to include in a treaty. Our delegation feels that we do not have the power to oppose him any longer."

Worcester adjusted his glasses, took the papers over to the window, and squinted at the proposed agreement. Completing his reading, he sighed heavily and handed the papers back to Ross. "It looks bad, but don't give up hope. Would you be able to join me for dinner this evening, Mr. Ross?"

＊　　　＊　　　＊　　　＊

As Ross elbowed his way through the smoke and haze of the hotel dining room, he spied Dr. Worcester in a leather-covered, easy chair by the fireplace. Worcester was engaged in a conversation with a handsome, middle-aged man sitting across from him. Seeing Ross, Worcester and his companion rose.

"Ah, Mr. Ross, right on time. I'd like for you to meet Mr. William Wirt, Attorney General for the United States."

As Ross extended his hand in greeting, he was jostled by a tall, gangling man in his mid-forties. Smiling in embarrassment, the man turned to apologize.

"Well, Justice Marshall, up to his usual gracefulness," Wirt said in a bantering tone. "Please join us."

"Ah, William, I am so sorry for my clumsiness. Do forgive me. Don't let me interrupt…"

"Mr. Ross," said Wirt, "let me introduce you to John Marshall of Virginia, Chief Justice of the Supreme Court."

Marshall shook hands with Ross and Worcester, apologizing all the while. "Well, if you're sure I'm not intruding." He looked around the smoky room. "I was supposed to meet my good friend, Justice Story. Ah, there he is now."

A balding, bespectacled man, considerably younger than Marshall, approached the group. Marshall introduced him to Ross and Worcester as Justice Joseph Story, adding "Of course, you know Wirt."

"Yes, indeed," replied Story. "And I also know of Dr. Worcester. What brings a fellow Yankee to the swamps of Washington City?"

"Our friends, the Cherokee, seem to be in need of help. I thought Attorney General Wirt could provide them insight into how our judicial system works."

"The court will be sitting next Monday, Mr. Ross," said Marshall. "If it will help you understand our judicial system, it would be my pleasure to have you attend the session."

"By all means, do that Mr. Ross. It so happens that I am arguing that case for the government. Now, if it presents no conflict of interest, or suggests buying influence, I'll be happy to stand for a round of drinks." Wirt signaled a waiter.

"Kin ah fetch you gennlemen some refreshmens?"

"Yes," replied Wirt. "Bring us some Madeira."

"Yassuh." The waiter cast a toothy smile toward Marshall. "You mean some of The Supreme Court!"

Wirt broke out in laughter as Marshall grinned sheepishly. "Chief Justice Marshall's love for Madeira wine has become so well known here in Washington that the wine merchants have begun labeling their best brand The Supreme Court," Wirt explained to the others.

Seeking to divert attention from himself, Marshall turned to Ross. "I deem it quite admirable, Mr. Ross, for you to be so interested in jurisprudence. Law is the sinew that holds a society together…or a nation for that matter. It is the achievement of civilization for men to voluntarily agree to live by law rather than by their brute strength."

Ross nodded. "My people have a legal system; in fact, quite an old and complex system. But to convince the whites that we are making tribal progress, we are speeding up the process of systematizing our laws, as Thomas Jefferson advised us to do some time ago."

Marshall's brow knitted in a frown. "Ahem…ah…yes…Jefferson. Keep in mind, Mr. Ross, that law develops slowly. It is part of a time and place. Law does not develop in a vacuum."

"If I may be so bold, what is the nature of the case before the court next Monday?" asked Ross.

"The case is McCulloch vs. Maryland. The main issue turns on the legality of a state taxing federal property. It would not be prudent for me to say more than that. But I can freely state that you will not hear better lawyers than those who argue the case. In addition to Mr. Wirt, you'll hear Daniel Webster, and William Pinkney."

"For such praise, sir, I'll stand for another round of Madeira," said Wirt.

"Thank you kindly," replied Marshall, rising from his chair. "Joseph and I must be going. Mr. Ross, it was nice meeting you. I hope to see you in court."

After Marshall and Story departed, Ross turned to Wirt. "Did I notice some discomfort on Mr. Marshall's part when I mentioned Thomas Jefferson or was it just my imagination?"

Wirt shook his head. "It was not your imagination. You see, Marshall went through the hell of war. He wintered at Valley Forge with Washington. He saw soldiers barefoot in the snow, ill clothed, and starving to death. When that winter was over only three out of the forty soldiers in his Virginia regiment were still alive. Marshall blamed the misery on the weakness of the Continental Congress which sat back helplessly and watched its own army starve.

"Jefferson endured none of this; he never served in the army. Even though the two are distant cousins, Marshall considers Jefferson a shirker...and they are poles apart in their political differences. Marshall feels that we would have anarchy if we followed Jefferson's state's rights philosophy. Jefferson talks of democracy and the common man. Marshall looks at democracy as mob rule. He is an avowed Federalist who envisions a strong, central government; a government limited in power but strong enough to ward off encroachments by the states. Marshall is terribly concerned about the threats to national unity the Missouri question has presented."

"I also sensed some reluctance on the part of Mr. Marshall to discuss the upcoming case," Ross continued.

"As the presiding judge, it would be unethical for him to do so." Wirt paused to refill his glass. "To a large degree, the case is similar to the Missouri controversy...a question of state versus national power."

"My concern," replied Ross, "is this. Does the federal government have the power to protect the Cherokee from the state of Georgia?"

*   *   *   *

When Ross and Dr. Worcester arrived outside the capitol building on Monday morning, February 22, a crowd had already assembled. Washington ladies, legislators who had time on their hands, and idle onlookers gathered anytime Wirt or Webster appeared before the court. It was considered a special occasion. The turnout indicated not only the state of social life in Washington but great concern over the bank many blamed for the current financial crisis.

Ross and Worcester found seats in a cramped, semi-circular room in the lower level of the capitol building. "Unfortunately," explained Worcester, "when the capitol was designed, someone forgot to include housing for the Supreme Court of the land. This used to be the Senate chamber. After the capitol was burned, Jefferson redesigned the interior and moved the Senate chamber to the second floor. While this building was under repair, the Supreme Court met in the home of the court clerk, Elias Caldwell, on Pennsylvania Avenue."

Dr. Worcester's narration was interrupted when Chief Justice John Marshall and the other six justices entered the courtroom. After taking their black robes from pegs and donning them, they seated themselves on mahogany benches. Marshall swept the courtroom with penetrating black eyes and announced, "Due to the extraordinary nature of this case, the normal restrictions of two lawyers per side has been waved in favor of three per side. Also, there will be no restrictions on time in the arguing of this case."

Grandly dressed in tight breeches and a blue cutaway coat with big, brass buttons, Daniel Webster led off in favor of the bank. Called Black Dan ever since he was a boy, the young lawyer, just turned thirty-seven, had already made a name for himself.

"It is argued," he said, "that the Constitution created a government of delegated powers, and what is not delegated is reserved to the states and people. Nowhere in the document did it say that Congress could create a bank. Therefore, according to the states' rights interpretation, it is unconstitutional.

"Our Constitution clearly states that Congress has the power to coin money, to borrow money, to lay and collect taxes. It further states that Congress has the power to make all laws which shall be necessary and proper for carrying into execution of these delegated powers." Keeping his eyes focused straight at Marshall, he continued. "The grant of powers itself necessarily implies the grant of all usual and suitable means for the execution of the powers granted. Congress has duties to perform and therefore has a right to the means by which these duties shall be executed. A bank is a proper and a necessary instrument for the government in the collection and disbursement of revenue. In my view, it is a fit instrument to an authorized purpose and if not specifically prohibited, it may be used. Political power without economic power invites anarchy and despotism."

Webster then moved on to argue that a state could not tax a federal installation. "If the states may tax the bank," he asked, "to what extent shall they tax it and where shall they stop? An unlimited power to tax involves, necessarily, a power to destroy, because there is a limit beyond which no institution and no property can bear taxation."

*   *   *   *

On February 24 attention was diverted from the Supreme Court debate when the Senate issued its report on General Jackson. In spite of rumors that Jackson was prepared 'to cut off some ears', the report condemned his conduct on every count. "It is with regret that the committee are compelled to declare that they conceive General Jackson to have disregarded the positive orders of the Department of War, the Constitution and the laws and that he had taken upon himself the exercise of those powers delegated to Congress. The committee find the melancholy fact before them that military officers, even at this early stage of the Republic, have, without the shadow of authority, raised an army and mustered them into the service of the United States. Two hundred and thirty officers have been appointed. To whom were these officers accountable for their conduct? Not the President of the United States for he was not even furnished a list of their names…"

The report was tabled as Congress celebrated the treaty John Quincy Adams had signed with the Spanish Minister, Luis de Onis on February 22 in which Spain ceded Florida to the United States. The Senate hurriedly and unanimously ratified the treaty on the 24th thinking, surely, it must have been the relentless pressure of General Jackson on the Spanish that had brought the cession about!

In the House the treaty drew heavy fire from Clay and other westerners because it, in effect, relinquished all United States claims to Texas…a natural and desired space for expansion of slavery.

*   *   *   *

Ross was unable to attend the final days of the argument before the Supreme Court as he and the Cherokee delegation had to meet with Calhoun. On February 27 they signed a treaty in which they ceded to the United States virtually everything Calhoun had demanded.

Awaiting his turn to sign, thoughts spun through Ross's mind. In the short time he had been in Washington City he had seen the United States gain Florida. Missouri Territory would sooner or later become a state if the issue did not destroy the nation in the process. Congress was poised to make Arkansas Territory out of the southern county of Missouri Territory. This would require removal of the western Cherokee even further west. Now, as he waited, the eastern Cherokee were signing away another four million acres of their homeland.

Clearly, the United States was into an expansionist mode. How much time would this treaty buy before the tidal wave swept all the Cherokee westward?

When Congress adjourned on March 4 the Missouri question was still unresolved. The report on Jackson's misconduct was tabled, never to be resurrected.

Both Ross and Worcester had been preparing to depart Washington but on March 6 they crowded into the Supreme Court to hear John Marshall deliver the decision in the case of McCulloch v. Maryland. When Marshall came to the question regarding what powers the Constitution gave to the federal legislature, he declared. "...the government of the Union, though limited in its powers, is supreme within the sphere of action."

In regards to the power of the United States to establish banks he declared, "No axiom is more clearly established in law, or in reason, than that wherever the end, if required, the means are authorized...the States have no power to retard, impede, burden, or in any manner control the operations of the constitutional laws enacted by Congress to carry into execution the powers vested in the general government."

Worcester leaned over to Ross and whispered, "This decision will stir up a hornet's nest among the states' rights people."

"No doubt," replied Ross, "but, with this decision, I now have confidence that the United States can actually protect us from states like Georgia."

*   *   *   *

After Congress adjourned the exodus from Washington City began. Andrew Jackson left on the 9th of March for a triumphal tour of eastern cities. The last week of March President Monroe left for a four or five month tour of the south and west. Calhoun would accompany him as far as his plantation near Abbeville in South Carolina.

At the end of March Ross left for extended business dealings in Baltimore. On April 10 Clay borrowed twenty thousand dollars from John Jacob Astor to pay off his gambling debts and loans he had generously co-signed for his friends. Soon he would have to relinquish his role as Speaker of the House and return to Lexington to repair his law practice and finances. Thomas Jefferson, living in retirement at Monticello, fumed that Marshall's decision demonstrated the error of lifetime appointments for justices in the Supreme Court.

Awaiting the next session of Congress, the Missouri question hung like a sword of Damocles over the nation. Beneath it all, like a brooding nest of vipers, was the institution of slavery.

CHAPTER 9

LO! THE HEATHEN

John Ridge, sweaty and stripped to the waist, laughed and flinched at the icy rain. From his vantage point on Colt's Foot Mountain, all day he had watched the threatening clouds hanging low over Cornwall. Chimney smoke, reluctant to rise, merged with the clouds adding to the day's gloom. Now, late in the afternoon, the heavens opened up with a cold downpour. Shivering, John slipped into a warm, woolen shirt and took shelter under the long, protective branches of a hemlock tree.

It had been exhausting but fun-filled. Teams of Cornwall students had spent this November day in 1820 competing in cutting, sawing, splitting, and stacking firewood. As a result, several cords of freshly cut red maple and scarlet oak were piled high on the north slope of Colt Foot's Mountain waiting to be hauled to the missionary school. When hauled and restacked at the school, it would guarantee winter warmth. Although wood cutting was one of the assigned chores to Cornwall students, John failed to see how it contributed to his education.

The next morning he awoke with a head cold and a runny nose. No bother. It simply meant that he could avoid another day of wood cutting. The following morning his throat was so sore he stayed abed and skipped the six a.m. prayers. The school principal, knowing of John's aversion to spiritual matters, came to see him. Convinced that the illness was real, he ordered some chicken broth to be brought up to the cramped and smoky sleeping quarters under the gambrel roof.

In another day John's condition had deteriorated. His lungs were now congested and a high fever had set in. With no provision for nursing students at the school, Rev. Herman Daggett, the school principal, arranged to have John moved a block west to the home of John Northrup. Mr. Northrup was a steward of the school but it was his wife who would have to watch over the young man.

John was now delirious from the raging fever. In his delirium his mind drifted back in time.

*   *   *   *

A cold, northerly wind pierced his thin coat and flung dust into the eyes of John Ridge as he rode down Pine Street. In late November of 1818, gone were the blazing colors of oaks and maples. Scattered along the main thoroughfare, he could make out blacksmith shops, distilleries, shoemakers, a doctor's office, grain mills, a lumberyard, and a small woolen mill. Few people bothered to notice as the small mounted group rode down the street. After almost two months in the saddle, they had, at last, arrived at Cornwall. Nestled among the hills in the Hausatonic River Valley, this farming village in northwest Connecticut, was home to the Foreign Mission School.

The Town Green was located on the southwest corner of the intersection of Bolton Hill Road and Pine Street. Abutting the Green on the west side stood the Mission School. To John, the small, one and a half story, gambrel-roofed building was unimpressive.

"So, this is what we rode two months for," he said to no one in particular as he dismounted his weary horse. Before he could linger longer in his mood of disappointment, a group of boys noisily burst out the north door of the school, led by his cousin, an exuberant Buck Watie. His spirits rose immediately as he and his companions, John Vann, Darcheechee, and Dr. Dempsey, endured a barrage of greetings, questions, hugs, and back-slapping from his cousin, Buck, Leonard Hicks, and other Cherokee students. The Cornwall students suddenly fell silent as a thin, frail, middle-aged man emerged from the school.

"Well, Elias, where are your manners?" he snapped.

John's cousin flushed and stammered. "I'm sorry, sir—Dr. Dempsey, John Ridge, John Vann, Darcheechee, this is our school principal, Reverend Herman Daggett."

"Damned glad to see you, sir," said Dempsey, extending his hand. "I don't need to tell you how sore my ass is after settin' in that saddle for two months."

Daggett scowled. "Well...yes. Welcome. We don't take to profanity around here, Mr. Dempsey." He turned to John Ridge and eyed him from head to toe. "That's a fine looking watch you are wearing, Mr. Ridge."

"Why, thank you, sir. I bought it in Philadelphia."

"Hmmm. Rather ostentatious, Mr. Ridge. Such worldly goods do not become a Christian."

"But I'm not a Christian, sir."

Daggett's eyes popped. "Don't you want to be a Christian?"

"I'm not sure, sir. I haven't given it much thought."

Incredulity showed. "Isn't that why you came to Cornwall, to become a follower of Jesus Christ?"

"No, sir. I came to get an education. My father wants me to become a chief among my people someday."

Daggett stroked his chin and stared at John. "I see. We will speak more on this subject. Your pagan soul is in danger." He turned to John Vann.

"And I suppose you wish to become a chief also, my boy."

"No, sir." Vann laughed. "I just came along for the ride."

Daggett frowned at the giggles that Vann's remark produced. "Levity does not become a Christian, Mr. Vann."

Without waiting for a response, Daggett turned to the last of the newcomers. "Darcheechee...what kind of name is Darcheechee?"

"I don't know," replied the flustered young man. "I'm a full-blood Cherokee and that's the name I was given."

"Darcheechee is not a fitting name. We will give you a new Christian name." Daggett turned away to reenter the school. "Elias, show these people to their quarters."

As they climbed the stairs to the attic of the school that served as a dormitory, Ridge asked, "Buck, why is Rev. Daggett calling you Elias?"

"Here. This will be your bed, John, right next to mine."

"That's fine, Buck, but you didn't answer you question. Why did Mr. Daggett call you Elias?"

"Always call him Reverend Daggett, John." He cleared his throat, embarrassed. "The name change...Last summer as we rode north with Jeremiah Evarts, he took us to places like Monticello to visit with President Jefferson, then to Montpelier to see President Madison. We went to Washington and shook hands with President Monroe, then to Baltimore and Philadelphia. They are such great and grand places, John. Our poor people have nothing to compare with such cities. When we visited at a place called Burlington, New Jersey, we stopped at the home of a man called Elias Boudinot. He is the president of the American Bible Society and a true supporter of our education. He thinks we Indians are part of the lost tribes of Israel. Mr. Boudinot took such a personal interest in me…he even invited me to adopt his name. So, when I got here, I enrolled as Elias Boudinot."

"Are you ashamed of your own name, cousin?"

Elias flushed. "To tell the truth, I did not look forward to enrolling under my Cherokee name, Gallegina. Look what happened to Darcheechee."

John chuckled. "No need to get defensive, Buck…er, Elias. I'm so glad to see you I don't care what they call you. But tell me, why in the name of all that's holy, did they locate this school so far from the world?"

"The American Board of Commissioners for Foreign Missions founded the school in 1816. This building is a remodeled school put up by the town residents. It opened its doors for students in May of 1817. As to why they located it here…the missionaries considered this a moral community. It represents the ideal society that they wish to see us reproduce in our own lands."

"In other words, this is the place they wish to bring heathen into contact with Christians in the hopes that their goodness will rub off on us," mocked John.

✳   ✳   ✳   ✳

The clanging of a bell awakened John the following morning. "What the devil is that?" He groped for his watch in the gray light of dawn.

"That's the call for six o'clock prayers," Elias answered. "Get dressed."

Reverend Daggett led in prayer as the sleepy-eyed students assembled in the classroom. Then, one by one, the students read a verse from a chapter in the New Testament. After a plain breakfast, the students deployed to assigned chores.

"Mr. Ridge, I will need to work with you this morning to determine correct placement in your studies."

John followed the principal to his desk. After thumbing through some books on his desk, Daggett handed one to John. "Now, Mr. Ridge, let us see where you are in reading ability."

Recognizing the book as one written at the primary level, John snorted and tossed the book on Daggett's desk. Scanning the other books he selected one written in Latin. Opening it he read from "Concerning Old Age" by Cicero. He then closed the book, smirked, and handed it back to the principal, certain that the old man had understood the intended insult.

Daggett removed his glasses and polished them with his handkerchief. "It seems I have seriously underestimated your capabilities, Mr. Ridge. Be sure I will not repeat such a mistake." He adjusted his glasses. "Your cousin, Elias, is our best student. I shall place you with him in our most advanced subjects."

Seeing the smile starting to form on John's face, Daggett snapped. "You should also know, Mr. Ridge, that fraternization between students and the townspeople is strictly forbidden, especially young women. You will restrict yourself to the school grounds. You may not visit in any homes in this community without being invited."

"Is that because we might introduce immorality into the community, or be exposed to it?"

"Mr. Ridge, arrogance ill becomes a Christian. You must learn to walk humbly with thy God."

∗   ∗   ∗   ∗

John awakened to the touch of a hand on his brow. "Well, Mrs. Northrup, I think this one is going to live after all."

John opened his eyes to see a man bending over him. "I'm Dr. Samuel Gold, son. There for awhile you gave us quite a scare with that high fever and all."

Attempting to sit up, John winced as a sharp pain stabbed his right hip.

"Just take is easy, son. Your fever may have gone down but you've still got an inflamed hip joint."

"It's a problem I've had since childhood, doctor. It flares up from time to time."

Dr. Gold gathered up his bag and turned to Mrs. Northrup. "What he needs is considerable bed rest. Keep him off his feet. Let him get some strength back."

∗   ∗   ∗   ∗

John closed his eyes and lay back on his pillow, feeling the warmth of the spring sun filtering through the southern window. In the gray spectrum that separates sleep from wakefulness, John's thoughts drifted back to the day his father had left him at Spring Place, a frightened seven year old, who walked with a limp and spoke no English.

It was the first time he had ever been away from home and the first time he had been imprisoned in clothing that he had to wear constantly. The Moravian missionaries were unyieldingly opposed to seeing the human body naked. The fact that his sister, Nancy, and his cousin, Buck, were in school with him helped make the adjustment to a new and regimented environment. A quick learner, John became fluent in English within a year. The missionaries sent glowing reports about John's academic progress to his parents in Oothcaloga, although some concern was expressed about his superior attitude and lack of piety.

Now, here he was in the spring of 1821, eighteen years old and too ill to even travel home. Perhaps he would never complete his education; perhaps he would never be able to lead his people.

It was the touch of a soft hand on his brow that stirred him from drowsiness. Blue eyes and a smiling face, framed in reddish brown hair, looked down on him.

"Well, hello...and who are you?"

"I'm Sarah Bird Northrup, Mr. Ridge. My friends call me Sally."

John propped himself up on his elbows. "Alright, Sally...my friends call me John, not Mr. Ridge. But just what are you doing here...I mean, in a man's bedroom?"

"I'm your new nurse, Mr. Ridge...John. Mother is so busy looking after the other students, cooking, mending, and nursing, that she asked me to help out."

Rounded breasts the size of teacups held snuggly by her bodice, hips that were beginning to widen to womanly proportions. "Aren't you just a tad young to be taking on nursing responsibilities, little lady?"

"Now don't you fret, Mr. Ridge. I'm fourteen years old and perfectly capable of taking care of you."

John smiled and let himself back down on his pillow. "Alright Nurse Northrup, I'm completely at your mercy. In fact, I think I'm beginning to feel better already."

A few weeks later, following his examination of John, Dr. Gold remarked to Mrs. Northrup. "I'm amazed at his physical recovery. In fact, he has regained so much strength that we can dispense with further medication. However, I am concerned about his mental state. From time to time I find him in a state of deep depression. I don't know what is causing it but I'd suggest you try and find out."

Something in the doctor's tone nudged Mrs. Northrup into action. One afternoon, while Sarah was in school, she carried a basket of mending into John's room and sat down in a rocking chair to darn socks.

"Just thought you might like some company. I know being confined to a bed can make one terribly depressed."

"Oh, I'm not depressed," John replied. "In fact, I'm feeling much better."

"Dr. Gold thinks that something is troubling you. Is something troubling you, John?"

John flushed. "No, Mrs. Northrup, nothing is troubling me at all."

Mrs. Northrup peered over her glasses and rocked back and forth. "John, if you have something troubling you, you should tell me. I know I'm not your mother, but you have always trusted me."

John scowled and looked out the window down School Street to Colt's Foot Mountain. Words would not come.

"I think I know what is troubling you, John, and you'll feel much better if you unburden yourself. Just tell me. Are you in love with my daughter, Sarah?" She paused, afraid of what she would hear.

John's chin dropped to his chest and tears came to his eyes. "I'm so sorry, Mrs. Northrup," he blurted, "you and Mr. Northrup have been so good to me all these months...I've tried and tried to put Sally out of my mind but I'm not strong enough to do it...I do love her...I know I'm not supposed to but one can't help who they fall in love with...I want to marry her...with your blessings, of course."

Mrs. Northrup ceased rocking and sat quietly, her mind spinning. From time to time she had fleetingly recognized the possibility, with John and Sally being confined under one roof, something like this could happen. Now her fears had been realized. The passions of youth had broken down the barriers of puritan training. She gathered up her mending and stood. "John, hear me. You are a noble youth, handsome, and a perfect gentleman. But this dream of yours cannot be. My daughter must never marry an Indian."

When Sally came home from school that afternoon, she was met at the door by her mother. "Sally, I have one direct question and I want a direct answer. Are you in love with John Ridge?"

Taken aback for a moment, Sally gathered her composure and replied, "Yes, mother, I am."

"I see. Well, to be honest, I'm not too surprised. But, you must understand, Sally, this cannot be. You have no idea of the uproar that would take place in this community. We have our reputation to think of. So, your father and I have decided that you are to see no more of John. Tomorrow, we are sending you to your grandparents in New Haven."

*   *   *   *

"The future of our people will be determined, in large measure, by actions taken by those who hold political power in the United States government. If the union is to dissolve, we must consider the course of action which will best serve our interests. It is, therefore, exceedingly important that you keep me completely informed of what is transpiring in Washington City. I am, sir, yr.obt. servt." Jno Ross

Hanks folded the letter and returned it to his pocket. For two years the Congress had been deadlocked over the admission of Missouri as a state. Congressmen had become accustomed to eating by candlelight as debates raged on the floor from morning to night. Talk of disunion and civil war was common place. Political parties, once defined by principles, were now shaped by geography. Alabama was admitted as a slave state in 1819. Maine had been separated from Massachusetts and entered as a free state in 1820. It was of acute concern to the south that Missouri be admitted as a slave state in order to keep the balance; eleven free states in the north and eleven slave states in the south. The spread of slavery was the focus of debate but, thinly disguised, the primary concern was balance of political power. Unwilling to face the chasm before them, both parties crawled toward a final vote.

Now, Monday, February 26, 1821, Hanks settled into a gallery seat and found himself alongside John Quincy Adams, Monroe's Secretary of State. Although they had never met, Adams nodded courteously. As the House of Representatives gather to take another vote on the explosive Missouri subject, an overflow crowd, including fashionable ladies, filled the galleries and spilled over onto the floor of the stuffy chamber. Candles were placed all around as well as in the chandelier. Fires burned in four hearths.

For hours John Randolph of Virginia held forth. He pointed to the women and in his high pitched voice he screeched, "Mr. Speaker, what, pray, are all these women doing here, so out of place in this arena? Sir, they had much better be at home attending to their knitting." He went on to say, "I consider it the greatest misfortune to be born the master of slaves but I unalterably oppose any interference with its practice on the part of the federal government."

Adams shook his head in dismay and in an aside said to Hanks, "It's useless to call him to order. Like all his speeches, they have no end and no beginning. He can no more keep order than he can keep silence."

Finally, Speaker Henry Clay, gaunt and exhausted from sleepless hours, stepped into the well of the House to report the latest revision from the joint committee. After reading the resolution, Clay looked out over the House. His quiet words were spoken with pleading solemnity. "My friends, I wish that my country should be prosperous and her government perpetual. I am in my soul assured that no other government can ever afford the same protection to human liberty. Leave the North to her laws and institutions. Extend the same conciliatory charity to the South and West. Their people, as yours, know best their wants…know best their interests. Let them provide for their own…our system is one of compromise…and in the spirit of harmony let us come together."

Weary and tired of the issue, the House narrowly passed the compromise measure 87 to 81, mostly along geographical lines. By the compromise the North had secured the consent of the South to the exclusion of slavery from any territory north of 36 degrees, 30 minutes, the greater part of the Louisiana Purchase…but Missouri would enter the union with slavery.

As they left the gallery, Adams mumbled to Hanks, "Slavery is the great and foul stain upon the North American Union. What can be more false and heartless than this doctrine which makes the first and holiest rights of humanity depend upon the color of the skin? If the Union must be dissolved, slavery is precisely the question upon which it ought to break."

*   *   *   *

It was a warm day in mid-March. Under a shady weeping willow, Ross pored over the lengthy report from Hanks as he sat beside the cool and beautiful Poplar Spring on the west side of his home. Nearby his sons, James and Allen, sailed boats down the stream that flowed out of the spring. Recently, Ross's home had been designated as a United States post office and renamed Rossville. Weekly mail was now received by stagecoach.

Ross knew from information provided by Hank's report that the Missouri Compromise was not the final word on the slavery question. It was a smoldering stump just waiting for a brisk breeze to awaken it. If the United States ever abolished slavery and put pressure on the Cherokee regarding the matter, it would amount to a substantial property loss for Ross and his brother, Lewis. For now, it was comforting to know that the slave-holding states had prevailed.

Ross felt a tug at his sleeve. "Father, someone's coming." James pointed at two riders approaching on shaggy ponies. The taller rider was a middle-aged man. The second rider was a girl about six years old. The man dismounted.

"Si-yu' ginay'li"

The man wore a dirty, travel-stained homespun hunting shirt trimmed with red fringe. A red shawl was twisted around his head as a turban. A beaded belt held a large wooden-handled knife in a rough, leather sheath. He wore plain buckskin leggings and walked with a limp. Ross hurried to embrace him.

"Sequoyah! My old friend. It is so good to see you. James, fetch a chair for Mr. Gist. Allen, get him a glass of cold water." He turned to the child astride the horse. "And who might this be?"

Sequoyah eased himself into a chair in the shade of the willow. "She is my daughter, John. I call her Eye-o-kah."

"Ah, little one, let me help you out of the saddle." The little girl moved quickly to shyly stand by her father.

Quatie came out of the kitchen, quietly greeted Sequoyah then turned to the girl. "Come child, you look starved. Let's see if we can't find a glass of milk and some cookies."

Eye-o-kah looked questioningly at her father. "It's alright," he said, "Go along with Quatie."

"You boys might as well come and have some cookies too," said Quatie.

Left alone, Ross turned to Sequoyah. "Well, my friend, it's good to see that you have not lost it. Not too many men in their mid-fifties can produce such a beautiful daughter."

Sequoyah chuckled and reached for his pipe and tobacco. Ross waited while he filled the bowl of his long-stem pipe. From the kitchen Moses appeared holding a hot coal between tongs. He touched the coal to the tobacco and Sequoyah puffed. Once his pipe was drawing good, he leaned back in his chair and sighed contentedly.

"Sure good to get off that horse. After weeks in the saddle my backside was killing me."

"So, what brings you all the way from Arkansas country? When you left here three years ago I didn't know if I'd ever see you again."

"Didn't know if you wanted to see me. You were disappointed when I left with the others but I felt like the move to Arkansas was inevitable. Sooner or later the rest of you will have to join us. The whites won't let you stay here regardless of what you do."

Ross caught the accusatory tone. He knew that Sequoyah had left in 1818 rather than adopt any of the white man's ways. "Only time will tell, my friend. Right now I'm placing my trust in the laws of the United States and the men who administer them."

Sequoyah took another drag on his pipe and gazed absently toward Lookout Mountain. "They called me crazy, Little John…said it couldn't be done."

"Who called you crazy? What couldn't be done?"

Lost in his own thoughts, Sequoyah ignored Ross. "Years ago, when I was a boy, I first saw the white man's talking leaves. I would watch the missionaries at Spring Place as they read the talk of their god from the Preacher's Book. The white man reads the words and the deeds of their great men who were long dead…they read the big leaves about things that are happening by the big waters where the sun rises…they sent messages across the country on little talking leaves…" He turned to Ross. "You have many talking leaves in your house."

"Yes, of course…books, newspapers, letters…but what…?"

"When I told the head men that I could make a book, they called me crazy. They said when the Great Spirit first made a red boy and a white boy, they gave a book to the red boy and a bow and arrow to the white boy, but the white boy stole the book and left the red boy the bow and arrow and therefore an Indian could not make a book. But I fooled them, Little John. I made a book."

"What are you saying, my friend?"

Sequoyah smiled. "My friends laughed at me…said I was wasting my life. My wife got angry with me because I neglected the fields. She burned much work that had taken me years to create…so I had to start over. Turtle Fields said that I was making a fool of myself and no one would respect me. But I told him, if our people think I am making a fool of myself, you may tell the people that what I am doing will not make fools of them. They did not cause me to start and they will not cause me to stop…so I will go on, and you may tell our people. I heard no more from him. Now, Little John, my work is finished."

Sequoyah untied a roll of papers wrapped in leather skin. "Here is my book, Little John. I have made eighty-six letters that represent the sounds in our language. Take two or three days to learn these letters and you can read and write anything in our language. I can even teach you to read."

Ross smiled. "I already know how to read and write. Many of our people can. I'm not sure that your…what do you call it?…an alphabet?…is needed."

"Ah, but you read English, Little John. You say many can read and write, but in truth, only a handful of our people, a privileged few, the mixed bloods, can read it. Our people do not need to spend years toiling to learn the white man's language when in just a short time they can learn to read and write in our own language."

Ross said nothing.

"I can see you do not believe me," Sequoyah reached inside a bag and produced a quill, a small bottle of poke berry ink, and a scrap of paper. "Say something, John…say anything and I will write it down." He looked to where his daughter was now playing with the boys. "I will call my daughter and she will read what you have spoken."

After a moment's silence, Ross decided to humor his friend. "Alright, Sequoyah, write this down. 'Please stay for supper'."

Sequoyah smiled at Ross's patronizing manner and wrote. "Eye-o-kah, please come here," he called. When the girl presented herself, he handed her the scrap of paper and said, "Read this."

"Please stay for supper," she immediately responded.

Sequoyah turned to Ross who sat…stunned. "We will be most happy to break bread with you. It has been a long time since I tasted Quatie's cooking."

Ross nodded, still trying to understand what he had just witnessed.

*   *   *   *

The metallic buzzing of the cicada in the magnolia trees in late August signaled the approaching end of summer. Wisteria vines shaded the east veranda of Ross's home where he and Major Ridge sat discussing the implications of the Treaty of Doak's Stand.

Through his usual tactics of threats and temper tantrums, Jackson had bullied the Choctaws into an agreement to move from land along the Mississippi to Arkansas Territory.

"That cession will provide the government some of the richest cotton lands in Mississippi. The south will love Jackson for it. Add this to the millions of acres he has already forced us to give up and it will make him the most popular man in all the States."

"Such agreements only encourage him," said the Ridge. "What we need is unified opposition from all the Indian tribes as Tecumseh advocated."

"Too late for that now," Ross replied, "but it would help if we could only get unity among the Cherokee."

In the stillness of the hot afternoon, The Ridge fanned himself, then reached inside his shirt pocket. "I have a letter here written by a doctor by the name of Gold up in Cornwall. He says my son, John, is seriously ill. Susanna is insistent that I go to him at once. But, there is a problem…"

"What's the problem? Is there any way I can help?"

"I don't speak enough English to make such a trip alone. I was wondering if I could take your Moses with me as an interpreter?"

"I would consider it a privilege to help out and I'm sure Moses would enjoy a change of scene."

On the morning of September 4, 1821 The Ridge and Moses set out on horseback for Cornwall. With good weather they rode into Litchfield, Connecticut at the end of the month. Maples in blazing autumn splendor lined the dirt streets in front of sturdy salt-box houses. Past Tapping Reeve's law school they turned right at the Green on East Street to a large four-story building, Catlin's Tavern. After a night's rest, The Ridge rented a coach and four, the most splendid carriage he could find. Next he selected boots with white tops and a coat trimmed with gold braid to set off his physical appearance. "I can't have my own son ashamed of me," he joked with Moses.

Eyes popped among the locals as Moses drove the carriage the fifteen miles to Cornwall. No one had ever seen such a lustrous display of royalty in these New England hills…and a black man was an equal curiosity.

The Northrup family was equally awed by this colossus from the south who now strode among them. His commanding presence fairly exuded power and wealth. John, now on crutches, was swallowed up by his father's hug. Tears of joy streamed down The Ridge's cheeks.

"I have come to take you home to your anxious mother. Three years is a long time."

"That may not be possible, father. Dr. Gold does not think I am yet fit for travel."

"I must see Dr. Gold. I must thank him for taking care of you."

John Northrup interrupted the reunion, all of which had been taking place in the Cherokee language. "John, ask your father if he would like to spend the night, or at least dine with us."

John translated the Northrup's invitation. "Thank him for his hospitality," said The Ridge, "but I have a room at the local tavern. I will gladly accept the invitation to dine. After a month on horseback, I'm long overdue for a family meal."

"And…umm…what about your driver?" Northrup asked hesitantly.

"Slaves do not eat at the same table…"The Ridge blurted out, then caught himself. "But this is your house, Mr. Northrup."

During his two week stay in Cornwall, The Ridge was welcomed and lionized every where he went. He paid his respects to Dr. Gold and presented him with an Indian pipe carved of black stone. In turn, Dr. Gold gave him a small telescope.

The villagers, along with the Northrups, gathered around as The Ridge made ready to depart. Instead of his son, John, he and Moses would be accompanied by Leonard Hicks, who had received his father's permission to enter a school in South Carolina with a climate more to his liking.

The Ridge drew his son aside. "John, more than just your illness, I think I know what is holding you in Cornwall. I have seen that you and Sally have eyes for no one else. Your mother and I have always cherished plans for you to marry a daughter of some chief. By so doing, we feel that you will be of greater usefulness to our people. You can follow either your head or your heart but, before you act, think carefully of the consequences."

*   *   *   *

At the end of December Ross rode into Nashville to purchase one of the new cotton gins that were gaining popularity. Six thousand bales of cotton had been shipped from Tennessee to New Orleans the past season. Ross was planning to expand his cotton fields the coming year.

While sitting in the dining room of the Nashville Inn, he scanned the December 26 edition of the Nashville Whig. He noted that a fellow by the name of Martin Van Buren had arrived in Washington City on November 5 as Senator from New York and Thomas Hart Benton had been seated as the first senator from Missouri on December 6. Another item mentioned that a new missionary, by the name of Evan Jones, had recently arrived at Valley Towns, across the mountains in North Carolina.

His reading was interrupted by a cheery voice and a slap on his shoulder. Ross looked up to see his old friend, Sam Houston.

"You won't believe this, John, but you are looking at Nashville's newest lawyer. See, the announcement right there in your paper...'Sam Houston, attorney at law. Having removed to an office second below A. Kingsley's Esq. on Market Streets, can be found at all times where he ought to be'."

"Well, congratulations, Sam. I've also heard that you were elected major general of the Tennessee militia."

"All true," replied Houston.

"I've also heard that you were getting pretty deeply involved in political matters."

"Also true," Houston replied. "You won't like my saying so, John, but I'm supporting Jackson for president this next election. I expect the Tennessee legislature will nominate him for that office next July."

Ross said nothing but a warning signal registered in his mind.

CHAPTER 10

A TRAITOR
IN OUR MIDST

Rain in the spring of 1823 never ceased. Day after day soggy, gray clouds rolled up from the gulf and unloaded torrents of water in the Tennessee Valley. Streams over-flowed and fields flooded. By the time farmers were able to plant corn the season was far advanced. Leaders of the nation were anxiously concerned with finding supplies of corn that would see their people through the winter. Therefore, when Calhoun sent commissioners to negotiate sale of Cherokee land in early summer, they were met with little enthusiasm…in fact, they were not met at all.

Ross curtly dismissed the commissioners' suggestion that a meeting be held at Taloney, some miles east of the new Cherokee capital, New Echota. "I know of no instance of Ministers or Commissioners, to a foreign court, persisting in selecting a spot remote from the seat of government to which their embassy was directed. If there is to be a meeting, we will be the ones to decide the time, the place, and the agenda."

Duncan G. Campbell and James Meriweather, cooled their heels until finally, on October 16, Ross informed them that the Cherokee Council would receive their messages on the subjects of their mission…at New Echota.

As the council assembled in their new meeting house, Major Ridge stood and proudly introduced his son, John, who had returned from Cornwall to recuperate. John would act as an interpreter and thereby gain his first taste of Cherokee politics. Ridge also, recalling past misrepresentations, announced that all proposals from the commissioners must be submitted in writing.

Campbell, exuding good will, spoke first. "Under the kind protection of your first father, President Washington, and by those great friends of mankind who have followed him, you have been taught that you have a father to whom you are accountable. If the president practices towards you the kind treatment of a father, it becomes your duty to return the obedience and gratitude of children."

John Ridge hurried with his interpretation to the Cherokee. Campbell then continued. "We propose to purchase of the Cherokee nation the whole, or a part, of the territory now occupied by them and lying within the chartered limits of the State of Georgia. Clearly, you must see the rights of Georgia and the obligation of the United States. That these rights may be fulfilled, and these obligations discharged, is the important object of our present mission. We will now remove ourselves so that you may consider our proposals."

Soon as the Commissioners departed, young John Ridge sprang to his feet in fury. "What a pile of stinking horse shit they just unloaded…the ultimate gall of Campbell speaking to us as children."

His father chuckled. "Behold, what education can do for our children. I beg the Council's forgiveness for my son's impetuosity. John, you forget where you are…in Council the words of the elders are heard first."

"We all share your feelings, John," Ross injected, "but when negotiating with these land grabbers, never reveal your feelings. Any show of weakness or lack of unity only encourages them. Blood in the water only serves to attract more sharks."

For the next three days the Council deliberated the advantages of concessions and the possible consequences of refusal. On October 20 the Council and Commissioners came together again at New Echota.

As Speaker of the Council, Major Ridge made the reply. "Brothers and friends: The limits of this nation are small and embrace mountains, hills, and poor land which can never be settled. The Cherokees once possessed an extensive country but they have made cession after cession to our father the President, to gratify the wishes of our neighboring brethren, until our limits have been circumscribed. It appears from the desire of our brethren to obtain our lands, that it would be unreasonable for us to presume that a small cession at any time would ever satisfy them.

"You give us one reason why a cession is urged; that is, from the crowded settlements of the people of Georgia. We presume, if Georgia were in possession of the whole extent of her chartered limits, that it would not remedy the inconvenience complained of.

"Brothers, from the comparative view which you have taken of the population of Georgia and the Cherokee nation, you say that the difference is too great ever to have been intended by the Great Father of the Universe, who must have given the earth equally as the inheritance of his white and red children. We do not know the intention of the Supreme Father in this particular, but it is evident that this principle has never been observed or respected by nations or by individuals. If your assertion be a correct idea of His intention, why do the laws of civilized and enlightened nations allow a man to monopolize more land than he can cultivate to the exclusion of others?

"Brothers: we cannot accede to your application of cession. It is the fixed and unalterable determination of this nation never again to cede one foot more of land."

Flushed with rage at their inability to answer this eloquent aborigine, the commissioners rose to leave. Campbell spoke. "Let me urge the Council to continue in session until we have time to prepare a reply to your thoughts expressed today. Perhaps there is a solution..."

Campbell's solution appeared the next day.

William McIntosh was the son of a roistering Scot and a full-blood Coweta woman. In enjoyment of sumptuous living and beautiful women he had inherited his father's tastes. Yet he had risen to become one of the principal chiefs of the Creek Indians. On the 21st McIntosh rode into New Echota, along with his son, Chilly, and a half-dozen carousing Creek chiefs. He was warmly welcomed by the Cherokee and escorted to the White Bench, a place reserved in the Council House for those held in high esteem. Association between the Cherokee and the Coweta clan of the Creeks had long been amiable. In fact, one of McIntosh's wives was a Cherokee. The Ridge often served as advisor to the Creeks.

In the course of the day McIntosh managed to get alone with Ross. "You know," said McIntosh, "I think you should reconsider your stand on Campbell's offer."

"Why do you say that?" asked Ross.

"The white man is growing. He wants our land and is willing to pay handsomely for it. If we don't sell, by and by, he will take it anyway and our poor people will be left without home and hope."

"Am I hearing these words from a chief of the Creeks?"

"Listen," McIntosh spoke urgently, "we should sell now and move west to a new home. If you can bring yourself to favor this deal with Campbell, I can promise you a present of two thousand dollars…and the same to McCoy…and three thousand to Hicks. If you doubt me, I can get you paid before the treaty is even signed. What do you say, John? If I've left out anybody, any friends of yours, they will get the same amount. All you've got to do is say yes."

Ross peered intently at McIntosh. "Bill, how much will you get paid if we sign such an agreement?"

McIntosh hesitated. "Keep this between us, but if you sign, John, then I will collect seven thousand dollars."

"I see," Ross quietly responded. "Have you done this sort of negotiation before?"

"Oh, yes," McIntosh proudly replied. "For every treaty I've signed with the whites, I've been well taken care of."

Ross was silent for a moment. "Let me discuss your offer with a select few, then I'll get back to you. In the meantime, just so the others won't think I'm concocting a wild story, put the offer in writing."

"Consider it done," said a relieved McIntosh.

Early next morning headmen of the Council convened in secret. Ross related his conversation with McIntosh and read the contents of the letter. When he finished a solemn hush fell over the group. The implications of what was happening were apparent to all. A traitor within, or the erosion of will in other tribes, would eventually result in the dreaded calamity of capitulation of all to the whites. Finally, The Ridge broke the silence.

"He has signed his own death warrant. It was by his own motion in 1811 that his people made it a death penalty to sell Creek lands." He shook his head sorrowfully. "His people will never forgive him when they learn that he has taken bribes, that he has become known as the white man's chief."

"He will have earned his fate," said Ross. "Somehow, he got by with signing away more Creek lands in Georgia in 1821. Thirty eight Creek chiefs refused to sign but McIntosh ignored them all. My estimate is that he has already signed away fifteen million acres of Creek land."

"Is it the consensus of the Council that further talks with Campbell should be broken off?" asked The Pathkiller.

"I think not," said Ross. "If we break off negotiations, the blame for failure will be placed on us by the United States. The commissioners will soon know that their duplicity has been uncovered. They will be so embarrassed that they will break off talks."

Speaking in a firm voice The Pathkiller said, "We will have an immediate meeting of the entire Council. See to it that McIntosh attends."

Within the hour the entire Council convened in an air of questioning. McIntosh entered, smiling with expectancy. He was shown to a seat of honor beside Major Ridge.

The Ridge rose and addressed the Council. "You have been summoned with very short notice, and for that I apologize. A matter of utmost urgency has arisen, a matter pertaining to the treaty Commissioner Campbell has presented. I now yield to our President of the National Committee, John Ross, who will lay before you the issue at hand."

McIntosh smiled at Ross and winked. Ross rose, letter in hand, and straightened to his full five feet, six and a half inches. "My friends, a traitor, in all nations, is looked upon in the darkest color, and is more despicable than the meanest reptile that crawls upon the earth. It has now become my painful duty to inform you that a gross contempt has been offered to my character as well as to that of the General Council. This letter, which I have in my hand, will speak for itself. Fortunately, the author of it has mistaken my character and sense of honor."

Tension filled the air as Ross handed the letter to the Clerk of the Council, Alexander McCoy. McIntosh mopped his brow and loosened his black cravat, a look of panic in his eyes. Sentence by sentence, McCoy read and interpreted the letter.

As McCoy concluded, the Council sat stunned, all eyes fixed on McIntosh. In a high state of agitation he stood, wiped his brow and stammered. "Let me explain…"

The Pathkiller cut him short. Pointing a shaking, bony finger at McIntosh he said, "Set him aside."

The Ridge slowly rose. "The sorrow that I feel now in my heart is very, very, heavy. McIntosh and I have been friends…we were comrades in arms. We fought side by side at Horseshoe Bend…" He turned to look at McIntosh. "Chief McIntosh, who once stood erect, has betrayed our trust and the trust of his people. I now depress him. I cast him behind my back. I divest him of trust. I do not extend this disgrace to your own nation, the Creek people. You are now at liberty to retire in peace."

McIntosh hurriedly departed, goading his horse into a hard gallop. Even knowing that the exposure of McIntosh had scuttled their plans, Campbell and Meriwether continued to badger the Council for another three days. "The Cherokee," Campbell contended, "surrendered their sovereignty through the Treaty of Hopewell in 1785. You hold possession of your lands only by the generosity of the United States. You will not be permitted to exist as a separate, distinct, and independent government within her limits."

The Council members sat implacable. The Pathkiller nodded to Ross who rose to respond. "Brothers, Article Seven of the Holston Treaty says, and I quote, 'The United States solemnly guarantee to the Cherokees all their lands not herein ceded.' It says nothing about surrendering sovereignty. But we do not refer to the seventh article of the treaty of 1791 as a foundation of our title to the soil upon which we stand. Our title has emanated from a Supreme source which cannot be impaired by the mere circumstance of discovery by foreigners; neither has this title been impaired by conquest or by treaty. If our original title was lost, why did not the treaties of peace declare it in plain terms; and why should the United States purchase, time after time, lands to which you would wish to convince us we have no title?

"This session has now entered its twenty-seventh day. You have no grounds to complain of a sudden close of our negotiations; the subject has been fully discussed. We now consider this a final close to our negotiations."

As the commissioners departed, The Pathkiller, creaking with age, rose tremulously to his feet. "Too many winters have been borne on my shoulders for me to do the task that must be done. It begs credibility to think that Georgia will let this matter rest. They will besiege their lawmakers in congress until it is resolved in their favor. And so, once again, I must send you, you young members of the Council, to do battle in Washington City."

*   *   *   *

John Northrop sat slouched in his rocking chair, gazing at the glowing coals through half-closed eyes. Random thoughts glided across his mind then dissipated like the wisps of gray smoke that slowly rose up the chimney. His bible lay opened in his lap. Heretofore, whenever the steward had a problem, he had turned to his bible for strength and guidance. This night the long-held practice had failed. Social pressure from his neighbors was colliding head-on with his conscience. This very afternoon he had sat through a particularly painful session with the local governing board of the mission school.

"John, I implore you," said Rev. Herman Daggett, "as a friend, and as one concerned with the future of this school, do not let this marriage take place. It is our Christian duty to civilize these savages; it is not our duty to marry them. If you let Sarah marry this Ridge fellow, it will bring down a cascade of condemnation that we might not survive. Sustaining contributions will dry up overnight and we will lose this school."

"I understand, Reverend. Mrs. Northrup and I have made every effort to discourage this match. Two years ago, when the wife and I became aware of Sarah and John's feelings, we sent her to New Haven to be with her grandparents, with the hope that she would soon forget John. That didn't work. She refused to show any interest in other gentlemen and she refused to eat. In fear for her health, after three months, we brought her home. Then, as a last ditch effort to end the alliance, my wife sent John home."

"But did she send him home to stay? Our information tells us that she gave him conditional permission to return."

"Well, yes, in a way that's true. She told John that if he went home, regained his health, and returned in two years without his crutches, we would grant permission for them to marry. We thought that was the end of it. We never dreamed that he would return. Now, two years later, John Ridge showed up hale and hearty."

At this point, Rev. Timothy Stone, a former pastor of the First Church in Cornwall, but now a worker at the Mission School, weighed in on the side of Daggett. "John, this community is scandalized. You seem to have no comprehension of how it feels about a savage taking a gentle-born white girl into the filth of a wilderness wigwam."

Northrup chuckled. "I could hardly call John a savage. He is handsome, intelligent, and wealthier than most of us here in Cornwall. His prospects for the future look unlimited."

"I find absolutely no humor in this," said Stone. "Don't you realize that the source of Ridge's wealth is based on slavery? May God grant the election of John Quincy Adams to the presidency so that he can rid the nation of this curse."

Rev. Daggett sighed. "I see no further purpose that can be served by continuing this meeting. Let me impress upon you, John, the severity of this matter. Your congregation will not support you and the church will not sanction this marriage. If it takes place, it will be denounced in pulpits everywhere. I will not perform the wedding ceremony and, God forbid, when the press gets hold of this matter, there will be no one here to defend you from the devil himself."

Northrop laid his bible aside. Nowhere could he find scripture forbidding inter-marriage. Yet, Sarah was so young, so delicate, only sixteen. When Ridge took her to bed would he be gentle or brutal? Would their offspring be fair of skin like Sarah or swarthy as an aborigine? A flush of shame came over him. Never had he pictured his daughter so. He well knew that a good Congregationalist should not let his mind dwell on sex. It was accepted tenet that sex was sinful, a tool of the devil. In all the years he had been married to Mrs. Northrop, he had never seen her naked. In their acts of procrea-tion, which were carried out in the dark of the night, under the quilts, Mrs. Northrop never moved her flannel nightgown above her thighs. It would never have occurred to him to whisper sweet words into his wife's ear, to caress her smooth and ample breasts and tease the nipples. Sex was not to be enjoyed. It was a duty. And so, Sarah must be prepared to render to her husband her wifely duty.

Later that week John Ridge came storming into the Northrop household waving a copy of the Litchfield American Eagle. "Who is this Isaiah Bunce?" he raged.

"Calm yourself, John," soothed Mr. Northrop. "Bunce is the scandal-mongering editor of the newspaper you hold. As you may have gathered, he has little sympathy for our missionary endeavors."

"This article is despicable. How can you permit such vulgar and evil thoughts to be printed?" Ridge stormed. "It seems that race prejudice is the ruling passion in this community. An Indian is considered accursed. He is frowned upon by the meanest peasant. Scum of the earth are considered sacred when compared to an Indian. If an Indian is educated in the sciences, has a good knowledge of the classics, astronomy, mathematics, moral and natural philosophy, and his conduct is equally modest and polite, yet, because he is an Indian, the most stupid and illiterate white man will disdain and triumph over him. It is disgusting." He threw the paper to the floor.

"John, do not take this personally," Northrop said gently. "Bunce's vitriolic campaign is against the missionary effort, not you."

John Ridge and Sarah Bird Northrop were married in the Northrop home on January 24, 1824 in the company of her parents. Walter Smith, pastor of the Second Congregational Church, in the face of public condemnation, had the courage to officiate. Beginning their journey to the south, the couple rode off in a magnificent coach driven by a black coachman in livery and pulled by four white horses. Because, at almost every stop they were met by threatening mobs, Mr. and Mrs. Northrop kept them company the first part of their journey.

The missionary agents who managed the Mission School scurried to recover. They condemned miscegenation and forbade further marriages at Cornwall across the race line. There were some difficulties in making the doctrine of racial pride conform to Christian teachings but Lyman Beecher and Timothy Stone carried it off. Good people of Cornwall, who advocated spreading their culture, had found more than they had bargained for.

*   *   *   *

On the night of January 8 the house at 1333 F Street was ablaze with candle-light, the small orchestra played, and wine flowed. Host, John Quincy Adams, and wife, Louisa, were giving a party in honor of General Andrew Jackson on the tenth anniversary of his victory at New Orleans.

"Everyone in Washington must be here tonight," observed Ross.

"Everyone who is someone, with a few exceptions," replied Hanks. "There must be a thousand in attendance. For one who claims that he doesn't want to be president, Adams is putting on quite an affair."

"Our friend Jackson has made quite a name for himself since Horseshoe Bend," Ross wryly answered.

"He intends to have a bigger name. A name like president of the United States. Only Adams would have a different arrangement. He wants to be number one and he would like to have Jackson as vice-president."

"Jackson take the number two spot? You can't be serious!"

"That's the whole idea behind this party. Adams wants to curry Jackson's friendship and support. With Jackson on his ticket, Adams would win the support of the western states and leave Clay's candidacy high and dry. The old geezer is pretty cagey. And speaking of geezers, here he comes now."

"Ah, good evening, Mr. Ross. So happy you were able to join us." Severe and stooped, Adams gamely worked his way through the crowd, attempting to be outgoing.

"It was good of you to invite us. When we met at the White House this morning, I had no idea it would be such an elaborate party."

"Well, we must pay due homage to our heroes."

"I'm disappointed that President Monroe is not in attendance. I had hoped to press our cause with him on an informal basis."

Adams fidgeted with his collar. "President Monroe declined my invitation as he wishes to remain impartial about the upcoming election. Well, thank you again for coming. If you will excuse me, I must see to my other guests."

As Adams shuffled away, Hanks leaned close to Ross's ear. "What he didn't tell you was that Monroe would be mincemeat at this party. With Adams, Calhoun, and Crawford, all members of his cabinet, and all dying to be the next president, this is a party Monroe would just as soon skip."

"What about Clay? I don't see him here...nor Calhoun or Crawford."

"Calhoun probably chose not to attend," Hanks replied. "Adams has been miffed at the electioneering that Calhoun's wife engages in at all social affairs. Since Adams got appointed Secretary of State over Clay, relations between those two have gone from bad to worse. Much the same with Adams and Crawford."

*   *   *   *

Calhoun paced irritably back and forth. He was not enjoying the stinging criticism the delegate from Georgia was delivering.

"Mr. Calhoun," said Thomas Cobb, "I speak with the authority of Governor Troup and I say your civilization program with the Cherokees has worked too damn well. Those savages now know the value of land. Those gut-eating, root grubbers have the unmitigated gall to think that they can have an independent state within the boundaries of Georgia. This we will never tolerate. Unless you bring more pressure to bear on them, the sovereign state of Georgia will be forced to take matters into her own hands. You will either join us in ejecting the Cherokees from lands that rightfully belong to Georgia or you must make war upon us and shed the blood of your brothers and friends."

Calhoun waved his hands in denial. "You are too impatient, Mr. Cobb. It takes time…"

"I understand your timing problem, sir. You do not wish to alienate any northern votes by action against the Cherokee. But it is necessary that these misguided people be taught that there is no alternative to their removal. You will deceive them grossly if you lead them to believe that their consent is necessary to Georgia's actions."

"But there are treaties, Mr. Cobb…"

"Treaties, my ass. The Indians are simply occupants, tenants at will, and so ignorant that they are incapable of understanding the meaning of a treaty. The time must come when the soil of Georgia shall no longer be imprinted with the footstep of the savage. Removal beyond the Mississippi will give these sons of nature the wilderness congenial to their feelings and appropriate to their wants."

Calhoun struggled for control. "Mr. Cobb, I have an appointment tomorrow with these gentlemen…"

"Gentlemen? You call them gentlemen!! Your proposition that these "gentlemen" be incorporated into our society…bah! If such a scheme is practicable at all, the most rights and privileges that public opinion would permit them would be somewhere slightly above the status of the Negro. It hardly seems feasible." Cobb picked up his hat before a parting shot. "You should know, I have today delivered a letter to Congress conveying the thoughts I have just laid before you."

*   *   *   *

Caught between the demands of Georgia and the pressure from the Cherokee, Calhoun was in a vile mood. Things had not gone well in the last four meetings with the Cherokee. Led by a very stubborn John Ross, the Cherokee delegation had refused to budge on any concessions. Dealing with Ross was consuming an inordinate amount of time; time that could be better spent talking with representatives from different parts of the nation who could advance his presidential aspirations. There must be a way that would free him from these fruitless negotiations...

A light tap on the door interrupted his thoughts. Aide Hanks stepped inside. "The Cherokee delegation is here to see you, Mr. Secretary."

Seated behind his desk an impatient Calhoun moved the discussion quickly to the point. "Gentlemen, you must be sensible to the fact that it will be impossible for you to remain in your present situation. You cannot exist as a distinct society, or nation, within the limits of Georgia."

"And why not, Mr. Secretary," asked Ross, "if the United States will honor its treaties? We are sensible to the fact that the United States, in its compact with Georgia, said it would not extinguish Indian title unless it could be done peaceably and on reasonable conditions. Without the free and voluntary consent of the Cherokee Nation, the United States cannot comply with that treaty."

Warming to his subject, Ross stood and placed his hands flat on the desk and looked Calhoun straight in the eye. "The Cherokee Nation never promised to surrender at any future date, to the United States or Georgia, their title to any lands. On the contrary, the United States have, by treaties, the highest law in your nation, solemnly guaranteed to secure to the Cherokees forever, their title to lands which have been reserved for them.

"You say it will be impossible to remain for any length of time in our present situation. Sir, to these remarks we beg leave to observe, and to remind you, that the Cherokees are not foreigners but original inhabitants of America and that they now inhabit and stand on the soil of their own territory."

Ross removed his hands from the desk and stood erect. "Forgive my temperament, Mr. Secretary, but we have been toyed with enough. Our predicament and our wishes are ignored or lost in the floodtides of greed and politics that consume your people. We ask for little…we ask that your government honor its treaties with us…nothing more."

On March 10, 1824 Calhoun removed himself from further direct negotiations with the Cherokee. On that date, without a hint of legislative sanction, he designated a favorite of his, Thomas L. McKenney, to be in charge of Indian Affairs.

The Cherokees were upbeat that night as they gathered around the dining table in the Tennison Hotel.

"I'd suggest we make an appointment with McKenney as soon as possible. He has been a friend and, through him, maybe we can get something done. Pass the chicken, please." So spoke Major Ridge.

"Yes, I agree. We will meet with McKenney," replied Ross, "but remember, even though he is our friend, he is a closer friend to Calhoun and can do only what Calhoun permits him to do."

Ross was disrupted by his friend George Lowrey. Pointing to a dish of sweet potatoes, Lowrey in a loud voice said to the black waiter, "Bring me some of those roots. We Indians are very fond of roots." He caught the attention of the entire dining room. Several times he called for "more roots" adding at each request, "We Indians are very fond of roots."

Ross soon detected the object of Lowrey's sport. A member of the Georgia congressional delegation, now seated at their table, on the floor of the House had referred to the Cherokee people as "savages subsisting upon roots, wild herbs, and disgusting reptiles." Soon the Georgia delegate, flushed with anger, stalked out of the room to the hoots of laughter from the other diners.

Negotiations with McKenney during the months of March, April, and May were no more productive than they had been with Calhoun. On April 29 Ross presented to McKenney case after case where the Agent to the Cherokee, McMinn, had failed to act in the best interest of the Cherokee.

"Your lack of confidence in McMinn," replied McKenney, "is not considered a satisfactory reason for his removal."

"And what about compensation for use of the Cherokee light horse in 1820 to remove white intruders?" asked Ross.

"Unfortunately, there is no money available for that," answered McKenney.

"And money for the education of our female children here in Washington?"

"Sorry, that fund is depleted."

"I suppose there are not a thousand dollars to pay the annuity promised in the Tellico Treaty?"

"Tellico Treaty? I know of no such treaty," responded McKenney.

Ross smiled as he unrolled a document. "This might refresh your memory," he said, handing a copy of the treaty to McKenney.

Flushing with embarrassment, he returned the paper to Ross. "I'm sorry. I never knew such a treaty existed. Excuse me. I must confer with Secretary Calhoun."

McKenney returned in a few moments with an obviously agitated Secretary of War. "Even though this treaty is twenty years old," said Calhoun, "it appears to be valid and still in force. I will approve payment of the annuity but a third of it must go to your brothers who have relocated west of the Mississippi."

Ross bristled. "I must strenuously object, Mr. Secretary. Those individuals have withdrawn and formed a distinct community in another country. They can have no pretensions or claims to the property of our nation."

"If you will read article six of the Treaty of 1819 you will find that manner of payment is so ordered," Calhoun countered.

His jaw tightened, but knowing Calhoun would not relent, Ross nodded. "We may desire to discuss the matter at length sometime in the future. For now, we will settle for the expenses incurred during our stay here in Washington."

"I'm sorry, Mr. Ross," injected McKenney. "The government cannot be responsible for your expenses for this visit as the government did not request your presence. Your six month stay will have to be out of your pocket."

Ross replied with withering sarcasm. "We did not suppose that it was the policy of this government to extend its bounty exclusively to those who make visits here for the object of selling their lands."

Back at their hotel Ross continued to vent his wrath. "What we are seeing, Major Ridge, is a blatant attempt by the United States to promote division among the Cherokee. Our unity is our greatest strength…and the greatest fear of the United States."

The Ridge wearily dropped to a chair and kicked off his boots. "Face it, Little John, we got our ass kicked this trip. There is as much interest in our problems here in Washington City as there is sex drive in a mule. Politics is not to my liking."

"Politics," replied Ross, "is the only weapon we have left. We must learn to use it."

∗ ∗ ∗ ∗

He removed his cap and let the warm, southern April breeze tease the few strands of hair that remained as the two keelboats moved slowly up the clear, blue-green waters of the Grand River. His eyes scanned the east bank where an extensive canebrake bordered the river. Red-winged blackbirds trilled from the top of the reeds. Beyond the shore was a valley densely timbered with oak, ash, and hackberry. Open areas were overgrown with nettles and tall weeds. Suddenly they came upon a rock ledge that extended into the river from the east bank; a natural landing place.

"Put 'er ashore here, sergeant."

"Yes, sir, Colonel."

Only three weeks ago he had received General Winfield Scott's directive to abandon the post at Ft. Smith and move the army upriver to the mouth of the Verdigris. Controlling hostilities between the Cherokee and Osage could be better effected if the army presence was closer. On April 9 the Seventh Infantry left the unhealthy post at Fort Smith. Two keel boats, with supplies and a hand full of soldiers, moved upstream. Most of the soldiers would follow the regiment's wagons along a trail already well marked.

In the Three Rivers area, where the Arkansas, the Verdigris, and the Grand came together, he decided the area too cluttered with the tents of traders and Indians. He chose the eastern branch and moved up the Grand for three miles. Now, on April 22, Colonel Matthew Arbuckle stepped ashore at the site where his men would build a new garrison. Temporarily housed in tents, the soldiers set about felling trees, sawing and hewing logs. By May 1824 work was nearing completion. No one suspected that malaria and other maladies would soon give the post, named Cantonment Gibson, the distinction of being the Charnel House of the army.

CHAPTER 11

CORRUPT BARGAINS

Early January of 1825 found Major Ridge back in Washington City with his son as hired agents for the Creek Indians. Understanding that his old friend, Andrew Jackson, had been elected president of the United States, The Ridge decided to pay him a visit. He found the general comfortably seated in a rocking chair in the parlor of Gadsby's Tavern, smoking his corncob pipe, sipping whiskey, and listening to the piano playing of Margaret O'Neale. Happily seated nearby, smoking her clay pipe, was his wife, Rachel. The Ridge greeted Jackson, his son translating.

"My heart is glad when I look upon you. Our heads have become white. They are blossomed with age. It is the course of nature. Friendship formed in danger will not be forgotten."

As John Ridge finished translating his father's remarks, he added, "We also wish to extend our congratulations upon your being elected president."

Jackson blew a plume of smoke into the air and smiled sardonically. "The congratulations are a bit premature, I'm afraid. I do have the most popular votes but it's the electoral votes that count. In our system of elections, if you don't win by the electoral votes, the selection of the president is passed to the House of Representatives. They select from among the three persons who receive the highest count, which in this case, means Adams, Crawford, and me. I'd support the devil before I'd support Crawford. He's had several strokes and probably couldn't serve even if he got elected. Looks like the real squeeze is between Adams and me. The

House will decide…and Clay controls the House…and that is my worry. That gambling sonofabitch will play all the cards he holds to his future advantage."

He took a sip of whiskey and let a short, bitter chuckle escape. "Thank God, Henry Clay didn't make the cut. I'd see the earth swallow me up before I'd fraternize with him. But…the bastard can still make trouble. My informers tell me he met with Adams last night." He shifted in his chair. "Where are my manners? Let's not talk politics. Margaret, my dear, please pour these gentlemen some smooth Tennessee whiskey."

Having nothing better to do, on February 9 John Ridge accepted the offer of Tom Hanks to attend the election ceremonies. They waded through a wet snowstorm to find a seat in the overflowing gallery of the House. Spectators crowding the galleries included foreign ministers, governors, judges, and other distinguished persons. Negroes crowded outside the hall.

At exactly high noon the members of the United States Senate filed into the House of Representatives and took their seats in front of the Speaker. For over two hours the business of opening electoral certificates and counting the ballots proceeded. Finally, to no one's surprise, it was announced that John C. Calhoun had been elected Vice-President but that no candidate for the presidency had received the necessary majority of votes. With that announcement, the Senators filed out of the chamber to allow the Representatives the privilege of selecting the next president. Tension swiftly mounted.

Speaker Henry Clay took his place at the podium and appointed Daniel Webster and John Randolph as tellers. It would be their duty to notify the next president of his election. Clay then called for a roll call of the states. Representatives of each delegation took their seats together in the order of which the states would be polled.

"This is gonna be interesting as hell," Hanks commented.

"Would you enlighten me on these procedures?" Ridge requested.

"Well, the order of voting will run from north to south along the Atlantic seacoast and then south to north along the Mississippi Valley. Each state gets one vote and that vote is determined by the majority of the state's delegation."

As they watched, Clay left the podium. Smiling and confident he walked down the aisle. He paused by an old man, bent and whispered in his ear.

"That man," explained Hanks, "is General Stephen Van Rensselaer, representative from the state of New York. They say he has been under godawful pressure from Van Buren, who wants him to vote for Crawford, and from Clay and Webster who want him to vote for Adams. Since his state is split almost fifty-fifty, Van

Rensselaer will be deciding the vote for New York. Thirteen states are all that is needed to win...and New York is that thirteenth state."

As they watched, Van Rensselaer lowered his head to the edge of his desk, covered his eyes, and appeared to be praying. When the ballot box reached his desk, he picked up a piece of paper from the floor and stuffed it into the box.

The voting completed, Webster stood to announce the results. Thirteen states had voted for Adams, seven for Jackson, and four for Crawford. For a moment the House and gallery sat in stunned silence. Speaker Clay turned to the House and declared, "John Quincy Adams of Massachusetts, having received the majority of votes of all the states of the Union, was duly elected President of the United States for four years, to commence on the fourth of March, 1825."

A rumble started in the gallery followed by a stream of hisses. Clay, taking no chances on a demonstration, ordered the galleries cleared. Only the Negroes were smiling at the election results.

"Well, I'll be goddamned," said an unbelieving Hanks. "The man who had the most popular votes, the man who had the most electoral votes, the man who the American people selected has just lost this election. That scheming, conniving bunch of political bastards did him in. Come on. Let's go see Jackson."

It was three o'clock in the afternoon when Hanks and Ridge arrived at Gadsbys, located on the north side at the corner of Pennsylvania Avenue and West Sixth Street. Eaton and Donelson arrived simultaneously. Jackson, seated in his rocking chair, listened to the report with controlled anger.

"Tell me," Jackson demanded, "how did Kentucky vote?"

"Kentucky voted for Adams," replied Hanks.

Jackson lunged out of his chair, his rage out of control. "There, gentlemen...there it is...evidence of a corruption that could only be engineered by the likes of Clay. How the hell can Kentucky vote for Adams when he didn't get a single popular vote in that state, not a goddamned one." Saliva slid down Jackson's chin. "Everyone knows that the Kentucky legislature passed a resolution instructing its representatives in Congress to vote for the western candidate, and the western candidate was me."

Jackson, puffing furiously on his pipe, paced up and down the room while his friends looked on. "This is a farce," Jackson stormed. "If the people submit to this, they might as well bid farewell to their freedom. Mark my words, Clay has bartered away the rights of people for promises of office. And Adams? My God...how can any man accept election to the presidency knowing full well that the people do not want him...and knowing that sonsuvbitches like Clay fixed this election?"

One minute Jackson was an erupting volcano; the next he was calm and controlled. "It's a bitter defeat, gentlemen, but I am consoled by the knowledge that I have received the approving judgement of an enlightened, patriotic, and uncorrupted people. I made no secret deals; no secret conclaves were held; I attempted to persuade no one to violate pledges given. My hands are clean."

*   *   *   *

To honor the President-elect, Monroe gave a levee on February 10. The prospect of seeing Jackson, the defeated hero, come face to face with Adams was too much to miss. Washington turned out in force. Milling around in the crowd, the two men inevitably came together. Jackson extended his hand in hearty congratulations. His face showed no anger or disappointment. "How do you do, Mr. Adams? I hope you are very well, sir."

Adams accepted the extended hand and coldly replied, "Very well, sir. I hope General Jackson is well."

A murmur of admiration for Jackson passed through the party.

*   *   *   *

February 17 found John Ross, George Lowrey, and Elijah Hicks checking into the Williamson's Hotel in Washington. Topping their agenda was the matter of a new government agent for the Cherokee since Joseph McMinn had passed away the previous November. Before they were able to pursue their goal, a breathless John Ridge hurried to their hotel.

"You'll never believe what has happened," he panted. "The Creeks have given up their lands…they have signed a treaty with the commissioners."

"Slow down, John. Where did you get such information?"

"John Crowell, agent for the Creeks, and Big Warrior, just rode into town. They are in my room. Come with me."

Ross was dismayed at the dusty, exhausted appearance of the Creek delegation. Big Warrior seemed dangerously close to collapse but he smiled and extended a weak handshake to Ross.

"Big Warrior, it is good to see you," Ross said gently. "Ridge tells me that you have signed away your lands. Do you feel like telling me what happened?"

"Let me tell you. Big Warrior is too weak to speak." It was Opothle Yoholo, the Creek National Council speaker. "I don't know how he survived the trip. We rode hard, long days, trying to get here to stop the treaty."

Ross sat down and motioned for Yoholo to do the same. "Now, take your time...start at the beginning and tell me everything that happened."

With dark eyes flashing with anger, Yoholo began. "In spite of my warning, William McIntosh signed a treaty on February 12 at Indian Springs with those agents from Georgia, Campbell and Meriwether. McIntosh was the only member of the National Council. Georgia will get four to five million acres of our land...and within eighteen months all Creeks must be out of Georgia."

"So," Ross mused, "in spite of my warning to your Council, McIntosh has succeeded in selling out his people." He looked at Opothle Yoholo. "How do you plan to stop the treaty?"

"When Calhoun compares the signatures on the treaty with names on annuity receipts, the absence of names of the headmen will show the treaty to be a fraud. Corruption will be evident when he sees that two hundred thousand dollars will be paid to a tiny McIntosh group. We cannot believe that a treaty made with such a small minority of our people will be ratified."

Ross shook his head. "Don't underestimate the lust of white men for our lands."

True to Ross's expectations, the Senate, in the last moments of its session, ignored all protests, and, without examination, confirmed the Treaty of Indian Springs on March 3, 1825. With that out of the way, they were free to enjoy the parties and the presidential inauguration scheduled for the following day.

It was a grim party of Creeks and Cherokees that witnessed the installation of John Quincy Adams on March 4. The next day Adams named Henry Clay of Kentucky to be his Secretary of State, confirming suspicions of Jackson and his allies that a "corrupt bargain" had been made. One of the first acts of the newly installed president was to sign the Treaty of Indian Springs on March 7 and authorize its proclamation.

On March 8, Big Warrior of Tuckabatchee, head man of the Upper Creek Towns for nearly twenty years, died in Washington City. Age, infirmity, and the knowledge that the treaty spelled doom for his people, were too much for the old warrior to withstand.

*   *   *   *

In the blackness of night the National Council of the Creeks met in great secrecy. Little Prince of Broken Arrow, headman of the Lower Towns, spoke quietly. "Listen to what I tell you. William McIntosh was the son of Captain William McIntosh, a loyalist officer during the American Revolution. His mother was a Coweta woman of the prominent Wind clan. One of his half-brothers, William R. McIntosh, served in the Georgia legislature. John McIntosh, another half-brother, worked for Crawford as the Treasury Department's collector for the port of Savannah. George Troup, United States Senator and Georgia governor, is a cousin. I relate all of this so that you will be prepared for any consequences likely to take place when sentence is carried out. William McIntosh is a traitor of such enormity that I cannot describe. Fraudulent by the standards of any society, concluded in violation of the clearly expressed orders of this Council, the Treaty of Indian Springs is riddled with bribery and deceit. In this treaty, McIntosh has sold the country of his people and the legacy or our children...that is why this Council has decreed that he must die. To carry out the sentence, the Council has chosen a warrior whose battle scars gained in the defense of his people attest to his loyalty...Menawa, Council Chief of Okfuskee."

*   *   *   *

At daylight on the morning of April 30, 1825, Menawa led a force of about one hundred fifty warriors to McIntosh's plantation on the banks of the Chattahoochee River. They quietly surrounded his house and outer buildings and piled bundles of kindling wood against the walls. In a matter of moments, the buildings were aflame. Chilly, the son of McIntosh, jumped through a window and swam the river to safety.

From a second story window McIntosh shouted, "Let the women come out."

"They are free to come out. They will not be harmed," replied Menawa.

Two of McIntosh's wives, Peggy and Susannah, with their children, quickly emerged. In a few moments the fire drove McIntosh down the burning stairs. A volley tore into his body. Several warriors rushed inside, seized him by the legs and dragged him into the yard. With blood gushing from his wounds, McIntosh raised himself on one arm and looked defiantly at his executioners. At that moment an Okfuskee Indian drove a knife into his heart up to the hilt. With that, McIntosh gurgled on his blood and died. The warriors continued to fire into his body until they had put more than fifty balls into his head. He was buried naked in the ground. Creek justice had been carried out.

*   *   *   *

Ross paced back and forth attempting to bolster the Creek and Cherokee delegates seated in his room.

"Gentlemen, I do not need to describe to you the desperate plight we now face. A weakening of the Creeks by the Treaty of Indian Springs makes the Cherokee all the more vulnerable to the demands that they too remove. Tomorrow I will make one last plea with President Adams to rescind the treaty. After that, I must return immediately to New Echota for a special meeting of our Council. Governor Troup has called out the Georgia militia and there is much concern at home that we will be attacked. Chilly McIntosh is doing mischief in trying to get revenge through the Georgia militia.

*   *   *   *

The president shifted his pudgy body uneasily and dabbed his red, watery eyes with a handkerchief. "I'm truly sorry if the treaty is a fraud, Mr. Ross, but the laws must be obeyed. The treaty is a law and no white man can break it. There is no precedent for declaring null and void a treaty that has been ratified by the Senate and proclaimed by the president."

Ross silently studied Adams for a moment. "Mr. President, I understand you are a student of your Bible."

Adams, surprised at the shift in direction, responded. "Yes, I begin every day by reading my Bible. I find it gives me comfort and courage."

"You are familiar with Psalms 89?"

"You might wish to refresh my memory…"

"Verse 14 says, 'Righteousness and justice are the foundation of thy throne…' I feel that verse applies to you, Mr. President. You are a fair man; you recognize injustice when you see it and you are not comfortable with it. It is obvious to you that the Treaty of Indian Springs is corrupt to the core. Why is it always the rights of the Indians must yield when their rights are equally protected by the United States Constitution?"

Adams shifted again in his chair and moped his bald head with the handkerchief. Ross stood to take his leave.

Adams rose from his chair and extended his hand. "You overestimate my powers, Mr. Ross. With Governor Troup out of control in Georgia, the United States has rarely been so close to constitutional disaster. I cannot foresee the outcome, but I can assure you that whatever is done, it will be done legally. There is no way I can predict how the upper house of Congress will respond…but perhaps they will receive a new treaty."

*   *   *   *

During the second half of the year, Ross worked at strengthening the resolve of the Cherokees and kept his eye on national events.

The month of October proved to be an eventful one. Even before the Adams administration had an opportunity to reveal its program, the Tennessee legislature passed a resolution endorsing Andrew Jackson for president in 1828.

Also, that month, Ross received a puzzling and shocking letter from Jeremiah Evarts, dated 17 September 1825, in which Evarts announced that no more Indian students would be received at Cornwall. Ross immediately summoned Boudinot to get his reaction to the letter.

"Boudinot smiled ruefully. "I suspect John Ridge and I bear most of the responsibility for this action." He pulled a couple of letters from his pocket. "This first letter is from Dr. Benjamin Gold, Harriett's father, in which he refuses to let us wed. Harriett must have persuaded him for in the second letter he gives his permission. When John Ridge married Sarah Northrop the town of Cornwall erupted into a volcano of rage. Now that the word is out that Harriett and I plan to marry next spring, I suspect the town is even in worse shape."

Ross pondered for a moment. "You mean to tell me that the Christians would close down the school just over a matter of marriage?"

"Yes, if the marriage is between people of different complexions."

"And how does that make you feel?"

"I would hate to see such excellent educational opportunities lost to our people but nothing they do will deter Harriett and me from marriage. Beyond that, I'm convinced that the Indian and the white man simply cannot live together."

CHAPTER 12

CRISIS IN CORNWALL

Outside a summer storm raged. A fierce, wind-driven rain blew down the Housatonic Valley lashing the three-storied residence of Dr. Benjamin Gold. Inside the house another storm held sway. For hours Harriett Gold had endured threats, pleas, and insults from family and church officials. Her brother-in-law, the Rev. Herman Vaill, was holding forth.

"The marriage will occasion so much evil you might as well die as marry an Indian," he raged.

Mary Brinsmade, Harriett's sister, bristled in defense. "How can you, a minister of the gospel, speak such invective words? If you can say nothing positive, then you best not speak at all."

Vaill retreated. "Let me clarify my position. Harriett can marry a man of any color she chooses so long as it does not injure the cause of religion and our Foreign Mission School. She must realize that she has to accept responsibility for what will happen if she marries that Indian. Old friends in this community are shunning her and speaking of her 'animal feelings'. The church choir leader has banned her from sitting with the other girls and has asked the choir to wear black arm bands…"

"Which they refused to do," Mary injected.

"Nevertheless," Vaill continued, "Harriett's course of action is going to hurt, not help, Indian missions. She knows that friends of the school oppose such a marriage. If she continues with such plans, she will be nothing more than a Judas, a betrayer of the cause. Another event such as the Ridge and Northrop marriage will annihilate the Foreign Mission School."

Harriett stood impassively at the south window watching the driving rain shred rose petals.

Vaill moderated his approach. Lowering his voice, he spoke to Harriett. "Just for a minute, think of your reputation...think of my reputation...think of your family's reputation...you are the daughter of Cornwall's most prominent family. Of the fourteen children, you are the apple of your parents' eye, the idol of the family. You are one of the fairest, most cultured ladies of this community, a very pious, amiable girl, the nearest to perfection of any person I ever knew. Your sisters have married in high rank; some rich, one to a lawyer, another to a judge, one to a Congregationalist minister. All have married so well that it would be a dreadful stroke if you married an Indian."

Harriett slowly turned from the window. Clutching a damp handerchief, she lifted her reddened eyes and faced Vaill. "Elias and I have vowed and our vows have been heard in heaven. Color is nothing to me. His soul is as white as mine. He is a Christian and ever since I embraced religion I have prayed that God would open a door for me to be a missionary...and this is my way. I can do more good for the Indians if I become one of them. That is my final word on this subject."

When the forthcoming wedding became public knowledge, an explosion rocked Cornwall. On a warm, June night a mob assembled on the village green and burned Harriett, Boudinot, and Mrs. Northrop in effigy. Harriett's brother, Stephen, set fire to a barrel of tar as a funeral pyre.

Fearing that Harriett might be harmed by the crowd, she was spirited away to a friend's home on Dibble Hill, about a mile northwest of Cornwall. From there she could see the flames and smoke and hear the mournful tolling of the church bells marking the departure of a soul.

In late April of 1826, disguised to avoid recognition and possible harm, Elias Boudinot arrived in Cornwall. On May 1, at two o'clock in the afternoon, Elias and Harriett were united in marriage in the Gold home by Harriett's brother-in-law, a contrite Rev. Herman Vaill. No young people were invited. Stephen could not stand to see them married and worked in the sawmill all afternoon. Soon after, the newly weds left New England for Philadelphia. Their honeymoon was to be carried on during a fund raising campaign which the Cherokee Council had appointed Elias to conduct.

*   *   *   *

In October a committee from the ABCFM met to act on the fate of the Mission School at Cornwall. In its annual report the racial controversies created by Indian-white marriages were barely acknowledged. It did admit that discrimination against the Indians 'results not merely from the difference in complexion, but from the hereditary feelings of our people in regard to the Indians.' In November the school's fate was sealed. It would close.

*   *   *   *

The eastern sky was tinged with pink as the president turned toward home. Having risen an hour and a half before dawn, he would complete his daily four mile walk in time to see the sun rise from the eastern chamber of the White House. The solitary walk helped keep his bowels regular and provided time for much needed reflection.

He had just returned from his home in Quincy, Massachusetts where he had buried his father. John Adams, second President of the United States, had died on Tuesday, July 4, 1826, completing almost ninety-one years on earth. Hovering near death, he had brightened when reminded that it was the fourth of July, the fiftieth anniversary of independence. "It is a great day. It is a good day," he said.

The president entered the White House, made a fire in the fireplace, and sat down to read three chapters in the Bible, a part of his daily routine. He then turned his attention to a problem that had been gnawing at him all the while he had been out of Washington, the Treaty of Indian Springs. This occupied him until breakfast at nine.

Following breakfast the president met in his office with members of his cabinet. "Gentlemen," the President began, "we are once more faced with a dilemma, of which there seems to be no shortage these days. The Creeks refuse to abide by the Treaty of Indian Springs. On the other hand, Governor Troup of Georgia, refuses to accept the revision, The Treaty of Washington. The Indian Springs Treaty gave the Creeks until September 1 to relinquish their lands in Georgia. The Treaty of Washington gave them a January 1, 1827 deadline for removal. Some violence has already issued, enough to justify my sending General Pendleton to intervene. Troup considered that a threat to what he calls states rights. He has called up his state militia and is making threats. Right now, gentlemen, Georgia and the United States may be headed for a confrontation. Your president invites, nay, welcomes, your suggestions for resolving this issue."

Secretary of War, James Barbour of Virginia, was the first to respond. "As you know, Mr. President, for a long time I held out for incorporating the Indians into the several states as citizens. I now feel, as Mr. Calhoun has advocated, our only option is to remove them all to a territory west of the Mississippi."

"Bygod I agree with that." Clay leaned forward toward Adams. "It is impossible to civilize those Indians. There never was a full-blooded Indian who took to civilization. It's not in their nature. They are clearly inferior to the Anglo-Saxon race and they can't be improved. Without doubt, in fifty years they will be extinct. And I can't say that their disappearance from the human family will be a great loss to the world." He leaned back and reached for his snuff.

Adams too leaned back. Clay's breath, impaired by tobacco, whiskey, and bad teeth, was repulsive.

"I'm shocked, Mr. Clay, by your blatant contempt for the 'inferior' human beings,' retorted Barbour. "If what you say is true, then why bother quarreling with our southern friends over a disappearing race? Why not yield to Georgia? It's obvious, if we pursue our present course, Georgia will be driven into the arms of General Jackson in the next election."

Adams hurried to head off a clash. "Your conclusions are probably correct, but I would remind you, Mr. Clay, John Ross might take exception to your thoughts. Be that as it may, I'm prone to agree with Mr. Barbour. In the long run, I, too, feel there is no practicable plan by which the Indians can be organized into a civilized or even a half-civilized government. Even though I might agree with Governor Troup on the need to remove the Creeks, I insist that it be done legally. There can be no harm in having Creek Agent Crowell encourage a quickened removal. At the same time, please remind Governor Troup that the Treaty of Washington is the law of the land and the president expects him to abide by that law."

*   *   *   *

As Vice-President Calhoun rode west out of Washington City, a cold December wind watered his eyes and nose. He had been invited to spend the Christmas holidays at Ravenswood, the home of his old friend William Henry Fitzhugh, a rich Virginia planter in Fairfax County. But this was more than a pleasant holiday diversion. He also knew that Fitzhugh had invited Senator Martin Van Buren, and Van Buren's friend, Stephen Van Rensselaer. The fewer people who knew of this meeting the better. Riding alone with his thoughts, Calhoun had already crossed one bridge in his decision making. With Van Buren he would see about crossing the next.

Politicians, once infected with the fever of power, were never far from thoughts of the next election. He was convinced that Adams and Clay were already laying groundwork for the presidential election of 1828. He was certain that Adams, who made no secret of his anti-slavery feelings, was planning to bring the slavery issue before the Congress, to reopen, in effect, the "Missouri Question" in order to make political gains in Pennsylvania. If they could accomplish such a feat, certainly their next move would be to end slavery throughout the nation. That must not happen.

No, he would not continue an appearance of supporting Adams, whose administration was already in shambles. Certainly its inert Indian policy would easily deliver the votes of Georgia, Alabama, and Tennessee to Jackson in the next election.

"Be partisan. Award your friends. Partisanship is the only way to build loyalty, support and organization...and win elections." It was something Clay had said. As much as he detested Clay, it was a sentiment he now shared. Yes, he would feel much more comfortable with Jackson and his belief in states' rights. But, with Van Buren he could not be obvious about his feelings...his support for Jackson would come with a price; the vice-presidency. If he meant what he said, and his poor health seemed to add credence to his words, Jackson would serve no more than one term. If Calhoun were his vice president, then...

*   *   *   *

Ross stood looking down at the face of the Moravian's first convert. Charles Hicks, friend and mentor, lay arrayed in funeral finery in a black walnut coffin fashioned by a Moravian carpenter. First, it had been the aged Path Killer who had died on January 6. Then two weeks later, on Saturday, January 20, Hicks, the second chief of the Cherokees, succumbed to pneumonia.

Ross felt a hand on his shoulder. "They will look to you now, Tsan-Usdi, more than ever."

"No more than to you, Major Ridge. Bye the way, the Moravians want you to deliver his eulogy. These Christians have a different way of dealing with death."

"Since I knew him longer than anyone else, I guess I'm the logical one to do that. Come on. Let's go over to Vann's house. We can spend the night there. There's something I wish to discuss with you."

Stretched out in comfortable chairs in the twenty by thirty foot living room, Ridge and Ross and their host, Joe Vann, soaked up the warmth of a roaring fireplace. One of Vann's slaves served a hot punch spiked with whiskey. The Ridge took a sip and let out a whistle. "Whatever is in this sure takes the chill out of my bones!"

Vann chuckled. "What's in it is what got my father killed. He just couldn't leave the hard stuff alone. In 1805 when he moved into this house, he was living high. When he was sober he was a prince of fellows, but when he was drunk, he was one vicious son-of-a-bitch. Once he killed a brother-in-law in a duel over money. Another time he tied up a fellow that wanted to live with his sister and horse-whipped him. He forced a white woman to confess to theft by stringing her up by her thumbs. Even if he was my father, I'd have to say he was a thoroughly godless man...but...he did encourage the Moravians to locate here at Spring Place. Even helped them secure the land. He would raise hell with everyone else but never the Moravians. So, I guess there is some good in the worst of us." Standing, he stretched and yawned. "And now, gentlemen, if you will excuse me, I'll be turning in."

After Vann left the room, The Ridge stood and warmed his backside at the fireplace. "As you know, Little John, the Council will not meet until October, at which time it will elect a new principal chief. I expect they will name you."

"But why me, Major? You have the experience, the maturity, and the respect of the Council. Why shouldn't you be the one elected?"

"Because I'm too old, John. The future of our people will depend upon men like you...men who read and speak the language of the whites, who understand their laws, and their way of doing business. Now, if my predictions come true, and you are elected Principal Chief, I suggest that you consider moving from Rossville to a more central site in the nation...a place near me, for example."

"I will certainly give that some thought."

Ridge turned from the fireplace. "It is getting late and we need to turn in, but there is one more thing that needs attention...and soon. The missionaries are showing much concern over the actions of White Path. They fear he will lead a revolt and attack them. Everyone knows how much he hates missionaries.

"When he was expelled from Council last year, I never figured the old man to create such a fuss. He is calling a meeting next month at Ellijay. No one will attend who has any authority. Nevertheless, it would be good if you talked to White Path. He knows you, trusts you...and I think you can settle him down. Governor Troup knows that we have lost Pathkiller and Hicks. He will see that as a weakness and will move in with the Georgia militia at the least provocation. It is imperative that White Path cause no trouble at this time. You need to confront him as soon as possible."

Ross stood up and placed his glass on the mantel. "I will meet with him, and soon, but not in a confrontational manner. Do you realize, Major, what we are doing to some of our people? The old ones, the uneducated, the poor...we are asking them to give up their values, their traditions, their religion. We have passed laws contrary to their ancient customs. We have permitted the missionaries to push too far, too fast. Our people cannot survive if divisions are created and widened. The federal government has been playing the dividing game for years...now it's the missionaries."

The Ridge nodded. "I fully understand what you are saying, Little John. But our people have to change. If we don't educate our children, if we can't demonstrate that we can govern ourselves, then we stand no chance of being accepted as a nation by the white people...and if we are not accepted as a nation, we will be treated as savages and pushed beyond the Mississippi."

*   *   *   *

In late February, fed by the rapidly melting snow on the mountains that sheltered Ellijay, the Coosawatte River danced and splashed on its way to the level plain that Ross had just left. Ellijay sat on the banks of the Coosawatte in a protected valley formed by surrounding mountains. This was White Path's town. As he rode in, Ross saw that many warriors from various Cherokee towns had gathered for White Path's council meeting.

Comfortably seated in a place of honor, Ross listened as White Path opened the meeting. Dressed in a shirt of buckskin which hung to the knees, a robe of old buffalo skin, and leather moccasins, White Path seated himself. As if resurrecting the old days, tobacco and pipes were brought. White Path selected a pipe, one whose stem was three feet in length, covered with beautiful rattlesnake skin, and adorned with porcupine quills and bird feathers. With a hot coal from the fire White Path lit the pipe and smoked. He puffed some smoke toward the sun, then to the four cardinal points, before passing the pipe. Once a proud warrior and member of the Cherokee Council, he was now shrunken by years and bent with arthritis. He stood and in a shaky, shrill voice declared, "I have called you together to save our people. For too long many of our leaders have acted as though they were ashamed of being Cherokee. I am proud to be Cherokee, but I no longer feel at home among some of my own people. They have forsaken our language and our traditions. From all time past, no matter what the station in life, we have ruled ourselves by sitting together in council and talking until we came to agreement. Now, we are being saddled with rules made by a few pretentious rich brethren. All authority is being centralized. I was even told that I had no power to call a council even in my own town.

"The white missionaries speak of us as polluted, ignorant, and backward. Is our Great Spirit less than their Christian god? Are we to be excluded from our councils because we do not believe in the Christian god? Is this the handiwork of white missionaries?

"In the old days we lived in harmony, in community, and no one went without food. Now we are encouraged to accumulate possessions in the ways of the white man. We cannot save our nation by taking on the behavior and dress of the whites. We must reject the ways of the whites and return to our old tribal law and customs. We have not only sold our land to the whites; we have sold our souls."

White Path turned and through rheumy eyes peered at Ross. "We appreciate your riding all this way to hear our concerns. We do not accuse our chiefs of treason in the manner of the Creek McIntosh. We plan no armed rebellion so the missionaries should have no fear of us…but we do have fear of them. We fear the deep division among our people that has been brought about by the missionaries. Help us heal that division. We know you, Chief Ross. We put our confidence in you. Let us reject the white man's religion, his laws, and his values. Let us regain our self respect. Let us be Cherokee!"

*   *   *   *

Sam Houston leaned back, an amused smirk on his face, surveying his fellow members of the House of Representatives. It was March 4, the last day of the first session of the 19th Congress and the members were impatient to be on their way home. But before they could adjourn, they needed to attend one final item of business…a special message from President Adams.

Never an example of decorum, the House was exhibiting its irritation. Edward Everett of Massachusetts, trying to be heard above the hubbub, finished his lengthy report with a resolution: 'Resolved: That it is expedient to procure a cession of the Indian lands in the limits of Georgia and: That until a cession is procured, the laws of the land as set forth in the Treaty of Washington, ought to be maintained by all necessary and constitutional means'. "Considering the lateness of this period of the session," he said, "and the unwillingness of the committee at this moment to engage in discussion…I move that the report be printed."

Representative William Drayton of South Carolina loudly voiced his objection. "When the maintenance of the conflicting doctrines, reported by the President and the Governor of Georgia, may lead to the employment of force against our fellow citizens, which may shake the solid fabric of the Union to its center, and involve our country in the throes of civil war, it is difficult to conceive of any matter which could be more important and critical in nature."

Everett wearily responded. "In the few moments that remain before we must adjourn, I cannot respond to the gentleman from Georgia. But it is clear that the report contains evidence representing the claims of Georgia as well as those of the Creeks. I move the resolutions be printed."

Houston fidgeted in his seat. The outcome of this useless debate was obvious to him. The House would pass the resolutions demanding further cessions of land from the Indians. The South needed more space for slavery. The North knew the government needed the income from the sale of Indian lands. In a few moments, his hunch was borne out when the House passed the resolutions 61 to 57. Final disposition of, and unity on, the Indian question was clearly not near.

Houston yawned, stuffed his papers in a bag, and cast a farewell glance around the House chambers. Outside, he glanced up at the rotunda dome that was nearing completion. He mounted his horse. He was going home to Tennessee to run for governor.

*   *   *   *

"Papa, are we really moving?"

Ross looked up from the Nashville Banner and Whig. He and his son were sitting in the shade of the backyard willow tree, enjoying the early April breeze. "Yes, James. Our new home on the Coosa should be finished and we will be able to move in another week or so. It will be near Major Ridge's place. I think you will like it."

The boy sat with his chin resting on his knees, watching the creek slowly flow out of Poplar Spring. He tossed another pebble into the water. "It may be new and nice, but I'm sure gonna miss this place."

Ross leaned back against the tree and looked at his son, now a strapping thirteen year old. "I'll miss it too, James. My grandfather built this house in 1797. He came here as a young trader and met and married grandmother Anna Shorey. With his own hands he hewed the logs for this house. He shaped the stones that formed the three chimneys. Did you know, there's not a single nail in it?"

James merely grunted as his father continued to reminisce. "My father was born here just as you were. And when my mother died, I came here to live with my grandparents. It's the only home we've ever known. With grandpa and grandma McDonald both buried here, it won't be easy leaving."

"Then why are we leaving?"

Ross sighed. "Well, Jimmy, it might not make sense to you right now, but someday it will. We are given only one life to live. We have the choice of squandering it or using it for some noble purpose. I am dedicating my life to the good of our people, and since it will demand more of my time, the most sensible thing to do is move to a more central location where I will be more available."

"What will happen to this house when we move?"

"I've arranged to sell it to Rev. Nicholas Dalton. He is a Methodist preacher who married my niece, Mary Coody. He will also be taking over our business at the landing. So, in a way, things will sorta stay in the family."

"The land will always be ours, won't it, papa?"

"Yes, son, I promise you it will."

In his heart Ross was not as certain as he sounded. To the south, in Milledgeville, the capitol of Georgia, tremendous political pressure was building under the leadership of Governor George Troup, to physically take over Cherokee lands.

*   *   *   *

The reverend stopped to let his horse drink from the small stream that flowed along the eastern flanks of Turnip Mountain. The hot, late April sun beat down causing sweat to seep through his black, broadcloth coat. He would have liked to loosen the napped, woolen fabric but appearances must be maintained.

Just ahead, on the south side of Turnip Mountain, was his destination, the Haweis Mission. Pleased with its success at Brainerd, the American Board had opened the Haweis Mission in 1824, along with schools at Hightower, Candy's Creek, and Willstown. As with most mission schools, a mission church was organized at each station, consisting of the white mission family and local Cherokee converts. The missions included small farms and, usually, a blacksmith shop.

For some reason, things had not gone well at the Haweis Mission. Church meetings had been disrupted. Missionaries, who were determined to save the natives from the fires of hell, had been stoned and threatened with whippings by some of the Cherokees who clung to the old traditions. This was a journey of reassurance and encouragement by the reverend.

But that was not his real reason for this tiring ride. He needed to see John Ross and expedite the purchase of a printing press. He knew the Council had set aside $1500 in 1825 to purchase a press but no action had taken place since. He understood that Ross had been preoccupied fighting off the land acquisition efforts of the federal government and Georgia, but, in his mind, the press was a project that could no longer be neglected. As a missionary tool, the press presented unlimited possibilities; psalms, sermons, perhaps the entire New Testament, could be printed and the gospel could be made available to all the heathen. It was imperative that he move Ross to action.

He had stopped at Ross's new home about ten miles or so back. His slaves had done an excellent job in building the comfortable two-storied house on the north bank of the Coosa River. Seventy by twenty feet, the weather-boarded home was topped with an ash shake roof. A porch ran the length of the front and on either end were tall, red, brick chimneys. It had twenty glass windows and four fireplaces. Outside the house was a kitchen, smokehouses, slave quarters, corn cribs, a blacksmith shop, and stables. Having been fed a hearty lunch by Quatie, and told where Ross could be found, the reverend had continued his journey.

"Well, Reverend Worcester, how are you coming along with your study of the Cherokee language?" Ross and the reverend were sitting under a brush arbor overlooking the Coosa River. Because of the oppressive heat, religious services were usually conducted out of doors under a shady brush arbor made from poles and tree branches.

"Slowly and with much difficulty," confessed Worcester. "Greek and Hebrew were never this much of a problem at Andover. But Boudinot is a patient teacher."

Ross chuckled. "I have trouble with it myself and I've lived with it all my life. Guess I never really applied myself to language. With my father, business was always the important thing. Guess that's the Scotch in me."

"By the looks of your new home and holdings, I'd say you've done quite well in business." Worcester knew that Ross's wealth was based largely upon slavery, an institution he disapproved of, but this was neither the time nor place to bring up the subject.

Ross passed over the remark. "You are a long way from Andover, Rev. Worcester. Tell me, how did you become a minister?"

"You may not believe this, Mr. Ross, but my father was one of four brothers who were ministers. My mother was one of four sisters who married ministers. My mother and father had fourteen children. I am one of four brothers who are ministers. You might say it's in my blood."

"And you think the Cherokee are worthy objects of your efforts?"

"Mr. Ross, the American Board, for whom I work, stated very clearly in 1816 that its goal for the Cherokee was to make the whole tribe English in their language, civilized in their habits, and Christian in their religion. Which brings me to the purpose of my visit."

Ross slapped at a mosquito. "I didn't think you rode all the way down here from Brainerd just to enjoy these devils."

Eager to make his case, Worcester leaned toward Ross. "Two years ago your Council set aside money to purchase a printing press. I have already corresponded with the Secretary of the Board, Jeremiah Evarts in Boston, regarding the availability and costs of a press and type. With the funds you have set aside we can purchase a press with two sets of type, one in English and one with Mr. Guess's alphabet. We can print a newspaper in English and in Cherokee. We can make the gospels available to everyone. We can print religious tracts, hymns, translate the New Testament into Cherokee...we can sell subscriptions to defray expenses...never has such a glorious opportunity existed for spreading the word of God..."

"Hold on, hold on," Ross interrupted the breathless minister. "I can see you have given much thought to this matter. How soon can this press be available?"

"I don't know but I will write Mr. Evarts just as soon as I return to Brainerd, if you'll just give your approval. It will take some time for it to be shipped from Boston to Augusta. It will be up to you to arrange delivery from Augusta to New Echota."

"Once you get the press, you'll need someone to operate it. Have you given thought to that problem?"

Worcester frowned and hesitated. "I would be delighted to have Elias Boudinot as the editor. He is educated and has an expert knowledge of both languages. But the Board in Boston is not convinced. They are concerned with his attendance at the Sabbath ball play and other evidences of backsliding."

Ross smiled. "Backsliding...what an interesting term. Elias would be an excellent choice. But, tell me, Mr. Worcester, with you living at Brainerd and Elias in New Echota, how will you be able to work together?"

"Without hesitation, I will move to New Echota...although, the Board really does not approve of my moving to a place where there is no school, no church, and no mission work."

"I would not dampen your enthusiasm, Reverend. Go ahead and purchase the press. But, keep in mind, the Council would not invest a fifth of our annual income in a press if we were not interested in publishing our laws, promoting culture, and unifying our people. Missionaries were invited to assist in educating our people in the language and manners of whites but the Cherokees have minimal interests in your religions."

*   *   *   *

In the last week of May in 1827 the Cherokees elected delegates to the constitutional convention which was to be held at New Echota come July 4. Of those elected from the eight Cherokee districts, a disproportionate number were from well-to-do, English speaking, mixed bloods. Of the twenty-one elected, only four were full bloods. All but nine, those from the rebel group, could write their names in English.

The most highly contested race was in the Coosawatte District between John Ridge and Kelachulee. This was White Path's district. In the first race Ridge and Kelachulee ended with tie votes. In the run off, Kelachulee defeated the young Ridge. Kelachulee was an aged chief, a full blood married to a full blood. He owned no slaves, spoke no English, and had nothing to do with the missionaries.

To heal the rift, Ross spoke urgently and persuasively about the need to convince the whites that the Cherokees were civilized, and, above all, if they were to survive as a nation, they absolutely must stay united. To reassure the followers of White Path, he promised that the missionary aggression would be checked and that religious practices of those who held to the old ways would not be hindered.

As scheduled, the constitutional convention met at New Echota on Wednesday, July 4, 1827. John Ross, after being elected president of the convention, presented a draft copy of the constitution for debate and amendments. On July 8 the delegates took a brief recess and some attended church services under the pines where Rev. Samuel Worcester was preaching.

On Thursday, July 26, after three weeks of debate, twenty-one weary delegates signed the final draft of the constitution, which was modeled very much after that of the United States.

Originally designed to go into effect at once, its implementation was postponed because of the uproar it aroused in Georgia. Governor Troup sent a copy of the constitution to President Adams and angrily demanded that Adams denounce the act. The Cherokees, expecting Adams to approve their works, sat back to await his verdict.

*   *   *   *

Jackson took a long pull on his pipe. Fanning with a newspaper in the August heat, he exclaimed, "Well, Sam, or should I say Governor Houston, you are to be congratulated. You stomped the hell out of Newton Cannon."

Houston's six foot two frame was sprawled on a couch, his ruffled shirt and glossy, black trousers dulled by travel dust after his nine mile ride from Nashville. "General, I attended every barn-raising, log-rolling, cock fight, and barbecue in this state. I kissed every baby, charmed every woman, and shook every hand that showed up. But, your support didn't hurt either. My strong win tells me that Tennessee will go all out to elect you president."

Jackson grunted in satisfaction. His protégé, Sam Houston, would go a long way.

He pulled a paper from his inner coat pocket. "Got a letter here from a fellow by the name of Amos Kendall. Seems he was in the employ of Clay over in Lexington. He and Clay must have parted ways...but if we had any doubts about Clay and Adams and their corrupt bargain, this letter should remove them."

*   *   *   *

Houston stepped out of the Nashville Inn into the bright autumn sun. The Inn with its imposing three-story colonnade was the headquarters of the Jackson party. It was also home to Houston. Across the square was the City Hotel where the Whigs hung out. Sam glanced at a cock fight taking place in a vacant lot next door to the inn, mounted his dapple gray horse and trotted off down the street.

Much was on his mind this morning. Life had been good to him. He had survived the Battle of Horseshoe Bend; he had been elected to Congress and it was common talk that he just might occupy the white castle on Pennsylvania Avenue some day. Maybe he was the man of destiny that many were looking for. He was thirty-five years old and could have his pick of the many eligible damsels who graced the cotillions of Mrs. James K. Polk. In fact, this was a cause of concern among his friends. He had toasted too many of the ladies. He had been too cozy, some said, with the dark-eyed Cherokee maidens. His friends earnest counsel was that he settle down and get married. But, that could wait. This was October 1, 1827 and Sam Houston was on his way to be inaugurated as Governor of Tennessee in the pulpit of the impressive Baptist Church of Nashville.

*   *   *   *

The story in the paper was not good news. According to the report, the Creeks had signed the Treaty of Fort Mitchell on November fifteenth in which they gave up all their land in Georgia. With another success for the Georgians, it was predictable that they would now increase pressure on the Cherokee. Ross's reading was interrupted by one of his servants announcing that the Reverend Samuel Worcester had arrived. It was December 10, the day Susan Henley and William Shorey Coodey were to be wed.

"Come in Reverend. You looked soaked. Dry yourself by the fire."

"Gladly, gladly," responded the shivering minister. He stood before the fireplace and rubbed feeling back into his hands. "The rain just won't let up. It rained all day yesterday and nobody came to Sabbath service. Just my family and Boudinot's. It rained constantly all the way down from New Echota. But I couldn't miss this glorious occasion. I'm so happy that Susan asked for a Christian marriage."

"My stepdaughter is nineteen. She made her own choice."

Worcester coughed and cleared his throat. "Bye the way, Mr. Ross, I read your constitution. I must say it is a remarkable piece of work. Much like that of the United States. But, I noticed there was no mention of God in your oath of office."

"Well, no mention of your god, at least. All we ask is that the office holder adhere to the constitution and profess loyalty to the interests and prosperity of the nation."

"But you prohibit ministers of the gospel from holding any political office!"

"Surely, Reverend, you believe in the separation of the church and state," Ross teased.

"And I noticed you did not ban the practice of having more than one wife. Does the young man, William Coodey, that Susan is marrying have any such inclinations? If so, I cannot be a party to the wedding ceremony."

Ross chuckled. "If he does, I'm confident that Susan can change them."

"I do not mean to offend you, Mr. Ross, but these are matters of some concern to Christians...and to my Board, I might add. But on this day, I should never have inquired. You probably have other matters on your mind."

"Indeed I do, Reverend." Ross brandished the newspaper. "The Georgians are winning in evicting the Creeks and it appears that Andrew Jackson will win the presidency in next year's election. This cannot good news for the Cherokee."

"Well, that is certainly something worth praying about, isn't it?"

"I would not offend you, Reverend Worcester, but I have observed that contented majorities, conscious of their strength, are never found praying for a redress of grievances."

As Ross was to learn later, on December 13, Wilson Lumpkin, Representative from Georgia and member of the House Committee on Indian Affairs, introduced a resolution: "Resolved, that the Committee on Indian Affairs be instructed to inquire into the expediency of providing, by law, for the removal of the various tribes of Indians who have located within the States or Territories of the United States, to some eligible situation, west of the Mississippi River…"

This was the first attempt ever made by any member of Congress for such action!

CHAPTER 13

JACKSON'S REIGN BEGINS

New Echota was in a festive mood. It was February 21, 1828 and the first issue of The Cherokee Phoenix, was off the press. The publication of the four-page paper, printed in English and Cherokee, marked the beginning of a new chapter in Cherokee history. In their eyes, the modest journal was more precious than the Gutenberg Bible.

After a ten-week voyage from Boston, the thousand pound press lumbered two hundred miles up wagon trails from Augusta to New Echota. The press was installed in an unheated, twenty by thirty foot shop, purposely built for it.

The construction of the press was simple. A cast-iron base held a tray for the hand-set type. Over this a single sheet of paper would be laid. Just above the tray a horizontal metal plate hung from the end of a grooved shaft passing through a spiral-threaded cylinder. A huge extended handle, swung full around, turned the shaft which lowered the plate which pressed the paper evenly against the type. Only one page could be printed at a time.

"This is a fine editorial, Elias," Ross commented. "Looks like we picked the right man for the job."

Boudinot wiped ink from his hands with a wad of rags. "The right man should be worth more than $350 a year."

Ross put down the paper. "I know you are sore that the printer is being paid more than you. Be glad that Worcester was able to get his Board to up your salary by a hundred."

"Worcester's Board is unhappy that I attend ball games. Even though I have a white wife, and a white education, they just know that an Indian couldn't be worth what they pay a white man."

"Elias, with your education, as editor of this newspaper, you have the power and the means to persuade influential people. You command the words which can elevate the cause of the Cherokee people near and far. Who will remember the name of the man who inks the press?"

In the coming weeks the bilingual paper, printed in columns of English and Cherokee, was read in homes in Boston and Philadelphia, by Congressmen in Washington, and by irate Georgia senators in Milledgeville.

The first edition of the Phoenix caught up with Sequoyah at the Williamson's Hotel in Washington where he was representing the Western Cherokees in treating with the government. This modest but authentic Indian genius, who had given his people their greatest gift, was now a celebrity sought out by influential people. The noted artist, Charles Bird King, painted his portrait.

*   *   *   *

The Osage watched with awe and apprehension as the huge, smoking canoe, with two small boats in tow, tied up on the east bank about three miles above the mouth of the Verdigris. The landing was the site of a trading post built by Colonel A.P. Chouteau. The Facility, the first steamboat ever to ascend the Verdigris, discharged seven hundred eighty men, women, and children before returning to New Orleans with a cargo of furs, hides, cotton, and five hundred barrels of pecans taken on at the Verdigris trading houses.

Among the crowd watching the Creeks disembark was Colonel Matthew Arbuckle, commander at Fort Gibson, and Clermont, son of the great Osage warrior, Clermont. Ever anxious to preserve peace, Arbuckle proposed a conference between the Osage and the newly arrived Creeks. The Creeks were the first strangers from the east to come so far west to locate on land claimed by the Osage. Arbuckle knew, and the Osage feared, the Creeks would not be the last to come. It was February 12, 1828. The federal government had finally breached a hole in the dike on Indian resettlement.

*   *   *   *

Ross studied the copy of the Southern Recorder out of Milledgeville then pushed the paper across to Boudinot. "Here, read this."

Boudinot saw that the item indicated referred to an act passed by the Georgia legislature on December 26, 1827. He skimmed. '...the policy which has been pursued by the United States toward the Cherokee Indians has not been in good faith toward Georgia...All the lands which lie within the conventional limits of Georgia belong to her absolutely; that the title is to her; that the Indians are tenants at will...and Georgia has the right to extend her authority and her laws over the whole territory and to coerce obedience to them from all descriptions of people, be they white, red, or black...Georgia will not use force unless compelled to do so.'

"Well, what do you think?"

"It's something we cannot ignore," responded Ross. "One should not under-estimate the implications of Georgia's resolutions...nor should we panic. Sooner or later Georgia will resort to stronger measures, especially if Jackson is elected."

In the March 6 issue of The Cherokee Phoenix, editor Boudinot lashed out against the Georgia manifesto. "Who will expect from the Cherokees a rapid progress in education, religion, and agriculture when resolutions are passed in a civilized and Christian legislature (whose daily sessions, we are told, commence with a prayer to Almighty God) to wrest their country from them, and strange to tell, with the point of a bayonet, if nothing else will do."

Ross was just finishing the paper when he was interrupted by his servant, Moses.

"A gentleman by the name of Ramirez wishes to see you, Chief Ross."

"Benito Ramirez? Here? Send him in."

Ramirez entered smiling and extended his hand. "Chief Ross, it's good to see you again."

Ross stood, shook hands, and motioned toward a chair. "Señor Ramirez. How long has it been...fourteen years? I last talked with you at Will Webber's place. As I recall, you were more than a little interested in his granddaughter."

"You have a good memory, my friend. I'm happy to tell you that I married Will's granddaughter and we now have four beautiful children."

"Wonderful. But what are you doing all this way from your family and Mexico?"

Ramirez pointed toward the paper Ross had laid aside. "Your plight grows worse by the day and so does that of Mexico. I told you once before, when Americans see vacant land, their tendency is to occupy it. Our lands across the Mississippi are deep and fertile, excellent for growing cotton. Planters of the south covet those lands. They keep encroaching year by year. We must settle the lands with people who are friendly to Mexico."

"But don't you already have Cherokee settlers on those lands, Duwali and others?"

"Already we have members of the Choctaw, Quapaws, and Chickasaw, Caddo, Anadarko, and Cherokee tribes now living between the Arkansas and Sabine Rivers. But we must have many more of them. The whites have already established settlements along the Red River, not always with my government's approval."

"Where is Duwali settled?"

"His village is now on the Sabine River and he is prospering."

"I cannot imagine that he would welcome us as his neighbors."

"I realize there have been differences between you two, but that is no problem. We have so much land…you would not need to settle anywhere near him."

"Do the Texas Cherokees hold title to their land?"

Ramirez obviously was not expecting Ross's question. "No…no…" he stuttered, "they do not hold title…but my government will make them citizens of Mexico."

Ross shook his head. "Señor Ramirez, you cannot solve your problems by using Indians as a buffer between Mexico and the Americans. If we cannot retain land here, which has been ours for centuries, we would have even less chance of maintaining ourselves as transplants on new and strange soil, especially if we held no title to the land. In spite of Georgia's threats, I still cling to the hope that we will receive justice from the American government."

Ramirez soberly shook his head. "Justice from the Americans? I don't think so. I fear for your people, my friend, just as I fear for mine."

✳   ✳   ✳   ✳

The May morning was cool. Clay manned the oars while the president removed his clothing and slipped into the waters of the Potomac. After about fifteen minutes of swimming, Adams returned to the boat.

"I find myself much fatigued these days. I must be getting old," said Adams as he dressed.

"Don't let the Jacksonians hear you say that," chuckled Clay as he eased the boat ashore. Mounting their tethered horses, they cantered back toward the White House. "In the days of the early republic," mused Adams, "a gentleman would not seek public office. If he was qualified, the office would seek him. This election campaign is revealing a new type of politics. Mudslinging and character assassination are reaching an all-time low. The Jackson forces are accusing me of pimping for the Czar of Russia when I was the United States minister to that country. It is being claimed by them that I offered up my wife's maid as a sacrifice to the sexual desires of Emperor Alexander. Sometimes I wish to be spared the agony of witnessing the futurity before me."

Arriving at the White House they turned the horses over to stable hands. "Let's visit the nursery," suggested Adams. "I have some plantings that should be sprouting."

Clay nodded in assent surmising that Adams had other things on his mind. "If party warfare continues to develop," Adams continued, "and violent sectional tensions rise, a politician of strong conviction, who takes a sensible and courageous stand, is likely to be shunted aside." He stooped to pull some weeds from around his black walnut sprouts.

"Mr. President, you aren't suggesting that you might lose?"

"I'm merely suggesting that voters often fail to elect superior men to public office. The candidate the Democrats are supporting has neither an education nor a brilliant mind. Yet, Jackson's instincts are superb. He seems to sense the common man's discontents, their economic fears, and their prejudices. To win their votes he gives them slogans and whiskey barrels. The man has put forth no platform at all."

"I can agree with all you say, Mr. President. I am totally convinced that election of Jackson will lead to a lower quality of government."

Adams straightened and brushed dirt from his hands. "I do appreciate your taking on such great responsibilities in this campaign, especially in light of your health." He extended his hand. "I wish you well in your meeting with the National Republican rally in Baltimore."

"I shall do my very best, sir. Your reelection and my prestige are at stake. I remain optimistic. The American people will see through the false accusations fostered by Jackson's people."

Clay arrived in Baltimore on May 13th sick in mind and body from his intense campaigning. Yet when he spoke from the platform, his animosity toward Jackson and Caesarism poured forth from his silvery tongue.

"If it were physically possible, and compatible with my official duties, I would visit every state, go to every town and hamlet, address every man in the Union, and entreat them by the love of country, by their love of liberty, for the sake of themselves and their posterity…to pause solemnly and contemplate the precipice that yawns before us. If we have incurred divine wrath and it is necessary for God to chastise his people with the rod of vengeance, I would humbly prostrate myself before Him, and implore his mercy, to visit the land with war, with pestilence, with famine, with any scourge other than military rule or a blind and heedless enthusiasm for mere military renown."

Totally exhausted, Clay returned to Washington. If his health was to improve at all, he must get away. He would take the President's advice and take a medical leave. He would return to Kentucky, to his beloved blue-grass country, his English race horses, his blooded sheep, and his imported Hereford cattle just as soon as he could break away.

*   *   *   *

Laying the pen aside he ran his fingers through his dark, thick hair. The heat of June had descended upon New Echota. "Ann, I'm a minister of the gospel, not a book-keeper. I just cannot make these books balance."

"What is perplexing the Reverend Worcester now?" his wife teased.

"Oh, I don't know, Ann. There is just so much to do…preaching, translating the Bible, supervising the missions and the printing press…and then having to account to the Board for every penny we spend."

"You are too much of a perfectionist, Samuel, and you do take on too many responsibilities."

"It would be much worse if we didn't have help from the Boudinots. Letting us live here with them until our house is finished has been a God-send."

"It will be a beautiful home, Samuel. How soon can we move in?

Worcester looked out the door to the east where carpenters were erecting their house.

"September, they tell me. The Board can't understand why we didn't settle for a log house but I told them one of clapboard would set a fine example for the Cherokees. Besides, I want you and Ann Eliza to have the finest possible here in the wilderness. I know it has been difficult for you, Ann…the cooking, sewing, knitting, soap making. All so different from the culture we left behind in Boston."

"Samuel, you mustn't speak so. I'm happy with your love and the love of God. Besides, it will be much easier when Sophia Sawyer joins us."

"I hope so, but I can't help but wonder why she is being transferred to us from Brainerd. I've heard that her behavior is, well, just a little unorthodox."

"Speaking of unorthodox behavior...," Ann nodded toward the door.

Worcester looked up to see one of his parishioners coming up the walk. "You'll have to excuse us, my dear. What I have to discuss with John McPherson is rather sensitive."

Worcester met McPherson at the door and offered him a chair in the shade of the porch roof. He cleared his throat. "John, it has come to me that you have engaged in fornication. Is that true?"

The Cherokee dropped his head sheepishly. "I don't know that word, preacher...fornication. What does that mean?"

"It means criminal intercourse, John."

"I don't know what that means either."

Flustered and uncomfortable in discussing the topic, Worcester replied. "John, it means that you have been sleeping with another man's wife. That's against the word of God."

"Oh, you mean fucking. Why didn't you say so...and who told you?"

"Never you mind who told me. It's a sin!"

"How can something that feels so good be a sin? You told us that sinning made you feel bad. Well, I don't feel bad, I feel good."

"That's part of the problem, John, you feel no remorse..." Catching himself, Worcester said, "I mean, you should feel sorry for what you've done. After all, Mary Quaqua is not your wife."

McPherson studied his moccasin for a time. "Can't see what that has to do with it, preacher. She was more than willin'."

Worcester heaved a sigh. "John, I know that it is hard for you to change. But to be a Christian you must give up your pagan ways. I see no out but to suspend you from communion."

McPherson stood up, silent for a moment. Then he shook hands with Worcester. "I don't mind givin' up that cheap wine you serve, but I'm shore gonna' miss the singing."

*   *   *   *

It was July 4, 1828 and Andrew Jackson and Tennessee Governor Sam Houston were observing the anniversary in Lebanon, a few miles east of Nashville.

They had been escorted into town by a military company where they were greeted by 3000 citizens. A sumptuous dinner was served to 250 people in the backyard of Wynne's Tavern.

After attending a ball that evening, Jackson and Houston retired to their room in the tavern. The subject was, of course, the presidential campaign. Joining them were John Overton, Major William Lewis, Hugh Lawson White, and John H. Eaton. These men, intensely devoted to Jackson, had come together shortly following the election of Adams with the intention of securing the nomination and election of their friend in 1828.

Jackson wearily seated his frail, sixty-one year old frame in an easy chair and reached for his pipe. Stuffing tobacco into the bowl of the long-stemmed Powhatan, he nodded to Houston. "Might as well get on with it, Sam."

"Like I said before, General, I'd get rid of Calhoun. I don't trust that sunovabitch."

Jackson leaned his graying head against the chair and puffed great, white, plumes of smoke into the air. "I understand your personal animosity toward Calhoun, Sam, but Calhoun speaks for many in the southern states. We can't risk alienating them. But I don't want to talk about Calhoun right now. I want to hear about the latest conspiracy the Adams party is…" His voice trailed off as he went into a coughing spasm that shook his lean frame.

Not wanting to be the bearer of ill tidings, no one spoke for a moment but all eyes shifted to the oldest and most intimate friend of Jackson.

Knowing Jackson always framed any opposition to him as a conspiracy, Major Lewis cautioned, "You won't like it, General."

"There's a whole damn lot that I don't like about politics but knowing the intent of your enemy is vital if you're going to whip his ass."

"Well, to start with, Jefferson is rumored to have told Webster that you are one of the most unfit men for the presidency…and Madison feels the same."

"I've heard that one," Jackson snorted. "Those dandies have lived on a soft carpet all their lives. I've also heard that I'm ill-tempered, arbitrary, and ambitious for power. Tell me something I don't already know."

"Well, you've been accused of every crime, offense, and impropriety that man was ever known to be guilty of. Your duels, your connection with Aaron Burr, your horse racing, gambling on cock fights, the eleven military executions you ordered, the killings of Arbuthnot and Ambrister, your mother, and the peculiar circumstances surrounding your marriage to Rachel."

"My mother?" Jackson interrupted, "my mother? How did she get dragged into this?"

"Well," Lewis hesitated while taking a clipping out of his pocket, "according to the National Journal, General Jackson's mother was a common prostitute, brought to this country by British soldiers. She afterwards married a mulatto man, with whom she had several children, of which number General Jackson is one." Lewis paused. "Shall I go on?"

Jackson's head was bowed. With a trembling hand he signaled to Lewis. "Go on."

"The Journal also accuses you and Rachel of living in adultery…"

The General flexed his fist. "The National Journal is the Washington paper special to Adams, is it not?"

"Yes, it is."

In a rage Jackson propelled himself out of his chair. Turning his head, he quickly wiped a tear from his cheek. He walked to a window where he stood visibly shaking. "Myself I can defend. I can defend Rachel, the purest woman God ever created. But my poor sainted mother…how can anyone…how can any man permit a public journal which is under his control, to assail the character of any respectable female. Such vile, vulgar, gutter politics! Those tactics prove beyond a shadow of a doubt that Adams is not entitled to the respect of any honorable man. By the eternal, I'll pin the lie on him for every accusation he's made…"

"Best that you not, general." Jackson spun to confront John Overton, Chief Justice of the Tennessee Supreme Court and Chairman of Jackson's election committee. Jackson, now in full control of his emotions, eyed Overton through a cloud of smoke. The small, profane, bald-headed man had stood at Jackson's side for years, helping write his public letters, building up his organization, and ever plotting for his advancement. Overton had lost his teeth and his prominent chin seemed to almost meet his sharp, Roman nose. Lawyer, judge, banker, and land speculator, he was reported to be one of the wealthiest men in Tennessee. His advice was valued by Jackson.

"General, the purpose of this group is to rebut all those goddamn malicious charges. Leave it to us. You…you must keep yourself above the fray. The fewer positions you take, the fewer your chances of offending. If you speak out against the bank charter, you risk offending. Taking a position on slavery is a loser. Even though everyone knows you own slaves, let that issue lie. That pot will boil over in its own time. Speaking on Indian removal is probably safe, but for the love of God, if you want to win this election, don't even mention the goddamn tariff. That issue is so hot right now that it alone could determine the election. Any indication that you favor it and you lose the votes of the South; speak against it and you lose the manufacturing states."

*   *   *   *

From the shade of the magnolia tree that stood alongside the single room structure that he called his office, Calhoun looked out over the 500 acres of his plantation. On the south the rich bottomland was bounded by the Seneca River. To the north lay rolling mountains. In the fields he could see hands at work under a sultry, July sun. The warm air was heavy with the scents of magnolia and wild plum.

"It's a beautiful land, Mr. Vice President."

"Indeed it is, Hanks. But all that you see I stand to lose if we cannot change the tariff legislation. My property has ceased to give profits and I believe the same is true of nine-tenths of the planters. Our staples hardly return the expense of cultivation. The tariff adds 45% to the cost of tools and supplies. On the one hand, world competition forces us to sell low; on the other, the tariff forces us to buy high."

"Sounds quite serious…"

"Lieutenant Hanks, I consider it by far the most dangerous question that has ever sprung up under our system. The tariff issue has caused universal excitement even among men of the deepest character."

"Can you expect some relief if Jackson is elected president?"

"It is our hope that he will use the influence and power of his office to bring about a reduction in the tariff but we realize that the election of Jackson may not arrest the evil. He cannot repeal a law. The government of this country is not in the executive."

"Then your relief must be found in Congress?"

Calhoun's grim countenance tightened. "We have found getting such relief impossible. Remember this, Hanks, men do not come to Congress to weigh in intellectual detachment the best interests of the human race. They come as advocates for the special desires of those who elected them.

"Population has given preponderant strength to the manufacturing states and they use their power, as power is always used, for their own gain. Through the tariff, the domestic manufacturers seek a monopoly of the home market by eliminating foreign competition. The staple states, however, must compete on the world market. We have no choice."

Hanks, trying to take this in, asked, "Has anyone ever considered developing industry in the south?"

"Young man, your life has been sheltered from the realities of economics. All the capital of the south is tied up in land and slaves. For the south to go in for industry on a large scale would require borrowing from northern banks. We would merely supplant one form of subservience with another."

Clearly out of his depth, Hanks mulled, "Surely, there must be some solution…"

"Yes, there must be a solution, but it must be brought about by the orderly process of law, not by force or violence. Emotionally, South Carolina is becoming an armed camp of great discontent. We must find, under our constitution, a way to protect the minority from the tyranny of the majority. If the manufacturing interests can impose an unfair and oppressive tariff upon us, what is to prevent other impositions?"

"I gather you are referring to slavery?"

"I am. I tell you in confidence, Hanks, it is despotism which constitutes evil and until this government is made a limited government, and is confined to those interests which are common to the whole nation, there is no liberty, no security for the south. Every government based on power acts the same. It goes on and on, increasing and increasing, always getting what it can and never giving up any."

"But, isn't there some law…?"

With an edge of irony in his voice, Calhoun interrupted. "Alexander Hamilton, in the 51st number of The Federalist said, 'It is of the greatest importance in a republic not only to guard society against the oppression of its rulers but to guard one part of the society against the injustice of the other part.' Remember this, my boy, laws, so far from being uniform in their operation, are scarcely ever so."

One of Calhoun's servants approached to announce that dinner was ready for serving. As he guided Hanks into the large dining room of the mansion, Calhoun continued. "I want to thank you, Lieutenant, for the long ride you made from Washington to bring me needed information on exports and imports. It will be very helpful as I construct my paper for the Committee on Federal Relations, something I agreed to do at the request of the South Carolina legislature. Now, you will need a good meal and a good night's rest before you return."

After a wholesome fare of ham, beef, chicken, cornbread, potatoes, fresh vegetables, and fruit, they sat enjoying a glass of claret. With glass in hand they retired to the study where the walls were lined with book shelves. Calhoun sat at his huge rolltop desk, imported from Switzerland. Never one for small talk, Calhoun continued intoning thoughts on his passion, politics. During the course of the meal he had mentioned the Hartford Convention, Madison's Virginia Resolutions, and the Kentucky Resolutions of Thomas Jefferson. Only much later would Hanks understand how important these topics were in shaping Calhoun's thinking on states' rights.

Tired, sleepy, and quite relaxed from the wine, Hanks asked to be excused. "I deeply appreciate your hospitality, Mr. Vice President, and the conversation has been most enlightening, but you know I must be up and on the road early tomorrow. I bid you a most pleasant goodnight."

As he started to leave the study, Hanks turned. "One last question, Mr. Calhoun. What happens if you cannot find an acceptable solution to the tariff issue?"

For a moment Calhoun sat in silence, his brow deep in furrows. "If I cannot find a solution, Lt. Hanks, then I fear for the state of the Union."

*   *   *   *

Balloting for the presidency began in September and ended in November. In each state the balloting occurred over several days and the polls opened at various times even within a single state. By the middle of October partial returns from states with early elections caused many to wonder if a revolution was in the making. First returns indicated a landslide sweep for Old Hickory. Shrewdly, Jackson asked his friend, Major Lewis, to pass along such information to other western states that had not yet voted so these results might be used to his advantage.

When all the votes were in, Jackson had won with a total of 647,276 popular votes and 178 electoral votes. Adams had received 508,064 popular votes, mostly from New England states. For the first time in American politics, the value of intense political organization had been demonstrated.

Knowing that General Jackson would be in the presidential chair at the next session of Congress, and that the general's views coincided with his own on the Indian question, Wilson Lumpkin slept soundly.

*   *   *   *

On October 13, 1828 the Cherokee legislature assembled in New Echota where they proceeded to elect John Ross as first principal chief and George Lowrey as second principal chief. Addressing the General Council, Ross stated: "The pretended claim of Georgia to a portion of our lands is due to a potentate of England, whose eyes never saw, whose purse never purchased, and whose sword never conquered the soil we inhabit, presumed to issue a parchment, called a Charter, to the Colony of Georgia, in which the boundary set forth included a great extent of country inhabited by the Cherokee. The claim now advanced by Georgia is preposterous. Our ancestors from time immemorial possessed this country, not by a Charter from the hand of a mortal king, but by the will of the King of Kings who created all things. A respectful memorial should be submitted to the Congress of the United States, expressing our true sentiments, and praying that measures may be adopted on the part of the United States for the adjustment of their compact with the state of Georgia, lest they anticipate any further cession of land from this nation."

On November 4, in a message to both branches of the Georgia legislature, Governor John Forsyth stated: "If the United States are unable...to induce the Cherokees to remove, and unwilling to vindicate our rights over the persons and territory within our sovereignty, in the only practicable mode, our duty to the people and posterity requires that we should act."

While many in the nation celebrated the election of Jackson, dark gloom hung over The Hermitage. In ill health and in deep depression over the prospect of moving to Washington, Rachel had forced herself in early December to go into Nashville to purchase clothing suitable for her new position. While in the city she happened to pick up a campaign pamphlet that described her behavior prior to her marriage to Jackson. She was overcome by what she read. For the first time she realized the extent of slander directed against her. At home she attempted to conceal her disturbed state of mind by pretending gaiety. Suspicious, Jackson questioned her. At that point, Rachel broke down and sobbed out the story. Trying to hide his rage, Jackson comforted her.

On Wednesday, December 18 Rachel felt a stabbing pain in her chest and fell into the arms of her servant, Old Hannah. Hearing the commotion, Jackson rushed in from the adjoining room. As the pain intensified, a rider was dispatched to bring Dr. Samuel Hogg, the family physician. Hogg responded, accompanied by his friend, Dr. Henry Lee Heiskell, who was visiting from Virginia. Following standard procedure, they bled Rachel. With no release from the pain, they bled her again...and then a third time. Only then did the pain subside.

For sixty hours Jackson and the doctors stood by. Rachel rallied enough to urge her husband to get some rest. He went into the adjoining room to rest on a sofa. Shortly after nine o'clock he heard Rachel let out a long, anguished cry. He dashed through the door to see Old Hannah holding Rachel's head on her shoulder. At age sixty one, Rachel was gone.

At one o'clock on Christmas Eve, December 24, 1828, with some ten thousand people surrounding The Hermitage, her casket was slowly carried along the curved garden walk to the chosen spot in her lovely garden. Sam Houston led the pallbearers.

Back in the house, Jackson spoke to a small group. "Friends and neighbors, I thank you for the honor you have done to the sainted one whose remains now repose in yonder grave. I am now President of the United States and in a short time must make my way to the metropolis of my country. I go alone to the place of new and arduous duties. I shall not go without friends to reward…and I pray God that I may have enemies to punish."

CHAPTER 14

SHARP KNIFE TAKES COMMAND

On the evening of New Year's Day, 1829, in the living room of William O'Neale, located across the street from the Franklin House at 2007 I Street, thirty-nine year old John Henry Eaton took to wife the widow of John Bowie Timberlake. With dark eyes, sensuous lips, and a well-rounded, voluptuous figure, the thirty-year old, much-courted Margaret O'Neale Timberlake, still looked radiantly beautiful in the candlelight. The Reverend William Ryland, Methodist minister and longtime chaplain of the Senate and House, conducted the ceremony.

Another candlelight wedding took place on January 22 when Tennessee Governor Sam Houston stood beside blonde, violet eyed Eliza Allen in the drawing room of Allendale, the home of her parents, John and Laetitia Allen. Colonel Allen, a prosperous and politically powerful landowner in Gallatin, beamed with pride as the socially elite of the county witnessed the ceremony. For a son-in-law he could not have chosen better. Houston, only thirty-five, and almost certain of reelection, was a good friend of President Jackson. It was rumored that he would follow Jackson into the presidency. No, he could not have made a better match for his seventeen year old daughter.

Houston had an eye for pretty women, be they dusky Cherokee maidens or the raunchy ladies of the evening down along River Street. But this lovely virgin with long blonde tresses was purely special. The fact that she was a member of a wealthy and prominent Tennessee family would not hurt his political ambitions. Eight days after the marriage, Houston announced that he was a candidate for reelection.

*   *   *   *

Ross watched the heavy, wet snowflakes plaster against the windowpane. For a moment they clung, then slithered slowly, reluctantly downward in icy rivulets. A driving snow storm had turned the Potomac into a sheet of ice. Across the way Ross could see the smokeless chimneys in the unheated houses of the city's poor. It had been one recurring snowstorm after another since his arrival in Washington City in late January. The fireplace in his cramped room at the Williamson Hotel did little to fend off the bone-penetrating cold of 1829.

"You spoke with the president himself?" he asked without turning.

"Yes, and he is one miserable cuss. For a New England aristocrat to be defeated by a card-playing, whiskey drinking, illiterate is more than he can handle. He thinks the sun has set on his political career."

"Did he comment on Georgia's actions against the Cherokee?"

"No, not directly, but he did mention a recent conversation with Clay in which Clay warned of threats of disunion from the South. Those threats probably scared the hell out of Adams."

Ross turned from the window. "Adams seems to think his Indian policy has been a failure. Why is he suddenly calling alarm to Congress about our being an independent nation? What has come over the man? He expressed no such qualms when we adopted our constitution."

Hanks rubbed his hands before the struggling fire. "Adams thinks he lost the election because the South knew of his antislavery view…and because of his inaction in removing the Cherokee he alienated the land-hungry speculators."

Ross nodded and sighed. "I know Adams has been under tremendous pressure from Senator Benton for greater sales of public lands. Now that Jackson has been elected Benton will get his way."

"It's too late to expect anything from Adams. He is a broken man, a lame-duck president without influence. The rest of Washington is hunkering down, scared to death they'll be fired with Jackson takes control."

"I had such great hopes that we might exert some influence beneficial to our people before Jackson takes over. When do you expect him to arrive?"

"Talk is he will arrive here around mid-February."

"Well, in a way I feel sorry for the man—age sixty two, taking on such responsibilities. And I'm sure he is unaware of the hornet's nest that John Eaton's marriage has stirred up."

"Sorry? You feel sorry for a man who is intent on removing your people from their homeland?"

Ross smiled. "I know it sounds crazy, but the man has lost his wife...just when he needs her support most. She is the only one who could help control Jackson's temper."

"If I were you, John, I'd be more concerned with finding support for yourself here in Washington."

"I would like nothing better, Hanks, but Washington seems to be at a standstill until Jackson takes office. Secretary of War Porter is the only able body around. Clay is laid up with a bad cold, Webster is mourning the loss of his wife, Wirt is suffering with something like vertigo, and who knows where Calhoun is. Anyway, we already know where he stands."

"You really don't expect any of those to be your strong supporters, do you?"

Ross shook his head. "No, of course not...unless it suits their political purposes.

I know none of them really like us. They don't like each other, but they like Jackson even less. Clay is bitter at being defeated by Jackson. Calhoun thinks he should have been selected as president and now he fears that Jackson will name Van Buren as Secretary of state. So, we need to use their prejudices to our advantage."

"If none of the political powers can provide support, you might as well pack it up and go home," said Hanks.

Ross's jaw clenched. "You know I can't do that. My people have placed their trust in me. I can't go home before doing what I came here to do. If I am forced to do business with Sharp Knife, I'll do so when he arrives."

*   *   *   *

On February 11, about mid-morning, after three weeks of travel from The Hermitage, Jackson quietly arrived in Washington. He and his party, William B. Lewis, his nephew, Andrew J. Donelson and wife, Emily, took up residence in the National Hotel. The National, located on the northeast corner of Pennsylvania Avenue and Sixth Street, represented the newest and most fashionable that Washington had to offer. No sooner was his arrival known when cannon were fired, drums rolled, and raucous crowds filled the slushy, muddy streets.

After a brief stay at the National, Jackson moved to more familiar surroundings, his old haunt, Gadsbys.

Hearing of Jackson's arrival, Ross went to Gadsbys and sought an audience with the president-elect. He was turned away; Jackson was too involved forming his cabinet.

Stinging from the rebuke, Ross shouldered his way through a melange of people who crowded the boardwalk on Pennsylvania Avenue. Clearly, Jackson would be a formidable opponent in the future.

Head down, and hat pulled low against the driving snow, Ross collided with a member of the mob. Apologizing, he looked up to see the face of Thomas McKenney.

"John!" McKenney exclaimed, "what in the world are you doing out in this weather?"

"Trying to find my way back to the hotel. I've never seen so many people in one place."

McKenney laughed. "You must be the only person in Washington who isn't looking for appointment to public office. All these people are office-seekers and people seeking political plums. They've heard that Jackson plans to clean house. They've come from all over the country hoping to be one of the replacements. Look, let's go inside where we can talk."

They ducked around the corner to the 3rd Street entrance of the St. Charles Hotel. Inside, they beat off the snow and elbowed their way through the packed lobby to the bar.

"This is a favorite rendezvous for your people when they come to Washington. By the way, where are you staying?"

"At the Williamson."

"With Congress back in session and all this rabble in town for Jackson's inauguration, it's lucky you found a place at all." McKenney took a sip of hot toddy. "Since I know you didn't come here to celebrate Jackson's election, what did bring you here?"

"The usual, Tom. To get justice from your government. But, with Jackson taking over, my chances are slim."

"Yours and mine. Since I backed Calhoun, and Jackson knows it, I may soon be out on my ear. Yes, the Office of Indian Affairs may soon have a new head."

"I'd hate to see that. I think you have tried hard to be fair in all your dealings with us."

"I appreciate that remark, John, but maybe it's time I moved on." He took another sip of toddy and looked out on the murky streets. "Don't know when

I've seen this town so dull, so gloomy, so utterly lacking in social life. The losers are sulking…certainly not in a party mood. Jackson is still in mourning so there is no life with his people. One bright spot though…Maggie Smith is having a party in honor of her friends, the Calhouns. Want to come along?"

"Who is Maggie Smith…and who are her friends?"

"Maggie is Margaret Bayard Smith…the best party-giver in Washington. She also happens to be the wife of Samuel Smith who runs the branch bank of the United States here in Washington. Her friends include the elite of this city…Jefferson, Madison, Clay, Calhoun, Wirt, Porter…come to think of it, there might be people at her party that can be of more help to you than anyone else in this town."

"Meeting the people who write the newspaper that I read would be interesting. There's nothing else to do now but wait, so, if it's no imposition, I'd be happy to come along."

∗   ∗   ∗   ∗

The Smith residence was located in the square between Pennsylvania Avenue, 15th Street and H Street, near the Dolly Madison home and the White House. The new home, which the Smiths moved into in early November of the previous year, was aglow with candlelight. As they entered from the Fifteenth Street entrance, McKenney and Ross were greeted by Mrs. Smith, a vivacious woman of striking beauty who Ross guessed to be in her early fifties.

Looking around at the party, Ross remarked to McKenney. "I'm told that politics makes strange bedfellows. Now I believe it. There's Federalists, Republicans, and even some Jacksonians here, all under one roof."

"Mrs. Smith is not your usual partisan. She is a saucy lady not afraid to mingle the old and new regimes," McKenney responded.

"Well, bless my soul, if it ain't John Ross."

Ross turned to greet a tall, lanky, smiling Henry Clay, whiskey in one hand and Mrs. Smith in the other.

"I see you two have already met," said Mrs. Smith.

"Indeed we have," replied Ross. "I never expected to see you here, Mr. Clay. I heard you've been under the weather."

"A little flu from foggy bottom and a little wounded by the election, but otherwise fit as a fiddle."

"How I pity these public men," smiled Mrs. Smith. "Mr. Clay fell on his own sword in service to President Adams, yet he can still smile."

"To paraphrase Cardinal Wolsey," Clay laughed, "Oh! Had I served my God half as devotedly as I served my King, I should not now in my old age, thus have been left…"

A new voice chimed in. "We can laugh now but I shall cry more than I laugh on the fourth of March. You know, we almost had a pipe-smoking first lady in the White House. Imagine what our social life would have been like had Mrs. Jackson lived."

Somewhat embarrassed, Mrs. Smith made introductions. "Mr. Ross, may I present my good, but irreverent friend, Mrs. Peter B. Porter, wife of General Porter, the Secretary of War."

Ross bowed to this sparkling beauty. "Yes, I've had the pleasure of meeting your husband."

"He couldn't have been much of a pleasure, knowing he will be out of office in a few weeks. But, I say to the Jacksonians, if we must go now, we will be back in four years so enjoy yourselves while you can."

"I wish I shared your optimism, Mrs. Porter. What a pity that all the ladies cannot carry off the election results as charmingly as you."

Hearing the familiar voice, Ross turned to see John C. Calhoun with his pregnant wife, Floride, on his arm.

"Ah, the reluctant Jacksonian," laughed Mrs. Smith. Again she made introductions. "Mr. Ross, may I present my honored guests, Vice-President elect Calhoun and his wife."

Ross bowed slightly and crisply replied, "Mr. Calhoun and I have met."

Clay slipped away to get another drink. Calhoun, ignoring Ross, turned his charm on his hostess.

"What's the latest rumor on the make-up of Jackson's cabinet?" inquired Mrs. Smith. "Mr. Wirt calls it a millennium of minnows."

"I can assure you, General Jackson did not consult me regarding cabinet appointments. Knowing Jackson, he will be his own cabinet," replied Calhoun. "The General has a very decided will of his own."

"And," sniffed Mrs. Calhoun, "how does he expect Mr. Eaton to fit into our social life being married to that tavern keeper's daughter? It's simply scandalous."

In a few minutes, bored with such chatter, Ross moved across the room to join Clay who was standing, drink in hand, by the fireplace.

"Calhoun doesn't seem to think Van Buren will accept the Secretary of State position," said Ross.

"That's just Calhoun's wishful thinking. Van Buren will accept alright because he knows, historically, the Secretary of State has moved on to the presidency. That has Calhoun very worried."

"Why do you think Attorney General Wirt is being replaced?"

"No offense to you, Mr. Ross, but Jackson feels that Wirt is too soft on the Indian question. And, it cannot be good news for you to know that Jackson will probably replace him with John Berrien of Georgia. As you well know, Berrien is a strong advocate for Indian removal."

Ross stood silent, his back to the fire, eyeing the crowd. So, this is Washington politics; this is how a noble country is to be governed, not by men of exalted talents but by seekers of political power to advance their own interests. Yet, surely, there must be some men of integrity in the halls of Congress.

Back in his hotel room, Ross wrote feverishly through the night. Using undisputed historical records, and an appeal to the honorable traits of men, he compiled his memorial. On February 27 he submitted it to both the Senate and House of Representatives. In it he questioned the power of a state over that of the federal government.

"We cannot admit that Georgia has the right to extend her jurisdiction over our territory, nor are the Cherokee people prepared to submit to her persecuting edict. We would, therefore, respectfully and solemnly protest, in behalf of the Cherokee nation, before your honorable bodies, against the extension of the laws of Georgia over any part of our territory, and appeal to the United States Government for justice and protection."

No action was taken by either house of Congress on the memorial. Congress would delay facing the matter of "states' rights" until a later day.

*   *   *   *

A loud boom shattered Margaret Smith's slumber. A thirteen gun salute was ushering in the 4th of March, inauguration day. Peering through window curtains, she could see that the day was dawning bright and sunny. After a long season of cold and rainy weather, nature was now smiling on the incoming president.

After dressing and a hurried breakfast, on the arm of Francis Scott Key, she and two other ladies got into their carriage and joined the living stream of wagons, carts, buggies, coaches, and walking humanity heading for the capitol. Some were in finery and some were in rags but all were in a jocular mood. As they approached the capitol, Margaret could see that the terraces, balconies, and porticos were already filled with people. The masses pushed and shoved to get closer to the East Portico where Jackson would speak. On the south steps of the terrace they left the carriage. There Mrs. Smith encountered John Ross who had also come to witness the spectacle.

At eleven o'clock Jackson emerged from his quarters at Gadsby's and joined his escort of soldiers from the Revolutionary War and veterans who had served with him at New Orleans. Dressed in a plain black suit, black tie, and a long black coat, Jackson, stooped with age and grief, slowly made his way through the throngs down Pennsylvania Avenue. Being the only one not wearing a hat, his height and white hair made him easily visible.

At last Jackson and his escort reached the gate at the foot of the hill and he turned up the road that led to the front of the Capitol. He bowed to the ladies who filled the East Portico and the steps leading to it. Plumes of every color and draperies of red, purple, blue, yellow, and white added to the grandeur of the Capitol.

On reaching the Capitol, Jackson entered the Senate chamber at 11:30 to witness the swearing in of Vice-President Calhoun. He was conducted to a chair in front of the secretary's desk. A seat had also been provided for the retiring president but Adams disdained to attend. Henry Clay was also absent.

At twelve o'clock a procession formed and slowly made its way to the East Portico. As Jackson emerged the crowd exploded with shouting and screaming. Two artillery companies fired a twenty-four gun salute and the Marine Band played "The President's March". Then Jackson rose and stood in silence behind a table covered with red velvet. For a moment he looked out over the thousands, his tousled hair blowing in the wind, then he slowly bowed low to the people. Adjusting his glasses he began to read his inauguration message. The crowd was hushed. Jackson's speech, hampered by rotten teeth, was almost inaudible.

"Fellow citizens," he began, "as I am about to undertake the arduous duties that I have been appointed to perform by the choice of free people, I avail myself of this solemn occasion to express my gratitude." It was an address that lasted no more then ten minutes but he stood longer as the thousands roared their approval.

A deeply troubled Chief Justice John Marshall then rose to administer the oath of office. A strong Federalist, Marshall saw Jackson's election as a threat to the nation. For twenty years he had not voted but he had considered it his solemn duty to vote against Jackson.

Placing one hand on the Bible and raising the other, Jackson repeated the oath of office. He then shook hands with Marshall and raised the Bible to his lips. As the crowd erupted with acclaim, Jackson turned and once more bowed. The ceremony concluded, he walked down the hill to the gate and found a handsome, white horse waiting to take him to the White House. As he mounted, the waiting crowd let out a shout and surged down the street after him. The crowd had now become a mob, a torrent of rabble that would invade the "President's Palace" as a matter of right.

"Will you join us, Mr. Ross?" asked Mrs. Smith. "A modest White House reception has been planned and we are invited."

"Thank you, but no," Ross replied. He stood alone on the Capitol steps for a half hour watching the farmers, gentlemen, boys, women and children, black and white…a stream of humanity following the President to the White House. As Ross walked down the steps he encountered Daniel Webster coming up. Ross nodded in passing and, half to Webster and half to himself, asked, "What kind of hold does this man have over people?"

Webster shook his head. "I've never seen anything like this before. People have come 500 miles to see General Jackson. They really seemed to think that the country is rescued from some dreadful danger."

On March 13 Henry Clay rode out of town heading for Lexington. He waved as he passed John Quincy Adams in his carriage on Pennsylvania Avenue. In Clay's mind, he would return four years hence as president.

On March 18 Calhoun and his wife, Floride, said goodbye to their good friend, Margaret Bayard Smith, as they prepared to set out on the long journey to South Carolina where Floride would give birth to her baby.

On April 6, as spring was in full flower in Washington, Ross had received no response from the White House. Taking pen in hand, he submitted another request for the removal of Agent Hugh Montgomery, this time citing numerous instances where the native Georgian had failed to act on behalf of the Cherokee.

A few days later McKenney stopped by Ross's hotel. "John," he began, "Secretary of War, Eaton, seems too busy learning his new duties to see you. So, he sends you this message; he says that agent Hugh Montgomery has been directed to comply with orders hitherto transmitted. Eaton says intruders into your lands will be expelled, by force, if necessary.

"As to the question of Georgia extending its laws over your people…well, he says he is not prepared to decide that question. In fact, he says no remedy exists unless Congress wants to take it up."

"Eaton's incompetence and lack of backbone is showing early. He feels perfectly safe in passing the matter over to Congress," Ross retorted.

McKenney ran his fingers through his long, graying mane. "Eaton isn't in the best spirits these days. Seems the ladies of Washington refuse to socialize with his darling Peggy. The Eatons were particularly offended at being snubbed by Mrs. Calhoun."

"So I hear," chuckled Ross, "but regardless of his mood, I will not be put off."

"You are a stubborn man, John. Why don't you ever consider the idea of voluntary removal across the Mississippi before you are forced to go?"

"Never! It is no secret that you favor the idea and it is easy for you to consider because, to you, it is merely an abstract idea. Your people are not the ones who would be uprooted from homes and land they have inhabited as long as we can remember."

McKenney nodded in understanding. After a pause he said, "John, Congress is made up of people...and people who are elected are people who can be influenced..."

"What are you trying to say? I've submitted memorials to Congress and I haven't influenced anyone."

"Public opinion, John. You've got to have public opinion on your side. Your only chance of success is to secure strong public support for your cause, then Congress might be persuaded."

"Sounds great, but just how do I go about securing this grand, persuasive support?"

"I have a friend...name of Jeremiah Evarts..."

"Yes, I know Evarts. Spent considerable time with him when he visited the mission at Brainerd some years back."

"Good. Why don't you arrange a chat with him?"

*　　　*　　　*　　　*

Crockett drained the last drop of whiskey from his glass. "You're a goddamned fool, Sam, throwing you whole political life away over a damned girl who won't fuck."

Houston shook his head. "There's no other way, Davy...no other way."

Crockett put down his glass and picked up his hat. "Have it your way, Sam. As for me, I've got to get home and start campaigning." At the door he turned and looked at the slumping figure. "You know this is just gonna kill Jackson when he hears about it."

For a long time Houston sat stoop-shouldered at his desk. Through bleary eyes he watched the candle flame flicker in the warm spring breeze, then, with a heavy sigh, and another jolt of whiskey, he picked up his pen. To William Hall, Speaker of the Senate, he wrote: "Sir, it has become my duty to resign the office of Chief magistrate of the state and to place in your hands the authority and responsibility, which on such an event, devolves on you by the provisions of the constitution." Signed, Sam Houston.

On April 16, 1829 the political shock wave hit Tennessee. With his letter of resignation Houston's political career in Tennessee vanished and, with that, any hopes he might have held for one day residing in the White House.

Word spread quickly throughout Nashville that General Houston and his wife had separated. Rumors and speculation abounded: Houston had found his wife in the arms of another man…some said he had found her weeping and burning old love letters…Scandal mongers spread stories of Houston's bedroom brutality. Quickly a howling public formed against him.

He spent the rest of the week at the Nashville Inn putting his personal affairs in order, burning personal correspondence, and selling most of his possessions except for two saddles. Whatever the truth regarding his domestic troubles, Houston remained tight-lipped.

On the morning of April 23 he boarded the packet Red Rover and began his journey to the Cherokee Nation in the Arkansas Territory. On board he met a fellow by the name of Jim Bowie and an Irishman by the name of Haralson who invited Houston to share a bottle. Despondent, he drank heavily. Remorsefully, he contemplated the bitter disappointment his actions would bring to his good friend, Jackson. One day, as he was considering suicide by jumping overboard, an eagle swooped down nearby. It soared aloft with the wildest screams and was soon lost in the rays of the setting sun. Suddenly, Houston was at peace. He knew a great destiny awaited him in the west.

As the Red Rover slowly made its way down river, the subject of Texas was frequently discussed between Bowie and Houston. Bowie was returning to his cotton plantation and sawmill in Arkansas but he had visited Texas several times. Houston was an eager listener.

On May 11 at Little Rock Houston took time to write a letter to his old friend in the White House. Expressing his unhappiness but assuring Jackson that, contrary to rumors, he had no designs on Texas. He would do nothing that would embarrass the United States. Then he, and his drinking partner, Haralson, boarded the Facility, a small steamboat that drew so little water that it could pass through the low river channels. It was night when the steamboat arrived at Webber Falls, two miles distant from the dwelling of the Cherokee Chief John Jolly. Houston walked from the ship into a clearing lighted by torches carried by Negro slaves of the chief. Jolly stepped forward to embrace his adopted son. At last Houston was home.

*   *   *   *

"This is an absolute outrage. This is in defiance of the laws of treaties and morality. If Jackson can get away with this, then we are no longer a nation of law." He returned the paper to Ross.

"I agree with you, Mr. Evarts, but that is Eaton's response to our petition. We have been refused an audience with either the president or Mr. Eaton."

His long nose and protruding ears silhouetted against the sun, Evarts stood angrily before his window overlooking Washington. "For Eaton to claim that the government of the United States can do nothing to prevent Georgia from extending its laws over the Cherokee people is utter nonsense. As a lawyer I know that. Obviously, Jackson intends to ignore treaties with the Indians. I cannot, I will not, permit him to do that. Treaties are the supreme law of the land."

"I've tried to work through Congress and I've tried to work through the president, to no avail. What options are left?"

Evarts spun on his heel. "Mr. Ross, the great principles of morality are immutable. They bind nations, in their intercourse with each other, as well as individuals. The American Board will not readily write off the time, money, and Christianization effort among the Indians for the greed of land grabbers or small minded politicians. God has called this nation to a special mission. It is to be a special beacon of goodness in a corrupt world and God, in his vengeance, will rain disaster and destruction on America if it, as a nation, sins against that covenant. I will raise an outcry of Christians throughout this nation. I will arouse the national conscience and direct its indignation and sense of outrage into effective channels in the national councils. With God's help, I will instigate a campaign of petitioning the House and Senate that will create a flood of memorials from across the country that Congress will be forced to heed."

*   *   *   *

"I'm sorry, Chief Ross, that you were not able to secure the objects of your mission with the general government. Maybe better luck next time."

"Thank you, Hanks. I'm sure there will be another time but right now I'd better get home. I need to reassure my people and, unless I miscalculated, I may be father again before I get there. Thank you for helping sell our horses, and good luck on your new assignment."

"Working as an aide to Calhoun was a challenge. I don't know what it will be like working for Jackson. But when the president requests your services, you don't decline."

With all baggage stowed, Ross and his party left Washington City by stage the first week of May. In Philadelphia they decided to take the fastest route home, by stage to Pittsburg, then down the Ohio to Nashville. By June 24 Ross was at home, The Head of Coosa.

On June 13, before Ross arrived home, an article appeared in the Cherokee Phoenix reporting that Jackson's expressed attitude almost amounted to a command to the Cherokee to abandon their homes and take up new residence in regions west of the Mississippi. After reading the article, Ross sought out Boudinot.

"Elias, don't you feel this story was a bit inflammatory…it has frightened our people."

Boudinot, busy correcting proofs, retorted defensively. "Did the story reflect the truth? We have nothing to recommend our paper if we do not speak the truth."

"Yes, truth…as far as it went. As editor, you should reassure our people. Tell them that the president and the secretary of war do not run the United States. It is Congress that makes the laws, and the treaties between us the general government are very strong and will protect us in our right of soil."

Boudinot straightened up from his task and looked condescendingly at Ross. "Harriet fears that we Cherokee will see evil days. Sometimes I believe my wife has a better understanding of white intentions than you."

Before Ross could respond an exhausted rider on a spent pony slid to a stop before the print shop. The news he bore sealed the fate of the Cherokee Nation.

CHAPTER 15

GOLD, GEORGIA, AND GREED

The tracks led upstream on Ward Creek, a west branch of the Chestatee River. If he continued to follow the deer's spoor, he would be encroaching on tribal lands of the Cherokee, but who gave a shit about Indian claims. Fresh meat in place of hominy grits was well worth the risk. Counting on the gurgling of the stream to cover his footsteps, he quietly pushed ahead following the deer imprints. Through the pines he saw a buck and two does browsing on low-growing brushwood. Slowly he brought the rifle to his shoulder and aimed at the buck's flank.

"Virg, look what I found!"

In an instant the deer bolted. Virgil angrily turned on his brother. "Dammit, Junior, what th' hell are you yelling about. I told ya to keep quiet. Ya shithead, you've just cost us fresh meat."

Junior cowed. "Don't hit me, Virg. Just look at this pretty rock I found."

"Ya got rocks in your head, Junior. Gimme that damned thing." Exasperated, Virgil wiped his brow and sat on the trunk of a fallen pine. He cocked his arm to throw the rock into the river.

"Look at it, Virg. Ain't it purty?"

He was ready to throw when a gleam caught his eye. Peering closely at the rock, he asked, "Junior, where'd ya find this?"

Junior grinned. "Right there where you're sittin'…in the roots of the tree."

Reaching down, Virgil came up with a fistful of dirt. Methodically, he sifted the sand and gravel through his fingers. He held out a pebble between his thumb and forefinger. "Holy shit, Junior, this looks like gold!"

The deer now forgotten, Virgil, on hands and knees, groped through the mound of dirt created by the uprooted tree, sorting out what glinted. Abruptly, he stopped to look up at Junior who was befuddled by his brother's excitement over pretty rocks.

"Junior, this is shure 'nuf gold. We gotta keep this a secret. You must never tell anyone."

"Gold? Does that mean we're rich?"

"Yes, Junior, bygod we will be rich. No one will look down on the Brills anymore. But, remember, tell no one, not even Pa."

"I promise, Virg. Cross my heart."

*   *   *   *

Obadiah Speeks flicked ashes off his cigar with a wave of dismissal through the smoke. "The Boston-Georgia Land Company is not a bank, Mr. Brill. We are in the land business. We don't lend money."

Virgil smiled confidently at the obese northerner. "You don't understand, Mr. Speeks. My land ain't just any land, it's special."

"Your land is located in hill country, no good for farming. So what makes your land special?"

From his pocket Brill took a small pouch and poured its contents on Speek's desk. Speeks put down his cigar, leaned forward, squinted, and poked his finger into the small heap. Beads of sweat that appeared on his brow were formed by more than the July heat. In a hushed voice he said, "Boy, do you know what you've got here? It's gold!"

"That's what makes my land special."

Speeks leaned back in his chair and eyed Brill through hooded eyes. He waved to a map hanging behind his desk. "Show me exactly where your land is located, Mr. Brill."

Virgil stood and pointed.

"You're lying to me, boy. You can't own that land. That's in Cherokee country."

Brill flushed. "Makes no never mind. Gold's there and I'm gonna dig it."

Speeks sat, pressing his fingertips together. Finally he spoke. "Tell you what, boy. I'll make you a loan out of my own pocket so you can buy picks, pans and shovels. If you find more gold, we split it fifty-fifty."

"That's pretty steep..." Brill started to protest. But then he remembered why he had come to Speeks in the first place. No one else in Gainesville had any money.

After Brill departed, Speeks sat alone, fanning himself and envisioning the possibilities. Reaching a decision, he ordered his horse and buggy made ready. It was time to get down to the state capitol at Milledgeville and put some pressure on the legislature. That Cherokee land needed to be opened to white settlers and there was a special piece he wanted for himself.

On August 1, 1829 a notice appeared in the Milledgeville newspaper, the Georgia Journal: GOLD—A gentleman of the first respectability writes us thus under the date of 22d July: "Gold has just been discovered in this county and preparations are being made to bring these hidden treasures of the earth to use."

First it was a trickle but soon became an uncontrollable torrent. Thousands of whites, gold diggers, gamblers, swindlers, and prostitutes poured in from surrounding states. They came on foot, in wagons, and on horseback, crazed with the idea of instant riches. There was no law in this modern Sodom.

As the news came in, Ross reflected: had the Cherokee been able to control their land, and mine the resources, their nation would have entered upon an era of great prosperity. Under the circumstances, the gold rush only added civil disorder and a greater outcry from Georgians who felt they were being deprived of properties of untold worth.

*   *   *   *

"It's a goddamned conspiracy and I'm sure Clay is behind it." The president slammed his copy of the National Intelligencer on the table, stood and rubbed his arthritic fingers. Filling his pipe with tobacco, he turned to Hanks. "Lieutenant, you've been around this town long enough; tell me, what do you know about a William Penn?"

"You must be referring to the article in today's paper."

"Correct...so who is he and whose ax is he grinding?"

"From what I understand, the real writer is Jeremiah Evarts, Secretary of the American Board of Commissioners for Foreign Missions."

Jackson tossed a taper into the fireplace and puffed a cloud of smoke into the air. "In other words, another goddamned misguided clergyman."

"No, Mr. President. Evarts is a lawyer from Boston...and a very influential person here in Washington City."

"Is he in the employ of Clay?"

"They know each other but I don't think they are close friends."

"Well, someone sure'n hell is stirring the shit," Jackson snorted. "I'm not in office a month before I've got the society ladies of this fair city telling me who should be in my cabinet. They don't like the idea of John Eaton marrying Peggy Timberlake. They won't invite the Eatons to their parties and they refuse to call on the Eatons."

"Politics takes many peculiar forms, Mr. President."

Jackson snorted. "I consider it an insult not only to Eaton but to me. I've known Eaton most of my life and there is no finer fellow on earth...and there is no woman more virtuous than dear, sweet Peggy. I've watched her grow up...this matter must be brought to a head."

Hanks stared in disbelief. "And just how do you plan to accomplish that?"

Jackson ignored the question. "Now, I've got this confounded yankee, who isn't man enough to write under his own name, telling me how to deal with the Indians. He acts as though he knew more about Indians than I."

*   *   *   *

An angel shimmered in the glass of whiskey resting on the Ft. Gibson bar; an angel with deep-blue, teasing eyes and long golden tresses. Pouty lips, sweet and moist, inviting intimacy...a willowy figure, so warm and curvaceous around the hips and nubile breasts...his blood stirred, a tightness built in his throat, his temples throbbed. Why couldn't it have been as he had dreamed? God! How he had loved her! But why had he let himself love her? Why had he let himself become so vulnerable? How could he have been such a blind fool? In the end, he had been spurned, laughed at, his love rejected. The empty ache in his chest returned as he recalled her tearful admission that she loved another. His pride would not let him live with such scorn and rejection...not in Tennessee. Clutching the glass with shaking hands, Houston downed the whiskey and reached for the jug.

"Ah! t'is where I expected to find you," exclaimed the Irish accent. Houston turned from the bar to face Haralson.

"Our friend here, John Linton, wishes to learn the intricacies of the Green Corn Dance," said Haralson with a twinkle in his eye.

"Bygod, I'm just the person to teach him. Follow me." With a crooked grin and swaying steps, Houston led them outside into the late May sun.

"First, you gotta have a fire," he proclaimed. Within a few minutes some dead branches were piled on the bare ground. With the flames reaching skyward, Houston pulled out a full bottle. "Then you take a drink and dance all the way around the fire. Then you take another drink, throw a piece of your clothing on the fire, and dance around the fire again."

Linton asked apprehensively, "Why do we throw our clothes on the fire?"

"It's to appease the wine god, Bacchus," Houston replied. "Let the dance begin!"

A newcomer to the frontier, Linton was unequal to the challenge presented by Houston and Haralson, both seasoned imbibers. Whooping, chanting, sweating, and drinking, the trio circled the fire. As the dance went on, Cherokees gathered to frown on the white man's drunken spectacle. As they shed their last articles of clothing, Linton collapsed and passed out. Roaring with laughter at the joke they had played, Houston and Haralson stumbled off to find more clothing knowing full well that Linton had only the clothes that were sacrificed to the wine god.

*   *   *   *

A probing sunbeam awakened Houston. His head throbbed and there was a fermenting taste in his mouth.

"Well, the big drunk finally awakens. Did Governor Houston enjoy his Green Corn Dance?"

Hearing the female voice, Houston struggled to sit up. Realizing that he was naked, he recovered himself with the sheet. "Where are my clothes?"

"With all the sweat and vomit on them, I thought they needed a wash. Surely, the Governor of Tennessee deserves clean clothes."

Even with the heavy sarcasm, there was something familiar about her voice that his muddled mind couldn't identify. "Where am I?" he asked.

"You are in the home of my uncle, Chief Jolly."

Houston sat on the edge of the bed and peered around. Before him stood a stately woman of uncommon beauty. Her luminous green eyes were framed by long stands of raven black hair.

Houston smiled as recognition dawned. "Tiana…little Tiana Rogers, the daughter of old Hell Fire Jack…Captain John Rogers…now an all grown up woman."

"No, not Tiana Rogers…Tiana Gentry. Here, take your clothes."

She turned her back as Houston dressed. "You're married?"

"I was. I married David Gentry before we left Tennessee. After moving here my husband was killed in a battle with the Osage."

"I heard back in Nashville that you were having some trouble with the Osage."

She spun toward him. "And of course you have come to save us, or did you just come here to lick your wounded ego and feel sorry for yourself?"

"Whoa, Tiana. Why so mean?"

Tears of anger coursed down her cheeks. "When we heard you were coming Uncle John and I had great hopes that you could use your influence to arrange peace, to secure the United States soldiers to protect us. But seeing a drunken fool desecrating the Green Corn Dance puts us to shame. It looks like you are the one who needs help. Why don't you just go back to Tennessee?" With that she stormed out of the house.

*   *   *   *

Between August 5 and December 19, 1829 a series of twenty-four articles appeared in The National Intelligencer under the pseudonym of "William Penn". In moral and legalistic terms the author set forth at great lengths his statement of the rights of the Cherokee to the land they occupied. Toward the end of the essays, the author pointed out that the Supreme Court had long since declared that the United States are bound by treaties with the Indians. How absurd to resort to treaty-making with the Cherokee if the land really belonged to Georgia! "In the case," William Penn concluded," that the decision go against the Cherokee, it will be necessary for foreign nations to be aware that the people of the United States are ready to take the ground of fulfilling their contracts so long only as they can be overawed by physical force."

Ross put aside his copy of the National Intelligencer and reached for his quill and ink. In a letter addressed to Jeremiah Evarts he said, "I cannot adequately express my grateful feelings to you for the very able manner in which you have so clearly and correctly elucidated the rights of the Cherokee Nation in the series of essays under the signature of "William Penn"; but the gratitude of the Cherokee people, and the thanks of good men, will be with you for your benevolent exertions. The present crisis in our affairs is truly distressing, and there are no free people on earth who can possibly feel a deeper anxiety for their destiny than the Cherokees."

*   *   *   *

Brilliant leaves of red and gold on oak and hickory trees trembled in the autumn breeze as the annual meeting of the General Council assembled at New Echota on October 14. The collective wisdom of the tribe rested with these elder members. They slowly filed by to warmly shake the hand of their chief and whisper their confidence in him. Yet their dark eyes mirrored anxiety. Ross tried to hide his own doubts and assuage their fears. He began his comments:

"The late administration of President Adams did not act upon any of the subjects submitted by our delegation. Instead, he referred them all to the consideration of the present administration. Those of you who have had long experience with Jackson know that he is not friendly to our cause. If it were his decision to make, we would all be sent post haste beyond the Mississippi. Fortunately, such a decree is not his to make.

"A crisis seems to be fast approaching when the final destiny of our nation must be sealed. We can only look with confidence to the good faith and magnanimity of the General Government, whose precepts and profession inculcate principles of liberty and whose obligations are solemnly pledged to give us justice and protection.

"Do not lose heart. We do have good and influential friends in Washington City who are working on our behalf. Despite President Jackson's attitude, I still believe the United States government will honor its commitments. But much depends upon our own unity of sentiment and firmness of action in maintaining those sacred rights which we have ever enjoyed."

Here Ross paused and looked into the worried faces of the Council members. "What I say now is most difficult for me to speak and for our people to accept. But, if, contrary to all expectations, the United States shall withdraw their solemn pledges of protection, utterly disregard their plighted faith, deprive us of self-government, and wrest from us our land, then, in the deep anguish of our misfortunes, we may justly say, there is no place of security for us, no confidence left that the United States will be more just and faithful toward us in the barren prairies of the West, than when we occupied the soil inherited from the Great Author of our existence."

For a moment silence reigned over the assembly. Then Major Ridge, powerful in physique as well as oratory, stood to address the Council. "We are aware of the white man's oft repeated complaint that, because of our ignorance and fondness for the chase, we are in possession of too much land for our numbers. What is the language of objection this time? The case is reversed and we are now assaulted with menaces of expulsion because we have unexpectedly become civilized, and because we have formed and organized a constituted government. It is too much now for us to be honest, and virtuous, and industrious, because then we are capable of aspiring to the rank of Christian and politicians, which renders our attachment to the soil more strong and therefore more difficult to defraud us the possession. Let us hereby individually set our faces to the rising sun and turn our backs on the setting. As our ancestors revered the sepulchral monuments of the noble dead, we cherish the sacred spots of their repose. This is our land and for any who would sell or negotiate away any portion of it then let his blood be required."

Chief Choonungkee stood. "I am fully in accord with the sentiments expressed by Major Ridge. Let us reenact our old law that prescribes death for anyone who sells Cherokee lands without authority of the nation."

Womankiller, with gray hair reflecting more than eighty years of life, spoke in favor of the blood law and seconded Coonungkee's motion.

John Ridge, who was serving as secretary to the Council, was charged with the responsibility of framing the law. On October 24 the Blood Law was passed by the Council. It read, in part "...any person or persons who shall, contrary to the will and consent of the legislative council of this nation, agree to sell or dispose of any part or portion of the national lands...he or they so offending, upon conviction before any of the circuit judges of the Supreme Court, shall suffer death..."

*   *   *   *

"Mr. President, we are facing major political crises...Georgia and South Carolina. Pick one." It was the voice of the hulking Major Lewis.

It was November 29 and the president had gathered his closest friends and advisors into his second-floor office, located on the south side of the White House, to polish his first annual message to the 21st Congress which would convene on December 7.

Jackson, stooping, held a taper in the fire, lit his pipe, and puffed vigorously. Clamping the pipe between his long, unsightly teeth, he scooted his chair closer to the fireplace and put his stocking feet on the warm stone. "I don't see any crisis, Major Lewis. Ours was intended to be a government of limited and specific powers. It is our duty to preserve for it the character intended by its framers. In cases of doubt, the real source of power lies in the states. Georgia is merely doing what is her perfect right to do. They need to remove those ignorant savages from

Georgia territory and I will lend complete support to her efforts. Indian removal is directly linked to our national security. We cannot afford to offer a weak flank on the southwest to any would-be adventurers."

"You are referring to Mexico?" asked Eaton.

Jackson nodded. "After the Louisiana Purchase, Jefferson made a big mistake in setting the boundary between us and Mexico. He should have insisted upon a natural boundary, one that could not become the subject of a dispute later. It should have included Texas. Back in August I offered five million dollars for Texas but Mexico rejected the offer. Must've pissed 'em off...they insisted we recall Minister Poinsett. But give me time; I never knew a Spaniard who was not a slave of avarice. By the eternal, I will have Texas."

Aware that he was not accustomed to the discussions of the high and mighty, Hanks nevertheless blurted out, "What's the difference between what Georgia wants to do and those South Carolinians who would nullify a federal tariff, saying they are only exercising their rights as a state?"

Controlling his irritation at the young man's interruption, Jackson blew out a cloud of smoke. "Georgia is not attempting to ignore a federal law; South Carolina is. Georgia is not attempting to torpedo a source of federal revenue; South Carolina is. Georgia is exercising legitimate rights as a state. What South Carolina does, if she carries out her threat, is treason."

"But what about the treaties the United States have with the Cherokees?" Hanks pressed.

"Treaties!" Jackson snorted. "I told Madison a long time ago that is was goddamned foolishness for our government to make treaties with a bunch of ignorant aborigines. I've got to put the interests of my country above everything else."

The president turned to a table on which were several pieces of paper. "I've thought about my first message to Congress since the day I took the oath of office. Each time I had an idea, I jotted it down on a scrap of paper and stuck it in my hat. I guess now is the time to put them in order."

While the wind and snow whirled outside the White House, the give and take of Jackson and his friends went on for some hours. Tariffs, Indian removal, foreign affairs, and sale of public lands were all subjected to scrutiny. At a late hour all the scraps, notes, and previous drafts were turned over to a friend, James A. Hamilton. It was his task to polish the final draft.

On December 8 the new Congress convened, representing twenty-four states and 12,000,000 people, to hear the clerk of the House read Jackson's message. Representing Georgia in the House were George Gilmer and Wilson Lumpkin. From Tennessee were John Bell, David Crockett, and James K. Polk. From Virginia, John Randolph. In the Senate, representing Tennessee, were John Eaton and Hugh L. White. From Georgia, Thomas Cobb. And from South Carolina, Robert Hayne.

The Georgia delegation lost no time in transmitting the content of Jackson's message to the governor in Milledgeville. Embolded by the speech, the Georgia Assembly enacted legislation on December 19, 1829 that extended civil and criminal law over the Cherokees effective June 1, 1830. In addition, the legislation nullified all Cherokee laws and declared that no Cherokee would be qualified to testify in a court of law.

In New Echota the Reverend Samuel A. Worcester read the news from the Georgia Journal. Particularly foreboding to him was Section 7 of the act which stated that all white persons residing within the limits of the Cherokee Nation, who shall not have taken an oath of loyalty to Georgia, would be guilty of high misdemeanor and subject to confinement in the penitentiary at hard labor.

CHAPTER 16

WEBSTER, HAYNE, AND DISUNION

As Hanks seated himself in the packed gallery, he could feel the crackle of tension as the deeply divided Senate was called to order on the morning of May 26, 1830. Today the final vote would be taken on the Indian Removal Act.

Since the first session of the 21st Congress had convened on December 7, 1829, an accumulation of hot issues, the tariff, sale of public lands, Jackson's threat to the bank, had set Senate members at each other's throats. To the uninitiated the events might appear quite unrelated but Hanks had learned that in politics everything was related.

While the Senate settled in for the business at hand, Hanks let his eyes rove. Presiding over the great amphitheater of democracy sat a dour, hawk-faced Vice President Calhoun. Humorless, deist in religion, and puritanical in habit and temperament, he would never admit his personal ambition for the presidency. Yet, Hanks knew, no man desired the position more fervently. Confident that all men were rational, Calhoun believed that he could win over any man with cold logic. His distaste for compromise and his contempt for party hacks ill served him. Too bad, Hanks thought, that a man as brilliant as Calhoun never understood, nor could he relate to, the lesser intellectual level of his fellow men.

Gazing across the floor of the Senate, Hank's eye fell on the obscure senator from Connecticut, Samuel Augustus Foote. It had all started innocently enough when, on December 29, 1829, Foote introduced a seemingly harmless resolution: "Resolved: That the Committee on Public Lands be instructed to inquire into the expediency of limiting for a certain period the sale of public lands."

Perceptive senators, from both the south and north, immediately recognized the explosive nature of the proposal. For several decades the West had been bleeding New England of many of its most promising and energetic citizens. Even more serious was the fear of northern Senators that an influx of slave-owning Southerners into the south and west would create so many new slave states that the North would be overwhelmed politically.

On January 18, "Bull" Benton had vented his displeasure with Foote's resolution. A large, heavily-framed man, Senator Thomas Hart Benton, representing Missouri and the land-hungry west, took to the floor to denounce what he considered a blatant conspiracy. Dressed in high, black, silk, neck stock, a double breasted frock coat and pantaloons, the senator lashed out in blind fury. His monumental ego was more than some could stand. Hanks had noted that when Benton spoke, visitors in the gallery would invariably leave and many senators would devote themselves to their correspondence. But on January 18 no one moved. With grandiose rhetoric Benton railed.

"Sir, the prevention of emigration to the West is an injury to that quarter of the union. It is an injury to the people of the Northeast who are prevented from bettering their condition by removal. The factories up North want poor people to do their work for small wages. These poor people wish to go west and get land, to have flocks and herds, to own fields and orchards. This is what the poor people want to do. The Northeast would prevent it."

Benton wiped his florid face and smiled at the discomfort showing on the faces of northern senators. He bored in. "The Northern states are looking out for their true interests. Their language has been 'Let us prevent any new states from rising in the west or they will outvote us...we will lose our importance and become as nothing. Sir, it is enough to cause the west to reconsider, and perhaps reverse, its position on the tariff. After all, what profits do we derive from supporting a subsidy of the eastern states?"

His last words landed on the receptive ears of Robert Young Hayne, Senator from South Carolina. Carefully coached by Calhoun, he seized this opportunity to form an alliance with the west.

The handsome, spare senator, barely old enough to meet Constitutional requirements, fingered the gleaming white stock around his neck and smoothed his London-tailored frock coat. This scion of one of South Carolina's richest families was well-bred, intelligent, and a match for any speaker in Congress.

With a self-assured smile, Hayne eased into his speech. "I can easily conceive that it may be extremely inconvenient, nay, highly injurious to a state, to have immense bodies of land within her chartered limits, locked up from sale and settlement, withdrawn from the power of taxation, and contributing in no respect to her wealth and prosperity.

"I am one of those who believe, with the honorable Senator from Missouri, that the very life of our system is the independence of the States, and that there is no evil more to be deprecated than the consolidation of this Government. I am opposed, therefore, in any shape, to all unnecessary extension of the powers, or the influence, of this legislature, or executive, over the States or the people of the States."

It had been a good day for Daniel Webster. Successfully representing a client such as John Jacob Astor before the Supreme Court could only enhance his reputation, not to mention his purse. He had just left the court downstairs and was returning to his desk in the Senate when he caught Hayne's shocking and disturbing remarks.

That evening Edward Everett paid a visit to Webster's two-story brick home on Louisiana Avenue where Webster was dining with his thirty-two year old bride of a little over a month.

"Mr. Hayne made a speech?" Everett asked anxiously.

Utterly calm, Webster replied. "Yes, he made a speech."

"Sorry I missed it. I was tied up in a committee meeting in the House. You will reply in the morning?"

"Yes," Webster smiled. "I do not propose to let the insult to New England go unanswered."

"Did you take notes of Hayne's speech?"

Webster took from his vest pocket a piece of paper the size of the palm of his hand. "I have it all, my friend; this is his speech."

Relieved, Everett extended his hand. "Then I shall take my leave and disturb you no longer. I look forward to hearing your reply."

Everett had noted the new Mrs. Webster's frown at his intrusion. For the life of him, Everett could not understand why Webster would marry such a plain person. Of course, the twenty-five thousand dollar dowry Webster received could have been a factor.

Tuesday, January 20th, 1830 Webster took the Senate floor. Always careful about his personal appearance, he wore that day the Whig uniform; a blue dress coat with bright buttons, a buff waistcoat, and a high, white cravat. Being sensible to the benefits to be derived from publicity, he had sent a personal request to

Joseph Gales to report what he was to say rather than send one of his stenographers.

As was his custom, he began slowly and quietly, with a long introduction to capture the undivided attention of the talent, intelligence, and beauty that made up his audience. He spoke at some length about the land issue but he had no intention of debating Benton; his intent was to focus upon Hayne. He now came to his objective.

"The East! The obnoxious, the rebuked, the always reproached East! The honorable member from South Carolina has recited the indictment against us with the air and tone of a public prosecutor.

"Sir, I rise to defend the East. I rise to repel both the charge itself and the cause assigned to it. I deny that the East has, at any time, shown an illiberal policy towards the West."

Within a half hour, Webster's spell-binding voice had produced a hypnotic effect on his listeners. Combined with his over-hanging eyebrows, deep-set eyes, and his Black Dan complexion, he had captivated the audience.

"I am aware," he rumbled, "that the honorable gentleman from South Carolina has espoused an opinion that, I confess, surprised me. I am also aware that similar opinions are espoused by certain persons outside the capitol and outside this government, but I did not expect so soon to find them here. I speak of consolidation. Consolidation!—that perpetual cry, both of terror and delusion. Consolidation! I adopt and cherish it. I confess I rejoice in whatever tends to strengthen the bond that unites us and encourages the hope that our Union may be perpetual."

Webster's intimidating gaze swept across the Senate with almost visible impact. "I know that there are some persons in part of the country from which the honorable member comes, who habitually speak of the Union in terms of indifference or even disparagement. They significantly declare that it is time to calculate the value of the Union. To them the Union is to be preserved while it suits local and temporary purposes and to be sundered whenever it shall be found to thwart such purposes. Sir, I deprecate and deplore this tone of thinking and acting. The honorable member himself is not, I trust, and can never be one of those."

Seeking to provoke a personal response from Hayne, Webster turned to the issue of slavery. "The Northwest Ordinance of 1787 was drawn up by one Nathan Dane, then and now a citizen of Massachusetts. The ordinance forbade slavery. It thereby fixed forever the character of the population in that vast region. Such a population could never ally itself with slaveowners of the South."

With these shots at slavery and nullification, Webster's hopes of luring Hayne into defending the South Carolina doctrine were realized the following day. Because Webster had to attend some legal business before the Supreme Court, Hayne waited until Webster came upstairs. As Hayne rose to speak he looked at Webster, sitting at his desk looking proud and haughty.

"Certain things have been said that rankled here." Hayne pounded his chest. "Mr. Webster has discharged his fire in the face of the Senate. I trust that the gentleman will now afford me the opportunity of returning the shot."

"I'm ready to receive it," Webster called out.

Hayne spoke for an hour before the Senate adjourned for the weekend. Hanks listened impatiently waiting for the Cherokee question to reach the floor.

On Monday, January 25, a high, cold wind whipped the streets with dust. Some of the coldest weather of the winter was visiting Washington. An angry Hayne took the floor of the Senate and spoke for another two and a half hours.

"Now, on slavery…sir, there does not exist, on the face of the whole earth, a population so poor, so wretched, so vile, so loathsome, so utterly destitute of all the comforts, conveniences, and decencies of life, as the unfortunate blacks in Philadelphia, New York, and Boston. Liberty has been to them the greatest of calamities, the heaviest of curses.

"The wealth and prosperity of every State of this Union is beholding to slavery. From 1818 to 1827 inclusive, the whole amount of domestic exports of the United States was five hundred and twenty-one millions, eight hundred and eleven thousand, and forty-five dollars. Of which, three articles, the product of slave labor, namely cotton, rice, and tobacco, amounted to two-thirds of the whole. It will be seen, therefore, at a glance, how much slave labor contributed to the wealth and prosperity of the United States; and how largely our Northern brethren have participated in the profits of that labor."

Now Hayne came to his primary objective. "The Senator from Massachusetts, in denouncing what he is pleased to call the Carolina Doctrine, has attempted to throw ridicule upon the idea that a State has any constitutional remedy, by the exercise of its sovereign authority, against a gross, palpable, and deliberate violation of the constitution. The States, being parties to the constitutional compact, and in their sovereign capacity, it follows, of necessity, that there can be no tribunal above their authority. If the Federal Government, in all or any of its departments, is to prescribe the limits of its own authority, and the States are bound to submit to the decision, this is a government without limitation of powers."

Mr. Webster rose to reply but since it was nearing four o'clock the Senate adjourned.

At home Webster was visited by an irritated Justice Joseph Story. "Hayne's speech was an acrimonious and disparaging tirade against New England. You must respond to him and I am here to help you."

Webster smiled and waved the offer aside. "Give yourself no uneasiness, Judge Story. I will grind him as fine as a pinch of snuff."

Hundreds crowded into the Senate chamber by eight o'clock the following morning, Tuesday, January 26. This was unusual. The Senate usually met at noon and concluded its day's work by three o'clock. Entertainment was at a premium in the city and often what was provided came from the Congress. Every seat, every inch of ground, even the steps, were compactly filled. The House of Representatives was deserted. In the two galleries, and on the floor of the Senate, over three hundred ladies, with their attendant beaux, came to observe the moral gladiatorship. Senate clerk, Benjamin Perley Poore, barely had elbow room at his small desk.

Webster sauntered into the Senate chamber appearing absentminded and unaware of the huge audience. Once the business of the Senate resumed, he rose and faced the horde of people. He began quietly summarizing what had brought them to this point.

"Mr. Hayne has argued that slavery is no evil. I differ with him. I regard domestic slavery as one of the greatest evils, both moral and political. But this is their affair, not mine. Neither the central government nor Congress has any authority to emancipate the slaves. It is the original bargain; let it stand.

"But I must defend Massachusetts, the state I represent, and New England. There is Boston, and Concord, and Lexington, and Bunker Hill. The bones of her sons, falling in the great struggle for independence, now lie mingled with the soil. It is where American Liberty raised its first voice and there it still lives."

Overwhelmed by Webster's hypnotic eyes and sonorous voice, the audience sat spellbound.

"I come now," he rumbled, "to our most grave and important duty, to defend the true principles of the Constitution. I understand the Senator from South Carolina to insist, if circumstances require it, a State Government may, by its own sovereign authority, annul an act of the General Government, which it deems plainly and palpably unconstitutional. This is the sum of what I understand to be the South Carolina doctrine."

Hayne rose and interrupted. "The South Carolina stance is no different from that in the Virginia resolutions framed by Thomas Jefferson."

Webster resumed. "I am happy to find that I do not misunderstand the Senator. The great question is, then, whose prerogative is it to decide on the constitutionality of the laws?

"This leads us to inquire into the origin of this Government and the source of its power. Whose agent is it? Is it the creature of the State Legislatures or the creature of the people? If the Government of the United States be the agent of the State Governments, then they may control it...provided they can agree on the manner of controlling it. What happens if, at the very moment when South Carolina resolves the tariff laws to be unconstitutional, Pennsylvania and Kentucky resolve exactly the reverse?

It is too plain to be argued. Four and twenty interpreters of constitutional law, each with power to decide for itself, and none with authority to bind anybody else, is totally unworkable. Now, however men may think it ought to be, the fact is, the people of the United States have chosen to impose control on State sovereignties."

Webster directed his gaze at the vice-president. Calhoun shifted in his chair and glared at Webster. "In truth, sir," Webster continued, "either the laws of the Union are beyond the discretion and beyond the control of the states, or else we have no constitution of General Government. No state law is to be valid which comes in conflict with the constitution or any law of the United States."

Webster's voice, as he neared his concluding remarks, rose and swelled throughout the Senate chamber. "When my eyes shall be turned to behold, for the last time, the sun in heaven, may I not see him shining on the broken and dishonored fragments of a once glorious Union. May I not hear words of delusion and folly, Liberty first and Union afterwards; but may I hear everywhere that other sentiment dear to every true American heart—Liberty and Union, now and forever, one and inseparable."

The audience did not applaud; people sat entranced. A whack of the gavel and an angry call to order by John Calhoun woke the audience from its hypnotic state.

As Webster finished, a southern senator leaned over and said, "Mr. Webster, I think you had better die now and rest your fame on that speech." Hayne overheard the remark and called out, "You ought not to die; a man who can make such speeches as that ought never to die."

A few days later, in New Salem, Illinois, a young Abraham Lincoln read the speech.

Finally, on February 22, debates on the land issues touched the Indian problem. Senator Hugh Lawson White, Chairman of the Committee on Indian

Affairs, submitted a report which recommended that ample means be placed in the power of the President of the United States to secure removal of Indians to lands west of the Mississippi. On February 24, Congressman John Bell, Chairman of the House Committee on Indian Affairs, introduced a similar bill in the House. Bell, as was White, was from Tennessee.

Keenly interested in this legislation, Jackson had ordered his aide, Lt. Hanks, to keep abreast of congressional proceedings. Unknown to Jackson, Chief Ross, pressed hard at home by Georgian intrusions, had written to Hanks requesting frequent reports of a similar nature.

Hanks had occupied a seat in the Senate gallery each time the issue was brought to the floor, somedays sitting with George Lowrey, head of the Cherokee delegation then in Washington. Lowrey had served his people long and well. He was a major in the Cherokee regiment at the Battle of Horseshoe Bend; he was a member of all the important treaty councils, and a framer of the Cherokee constitution.

"This is quite a meeting house you have here," he observed to Hanks.

"Chief, this is the only place on earth that, I know of, where Senator A can refer to Senator B as 'my esteemed colleague', then proceed, with impunity, to tell the rest of the world what a son-of-a-bitch Senator B really is." Hanks caught himself, remembering that Lowrey, one of the first Cherokees to convert to Christianity, was an elder in the Presbyterian Church. In fact, because of the seriousness of the situation for the Cherokee, before he left for Washington, Lowrey had called upon his people to set aside the first day of January in 1830 as a day of prayer. "Pardon my language, sir."

Lowrey smiled and waved it off.

Serious debate on Indian removal began on Friday, April 9 when the newly elected senator, forty-three year old Theodore Frelinghuysen from New Jersey lashed out at Jackson and Georgia in a six-hour speech spread over three days.

"It is greatly to be regretted, sir, that our present Chief Magistrate did not pursue the wise and prudent policy of his exalted predecessor, President Washington. In November of 1785, in the Treaty of Hopewell, the Cherokees placed themselves under the protection of the United States. No one branch of government can rescind, modify, or explain away our public treaties, not even the president. Treaties are the supreme law of the land, so declared by the constitution.

"We possess the constitutional right to inquire why, when some of these tribes appealed to the Executive for protection, according to the terms of our treaties with them, they received the answer that the Government of the United States could not interpose to arrest or prevent the legislation of the States over them."

The senators listened respectfully as the attorney presented his case. Webster sensed an ally; Hayne an adversary.

"I believe, sir, it is not now seriously denied that the Indians are men, endowed with kindred faculties and powers with ourselves. They are justly entitled to a share of the common bounties of a benign Providence. With this conceded, I ask in what code of laws of nations, or by what process of abstract deduction, their rights have been extinguished? Where is the decree or ordinance that has stripped these early and first lords of the soil? Sir, no record of such measure can be found. Where the Indian always has been, he enjoys the absolute right still to be.

"The confiding Indian listened to our professions of friendship; we called him brother and he believed us. Millions after millions of acres he has yielded to us. We have crowded the tribes upon a few miserable acres on our southern frontier. It is all that is left to them of their once boundless forests, and still, like the horse-leech, our insatiated cupidity cries, give! give! Now, when they have nothing left with which to satisfy our cravings, we propose to annul every treaty…to gainsay our word…and, by violence and perfidy, drive the Indian from his home.

"The Indian bears it all meekly. Now he finds that his neighbor, whom his kindness has nourished, has spread an adverse title over the last remains of his patrimony, barely adequate to his needs, and turns upon him and says, 'away, we cannot endure you so near to us! These forests and rivers, these groves of your fathers, these firesides and hunting grounds, are ours by right of power and force of numbers!'"

Frelinghuysen, hands on his lapels, swept the Senate with a level gaze. "Gentlemen, I fear that I shall oppress the patience of the Senate by these tedious details, but place the white man where the Indian now stands; load him with these wrongs, and what path would his outraged feelings strike out for? Do the obligations of justice change with the color of skin? Is it one of the prerogatives of the white man that he may disregard the dictates of moral principles when an Indian shall be concerned? We, whom God has exalted to the very summit of prosperity, whose brief career forms the brightest page in history…are we to turn traitors to our principles, to become the oppressors of the feeble, and to cast away our birthright? Sirs, I hope for better things. If my efforts prove to be fruitless, even then it will have its consolations. I had rather receive the blessing of one poor Cherokee, as he cast his last look upon his country, for having, though in vain, attempted to prevent his banishment, than to sleep beneath the marble of all the Caesars."

*   *   *   *

Lowrey stood staring out the window, watching the coming and going of carriages on the street. His hands nervously clasped and unclasped behind his back.

"Sit down and eat, George," said Ross.

"I'm sorry, Lewis…no appetite…not after I've just witnessed the Congress of the United States repudiate its own laws."

"George, the august Senate has bowed to the convenience of the Chief Executive and deliberately laid aside their treaties. They have declared that they will not be governed by these solemn instruments, made and ratified by their advice and consent." Then Lewis added sarcastically, "But by a margin of six votes. I'd say Jackson is in a shaky position with the legislative branch. Who knows, he may get ousted in the next election."

Lowrey ignored Lewis Ross's comments. "Those worthy advocates of Indian rights, like Frelinghuysen, will be remembered as long as there is a living Cherokee. Yes, the vote had only a margin of six, but a margin of one or one hundred…it's still the law. In spite of all our efforts, they pass a mean-spirited law, unfair, and unnecessary…which means my people will be uprooted from their homes." He pounded his fist into the palm of his hand. "My god, my god…I've failed them…and Chief Ross. How can I possibly report such news?"

"You underestimate my brother, George. More than likely, he realized something like this could happen. Else, why would he have given us a reference for an attorney?"

Hanks poured more milk gravy over his biscuits and sausage. "You two still think all this is about the Cherokees? Didn't you notice how sectional the voting was? Can't you see that the Indians are only incidental to what is happening? We are merely pawns on a chessboard in a power struggle between the northern states and the slave-holding states…God only knows where this will end."

CHAPTER 17

CORN TASSELS

It was May 29 and the summer heat and sticky humidity of Washington had set in. "Gentlemen, if I took your case, do you realize the predicament it would put me in? I would be taking on the state of Georgia; I would be guilty of impeding a project to which the President of the United States is totally committed." Wirt wiped the sweat from his broad brow with his kerchief. "When Congress is not in session, Washington is a city without an excuse for existence. If I weren't involved in Judge Peck's case, I'd be home in Baltimore."

"We heard that you were in Washington. But, since you have no interest in our cause, we apologize for taking up your time," said a disappointed Lewis Ross. He and Lowrey stood to take their leave.

"No, no, don't go." Wirt, with blue eyes twinkling, waved them back to their chairs. "I didn't say I wouldn't take the case. As a matter of fact, I'm very much interested in your cause."

"I'm relieved to hear you say that. Jeremiah Evarts told us that the Supreme Court would protect us if we would only secure eminent counsel to represent us. That's what brought us to you." Ross sat back, relaxed.

"Evarts and I have discussed this matter and we both are strongly impressed with the injustice that is being done to your people," said Wirt. He paused and hitched forward in his chair. "You should know, if we do go to court, and prevail, there is a high possibility that the State of Georgia will not respect the Supreme

Court's decision...and I should not be at all surprised if the President cooperates with Georgia."

"But how can a ruling of the Supreme Court be ignored by a state?" asked Lowrey.

"Over the past few months you both have observed the intense debates in Congress over the critical issue of states' rights. What you might not be aware of is the debate in Congress over the power of the Supreme Court. Many in Congress do not believe the Court should have the final authority in interpreting the law. The President is one who shares that feeling. The President, having declared in favor of the right of Georgia to extend her laws over the Cherokees, will place the Supreme Court in a delicate and fearful predicament if they should differ from him."

"From what you say, it appears that ours is a hopeless case," said Lowrey.

Wirt smiled. "To you it may appear hopeless. That's why Evarts brought you to me. Georgia is determined to make hay while the sun shines and carry out her plan of expulsion during the present friendly administration. What is needed is a case involving the Cherokee that will be admissible before the Supreme Court. Until then, there is little that can be done."

Back as his home in Baltimore, Wirt sat at his writing desk, took pen in hand, dated the letter June 4, 1830 and addressed it to the governor of Georgia, George Gilmer. In the letter he suggested that the matter of Georgia's jurisdiction over the Cherokee be brought before the Supreme Court as a friendly test case. He then wrote a letter to John Ross and enclosed a copy of his letter to Gilmer.

*   *   *   *

"So, you think Webster is our best choice?"

"I really do, John. I have never before heard such persuasive power as Webster's debate with Hayne."

"I agree with Lewis," Lowrey injected. "If we have to go to court, I'd like Webster as our counsel. But, if for some reason we can't get him, I'd feel very comfort-able with Wirt. Either one will be expensive."

Ross sat at the table fanning himself with a folded newspaper. In late June the heat was intense in Boudinot's home in New Echota. "Gentlemen, we played our political card and lost. In spite of powerful efforts on our behalf by friends in the east, and indisputable arguments on the floor of Congress, we lost. Yes, I know the vote was close...but, we lost. As I see it we have only one card left to play and that is an appeal to the Supreme Court of the United States. With our lives and our lands riding on the outcome, we must have the very best counsel available, expensive or not. This is no time for parsimony. I will recommend to the General Council that we try to secure Daniel Webster."

*   *   *   *

Out of the hills and valleys by the thousands they came. In wagons, carts, on horseback, and by foot, they braved the oppressive heat. Dressed in white man's clothing, frock coats and beaver hats, hunting shirts, blankets and turbans, and women in bright calico skirts, they rose from Haweis on the Coosa River, from Pine Log, High Tower, Talking Rock, and Elijay in the mountains and poured into their new capitol, New Echota. Camp fires surrounded the great brush arbor that had been built outside the Council House to shade sessions of the General Council. At other times, meetings of the General Council featured visiting, courtship, games, and feasting. Those who assembled on this second Monday, July 10, 1830, were frightened and subdued. Their destiny was at stake.

Already saddened that Secretary of War, John Eaton, had announced that the government would no longer subsidize missionary work, they recognized that it was retaliation toward missionaries who stood against Jackson's removal policies. But, at the heart of the meeting was the report from their trusted chief, John Ross. Under the brush arbor, and in a great circle surrounding the arbor, the Cherokees crowded around as he attempted to explain, to the schooled and the unschooled, that Georgia had assumed the power to exercise sovereign jurisdiction over a large part of the Cherokee territory and that the Chief Magistrate, Andrew Jackson, had declared that he possessed no power to oppose or interfere with Georgia in this matter. A rumble of anger rolled through the crowd when he announced that an arrangement had been entered into between the United States and the civil authority of Georgia which required the Cherokees now working their gold claims around Dahlonega be sent home.

Casting his eye upon the troubled assembly, Ross tried to conclude his report with a note of optimism. "We are being intruded upon by people who we have not wanted and it seems we have no power to resist them. In spite of these seemingly impossible obstacles, we can yet hope for justice. We will not be passive victims. We can defend our cause before the Supreme Court of the United States."

＊　　　＊　　　＊　　　＊

Wirt leaned back in his easy chair and ran fingers through his curly hair. Outside his office he could see leaves changing color in the sun of late September. "So, Webster declines to take on the Cherokee's case. Did he offer any reasons?"

"No, he didn't," replied Evarts. "I don't know if he was afraid of not being paid or if he feared appearing in such a case would jeopardize his presidential aspirations. I personally think it was a political decision."

"Ah, politics," laughed Wirt. "I have an utter distaste for politics. I hate, from my heart, all its vile intrigues and cabals. I am much obliged to Jackson. When he declined my services as his attorney general, he gave me, in exchange for a dog's life, that of a gentleman."

"Then you will accept the role of counselor for the Cherokee?"

Wirt rose to his full six feet and stretched out his hand. "Jeremiah, injustice has been done to the Cherokees. It is not in my nature to flinch. I hold it most prudent always to do my duty whether convenient or inconvenient. If I had declined this engagement from a cowardly fear of the consequences, I should never be able to hold up my head again. I fear for the plight of the Indians, as well as for my country, if legal instruments, covenants between honorable people, are cast aside."

Governor Gilmer of Georgia had spurned Wirt's offer of a friendly test case in the Supreme Court, saying that he expected the Cherokee to move and that he would have no part in letting the federal courts sit in judgement of Georgia law.

During the next few weeks Wirt sought advice from Daniel Webster, James Madison, and his good friend of over thirty years, Judge Dabney Carr of Virginia. He carefully digested the debates that had taken place in the House and Senate over the removal bill. He knew that he must find a way to avoid the Georgia courts and take the Cherokee case directly to the Supreme Court. In October he thought he had such a case.

George Tassels, a Cherokee also known as Corn Tassels, accused of waylaying and murdering another Cherokee within the limits of the Cherokee nation, had been arrested by Georgia authorities. In September of 1830 the judges of the Hall County Superior Court upheld Georgia's seizure of Tassels and sentenced him to death. Ross employed a local attorney, William H. Underwood, to appeal the sentence and dispatched a letter to Wirt informing him of the circumstances. Wirt immediately sought a writ of error from the Supreme Court. On December 12, 1830 Chief Justice John Marshall granted the writ.

On December 22, the Senate and Georgia House of Representatives, purple with rage, denounced interference by the chief justice in the administration of the criminal laws of their state. They promptly passed a resolution stating that the State of Georgia would never compromise her sovereignty as an independent state and instructing the governor to disregard any mandate received from the Supreme Court of the United States. It also authorized the sheriff of Hall County to execute the laws. In open defiance of the Supreme Court, on Christmas Eve, December 24, George Tassels was hanged.

CHAPTER 18

CHEROKEE NATION VS. GEORGIA

Low lying clouds hung over the Coosa Valley and cold December rains continued to fall. Streams were out of their banks and muddy roads were almost impassible. Ross, standing before the front window, observed to his guest. "I'm afraid your arrival in Congress will be delayed, Mr. Crockett, but I do appreciate your going out of your way to visit me."

"Hell, Mr. Ross, my fancy-pants colleagues in congress will probably appreciate my absence," laughed Crockett. "I don't stand very high in popularity in Washington."

"I understand. Your standing up for the Cherokee was a difficult thing to do. I just hope it doesn't cost you the next election."

"If the voters of the Ninth Congressional District of Tennessee expect David Crockett to trade his conscience for party views, they are sadly mistaken. If I were the only member of the House to vote against the bill, I would still do it and I would rejoice to the day I die for having made the vote."

"But doesn't this jeopardize your standing with Jackson and your fellow Tennessee congressmen?"

"They can go to hell, Mr. Ross. I'm my own man. Jackson campaigned saying he would restore the government to the people. Hell, he is the government. He has assumed more power than any previous president. If you disagree with him, you are his enemy."

Ross nodded. "I've known General Jackson from my boyhood. I fought by his side during the late war, but, I must say, his policy toward us has been unrelenting and ruinous to our best interests and happiness." He paused and looked at Crockett. "Weather permitting, I suppose you will be leaving for Washington tomorrow. I will depart for Milledgeville to serve notice on Governor Gilmer that the Cherokee Nation will carry its cause to the Supreme Court next March. Giving notice seems the honorable thing to do."

"You are always concerned with the honorable thing, Mr. Ross. That's where we differ. If I don't like the way things shape up in Washington, I'm liable to tell them to go to hell and light out for Texas. But as for you…don't give up. Jackson may not live out his term in office. His health is in a helluva shape. If he does live, I don't see him running for a second term. He has too many problems with the nullifiers and the bank problems. Clay may very well be our next president."

On December 20th, as the momentous year was winding down, Crockett left for Nashville, a boatride up the Ohio, then on to Washington.

Ross left on horseback for a slow, muddy trip to Milledgeville. On the evening of the 26th, exhausted from battling muddy roads, he registered at the Mansion House, a family oriented hotel convenient to the State House. Picking up a used copy of a local paper he noted that ex-president John Quincy Adams had been elected to the Twenty-Second Session of the House of Representatives.

Next morning, Ross walked to the State House from his hotel. He scraped the red mud from his boots, walked up the west steps, turned left and entered the governor's office. The slightly-built, forty-year-old governor rose to meet Ross and greeted him courteously.

"I doubt if you remember me, Mr. Ross, but we both fought against the Creeks in 1813." He waved Ross to a chair. "I have to address the legislature in a few minutes so, without appearing to be rude, I must ask you to state your business concisely."

"Thank you for seeing me, Governor Gilmer. I realize the Georgia legislature is in session and I will be brief." He took a paper from his pocket and handed it to the governor. "This is to officially notify you that on Saturday, the fifth of March next, at the City of Washington, the Cherokee Nation will, by their counsel, Mr. William Wirt, move the Supreme Court of the United States for an injunction to restrain the State of Georgia from extending her laws over the Cherokee people."

With a flickering, patronizing smile the governor glanced at the papers. "You have kept Mr. Wirt quite busy." He looked up at Ross. "Let me tell you about your friend, Mr. Wirt. His first wife was my kinswoman, the daughter of Dr. George Gilmer of Albemarle, my great uncle. Mr. Wirt was poor, unknown, and undistinguished when Dr. Gilmer took him into his house, gave him his daughter, and introduced him to society. My wife lived with Mr. Wirt's family in Richmond when she was going to school. All these circumstances induced Mr. Wirt to believe he could prevail upon me to enter into a friendly case before the Supreme Court. Sir, such a made up law case, however courteous the manner, can but be considered disrespectful to the sovereignty of this state."

Gilmer picked up a paper from his desk. "An amazing coincidence, Mr. Ross. I was served a subpoena this morning from the Supreme Court, purported to be signed by the Chief Justice of the United States, demanding that the State of Georgia appear before the Supreme Court on the second Monday of January next to answer to that tribunal for having caused a person who had committed murder within the limits of this State to be tried and convicted thereof. The Supreme Court has no jurisdiction over us. Any attempt to execute the writ will be resisted with all the force at my command. If the judicial power, being attempted to be exercised by the Courts of the United States, is submitted to or sustained, it must eventuate in the utter annihilation of the State Governments."

Breathing hard, Gilmer attempted to compose himself. "I refused Mr. Wirt's offer, Mr. Ross, just as I now must refuse to receive your notification. We have no influence over the lawyers of Maryland and they damn well have no influence over the laws of Georgia."

*   *   *   *

He filled the glass with Madeira, leaned back in his chair and gazed at the amber wine. "Ah, Joseph...the nectar of the gods...and one of the few pleasures left to one who is three quarters of a century old."

Story removed his thick glasses, wiped them with a handkerchief, wiped his eyes, then his balding head. He replaced his spectacles. "All in all, John, time has been good to you."

"Divine providence, my friend. I could have been killed at the Battle of Great Bridge, or at Brandywine. I could have frozen at Valley Forge...but for providence..."

Marshall shifted in his chair. "In '75, before you were born, I marched off to war...barely twenty. You might say I was midwife to the birth of this nation."

Story waited for the slow-speaking judge to gather his thoughts.

"At Valley Forge our soldiers went barefoot in the snow, were nearly naked and some starved to death...thanks to a weak, helpless Continental Congress. And so, during the thirty years I have served as Chief Justice of the Supreme Court, it has been my most fervent desire, in every decision rendered, to strengthen our federal government."

"In spite of Jefferson and his minions, you have done a splendid job," added Story.

Marshall smiled. "Ah, yes...Cousin Tom. He will never be a hero to veterans of the Revolution. While we were freezing our ass at Valley Forge, Tom stayed home, warm and cozy, reading books. I will admit his malignity, at times, has been a thorn in my side. But, Joseph, considering the issues we may soon face, it pales in comparison."

"You are referring to the South Carolina problem."

"Not only South Carolina and its fanciful notion of nullification, but now the Georgia situation." Marshall placed his glass on the table and rose from his armchair. "You'll have to excuse me, Joseph. These bladder stones are acting up."

The Tench Ringold boarding house, located on the corner of 18th and F Streets, about two miles west of the capital, was where Marshall and four of the other justices often lived while the Supreme Court was in session. It, like all the other homes in Washington, was equipped with an outhouse in back. Cold January winds discouraged leisurely visits.

Returning, Marshall picked up where he had left off. "You realize that Wirt has been retained by the Cherokees to plead their case against Georgia."

"Yes, Wirt will do a splendid job."

"Splendid is an accurate description. Going by his previous appearances before the Court, he will anticipate our every question and, with his Germanic mind, he will systematically present a case that Georgia will find difficult to refute."

"I, myself, don't see how Georgia can justify the actions she has taken," said Story.

Marshall refreshed their glasses. "Let me ask you, Joseph. Assume for a moment that the court renders in favor of the Cherokees. Will the Chief Magistrate enforce it?"

"He is bound by the Constitution to uphold the law," replied Story, "but we know his sympathies lie with Georgia...and we know he interprets the law to suit his purposes."

Marshall rubbed his chin and gazed at the crackling hearth. "As a soldier and as a judge I have worked to unify this nation. If I were to render a decision that would drive Georgia, and the hot heads in South Carolina, into rebellion, I would bring about the very situation that is counter to my life's efforts. Yet, I must render justice, Joseph. Nothing is more important than justice."

＊   ＊   ＊   ＊

When the capital was built in Washington City, the Supreme Court was completely overlooked. No building was erected for that tribunal. Instead, the high bench was assigned to an undignified committee room in the capital beneath the House Chamber. The room had two windows and was heated by a fireplace set in the wall. Later the Court moved to a room under the Senate Chamber, which was a damp, dark, low, subterranean apartment. The room's ceiling resembled half a pumpkin shell or half an umbrella.

At eleven o'clock, on March 5, 1831 Chief Justice John Marshall and the other six judges, in robes of solemn black, entered this room. Sweeping the courtroom with his dark eyes, Marshall, with a slight nod, acknowledged William Wirt and his co-counsel, John Sergeant, who waited to present their case on behalf of the Cherokee Nation. Marshall knew both men well. Sergeant, a graduate from the College of New Jersey, had fought some of his most notable legal battles before the Court. He was an advocate of national powers as opposed to states' rights. Marshall liked the fifty-two year old advocate.

Seated in the visitor's gallery Marshall noted three fashionably attired Cherokee delegates: John Ridge, Richard Taylor, and William S. Coodey.

"Although a subpoena was served on the governor December 27 of last year, it seems that Georgia has declined to attend these proceedings," Marshall observed with a slight smile. "Nevertheless, the justices are now seated and are ready to hear the petition on behalf of the Cherokee. Mr. Wirt, Mr. Sergeant, you have the ear of the court."

Sergeant rose from the counsel's desk and opened the argument. "The Cherokee come asking nothing from the United States, to claim nothing except fulfillment of the treaty on the part of the United States. We come seeking an injunction to restrain the State of Georgia from executing and enforcing the laws of Georgia within the Cherokee territory as designated by treaty between the United States and the Cherokee Nation."

On March 14, with John Quincy Adams, Representative from the State of Massachusetts in the gallery, Wirt concluded the case for the plaintiffs. His argument came forth clear, firm, and persuasive. The justices leaned forward in their high-backed chairs, listening intently.

"Your honors," Wirt pleaded, "this ancient people, the Cherokee Nation, a nation far more ancient than ourselves, and in all probability far more ancient than the Saxon and Norman race that people the land of our fathers, present themselves to you as a separate, sovereign state."

"And how do you define a sovereign state?" Justice Johnson asked.

"It is the right of self government, your honor, which is the test of sovereignty. Every nation that governs itself, in what form so ever, without any dependence on foreign power, is a sovereign state," replied Wirt. "The Cherokee are a state foreign to our nation in the sense of our constitution. They are not citizens of the United States, they owe no allegiance to our constitution, and they have no voice in our laws and are not bound by them. They can make war upon us without committing treason. If they are not citizens of the United States then they must be aliens and, if aliens, their nation must be a foreign state."

"But," insisted Johnson, "they have placed themselves under the protection of the United States so they must be a dependent people and, if so, not sovereign."

"Sir," retorted Wirt, "every state in this union has placed itself under the protection of the United States."

Rebuffed, Johnson sat back in his chair. Justice Baldwin then took up the questioning.

"Counselor, when we think of a foreign state we usually consider geographic separation…"

Wirt interrupted. "If the objection to their being a foreign state is that they are not a transatlantic state, then Mexico is not a foreign state. Is it the fact that they are entirely surrounded by the territory of the United States that destroys the Cherokee Nation as a state? Then what about the free towns in Germany? Sir, it is not the geographic position but the actual allegiance which determines the question of foreign or domestic."

"But the Cherokees lie within the chartered limits of Georgia," insisted Baldwin.

"Justice Baldwin, the Cherokees lie exactly where they have lain for a time long antecedent to the existence of Georgia, and, very probably, long antecedent to the existence of the monarchy from which Georgia derived its charter. The Cherokees have owned their land from time immemorial whereas the charter which gave being to Georgia is not yet a hundred years old."

Seeking to lower tension in the court, Chief Justice Marshall raised the next question. "Mr. Wirt, is it your belief that this court has jurisdiction in this matter?"

"Our constitution declares that the judicial power shall extend to all cases in law and treaties made. From the beginning of the existence of the United States as a nation to the present time, here have been fourteen public treaties made with the Cherokees. How could this be if the Cherokee were not a state? A treaty cannot be made with those who have no capacity to fulfill their promises."

"I see," said Marshall, "please continue."

"If it please your honors," said Wirt, "let me conclude by summarizing. If it be necessary to the political existence of a state that they should cease to be wandering savages, the Cherokee have ceased. They have become cultivators of the earth, herdsmen, and mechanics. If it be necessary to their political existence as a state that they should have a settled and organized government, and a regular administration of laws and justice, they have them all.

"So long as they were savage, the Cherokee were permitted to govern themselves by their laws and customs. But having now, under the tuition of missionaries, become civilized and established a regular and well-balanced government, and a code of just and rational laws, their right of self-government is at an end. So it would seem that their right to govern themselves diminishes in the ratio that their capacity for self-government increases.

"In our infancy, our nation was far more anxious for peace than were the Indian nations. Is it that the Cherokee are now weak and unable to call us to account that we hold ourselves absolved from the obligations of treaties? Are we to make a tacit admission that we hold ourselves bound by our engagements only so long as we can be compelled to fulfill them?

"If Georgia proceeds to act in open disregard of all the treaties, as well as the laws and constitution of the United States, to which she herself is a party…if this be permitted, then we are no longer a nation. The United States have undertaken, in the most solemn form, to protect the Cherokees. If the United States fails to do so, she is as guilty as Georgia; there is no moral difference between them. If these things shall be permitted, the faith and honor of this nation are gone.

"But if we have a government at all, there is no difficulty in this case. In pronouncing your decree, you will have declared the law; and it is a part of the sworn duty of the president to 'take care that the law be faithfully executed'. It is not for him to sit in appeal on your decision. The constitution confers no such power. It is your function to say what the law is. It is his to cause it to be executed. If he refuses to perform his duty, the constitution has provided a remedy.

"Sirs, unless the government be false to the trust which the people have confided to it, your authority will be sustained. At all events, let us do our duty and the people of the United States will do theirs. If they do not, there is the end of this government and the union is dissolved."

✳   ✳   ✳   ✳

Following the evening meal, the dining table at the Tench Ringold boarding house had been cleared and glasses refilled. Marshall raised his glass and smiled at the other justices seated around the table. "Gentlemen, our jurisdiction extends over so vast an area, certainly it must be raining somewhere. So, let us ward off the ill effects of weather."

Smacking his lips in satisfaction, he returned his glass to the table. There was no joviality in his next words. "Only two days before this session ends and we still have this Cherokee matter before us. The issue presents the greatest crisis this Court has faced since its inception…"

"It doesn't have to be a crisis, John," injected Justice William Johnson. "Simply declare that this Court has no jurisdiction in the matter, which is truly the case, and the whole issue will go away."

"I entertain entirely different views, Bill," Justice Smith Thompson chimed in. "The constitution clearly gives this Court jurisdiction in all treaty matters."

"Of course," Johnson responded. "Treaties with other nations but by no stretch of the imagination can you consider a people so low in the grade of organized society, as these Indians are, a nation."

"How can you deny their nationhood?" asked Joseph Story. "We have formed innumerable treaties with them on an equal basis. We have purchased land from them, so they must own the soil. They govern themselves; we have never conquered them. What else is required for status as a nation?"

Johnson ran his fingers through his thin, gray hair. Independent minded, the sixty-year-old South Carolinian was clearly irritated. "Come, come, Joseph. Give those Cherokees status as a nation and every petty tribe with a few hundred acres will be demanding recognition as a state."

"I agree completely with you, Bill." Justice Henry Baldwin turned to Thompson. "Tell me, when the Ordinance of 1786 was passed, which provided for the regulation of Indian affairs, why were they placed under the control of the War Department instead of the Department of Foreign Affairs?" The abrasive Baldwin rushed on. "In the Treaty of Hopewell with the Cherokees, the word 'nation' is used not once. They acknowledge their dependent status. Stipulations in the treaty are wholly inconsistent with Cherokee sovereignty."

Thompson, knowing that Baldwin was a Jackson appointee and a staunch states' rights man, had little expectation of persuading the most frequent dissenter on the Court. "There is nothing inconsistent with a weak nation placing itself under the protection of a strong ally. It has been done throughout history. It certainly does not impinge upon Cherokee sovereignty."

"Sovereignty," snorted Baldwin. "This Court cannot divest the states of rights of sovereignty and transfer them to the Indians by decreeing them to be a nation or foreign state. This would reverse every principle on which our government has acted for fifty-five years. I disclaim the assumption of such judicial power."

"Can you deny that all negotiations carried on with the Cherokee have been made by way of treaty?" retorted Thompson. "Where is the authority, either in the Constitution or in the practice of law, for making any distinction between treaties made with Indian nations and any other foreign power?"

"The validity of the treaty depends upon Cherokee status," said Johnson. "Either the Cherokee nation is a foreign state or it is not. If they are not, then they cannot come here; and if they are, then how can this Court extend its jurisdiction into their country? I will vote to reject Wirt's motion."

"And let us not forget," added Baldwin, "at this very moment there are men prowling the halls of Congress who are avidly advocating the restriction of the powers of this Court. Let's not give them more cause for such action. And, if we follow Wirt's counsel, we will be facing a head to head confrontation with the President."

"If the 25th section of the Judiciary Act of 1789 is repealed by Congress," Story retorted hotly, "it will strip the Court of all armor and the door will be open for nullification, anarchy, and convulsion. It is an extraordinary state of things when the government of the country is laboring to bring down the very power on which its existence depends."

"Gentlemen," Marshall said wearily, "we must tread the direct and narrow path prescribed for us. As this Court has never grasped at ungranted jurisdiction, so will it never shrink from the exercise of that which is conferred upon it." Then doubled over with pain in his bladder, he left the table to relieve himself.

For years, through the strength of his personality, he had been able to secure unanimous decisions from the Court. Now, in despair, he faced a troubling, foregone conclusion; the decision would not be unanimous...and he alone must write the majority opinion.

CHAPTER 19

A TEST OF
CONSCIENCE

On March 18, 1831, the last day of the Court's term, and only four days after the close of argument, Marshall rendered his decision. For twenty-five minutes he read from prepared remarks before coming to his conclusion. "Since they are not a foreign nation," he stated, "the Cherokees lack standing to sue, thus the Supreme Court has no jurisdiction to hear this case. They will have to look elsewhere for a remedy."

*　　　*　　　*　　　*

As the last piece of luggage was lashed to the stage for Richmond, Marshall turned to Story. "Well, my young friend, if providence continues to smile, I will see you at the next session. Right now, I'm looking forward to getting home to see my dear Polly and rest. If I cannot manage to dissolve the stones in my bladder, then I fear I will have to travel to Philadelphia and seek the aid of Dr. Philip Physick. But, before I go, there is one thing I request of you."

"Anything, my dear friend, just name it."

"I know you did not agree with my decision on the Cherokee case. I want you to write a dissenting opinion…and I want it published."

Story's jaw dropped. "But why, Mr. Chief Justice? Never before have you wanted dissenting opinions. You have always worked for unanimity in court decisions."

Marshall smiled and waved away the protest. "You should also know that I have encouraged Richard Peters to print a separate volume devoted exclusively to the Cherokee case."

With that, he painfully climbed aboard the coach and took his seat. Leaning out the window he shook Story's hand and said, "One more thing...I have also written a letter to John Ross apologizing to the Cherokee for my decision...but it was one I had to make."

*   *   *   *

The March first deadline for either leaving Georgia or swearing allegiance to it came and went. Worcester was much too preoccupied to give it thought. On February 27 Ann had given birth to their third daughter, Jerusha. The baby was not thriving and a fever had laid its grip upon Ann.

On Sunday, March 13, while Worcester and his printer, John Wheeler, sat before the fireplace in the kitchen, a group of horsemen rode up just at sunset. As they opened the door, a man, wearing a uniform of the newly formed Georgia Guard, greeted them. "Samuel Worcester, you are under arrest for violation of Georgia law."

"Who are you?" asked Worcester, "of what crime am I charged and where is your warrant?"

"I'm Colonel John Sanford, sir, and I don't need a warrant."

Worcester was silent for a moment. "Colonel Sanford, my wife has just given birth and she and the baby are doing poorly. Please, I beg you, let me remain with her."

"Sorry, Worcester, I'm just following orders."

*   *   *   *

On a writ of habeas corpus Samuel Worcester was brought before Judge Augustin Smith Clayton. Unhappy because their fees from the Cherokee were in arrears, counsel for Worcester, Thomas W. Harris and William H. Underwood, launched into a less than enthusiastic argument that the Georgia laws were inconsistent with the United States constitution. Judge Clayton wasted little time in shooting down that line of appeal. "I'm not interested in going down that trail, counselor. I enforce the laws of Georgia and broach no interference from any-where. Let me hear from the defendant himself." He turned to Worcester.

"Reverend Worcester, I understand that you are engaged in missionary work that is partly funded by the federal government. Is that true?"

"Yes, your honor, it is."

"And is it also true that you serve as a United States postmaster in your com-munity?"

"That is also true, your honor."

"Reverend Worcester, I would not have you think for a minute that this court is hostile to your work. Several local residents have testified to your character, men whose judgement I respect. Therefore, it is my ruling that, since you are an authorized agent of the federal government, this Georgia law does not apply to you. Case dismissed."

✳   ✳   ✳   ✳

The governor gazed upon an explosion of color outside his west window. Red bud and white, waxy dogwood blossoms were cradled in wreaths of green leaves covering the hills of Milledgeville. The beauty did nothing to mollify his mood.

"So, Col. Sanford, you see no sign of movement...no sign of compliance with our law?"

"No, governor, I do not. Ross and Ridge are riding all over the Cherokee country trying to assure their people that the Supreme Court ruled in their favor. They are showing everybody the letter of apology from John Marshall. And, with Judge Clayton dismissing the charges against Worcester..."

"So, Judge Clayton thinks the missionaries are here by the authority and pro-tection of the United States government," seethed the governor. "By god, it won't take long to fix that." He turned to Sanford. "Here are two letters, one to Postmaster General William T. Barry and one to John Eaton, Secretary of War. See that they are on the outgoing stage."

To Barry he wrote, "The object of this communication is to request that you dismiss Samuel Worcester from the office of postmaster. If he is not removed, he will continue his seditious conduct and, under the cloak of religious ministry, teach discord to our misguided Indian people..."

Barry complied. He sent a letter to Worcester dismissing him from office. Eaton assured Gilmer that the government did not consider the missionaries to be its agents.

✳   ✳   ✳   ✳

Worcester was not greatly surprised when Colonel Sanford delivered a letter from Governor Gilmer on May 31st announcing his arrest.

"Have the other missionaries received this notification?" Worcester asked.

"Yes," replied Sanford, "I personally delivered letters to Butrick, Proctor, and Thompson."

Worcester nodded. "I will need to make arrangements with my wife. How much time do I have?"

"I can give you ten days to get your things in order; no more," Sanford replied.

That night Worcester lay abed listening to the singing of the cicada and the fitful cries of his newborn daughter, Jerusha. Since birth the child seemed to have little strength. Ann's breasts were sore, as the baby was too weak to use the ample supply of milk. With a fever that refused to go away after the birth of the child, compounded with the high June temperatures, his wife tossed restlessly beside him.

News had recently arrived that his good friend, Jeremiah Evarts, had died on May 10. The death preyed on his mind. The efforts of such a man must not be wasted.

He slipped out of bed and quietly made his way into the kitchen. There he sat down at the kitchen table, lit a candle, and took up a sheet of paper and a quill. Dating the letter June 10, 1831 he addressed it To His Excellency George R. Gilmer, Governor of the state of Georgia. "Sir, you cannot fail to perceive that I could not conscientiously take an oath to the state of Georgia nor can I abandon my employment of making known the word of God among the Cherokee…If I am correct in the apprehension that the state of Georgia has no rightful jurisdiction of the territory where I reside, then it follows that I have no moral obligation to remove…Your excellency will accept the assurance of my sincere respect." S. A. Worcester

"Samuel, what are you doing up at this hour?"

Looking up, he saw Ann standing in the doorway. Saying nothing he handed her the letter. She sank into a chair and read it.

"You know they will arrest you," she said.

"Yes, I know."

"What will the other missionaries do? Will they stand with you?"

Samuel reached across the table to enfold her trembling hands. "My dear Ann, I know not what they will do. Each man must decide for himself. As for me, I am prepared to bear the full burden myself if I must. But, if I am arrested, take comfort in the fact that the Board in Boston has assured me that they will employ William Wirt on my behalf."

Thursday, July 7, just as the last rays of the setting sun filtered through the pines, Sgt. Brill and a detachment of the Georgia Guard rode up the short trail from New Echota to the Worcester home. Samuel met them on his front porch.

"You Wooster?" asked Brill.

"Yes, I'm Rev. Worcester. I've been expecting you."

"I'm under orders to arrest you," said Brill. "I'll give you time to get your hat."

The following day, lips parched and thirst draining strength, Worcester and other missionaries that Brill had rounded up, trudged under the blazing sun enduring insults and curses from Brill. About noon they came upon a stream where they were permitted to drink. Nearby a Cherokee preacher was in the process of baptizing converts. "Come on, boys," shouted Brill, "let's baptize our horses." With that, several of the guard plunged their horses into the stream dispersing the Cherokee worshipers.

When the grand jury in Lawrenceville, Gwinnett County, was called into session on September 15, Worcester and ten other missionaries were charged with residing within the limits of the Cherokee Nation without a license. Colonel John W. Sanford, commander of the Georgia Guard, was the prosecutor.

Representing the missionaries before the court was a young Lawrenceville attorney, Elisha W. Chester, a native of Vermont who was a friend of Worcester during their college days.

Tension in the courtroom was high. Word had recently spread that Nat Turner had led a slave uprising in Virginia which resulted in the slaughter of several whites.

Chester's best efforts were in vain. When the jury quickly returned a verdict of guilty, Judge Clayton turned to the eleven prisoners. "This court has no desire to inflict punishment on misguided men. It has a magnanimous heart. You can avoid imprisonment by taking an oath of allegiance to the State of Georgia or by leaving the state. Your choice."

Nine of the prisoners promptly accepted the offer of pardon by taking the oath. Worcester and Elizur Butler declined the offer.

"Alright, Mr. Worcester," fumed a frustrated Judge Clayton. "If you have anything to say before sentence is pronounced agreeable to the verdict, speak now."

Worcester rose to his feet. "Sir, I am a resident of the Cherokee Nation over which this court holds no jurisdiction. I am a citizen of Vermont and a duly authorized missionary of the American Board of Commissioners for Foreign Missions. At the time of my illegal arrest, I was engaged in preaching the gospel to the Cherokee Indians and in translating the sacred scriptures into their language. Before God and before the law, I have committed no crime."

Clayton waved away the comments. "I have already ruled on jurisdiction. Georgia laws will be enforced in this court."

"May it please your honor," continued Worcester, "if I am guilty of all or any of those crimes which have been laid to my charge, then I have nothing to say why sentence should not be pronounced against me; but if I am not guilty of all or any of them, which I solemnly aver before this court and my God that I am not, then I have to say what I have already said, the act charged in the bill of indictment was not committed within the rightful jurisdiction of this court..."

Clayton threw up his hands. "Alright, Mr. Worcester, I've heard enough. I hereby sentence the both of you to four years of hard labor to be served in the state penitentiary at Milledgeville."

WORCESTER
VS. GEORGIA

As Worcester and Butler were taken to prison in Milledgeville, a fellow Congregationalist missionary, William Potter, obtained copies of the court's proceedings and made the long ride to Philadelphia. There he obtained a writ of error from Associate Justice Henry Baldwin. Wirt and Sergeant then requested the Supreme Court to consider their appeal at its next session, beginning in January 1832.

In hopes of expediting the release of Worcester and Butler, The American Board of Commissioners for Foreign Missions sent a letter to President Jackson in November urging him to secure release of the prisoners. In reply, Secretary of War, Lewis Cass, said it was the firm belief of the president that he had no authority to interfere with the operation of the laws of Georgia.

*   *   *   *

"This story on Worcester and Butler should catch the attention of the Georgians." Ross was reading from a copy of the Cherokee Phoenix with ink not yet dry.

"I expect it to catch the attention of people far beyond Georgia," said Boudinot as he pulled another sheet of paper from the press and hung it to dry in the crowded print-shop. "Cattle are openly stolen from our people, we are forbidden to dig gold on our own lands, women are assaulted, and families are driven from their homes. It is my duty to inform the world of these injustices inflicted upon our people by Georgia."

"And you have done your duty with commendable skill, Elias. Newspapers across the country and congressmen in the United States government defend our cause. But, Georgia, knowing she has Jackson's blessings, defies them all. I didn't believe the state would go so far as to imprison Worcester and Butler."

Boudinot paused and wiped his ink-stained hands with a rag. "How much sacrifice can you expect from a man? Worcester went to prison, leaving two children and a sick, bereaved wife. Why? Because of principle. God send us more such men."

"Wirt is taking the case to the Supreme Court. He is more optimistic of winning this time."

"I wish him well, Chief Ross. In the meantime, Worcester and Butler languish in prison, our people are abused, and my wife and children can't sleep at night. The prospect of being forced from our homes and land is never out of mind. It's taking its toll on Harriett."

"A rare woman, your wife. Few would do as she did, leave the sheltered life in New England and take to the wilderness with a savage," Ross joked.

Boudinot smiled faintly. "When and how will this ever end?"

"Take heart, Elias. I keep hearing rumors that Clay might run for president in '32. If he wins, our lot could be a lot better."

"Hello, looks like we've got company," said Boudinot. He and Ross stepped out the south door of the printshop where Col. Nelson and a half dozen men reined up. The colonel took off his hat, wiped his brow with a bandana, and fixed a baleful eye on Boudinot.

"I'm here to warn you again, Boudinot, about the lies and libelous articles you've been printing. You are slandering Georgians and I won't have that."

"If it's the truth, it isn't libel, Col. Nelson. And truth is our object."

"Don't smart ass me, young fellow. I may not know libel but I can damn sure have you tied to that sycamore tree and give you a good lashing."

Boudinot looked at the dirty, unshaven guard sweating under the late September sun. "You may have the power, colonel, but you don't have the cover of legal authority."

Nelson spat tobacco juice on the dusty ground. "With your missionary brains behind bars, who'd run this paper?"

"Well, even we ignorant Indians have liberty of the press and I guess we'd manage somehow."

Nelson glared at Boudinot, spat again, and gathered up the horse's reins. He glanced at Ross, who had remained silent. Shaking a finger at Boudinot, he threatened, "Just remember what I've said, printer, else you'll wake up some morning and not have a print shop."

As they rode away Boudinot turned to Ross. "You knew they were coming, didn't you?"

"I'd heard rumors."

"Thanks. I might have got that lashing if you hadn't been here."

"Elias, you are a marked man. You have infuriated the governor and all the Georgians with your editorials. The guard will waylay you at the first chance. Why don't you get out of town for a spell."

Boudinot nodded. "Been thinking in that direction. As long as Jackson withholds our annuity, we can't keep publishing the Phoenix. Maybe I can go back east and begin a fund-raising effort. My brother, Stand, can run the paper in my absence. I'd sure like to be in Washington when Worcester's case comes to trial.

*   *   *   *

On February 20, 1832, a gloomy day of heavy rain, the case of Worcester v. Georgia began. Ladies, plumed and perfumed, gentlemen of society, fifty to sixty members of Congress, several Cherokees, including John Ridge, crowded the stuffy Supreme Court chamber.

The state of Georgia, again refusing to acknowledge the authority of a federal court, had not sent council to participate in the oral arguments. Standing before six justices, illness kept Justice Johnson away, John Sergeant and Elisha Chester appeared on behalf of Worcester. Wirt was bedridden.

For three days Sergeant laid out the case, asserting that Georgia's 1830 law un-constitutionally usurped powers that rightfully belonged only to the United States and the Cherokee Republic. To a hushed Court he boldly stated that the treaties between the United States and the Cherokees made all of Georgia's Indian laws unconstitutional. "I do not deny," he thundered, "the power of Congress to repeal their own laws, to violate and, so far as concerns themselves, to put an end to a treaty. But until repealed and annulled by Congress, they are obligatory upon everybody. No individual can violate, not state can abrogate them, no office of this government can dispense with them, no single branch can repeal them. Congress alone can change this system. If the power of Congress be thus plenary, there can be no power in the state."

*   *   *   *

On March 3, 1832 Chief Justice John Marshall read the court's decision to a packed chamber. Now seventy-six years old, and recovering from a severe operation, and the recent loss of his wife, in a barely audible voice, Marshall read his twenty-eight page decision. During the hour and fifteen minutes it took for the reading, Justices Duvall, Story, and Thompson listened with rapt attention. Justice McLean had voted with the majority but did not sign Marshall's opinion. Baldwin, the lone dissenter, had refused to sign Marshall's opinion, nor would he join in the condemnation of Georgia.

In this case, where the issue was whether the federal law or the state law had authority over an individual who was an American citizen, Marshall left no doubt about the court's duty. "This duty," he said, "however unpleasant, cannot be avoided. Those who fill the judicial department have no discretion in selecting the subjects to be brought before them."

"Worcester," Marshall noted, "had been arrested by Georgia while he was performing missionary duties which Congress had recommended. Furthermore, he was under the guardianship of treaties guaranteeing the country in which he resided. Not only was Worcester convicted under a statute repugnant to the Constitution, laws, and treaties of the United States, so is the whole system of legislation lately adopted by the legislature of Georgia in relation to the Cherokee Nation."

The Supreme Court was on record. The Indian laws passed by the state of Georgia were unconstitutional. Worcester and Butler should be freed.

As the justices filed out of the courtroom, Story clasped Marshall by the hand. "Thanks be to God," he said. "The Court can wash its hands clean of the inequity of oppressing the Indians and disregarding their rights. The Court has done its duty. Let the nation now do theirs. If we have a government, let its command be obeyed; if we have not, it is as well to know it at once and to look to consequences."

"Time will tell, Joseph," Marshall replied wearily. "As we both know, rumors say that Jackson has told Georgia he will do nothing. History will record whether Jackson and the state of Georgia acted to deprive people of their legal rights. If they did so, in a nation built on law, there can be no greater condemnation."

*   *   *   *

Pacing the floor at the White House, Jackson was in a towering rage. "The Supreme Court is part of a goddamned conspiracy. Wirt wants the presidency so he foments the Georgia problem to advance his cause. Clay wants the presidency so he is riding Biddle's horse for a recharter of the bank. South Carolina despises the tariff so she threatens nullification. They are all ganging up to embarrass me and my reelection bid."

He exhaled a cloud of smoke from his pipe and immediately assumed a calmer demeanor. "Georgia has her rights and I will not interfere. A precipitous act might trigger a confrontation with Georgia and push her into South Carolina's ranks and start a civil war."

"No need to get yourself worked up, Mr. President. The Supreme Court has finished its session and won't reconvene until its term begins in January of 1833. It didn't direct you to do anything. In fact, you are under no obligation to do anything until Georgia makes a response."

Jackson turned to look at the skinny man with an egg-shaped head who had just spoken. Preston Blair had worked for Jackson since November of 1830 when the fire-eating Kentucky editor had been brought to Washington to start up a new Jackson newspaper, called The Globe.

Jackson puffed thoughtfully on his pipe. "You're right, Blair. And I'm confident Georgia will not bow to the Supreme Court." He grinned. "Marshall's decision is as good as stillborn."

*   *   *   *

On March 7 news of Marshall's decision reached Elias Boudinot and John Ridge in Boston. John Tappan, who had just arrived from Washington, conveyed the joyous news. A few days later a courier delivered the good tidings to John Ross at his home at Head of Coosa.

Two days after the opinion had been read, the Court issued a mandate to the Georgia superior court ordering it to reverse its decision and free Worcester and Butler. Elisha Chester carried the message to the new superior court judge, Charles Dougherty, in Lawrenceville.

"I move," said Chester, "that the missionaries be released upon a writ of habeas corpus. They have been unjustly imprisoned for too long."

Dougherty looked up from the Supreme Court order and smiled. "I'm sorry, Mr. Chester, but I must refuse your motion. The habeas corpus law applies only to prisoners in custody under federal authority. These men do not qualify; they are prisoners of the state of Georgia." He tossed the order back across his desk. "I'm also declining to enter any record of these proceedings in the minutes of my court."

"But," sputtered Chester, "you can't do that. There is no provision for a writ of error if a state court refuses to make a record of its action."

"Exactly," responded the judge. "You are doing all you can for your clients, Mr. Chester, and I have the same obligation to do all that I can for my native state."

In Milledgeville the newly elected governor, Wilson Lumpkin, stormed. "I'd rather hang the missionaries than bow to the will of the Supreme Court. There are some rights which can never be surrendered by a free state or submitted to the arbitration of others."

*   *   *   *

Disturbed by newspaper accounts that Jackson intended to take no action in support of the Supreme Court, John Ridge and Elias Boudinot were back in Washington the first part of April. Ridge lost no time in securing an audience with President Jackson. They found him having a whiskey with his friend, Amos Kendall and discussing Sam Houston's recent attack on the Ohio Congressman William Stanbery. Ridge got right to the point.

"I must know, Mr. President, whether the power of the United States will be exerted to execute the decision of the Supreme Court and put down the legislation of Georgia."

Jackson, still recovering from a bout with influenza and irritated by the ill fit of his new teeth, raised his hackles at the impudence of the question. "No, by the eternal, it will not."

Ridge, standing slim and tall, visibly slumped.

Jackson, sensing an opportunity, immediately assumed a conciliatory attitude. "Our policy is benevolent, our treaty offer is generous. I earnestly plead with you, Mr. Ridge, go home…go home and advise your people that their only hope of relief is to abandon their resistance and remove to the west."

Back at the Indian Queen Hotel, Ridge found an invitation to meet with Justice John McLean before the judge left Washington for his home in Cincinnati, Ohio. Appointed by Jackson to the Supreme Court in 1828, McLean had lost favor with Jackson because of his opposition to Peggy Eaton and his pro-Indian decisions.

"I do not wish to be harsh with you," said the kindly judge, "but frankness will serve you best. I must tell you, do not expect to gain anything from the recent Court's decision."

"After our meeting with the president, your words come as no surprise," responded Ridge.

"By a nod of his head the president could enforce the Court's decision. But, he would run the risk of a Georgia revolt. As much as the president believes in states' rights, the union is more dear to him."

"But what about the missionaries? Must they forever remain in prison?" asked Ridge.

McLean sighed. "I deeply regret their unlawful imprisonment. The president says that he does not believe that he has the power to accomplish that objective. But, even their release will not prevent the operation of Georgia laws over your people."

Ridge threw up his hands in a gesture of helplessness. "Then what are we to do?"

"I say this with all sincerity, and with deep sorrow. There is no choice but for you to sign a treaty of removal."

Back at their hotel, a despondent Ridge and Boudinot met with Elisha Chester. Chester related the story of his futile meeting with Judge Dougherty in Lawrenceville. "I am now convinced that you must sign a treaty," he told them. "Once you agree to that I believe Worcester and Butler will be released."

Ridge bristled. "How can you even suggest such? Those good men are in prison because they truly believe in our cause. To sign a treaty of removal would not only be a betrayal of them but our nation as well."

"Secretary Cass has proposed some very liberal terms. Won't you even convey them to your people for consideration?" asked Chester.

Ridge spurned his offer. "You are a turncoat, Chester. You are still in the employ of the Cherokee and the American Board, yet you have been seduced by that chicken snake, Jackson."

*   *   *   *

The gleam of silverware on white linen, the sparkle of crystal wine glasses...here in the governor's mansion Ann had not seen such splendor since leaving Boston in 1825…and just a short distance away her husband languished in the Milledgeville prison.

"Mrs. Worcester, I invited you to dine with us tonight so that we could discuss the plight of your husband. Believe me, I do not enjoy his imprisonment anymore than you. Therefore, I beseech you…when you see him on the morrow, please persuade him to end his confrontation with the state of Georgia. No good can come of it."

"But Governor Lumpkin, my husband has committed no crime. Why should it be his responsibility to end what you call a confrontation?"

"He stands convicted of violating a Georgia law. That's why he is in prison."

"But, Governor, the Supreme Court…"

"The Supreme Court of the United States has no jurisdiction in this matter. The ground which this state has maintained on this subject can never be abandoned without dishonor to herself."

"Neither can my husband dishonor himself by turning his back on his beliefs and bowing to a law the Supreme Court has declared unconstitutional."

The governor considered a forkfull of food before replying. "Mrs. Worcester, I am fully aware that the course taken by Georgia toward removal of the Indians has met with severe censure by a large and respectable portion of the people of this Union. The opposition that has been arrayed against us has received great strength and zealous aid from an influential segment of the Christian community. These zealots are pursuing a course that could lead to conflict and disaster. Georgia knows her rights and will never retreat from them even though it leads to bloodshed." He turned to Ann Worcester. "Tell your husband to dismiss the proceedings now pending before the Supreme Court against Georgia and let him apply to the proper authority of the state, in a respectful and becoming manner, and he shall go free, and not till then."

＊   ＊   ＊   ＊

"Samuel, please…the men."

Worcester released his wife from a tight embrace and turned to the convicts who were watching, silent and smiling, at a respectful distance.

"Gentlemen, this is my wife, Ann. Ann, these are my friends. More than friends, they are my congregation. I minister to them when I am not making cabinets and each sabbath I preach the Gospel."

The convicts moved on to other business while Worcester steered his wife to a bench beneath a live oak tree.

"How are my daughters?" he inquired.

"They are just fine, Samuel. Ann Eliza and Sarah send their love,"

"And the Cherokees...what is the situation with them?"

"Deeply discouraged, Samuel. Already surveyors from Georgia are staking out Cherokee lands. On my way to see you I encountered a group of Cherokees. When they learned where I was going, they took up a collection to help with my expenses. They gave me forty three cents...every penny they had. They are pained that you are in prison. They know it is because of them that you are here."

Worcester sat with bowed head. Ann spoke gently. "Samuel, Governor Lumpkin asked me to..."

"I know what the governor is asking you to do, Ann. I am under excruciating pressure from all sides to withdraw my appeal to the Supreme Court. But if we now yield, who will hereafter venture to place any reliance on the Supreme Court of the United States for protection against laws however unconstitutional? And the Cherokee...it would be a betrayal if I fail them."

"But, Samuel," Ann said gently, "you must also think of our country. Governor Lumpkin speaks of bloodshed..."

*   *   *   *

"Elias, this article of yours is not acceptable...you cannot print it."

"I expected some resistance from you, Chief Ross, but the Cherokee people must be informed of their true plight. I do conscientiously believe it to be the duty of every citizen to reflect upon the dangers with which we are surrounded. Last March the Creeks signed a treaty of removal. In May the Seminoles signed a similar treaty. This past October the Chickasaw Nation ceded their lands in northern Mississippi to the United States. Only the Cherokees are left. How long do you think we can hold out?"

"We can hold out so long as we are unified," Ross replied firmly. "Articles such as this will only cause doubt, division, and weakness."

"This article," said Boudinot defiantly, "will convey the truth. Our people are entitled to the truth so they can decide their future. They already know that Congress passed a bill to evict us. Your hope of the Supreme Court protecting us has proved futile. We all know that Jackson will not fulfill treaty obligations and protect us from Georgia. His election to a second term crushes your hopes that Clay would be our salvation. The American Board is now counseling us to treat. How much more will it take to convince you that telling our people to resist in the face of these events is irresponsible. You cannot make such a decision on your own."

"Elias, the interests of our people demand the continued publication of this paper. It cannot be used as an instrument of division. That decision is not mine alone. It is the considered opinion of the General Council..."

Boudinot removed his apron and laid it upon the press. "Chief Ross, I will not consent to be the editor of this paper without the right and privilege of discussing these important matters. You can tell the Council, they will have my letter of resignation tomorrow."

CHAPTER 21

A FRACTURE
IN THE FAMILY

The president crumpled the paper in his fist. "Goddamn that Calhoun. I should hang the sonuvabitch for treason…hang him high as Haman. He resigns as vice-president, then, on January 4th, shamelessly walks into Congress to become a senator from South Carolina…which simply affords him more opportunity for mischief."

Amos Kendall looked up from his writing. "I don't see Calhoun's signature on that document."

"You don't see his name but his hands are all over it…his ideas, his thoughts. Calhoun has been flirting with the idea of nullification for a long time. If it hadn't been for his duplicity, his endangering the union, I would not have run for a second term. Now, by the action of the South Carolina legislature, his illegitimate child has been given cover. By the eternal, no state can ignore a law of the United States."

Kendall smiled. "Georgia seems to be getting away with it."

Jackson ignored the dig. "If Van Buren is to follow me to the White House, and that is my fervent wish, it is essential that we maintain our allies, the southern planters. To use force against Georgia would wreck everything. Lumpkin is a patriot. He is not for nullification and he will not side with South Carolina unless he is pushed. Amos, I must get the Georgia issue defused…and quickly so that I can deal with South Carolina."

"Maybe you should send Houston to see Lumpkin. That deal maker will secure the release of Worcester if anyone can."

"Houston had to get back to Ft. Gibson. Some Texas matters need his attention," Jackson said evasively. He stood, tossed the nullification document on top of the heavy mahogany table, and walked over to the window. Looking out into the darkness he quietly contemplated his course of action. "I'll send Hanks. That charming boy can convince Lumpkin." He turned from the window and picked up the nullification papers. "Right now, I must deal with this."

On December 11, 1832 Jackson's proclamation on South Carolina's nullification doctrine was published. His language was blunt but such that it gained him immediate and strong support from his political enemies, even Webster and Marshall. "I consider," said Jackson, "the power to annul a law of the United States, assumed by one State, incompatible with the existence of the Union, contradicted expressly by the letter of the Constitution, unauthorized by its spirit, inconsistent with every principle on which it was founded, and destructive of the great object for which it was formed…Fellow citizens of my native state…you are deluded by men who either deceived themselves or wish to deceive you. Mark under what pretenses you have been led on to the brink of insurrection and treason on which you stand."

*   *   *   *

In Milledgeville Hanks encountered a wavering but stubborn governor. "You are merely the latest, Captain Hanks, to pressure me into releasing Worcester and Butler."

"President Jackson considers you a patriot, your excellency. He is confident in your ability to resolve this issue expediently and justly."

Lumplin squirmed in his chair. "We have already repealed the law under which Worcester was convicted. And our legislature has issued a proclamation which declared our abhorrence of nullification. What more does the president expect of me?"

"Sir, release the prisoners."

Lumpkin shook his head. "Not until they withdraw their appeal to the Supreme Court, Captain Hanks. We have our pride. I will not abandon my position and let the good name of Georgia be sullied."

"Then let me speak with Worcester and Butler."

The governor eyed Hanks for a moment. "Alright, Captain. If you can get those two to apply, in a respectful and becoming manner, they will be allowed to go free."

*   *   *   *

A smiling Worcester brushed curls of wood shavings from his shirt and extended his hand. "Recently we cabinet makers have been visited by most everyone asking us to recant. Now it's the military."

"I am here on behalf of the president, Rev. Worcester. He would like to see you and your colleague, Rev. Butler, released."

"We would like that too," Worcester replied, "but duties are ours; events are God's."

"Then there are a couple of things you need to do," replied Hanks. "First, instruct your lawyers, Wirt and Sergeant, to withdraw your appeal to the Supreme Court. Second, you must write a contrite letter to Governor Lumpkin requesting release. It's as simple as that."

Worcester laid aside his wood plane on an unfinished cabinet. "Life has never been that simple, Captain Hanks." He rubbed his callused hands together. "After much thought, prolonged prayer, and at the urging of the American Board, Brother Butler and I have reached the conclusion that we should drop our appeal and accept a pardon from the governor. We do this with mixed emotions. To accept a pardon implies an admission of guilt...but, as loyal Americans, we do not wish to create consequences injurious to our beloved country. On the other hand, we cannot escape the feeling that we are abandoning the Cherokee."

On January 8, 1833 Worcester and Butler wrote a brief letter to Writ and Sergeant requesting them to make no motion on their behalf before the Supreme Court. At the same time they sent a letter to Governor Lumpkin informing him of their actions and stating that they now had a perfect right to a legal discharge. The tone of their letter offended Lumpkin and their release was not forthcoming...not until a more contrite letter was written. On January 14, 1833, sixteen months after their imprisonment, they were released.

Two days later, January 16, Jackson sent his message to Congress asking for powers to use coercive measures against the Palmetto State.

*   *   *   *

On March 2, 1833, two days before Jackson's second inauguration, and as Ross and his fellow delegates prepared to leave Washington for home, the temperature dropped to six degrees above zero, the coldest day of the entire winter. Snow covered the ground and a driving northwest wind swirled it into tall mounds around the unfinished capitol.

Calhoun did not stick around for the inauguration. Jackson had signed on March second a bill, engineered by Clay, that would gradually lower the tariff that had led to South Carolina's rebellious stance. On the same day he had also signed what was referred to as the Force Bill, which gave the president authority to use force against the rebels in South Carolina. Calhoun left Washington on March 3. The stage made slow headway over the icy roads and frozen ruts. A frustrated Calhoun knew he must get to Columbia before the nullification hotheads put South Carolina into a crisis.

Through the cold and high winds on March 4, Ross made his way to the House of Representatives. There Andrew Jackson, who had secured 188 electoral votes to Clay's 49, would be sworn in for his second term against a stately backdrop of fourteen marble columns rising forty feet to the vaulted dome. It was shortly after noon when Ross elbowed his way into the crowded hall. Jackson took the seat of the Speaker of the House. Martin Van Buren, the newly elected vice-president, took a position to the president's left. After everyone got settled, the President rose from his seat and was greeted by cheers from the audience. Jackson, appearing thin and frail, began to read his inaugural address. It was mercifully short. Finishing, he bowed low then turned to the venerable Chief Justice, John Marshall, who administered the oath. Viewing the president, Ross wondered if he would live out his second term.

On Sunday, March 17, Ross and his companions started for home via the National Road. On board the stage was fellow traveler, Henry Clay, who was returning to his home in Lexington, Kentucky. Wrapped in blankets, Ross settled back in silence con-vinced that his sojourn in Washington had availed nothing. Congress had been too caught up in tariff debate, Jackson's battle against the Bank of the United States, and the nullification issue. A memorial submitted to Congress regarding the plight of the Cherokee had been totally ignored. Equally depressing to Ross was a letter he had received from the American Board of Commissioners for Foreign Missions in Boston informing him that they now believed it was in the best interest of the Cherokees to accept removal. The last bulwark of American support for the Cherokees had fallen.

Clay fished for his gold snuff box, took a pinch of the aromatic Maccoboy, and offered the box to Ross. Ross shook his head.

"I'm sorry you lost the election, Mr. Clay. We were hoping for a different outcome."

A sardonic smile curved Clay's thin lips. "So was I, Chief Ross. Since the last two elections, I have grown less confident in the virtue and intelligence of the people. If Jackson were an enlightened philosopher and a true patriot, there might be some justifica-tion for such public adulation, but when we consider that he is ignorant, passionate for power, hypocritical, and corrupt, what can we think? The illiterate masses seem intent upon following a charismatic but igno-rant leader...but...it is a mistake to presume the public is well-informed on any given subject."

To keep his mind off the penetrating cold, Ross pursued the conversation. "Will you run again for the presidency?"

Again Clay smiled. "There's always another election, Chief Ross. Let's wait and see."

"Since Jackson cannot run again, who might some of the candidates be? Will Wirt run again?"

Clay's brow furrowed in thought. "I doubt it. Wirt's health has gone to hell. Besides, he is not a political animal. He doesn't enjoy the fight."

"What about Calhoun?"

Clay laughed. "Ah, the cast iron man...now that crusty old bastard loves the fight as much as I do. Sure, he will run again. He has nursed the ambition to be president all his life...but he can't win. His views on nullification masks his fears for the future of slavery. He feels that slavery is the inevitable law of society and that stance alienates the north."

"And Webster?"

"The great god, Daniel. Of course he aspires to the presidency. He's just wait-ing for the right time."

"Van Buren?"

Clay scowled, turned up the collar of his brown, broadcloth coat and shifted in his seat. "That little magician has never done anything to advance the honor, glory, and wel-fare of the American people. He is the hand-picked puppet who will jump at Jackson's command. He is nothing but the tool of that old repro-bate, happy to carry out his frightful policies and principles. If it comes down to it, I will do everything in my power to defeat him."

"If I may be so bold, Mr. Clay, your countrymen owe you a great debt. Had it not been for your eloquent and persuasive speech to the senate last month, which effected a compromise on the tariff, South Carolina and the federal government might now be in bloody conflict."

Clay smiled and reached under his coat for his flask. "Chief Ross, politics is not about ideological purity or moral self-righteousness. It is about governing, and if a poli-tician cannot compromise, he cannot govern."

*   *   *   *

Clay's words echoed in Ross's mind as he prepared for the regular council meeting. In 1832 the seat of Cherokee government had been moved from New Echota to Red Clay council grounds, located in Tennessee less than a half mile from the Georgia state line. The large open-sided council house was located near a deep, blue pool called the Council Spring.

According to the Cherokee constitution, the annual session of the General Council was decreed to start on the second Monday of October. Fall was the ideal time for such gatherings. The harvest was then complete and the weather was normally dry and warm enough so that people could camp out.

When Ross rode into the council grounds in late afternoon, he could see hundreds of camp fires in the trees surrounding the clearing. He was greeted by Major Ridge's personal slave, a black called Peter.

"Looks like we will have a good turnout this session," Ross said as he dismounted.

"Yessuh, Chief Ross. We got plenty of mouths to feed this time. Major Ridge sent me ahead to make sure everything was ready. We already slaughtered fifteen beeves."

It was the practice of the Council to provide food for those who attended the annual meeting. Beef and great quantities of corn were consumed as the meetings usually lasted two weeks. Fifteen beeves a day were prepared by several families employed to do the cooking.

On October 15 members of the Council seated themselves on rough-hewn benches in the council house. Outside the structure stood hundreds of listening Cherokees. They always had full access when the people's business was being conducted.

When his turn came, Ross delivered his annual message to the assemblage. "Friends and fellow citizens...as representatives of the people, you have again assembled at the great Council fire for the purpose of deliberating the important concerns of this nation."

His brief report revealed to the people that their last mission to Washington City had met with failure. Trying to end on an optimistic note, Ross said, "I cannot for a moment permit myself to entertain so unfavorable opinion as to lose all confidence in the justice and good faith of the United States."

Anticipating arguments to come, Ross concluded with a call for unity. "It is a self evident truth that no community can successfully survive an opposing difficulty and attain the object of desire unless the members thereof can and do exercise a controlling influence of common interest so as to ensure harmony and perseverance among themselves by unity of sentiment and action..."

John Ridge stood to address the council. "I think we all agree that time for definitive action is long past. Opportunities have been passed over. Is it true, Chief Ross, that President Jackson offered two and a half to three million dollars for our lands?"

Ross nodded. He had noted a recent change in the attitude of Ridge and had expected trouble from the ambitious young man. "Yes, that is true. I declined the President's offer. Our gold mines alone are worth more than that."

"Of what worth is the gold if we are unable to mine it?" asked Ridge. "I believe you misread the intentions of the United States government and, intentionally or not, you are deluding our people with false hopes. Georgians continue to evict our people from their homes and seize their property. I am opposed to any long and unnecessary delay in signing a removal treaty with the United States. We should send a delegation to Washington empowered to treat."

At this point Ross's nephew, William Shorey Coodey, presented a petition of protest. The petition, which demanded that Ross explain his reasons for a devious course of delay, bore the signatures of twenty-five Cherokees, including Major Ridge, Boudinot, and Stand Watie.

Try as they might, the Ridge faction failed to induce an angry council to choose a delegation favorable to removal and clothe it with the power to treat. A delegation was chosen, headed by John Ross...and it was not empowered to enter into a removal treaty.

CHAPTER 22

THE RIFT WIDENS

The gray skies of January 1834, and unrelenting rain outside his window in Brown's Hotel, matched Ross's mood. He was deeply saddened by his split with Major Ridge. The parting had been painful for both. The Ridge had been his friend, his mentor, and a constant bulwark of support. In fact, it had been The Ridge who had prodded him about duty to his people and set him on a course that had led to his becoming principal chief of the Cherokee. The Ridge, who had threatened that any man who sold Cherokee land would pay for it with his life, was now the head of the faction favoring a treaty of removal. But it was John Ridge, his son, who, in his obsession to become principal chief, had driven the wedge between his father and Ross. In a struggle for loyalty, a father's duty was to his son.

Elias Boudinot, a highly educated person, fluent in English and Cherokee, with high moral character, who Ross had promoted as the only logical person capable of editing the Cherokee Phoenix, had been one of the first to break ranks. Boudinot had no hope that the whites and Cherokee could ever live side by side.

Throughout their lives his brother, Andrew, had been a thorn in his side. Whatever the issue, Andrew would always take a position of opposition. Now, he learned that his brother was in Washington leading a committee of Cherokees seeking to make a treaty of removal with Jackson.

His good friend and defender, William Wirt, hovered near death. Clay, Calhoun, and Webster were back in town, involved in the social life in such homes as

Margaret Bayard Smith. In Congress Clay was aggressively attacking Jackson for assuming authority and power beyond what the Constitution allows. Since, on the orders of the President, deposits had been withdrawn from the Bank of the United States in the pre-ceeding September, the country had been thrown into a financial panic. Fearing that the United States was heading for economic disaster, Clay introduced a resolution in the Senate to censure the president for exceeding his powers.

Thus, thought Ross, the ambition of individuals is the main spring of the great political machine which the whites called The Government.

Ross now knew that in his next meeting with Jackson he could no longer lead from any semblance of strength. The president knew of the division among the Cherokee created by the Ridge faction. He also knew that Andrew Ross was in the city hoping to sign a treaty of removal.

Jackson was still smarting from the Senate's vote of censure on March 28. His long-standing hatred of banks, and his fear of the nation being held hostage by the Bank's control of currency, had culminated in his vetoing the renewal of the charter for the Bank of the United States. He had followed up by ordering the removal of deposits from the Bank and their placement in his selected state banks. Knowing that Clay was already on the Bank's payroll, and that Webster owed the Bank over a hundred thousand dollars, added to Jackson's pleasure in vetoing the bill.

When Ross next met with Jackson, the President was inattentive and testy. Weakened from a recent bout with flu, he remained seated. He nodded as the Cherokee delegation entered. "So, Chief Ross, you are back in Washington. I hope you are not bringing me new problems."

"If we could get your government to honor its treaties, Mr. President, our problems would go away. However, I have brought some new proposals for your consideration."

Jackson showed a flicker of interest. "Leave your papers, Mr.Ross, and I will get to them as soon as possible."

*   *   *   *

On April 9th, while awaiting a response from Jackson, Ross decided to pursue his quest with several members of Congress. As he entered the capitol building, he encountered John Quincy Adams, now representing his state of Massachusetts.

"Ah, Mr. Ross, how good to see you again. I suppose you have come to hear Senator Calhoun's speech."

Ross shook hands with the diminutive and balding congressman. "I had other business on my mind. I had no idea Calhoun was speaking."

"Well, it might amuse you," chuckled Adams. "It deals with his ideas of government. But, his learning is shallow and his mind argumentative. His insanity begins with his principles from which his deductions are ingeniously drawn."

His curiosity aroused, Ross entered the senate chamber just as Calhoun was un-limbering his rhetoric against the Force Bill. Standing six feet two inches tall, the Senator from South Carolina had pushed some chairs down to both ends of a long desk, thus enclosing himself in a sort of a cage where he could pace up and down as he spoke. Ross noted how rapidly Calhoun had aged in the past few months. The chiseled bone structure of his face was clearly visible; his dark eyes were sunken. His hair, short clipped and streaked with gray, was brushed back from his forehead.

"I introduce this bill from a deep conviction that the act which it proposes to repeal is subversive to our political institutions and fatal to the liberty of our country." His voice was hoarse, his delivery harsh and abrupt. "It is true the Force Bill will cease to be law at the termination of this session of Congress but these seeds will not remain in the system without germinating! How dangerous it is to vest such extraordinary powers in the Executive!"

There was no grace, no polish, no beauty in Calhoun's words. He was speaking to convince. "I had my full share of responsibility in elevating General Jackson to power. There once existed between us friendly relations, personal and political. But once he acquired ascendancy, he has disappointed the hopes of his friends and realized the pre-dictions of his enemies. How shall we explain his re-election after he had actually proved himself so incompetent, after he had violated every pledge which he had made previous to the election?

"In casting our eyes over the scene we find the country divided into two great hostile and sectional parties...and it has been such since the founding of this nation when one party favored a national, or consolidated government, and the other in favor of the confederative principal. Today, in this conflict, we find both Houses of Congress and the Chief Magistrate on the side of the dominant interest. But what of the minority, the weak? Is South Carolina to acquiesce? Where there is weakness, exploitation follows. To all practical purposes, the national government will have proven its superiority to the states that created it. The basic argument," Calhoun concluded, "is whether ours is a federal or consolidated government...the controversy is one between power and liberty."

"Strange," Ross later reflected, "that Calhoun could not see that the argument he made for his home state applied equally to the Cherokee…except the Cherokee were not planning a revolt."

On April 29th, a month after their meeting, Ross received from the President a curt rejection of his proposals, conveyed through a minor official of the administration. However, if the delegation were to submit a proposal connected with their removal, it would be considered without delay.

*   *   *   *

"You look discouraged, my friend. May I lift your spirits with some spirits?"

Ross looked up from his plate to see Henry Clay, a decanter in one hand and a glass in the other. He smiled and waved away the offer. Clay took a chair next to him at the table.

"You can't accept defeat, Mr. Ross. Jackson is counting on you to fold your cards. If you submit now it will feed his insatiable lust for power. He calls himself the sole executive in which all other officers are his agents; he has seized the power of the public purse, a power clearly granted to Congress by the Constitution, a seizure that has plunged this nation into a depression. He is leading these United States into a monarchy. No, by god, you cannot give in." Clay was breathing hard.

Ross laid aside his fork and lifted his hands in a gesture of despair. "You are aware of all my efforts…and they have availed nothing. What more can I do?"

"Hang on. Stall. Do anything…just hang on until the next election. There is a new party forming, the Whigs, that will clean the Jacksonian stalls. I swear I will work to stamp out Jacksonism as long as there is breath in my body." Clay paused to stir some brown sugar into his whiskey. "Tell you what, Ross. You submit another memorial to Congress and I swear to you, I'll make sure it gets a full hearing."

As the Cock of Kentucky walked away, Ross sat in the smoke-filled dining room of Brown's Hotel pondering: was Clay a true friend of the Cherokee or was he merely using their plight as another club against Jackson? The ever-optimistic Clay had been wrong in predicting the last election; he could be wrong again. Jeremiah Evarts was dead. His friend, William Wirt, had passed away on February 18th. It seemed he had no allies in Washington. Amidst the partisan warfare in Washington over the recharter of the Bank, and teetering on the edge of civil war over the tariff and South Carolina, the distress of the Cherokee was largely ignored by Congress.

With little hope for its consideration, on May 17 Ross submitted to the Senate and the House a memorial in which he summarized the indignities the Cherokees had endured for the past years and pleaded for redress of grievances. In the House the Committee on Indian Affairs, dominated by southern sympathizers, left the document on the table, unread. True to his word, on May 20 Henry Clay took the floor of the Senate.

Flourishing a copy of the Cherokee memorial in his hand, he launched his attack. "The President of the United States has not only refused to protect the Cherokee against the oppressions of the State of Georgia, but is exercising his power on the side of the oppressors…"

Clay was interrupted by Senator Forsyth of Georgia. "The Cherokee are not subjects of this nation, therefore, they are not entitled to a hearing before this Senate."

"It does not matter what the petitioners call themselves," Clay fired back. "A horrible grievance has been inflicted upon them by the President's arbitrary policy which tramples upon treaties and the faith of this nation. Unless the treaties which the United States have entered into with these Indians are to be disregarded, the Senate cannot possibly refuse to receive this petition."

Senator Frelinghuysen of New Jersey supported Clay. "To refuse to receive a memorial from people who have put themselves under the protection of this government is a monstrous political absurdity."

Senator Webster urged the petition be received. "The Senate regulates the Cherokee in every way. Why then cannot the Senate receive their petition?"

At a quarter of five, long past their usual adjournment time, the Senate referred the memorial to the Committee of Indian Affairs, ordered it to be printed, and adjourned. For all the time consumed, the heat generated, Ross could see nothing had been accomplished.

Andrew Ross, in the meantime, seemed bent on signing a treaty of removal at any cost. The president's crony, Major Eaton, carried on negotiations with the group. Before its adjournment on June 30 the treaty was rejected by the Senate.

From where he sat in the shade of his porch, Ross could see heat waves shimmering over the fields along the Coosa River. Cotton bolls were ripening under the relentless September sun.

"Looks like you will have a good crop this year."

Ross smiled wryly. "Yes, if I'm still around for the harvest. I guess you noticed in the Georgia Journal that my property is being offered for sale. Unfortunately, I don't have the protection which Governor Lumpkin extends to you."

The Ridge shifted uncomfortably in his chair. The Georgia lottery of Cherokee lands was well underway. "That isn't what I came to see you about, Little
John." He shifted again, wiped the perspiration from his broad brow, struggling
to find the right words. "Little John, for most of our lives we have been
friends…more than friends. Since John Walker was shot, rumors have circulated
that there are plans to assassinate you. I just want you to know that I have had no
part…not myself, not my son…in such plans." He moaned and pounded his fist
into an open palm. "I can't believe it has come to this."

"But it has come to this, Major. Friend has been set against friend; brother
against brother. Rumors have also spread that I am plotting against you. And
who benefits from these rumors? It is high time all such mischievous tales and
fabrications be silenced and the sinister men who delight in raising them should
be exposed. No, Major, you are an honorable man. Never would I believe such
thoughts originated with you."

The Ridge's shoulders sagged with relief. "I'm glad to hear you say that, Little
John." He looked at Ross with hope. "Is there any way we can bring our people
back together?"

Ross was evasive. "I sincerely hope so. The general welfare of our suffering
people requires it."

"I agree," said Ridge, "but how to secure the general welfare of our people
seems to be where the road forks…"

From the south lane, which led to the river road, a single horseman
approached. He dismounted, handed the bridle reins to one of Ross's slaves, and
removed his hat. It was Samuel Worcester.

Ross greeted him without enthusiasm and waved the guest toward a chair. At
his signal a domestic appeared with a pitcher. "Let me offer you a cup of cold
water, preacher." As Worcester drank, Ross continued. "What brings you so far
south, Reverend? I understand you are living at Brainerd now."

"That is true," replied Worcester. "There, I am beyond the jurisdiction of
Georgia, thanks be to God."

"It seems your god's power works only for the white man these days."

Worcester noted the caustic tone. "Your people certainly must think so.
Church attendance has declined sharply."

Ross stood and paced the porch. "And why wouldn't it decline, Reverend?
When the missionaries first came they promised the Cherokee that the surest way
to save their country was to become civilized and Christianized…to give up our
heathen ways and join mission churches. Now your board no longer defends our

rights. The missions at Hightower, Haweis, and New Echota have all been closed. My people feel that they have been abandoned."

"I can understand your sense of outrage, Chief Ross, but you should be aware that I myself was forced to leave the mission premises at New Echota. If we close a mission, the Cherokees feel betrayed; if we open a new one the United States government feels we are attempting to undermine it."

"But you lose nothing, Reverend Worcester. When you close a mission the federal government offers you remuneration…but the reimbursement comes from the funds due the Cherokee." Ross ceased his pacing. "I'm sorry for my outburst, Reverend, but you must understand that we are hanging on by our fingernails. Now, what was it that brought you to Head of Coosa?"

"If at all possible, Chief Ross, I would like to make use of your printing press. There are many hymns and much of the New Testament yet to be printed. I would, of course, pay for the privilege…"

"The press is no longer functioning. The Cherokee Phoenix ceased publication last May."

"But the Bible…we must print the Bible in the language of your people."

"Ah, yes, the Bible. When the white man came, he had the Bible and we had the land. Now, we have the Bible and he has the land. Do you consider that a fair trade, Reverend?"

✳   ✳   ✳   ✳

In the dark, frosty, October sky a star with a tail of fire held the Indians transfixed. Many clustered around the ada'wehi' seeking reassurance. The medicine man withdrew into the forest to build a small fire with wood that had been struck by lightning. At dawn he faced the east, held up tobacco in his left hand, recited a formula while kneading the tobacco in a counterclockwise direction with four fingers of his right hand. After blowing his breath across the tobacco, he added some spittle, then smoked the ancient tobacco. He held the smoke long in his lungs, rolled his eyes, then nodded…yes, the star was a bad omen.

In his report to the General Council Chief Ross had little new to offer. Speaking through an interpreter, which was his custom, he reported: "Owing to the peculiar situation in which our public affairs are placed by the position taken by the President of the United States, there is no alternative left the nation at present but to persevere in the peaceable course of asserting and maintaining our clearly acknowledged rights where we are, or to surrender them at discretion and remove west of the Mississippi."

Elias Boudinot, urbane, handsome, and articulate, rose to challenge Ross. "The peculiar situation of our people, of which Chief Ross speaks, cannot be relieved by a continued application to the federal government for redress under the treaties and laws of the United States. An arrangement with the government, by a general treaty, is the only remedy that can be applied to relieve the Cherokees. If we are to preserve the Cherokee people, if we are to relieve the increasing difficulties pressing upon us, we must flee the white man as we would a pestilence. We must have a speedy remedy…and that remedy is to make a treaty…and to treat is to sell the land."

A rumble of dissent rolled across the council.

"You disagree with Mr. Boudinot because of your ignorance." It was young John Ridge on his feet. "You are so ignorant because Chief Ross refused to let Boudinot provide you with accurate information on which you could make an intelligent decision. Thus the most educated and enlightened editor of The Cherokee Phoenix you will ever have, was forced to resign. Chief Ross himself, who, according to the requirements of our Constitution is serving illegally, has repeatedly refused to convey the truth to you. Look about you. What do you see? Our property is being confiscated, our women violated, our rights trampled. Who is there to protect you? No one! Chief Ross would have you ignore reality. President Jackson has offered a generous treaty…three million dollars for our lands and promises of comparable lands west of the Mississippi on which we can live in autonomy. Unless we remove from this place, we will not survive as a people."

His remarks were met with stony silence. Many, who had never been away from their mountains, could not conceive of starting life afresh in a distant and strange country. Perhaps the immortals, who dwelt in the forested mountain peaks, would still save them.

Thomas Foreman, a fiery opponent of removal, took the floor. Looking directly at John Ridge, he said, "It is not Chief Ross who bears the blame for our condition; it is your father, Major Ridge. He went to Washington with Andrew Ross to secure a treaty of removal. He is a traitor and an enemy of the Cherokee people. Once he went around our nation, making speeches, telling people to love the land. In his earnestness he stamped the ground. The ground is yet sunk where he stamped but now he talks another way."

Young Ridge lashed out against the attack on his father. "Major Ridge has with distinguished zeal and ability served his country. When he saw that it was on the precipice of ruin, ready to tumble down, he told the people of their danger. Did he tell the truth or not? Let every man here look at our circumstances and judge for himself. Is a man to be denounced for his opinions? If a man saw a cloud charged with rain, thunder, and storm and urged the people to take cover...is that man to be hated or respected?"

Then the old Major rose to defend himself. With calmness and dignity he spoke. "I do not have the vanity to hope for honors in my declining years. The sun of my existence is going down. It is now low and I have but a short time to live. It may be that Foreman has better expectations and, by slandering men, can establish his fame among you. But I have no expectation that he will enjoy it for long, for we have no government. It is entirely suppressed. Where are our laws? The seats of our judges are overturned." He turned a full circle, slowly, and looked at the council members. "When I look upon you all, I hear you laugh at me. When harsh words are uttered by men who know better, I feel oppressed with sorrow. I mourn over our calamity."

An unsympathetic Elijah Hicks chose this moment to speak. "I have here a petition, signed by 144 Cherokees from six districts. The petition requests that the Ridges, along with David Vann, be impeached for maintaining opinions and a policy to terminate the existence of the Cherokee community on the land of their fathers."

After deliberation, the council concluded that the accused were guilty as charged and voted that they be removed from office.

Amid the tension, all eyes turned to Ross as he stood. "It grieves me deeply that it has come to this. Jackson's strategy to divide and conquer has brought about a rift with my own brother. It has deprived me of old and deeply treasured friendships. It has brought bitterness and division to our people.

"John Ridge may consider my status as illegal, yet he knows, as do all of you, that the Council decided to suspend all elections when Georgia deprived us of our government, until we could fully and freely exercise our rights once again.

"As to President Jackson...yes, he did offer three million dollars for our lands...and I rejected his offer because I do not consider it an adequate, much less generous, offer. Certainly, the United States government will make a treaty with us. They have made many such treaties. Name one which they have kept. We are in our present predicament precisely because the federal government will not fulfill its obligations under existing treaties."

With a quiet gaze Ross swept across the council members facing him. "Let me leave you with this one last thought. Is there anyone here so naïve, so childishly trusting, who believes that if we agree to removal that it will sate the white man's lust for land? Is there anyone who believes that the United States will fulfill a treaty elsewhere if it will not enforce one here?"

The council meeting ended on November 3, 1834. In December the sun at high noon was darkened. Birds grew silent, dogs howled, and horses whinnied and pawed the earth. When the eclipse was followed by a winter of severe cold and heavy snow, a feeling of impending doom descended upon the Cherokee.

CHAPTER 23

AT THE MERCY OF WOLVES

The President leaned back in his chair, watched the January snow falling softly outside the south window of the White House, and smoked his pipe with contentment.

"So, Cass, we finally have some Cherokees who will sign a treaty."

"Yes, Mr. President. A group led by John Ridge is ready to deal."

"Never in my life did I countenance making treaties with those red heathen but, in this case, I'm happy to make an exception."

The President sucked noisily on his pipe then turned to his Secretary of War. "I don't want anything to blow this opportunity, Cass. Who can we trust to get this treaty nailed down?"

"Why not use John Schermerhorn? He was quite helpful in getting a removal treaty with the Seminoles."

Jackson chuckled and nodded his approval. "The Right Reverend Schermerhorn from Utica, New York...what better choice than an ambitious, renegade preacher. We can always tell our critics that we have a Christian negotiating with the Cherokee. See that he gets to work on it right away."

"I think you should know that John Ross and his delegation are also in town. Ross is scared that you will deal with John Ridge so now he wants to make a treaty proposal himself. I think we should hear what Ross has to say. He may be ready to cede more now that he knows Ridge wants to dicker."

Jackson knocked the ashes from his pipe. "I don't like Ross...don't trust him. He's not a real Indian. Why, he's got as much Scotch blood in him as I do. He's just a greedy little potentate who cares nothing about the welfare of his people." He paused for a moment. "Alright, hold up on Schermerhorn until we hear what Ross has to say."

✳   ✳   ✳   ✳

As Ross and members of the Cherokee delegation were ushered into the President's office, Jackson stood, shook hands, and showed his adversary every respect and courtesy.

"May I say, Mr. President, how relieved we are that no harm came to you at the hands of Richard Lawrence," said Ross.

Jackson gave a sardonic chuckle. "That poor dumb sunuvabitch...has two pistols pointed at my chest and they both misfire. The man's a lunatic."

Waving them to chairs, he looked to Ross. "I understand you have some new proposals regarding your people. I'd be interested in hearing them."

"Upon what terms, Mr. President, will you negotiate for a final termination of these sufferings?"

"You already know my answer to that...total removal."

"Please reconsider, Mr. President. I propose, on behalf of the Cherokee Nation, to cede to the United States, for the use of Georgia, an extensive portion of our territory lying within the charter limits of Georgia, and reserve to our people only a fractional part bordering on Tennessee and Alabama, so as to unite our people living in that area."

Jackson rubbed his chin thoughtfully. "You know very well that Governor Lumpkin would never agree to such an arrangement."

Ross paused. He was about to make a serious cession. "We would be willing to become citizens of the states. Would not such a community of the aboriginal descendants of this continent then be worthy of that common privilege which has been graciously conferred on the outcasts of the European shores?"

Jackson stared blankly for a few moments. Was Ross referring to him as a European outcast? "I'm sorry, Ross. Nothing short of an entire removal is acceptable."

Ross swallowed hard. "In that case, Mr. President, we would insist that your government pay us twenty million dollars for our lands, plus reimbursement for all losses sustained by violations of the United States of former treaties."

Jackson leaned forward, ice in his blue eyes and voice. "Such demands are entirely preposterous and totally unacceptable. I will not be trifled with, sir. I thought you were here to make a sincere offer."

"I am sincere, Mr. President. I came to work out a reasonable solution to our problems. You have always assured us that you would conclude a treaty with us on terms as liberal as any the Senate might offer. Let us do just that."

Jackson quietly studied Ross. He knew, as did Ross, that his relations with the Senate were precarious. But, he had a far greater understanding of the American commit-ment to acquisitive scramble. "Alright, Mr. Ross, I accept your offer. I'll go as far as the Senate."

Ross and his delegation returned to Brown's Hotel confident that Jackson's enemies in the Senate would provide highly acceptable terms to the Cherokee. The Senate Committee on Indian Affairs, chaired by John P. King of Georgia, gave the idea of twenty million dollars for Cherokee lands short shrift. In less than a week, Ross was informed by Secretary of War, Lewis Cass, that the Senate was not prepared to offer more than five million dollars for Cherokee lands.

*   *   *   *

"Well, Chief Ross, you gambled and lost."

Not answering, Ross stared gloomily out the window of his room in Brown's Hotel. Getting no response, Hanks continued. "It looks like the Ridge group has the inside track. If the War Department has decided to deal with them on a treaty, what can we do about it?"

Ross roused himself and grabbed his coat. "I understand Benito Ramirez is in town. I'll be making a call on him."

Reading his mind, Hanks cautioned. "Don't go do something hasty and fool-ish."

"What could be more foolish than trusting in the United States government?" Ross replied. "Ramirez has offered us land before. Now may be the perfect time to explore the idea of settling a colony there under Mexico's jurisdiction."

*   *   *   *

Ramirez tapped the ash from his cigar and rocked back in his chair. "I sympathize completely with your plight, Chief Ross, but moving your people to Mexico at this time might not be advisable."

"But on previous occasions you have encouraged such an idea."

"The situation has changed, my friend. Jackson is still trying to purchase Texas from Mexico. As I sit here, refusing his offer, his friend Sam Houston is in Texas organ-izing for a forceful takeover. I am convinced they are, how do you say it, in cahoots. But President Santa Anna has no intention of letting that happen. Nor will he permit the continuance of slavery among the Americans who have settled in Texas. So you see, relations between my country and the United States are not good."

"If, by any chance," Ross countered, "Texas were to be purchased by the United States, there would be an immediate clamor in the South to extend slavery into that territory, but I do not believe the North would permit that to happen"

"I would hope that you are right, Chief Ross. I see the question of slavery hanging like a dark cloud over this country. President Adams was correct when he called it the great and foul stain upon the American union."

*   *   *   *

On March 7, Secretary of War Cass informed Ross that intercourse in writing between them was closed. After making a final and futile round of protests to Cass about entering into a treaty with unauthorized Cherokees, Ross departed Washington in early March.

Jackson now directed Schermerhorn to reopen negotiations with the Ridge party and on March 14, 1835 a "draft treaty" was signed. Schermerhorn, large, flamboyant, crafty, with a bullhorn voice, acted on behalf of the United States. John Ridge and Elias Boudinot signed for the Cherokee. Congress and American newspapers were giddy over the acquisition of such staggering proportions. Seven million acres of choice land would now be open to speculators. It would be a financial bailout for the economy. But Congress would not ratify the treaty until it had been endorsed by the Cherokee people.

*   *   *   *

The warm April air was heavy with the scent of wild plum blossoms. In the distance Ross could hear the quiet gurgle of the Etowah and Oostanaula Rivers, as they joined to form the Coosa. He trusted his horse as the dirt road glimmered only faintly in the starlight. Tired and road-weary, he reached his home at Head of Coosa about ten o'clock at night. Handing the reins of his horse to a sleepy slave, he entered the living room where a single lamp was shining. Expecting the children to be in bed and Quatie waiting up, Ross was shocked to see a large man, smoking a pipe and sitting in his favorite chair.

"Come in, Ross. Heard you were comin' so thought I'd wait up for you."

Ross peered hard in the gloom. "Who are you and what are you doing in my house...and where is my family?"

"Figgered you ain't heard." The man stood and fumbled a crumpled paper out of his pocket and handed it to Ross. "This says this house is mine...you don't own it anymore."

By the dim light of the lamp Ross could see that the paper was signed March 17, 1835 by William N. Bishop, agent for the state of Georgia, conveying right of occupancy to Virgil Brill.

Ross placed the paper on the table. "Brill..." he murmured. "I remember that name from the Battle of Horseshoe Bend."

"You should remember it from Cedar Creek five years ago when yer fuckin' friend Ridge turned me out of my house and burned it down."

"Where is my family? What has happened to them?"

Brill jerked a thumb over his shoulder. "Out there in one of them slave cabins. You can spend the night but come mornin' haul ass and git...you and all your kin."

Next morning Ross visited his father's grave under the huge live oak tree and gazed out over the fields and orchards. Then he loaded his bewildered family, wife Quatie, his four sons, James, Allen, Silas, George, and his daughter, Jane, and a few possessions into a wagon and headed north.

"Are we going back to our old home in Rossville?" Quatie asked.

"No, brother Andrew has taken over the old place. Besides, the old home place is in Georgia. I need to get away from the jurisdiction of the Georgia Guard."

Quatie looked back, tears streaming down her cheeks. "Oh, John...what is to become of us? Is there nothing we can do?"

Ross reached to put an arm around her. "No, my dear, there is nothing to be done. We are at the mercy of wolves." Grim lines formed at the corners of his eyes. "What you are witnessing is probably the greatest transgression in history of a so-called civilized nation upon a helpless people. Somehow, we must outlive the Jackson administration."

Two days later, crossing the Georgia line into Tennessee, he settled into a rough-hewn log cabin of two rooms located a half-mile south of Flint Springs. He would suffer along with his people. Here in a small valley on the east side of Blue Springs Ridge, he was not far from the Red Clay Council Ground.

On the morning of April 7 Ross was surprised by a visit from Samuel Worcester.

"I have come to say goodbye, Chief Ross. Tomorrow my wife and I will load our children in a wagon and leave for the Cherokee Nation in the west to continue my work for God. Before I left, I wanted you to know that I harbor no ill feelings toward you. It is my unceasing prayer that the transgressions of my countrymen toward the Cherokee will be forgiven."

Touched by Worcester's words, Ross responded. "I have no conscious feelings of vindictiveness toward you, Reverend. May God give you a safe journey."

✻   ✻   ✻   ✻

Nearly a thousand Cherokees assembled at the Red Clay Council Ground on May 11. Jackson's old crony, former congressman Benjamin F. Currey, who Jackson had appointed Superintendent of Indian Removal, accompanied the Ridge party.

When finally recognized by Council, John Ridge vigorously launched into extol-ling the virtues of the proposed treaty. His words were met with stony silence. When he sat down, ancient White Path tottered to his feet.

"When I step in cow shit, I do not pretend it is sorghum molasses. John Ridge, you have stepped in it."

Ross hid a smile at the old chief's uncommon bluntness. The next person that rose to speak was the hotheaded, much feared Tom Foreman.

In August of 1834, John Walker, Jr. was returning to his home after a heated dispute with the Ross followers at Red Clay. Walker was a member of one of the most prominent Cherokee families. His father, Major John Walker, had distinguished himself at the Battle of Horseshoe Bend and had laid out a town on the north side of the Hiwassee River, which he named Calhoun in honor of the Secretary of War. But his son, John, Jr. strongly favored removal. A mile west of

Muskrat Springs on the Cleveland-Spring Place Road, he was ambushed. James Foreman, cousin of the tempestuous Tom, was indicted for the shooting but, after a full investigation, the Tennessee Supreme Court decided that the criminal laws of the state did not extend over the affairs of the Cherokee Nation. James Foreman was allowed to go free.

"How fortunate we are to be instructed on what is good for us by the erudite Mr. Ridge," Foreman sneered. "And to be honored by the presence of Major Currey...We have a remedy in our laws for those who illegally deal away our lands. We know how to deal with those bought by the State of Georgia."

Foreman's words released a wave of pent up fury in the Council directed against the Ridge faction. Ross quickly rose to calm the members and deflect their rage. When cooler heads prevailed, the assembly still refused to consider Ridge's proposal and passed a resolution condemning those who had agreed to it. Chagrined at the plummeting of his popularity among the Cherokee, John Ridge withdrew from Red Clay loudly proclaiming that there would be another meeting at his home at Running Waters on the third Monday of July.

In July Ross traveled north to the Cherokee Agency to consult with his brother, Lewis. Contrary to what had happened to him, times had been good to Lewis. His trading business continued to prosper as evidenced by the large, white, two-story house he lived in on Market Street across from the Cherokee Agency. Charleston, Tennessee, home of the agency, was located on the south bank of the Hiwassee River. Across the stream, in the rolling hills on the north bank, stood the town of Calhoun. As dusk settled over the river valley, John and Lewis sat on the veranda, trying to catch a cooling breeze.

"John, why don't you bring your family to live with me? Lord knows, there's plenty of room. There is no need for you and your family to live in squalor."

"If it's good enough for our people, Lewis, it's good enough for me. Now, back to the matter I came to see you about; do you think we should attend the July meeting at Running Waters, or do we boycott it?"

"The federal government will be conducting a census of the Cherokee to determine the allocation of the annuity. Boycott the meeting and they just might rig the count against you."

"I suppose you're right." John fanned himself quietly. "What's your guess regarding the upcoming presidential election?"

"From what I hear, Martin Van Buren is one cagey politician. With Jackson's support, he may be hard to beat."

John nodded. "With three horses in the race, Daniel Webster, William Henry Harrison, and Hugh Lawson White, I suspect the Whigs hope to throw the election into the House as it happened in '24. Jackson is fit to be tied at the support Tennessee is giving White."

"Hello", Lewis interrupted, "someone's coming over from the Agency."

"Well, bless my soul," the man wheezed, "Chief Ross, you're just the man I need to see." In a booming voice the black-coated stranger addressed Lewis.

"Sorry," replied Lewis, "this is the chief. I'm his brother. And who might you be?"

"I'm Reverend John Schermerhorn, specially appointed by President Jackson to finalize a treaty made last March in Washington...just arrived here to day."

Not bothering to rise, John Ross crisply replied, "There is no treaty to finalize, Rev. Schermerhorn."

"Well, the president thinks there is. With his blessing, I negotiated a very generous treaty with some of your finest people, John Ridge and Elias Boudinot."

"I repeat, Reverend, there is no treaty. Neither Boudinot nor Ridge hold an elected office in the Cherokee Council and are not authorized to negotiate anything."

Somewhat deflated, Schermerhorn persisted. "Brother Ross, let it not be said that you rejected what you have not heard. In the name of Christian fairness, I beg you, at least let me present to your people the proposals included in the treaty."

Ross studied Schermerhorn for a moment. The best way to convince this repulsive man of the Cherokee's true stance was to let him meet with them. "Alright, Reverend, I will take pleasure in inviting the most influential chiefs of our nation to hear you out."

$$*\qquad *\qquad *\qquad *$$

The rain poured down relentlessly, but still they came. Across swollen streams and up the muddy trails leading to the meeting ground near John Ridge's home, some four thousand Cherokees collected, men, women, and children. In a quiet line, one by one, the men passed by to greet their chief. Seeing his wet, half-clad, starving people, Ross let his tears mix with the rain. His heart swelled with pride at the suffering his people were enduring to preserve their homeland.

On the morning of July 19th the meeting, called by John Ridge, began with prayers by David Watie and John Huss. In the distance, the sound of fife and drums could be heard from the camp of the Georgia Guard. Mr. Currey had taken precautions.

In the opening speech, Currey aimed his remarks at Ross. "You are here to decide how the annuity of the Cherokees will be divided. Regardless of your vote, I take this occasion to say, you cannot save your country. Your chiefs are still disposed to delude you even when ruin is demanding entrance at your door. Why is this so?"

Following Currey, the loquacious Schermerhorn seized the floor. "Let each faction name delegates to meet with me and Governor Carroll at the Cherokee Agency on the 30th of this month and we will work out a treaty."

On July 29 John and Major Ridge, with twenty in their party, rode into the Cherokee Agency at Charleston to meet with Schermerhorn. Ross and his men failed to appear. The next day a messenger informed the Ridges that the chief was ill but Ross welcomed the opportunity to meet with them elsewhere to settle all difficulties providing that the meeting comprise only Cherokees. It was more than merely stalling tactics. Ross was deeply depressed upon learning about the death of the best friend the Cherokees had in Washington. Chief Justice John Marshall had died at six o'clock on the evening of July 6. Polly's locket was around his neck to the end.

In August the breach between Ross and the Ridge faction widened. Schermerhorn, determined to secure approval of his proposed treaty, suggested that fliers be printed on the press of the Cherokee Phoenix and distributed to all Cherokees. When Ross got wind of the scheme, he immediately dispatched Peter Hilderbrand with wagon and team to New Echota to secure the press. Unfortunately, a mounted detachment of the Georgia Guard, led by Boudinot's brother, Stand Watie, beat Ross's wagons to New Echota by a scant two hours. The print shop, which had been moved to the home of Elijah Hicks, was emptied of press, type, and bindery and hauled to Spring Place where it was held under the custody of Watie.

Ross protested the seizure to Currey but to no avail. Currey argued that Elias Boudinot had originally purchased the press with voluntary contributions from citizens of the United States and that the press was merely being restored to its original owner.

The Cherokee Phoenix was never revived. Some fliers advocating removal were printed but Ridge knew full well that a newspaper, to be successful, must reflect the interests of its readers.

In September, acting as if a treaty had already been signed, United States officials sent census takers into the Cherokee Nation. Ross immediately dispatched letters to the district chiefs advising that no one was to give the agents any information regarding families.

On September 29, as Ross was preparing for, perhaps, the most important council meeting in Cherokee history, an unexpected visitor rode up to his tiny, log hut at Red Clay. The stranger alit, doffed his hat with a flourish, bowed and in a melodious voice said, "Chief Ross, may I present myself? I am John Howard Payne. I have a letter of introduction from Colonel Samuel Blackwell, your former legal counsel."

Ross shook hands, took the letter and invited Payne to sit. "Payne? Payne? I've heard that name somewhere…"

Payne smiled. "Have you ever heard the song, 'Home Sweet Home'? I wrote it."

"Ah, yes, and what brings a song writer to these parts, Mr. Payne?"

"Chief Ross, I have been abroad for some years. I came home with visions of starting a new journal that would be published in London but would feature the wonders and ideals of this country. I knew little of Cherokees and their embattled condition until very recently. I am now considering writing a history of your people before they are ex-tinguished. I have been told that you possess documents that would be helpful in writing such a history."

Ross studied the narrow, bearded face of his visitor. The seriousness of his demeanor was impressive. "I wince at the suggestion that my race might be extinguished, Mr. Payne. I do not contemplate such a fate. I would be very pleased to have such a history written by an objective person as yourself. If you can accept these humble accommodations, you are welcome to stay."

✳   ✳   ✳   ✳

Payne was awakened by a muted noise. He stepped out into the crisp, October air. Emerging from the trees, now gorgeously tinted with departing foliage, he saw a long and orderly procession of Cherokees. He watched, fascinated, as the Cherokee halted at the humble gate of their chief who stood ready to receive them. They formed diagonally in two lines and each, in silence, drew near to give his hand to Ross. Their dress was neat yet picturesque; all wore turbans, except four or five with hats. Many of them had tunics tied with sashes; some wore long robes and nearly all some drapery. It reminded Payne of the patriarchs in the old scriptures.

Salutations over, the old men remained near their chief. The rest withdrew, some to sit Turk fashion against the trees and on logs. All fixed their eyes on Ross, anxiously awaiting his comments. After Ross finished explaining what Schermerhorn would likely present at the council meeting, White Path spoke a few words. The group then picked up cups, blankets, and packs and left for the Red Clay Council Grounds.

"They certainly gave you their undivided attention, Chief Ross."

"Some of these people walked sixty miles since yesterday and camped in the woods last night. It gets your attention, Mr. Payne, when your homes, property, and freedom are being taken from you."

*   *   *   *

To the council Ross reported on the loss of the Phoenix printing press. "The manner of the seizure of the press could not have been sanctioned for any other purpose than to stifle the voice of the Cherokee people and that the ear of humanity might thereby be prevented from hearing. But let us be united and leave a character on the page of history that will never dishonor the name of the Cherokee nation."

During the days of deliberation that followed, Payne roamed freely among the attendees, interviewing members of the Ross party and the Ridge faction. On the Sabbath, as the council recessed to hear an Indian preacher, he struck up a conversation with Rev. Elizur Butler who had come over from Brainerd. Discovering that Butler had been imprisoned with Rev. Worcester at Milledgeville, Payne asked, "Rev. Worcester has moved across the Mississippi to the Cherokees in the west. Yet you chose to remain here. Why?"

"If you are witnessing an immoral act against innocent people, one cannot be silent. I could not, in good conscience, desert these people. They are so dear to my heart. Brother Worcester did what he thought was right; I am doing what I think is right. Time alone will judge the wisdom of our choices."

Payne quietly considered Butler's comments then offered, "For the past twenty years I have lived in London and Paris pursuing fame and fortune and finding little of either. I wrote an opera for which I was paid fifty pounds. For the song, Home Sweet Home, which was featured in the opera, I received not a penny. But, in good times or bad, never did I feel shame for any actions of my country, not until now."

*   *   *   *

Outside a savage November rain hammered on the tiny cabin's shake roof. Inside, as the clock ticked toward midnight, Ross and Payne basked in the warmth of the fireplace. Ross, reading the Knoxville Register, commented. "This is an excellent article, Mr. Payne, one that should stir everyone's sense of justice."

Payne put down his pen. "Give credit to Rev. Butler. He reminded me that one with a conscience should not be silent."

Ross put down his paper. "What are those dogs barking about at this time of night? Sounds like riders..."

Before he could rise from his chair, the door burst open. Armed men, with bayonets fixed, poured into the room.

"What's the meaning of this?" Ross demanded. "Who are you and why are you breaking into my house?"

"Never you mind the questions, chief. You are under arrest...you and your abolitionist friend."

"It's Brill, isn't it?" Ross asked. What are you and your Georgia Guard doing in Tennessee? You have no authority here."

"Authority be damned. You and your nigger lovin' friend are gonna be taught a lesson. Get your coats...you're takin' a ride."

Gathering up all the papers that were laid out on the table, the guard thrust Ross and Payne out the door into the driving rain. On horseback, through mud and storm, they headed south. In the darkness one of the guards started humming a tune.

"Know the name of that song, soldier?" Payne asked.

"The name's Captain Absalom Bishop...and hell no, I don't know the name of the song. Why should I?"

"It's Home Sweet Home. I wrote it."

"And I'm the queen of Sheba," Bishop snorted. "We hang liars like you in Georgia."

Twenty-four miles later, as the gray dawn was breaking, Ross determined that they were approaching Spring Place. Drenched, muddy, and cold Ross and Payne were shoved into an improvised cell in the basement of a slave house. "Welcome to Camp Benton," Brill laughed.

Days passed, broken only from time to time by threats and interrogations. One day as Payne stood looking through the bars, across the fields to the Vann House, he con-fided. "You know, this is not the first time I've been imprisoned. Back in 1820 I defaulted on a loan and was thrown into Fleet Street Prison in London. Through luck, and the assistance of my good friend, Washington Irving, I got out of that predicament."

"A friend in need is a friend indeed, to quote an old saw," smiled Ross.

"Yes, Irving was a friend...in spite of the fact that a fair maiden in London told me she preferred him to me."

"Ah, the romantic Payne...a side of you I've never seen. Have you ever been married?"

Payne turned from the window and shook his head. "I am an incurable romantic, Chief Ross. Before I met up with you, I was the guest in the home of General Harden in Athens, Georgia. While there, I lost my heart to his daughter, Mary. Once I get out of this mess, I plan to ask for her hand in marriage."

"But...General Harden's daughter is only eighteen or so. You...you must be in your forties."

Payne chuckled. "Forty-four to be exact. But love knows no age limits, my friend!"

A week after imprisonment Ross was taken from his cell and brought before Col. Bishop, commander of the Georgia Guard. To his surprise, Ross found John Ridge with the colonel.

Bishop tapped some papers on his desk. "Ross, you and your friend are charged with plotting an insurrection...getting the niggers to join with your Indians in an uprising against the whites. You are working as agents for Henry Clay. Your friend is a foreign agent...it's right here in his code...which we ain't broke yet."

Ross looked at the paper. "That's no code, Colonel. That's written in French."

Color rose in Bishop's neck. "This article he wrote for the Knoxville paper is enough for me. I'll leave you alone with Mr. Ridge."

"I'm sorry, Chief Ross, to be so late in getting here," said Ridge. "I was away from home when you were arrested. I certainly don't believe these trumped up charges."

"We both know why I was arrested," Ross replied with coolness. "It's another attempt at intimidation. Currey does not want me to lead another delegation to Washington. Schermerhorn is getting even with Payne, his old enemy from their days at Union College."

"I deny any knowledge of such," said Ridge. "Let me talk with Bishop and see if your release can't be arranged."

On Monday, November 16, Ross, Ridge, and Bishop sat down for dinner and a long conversation. When they finished, to the surprise of Ross, Bishop ordered his release. After being confined for nine days, he was freed along with his papers. Payne was detained another three and a half days then released with threats to his life if he ever returned to Georgia.

*   *   *   *

As the Ross delegation was taking up quarters at Mrs. Arguelles' Boarding House in Washington, Schermerhorn was plunging ahead at New Echota with his scheme for a removal treaty. Success would assure him of a position in the Jackson administration.

On December 22 members of a council, led by Major Ridge, convened at New Echota. Only three or four hundred people trekked into the makeshift council. "I am here," said The Ridge, now in his mid-sixties, "because an intelligent minority has a moral right, indeed a moral duty, to save a blind and ignorant majority from inevitable ruin and destruction. I am one of the native sons of these wild woods. I have hunted the deer and turkey here all my life. I have fought your battles, defended your truth and honesty, and fair trading. But we can no longer remain here in safety and comfort. I know we love the graves of our fathers…We can never forget these homes, I know, but an unbending, iron necessity tells us we must leave them. I would willingly die to preserve them, but any forcible effort to keep them would cost us our lives, our lands, and the lives of our children. There is but one path of safety, one road to future existence as a nation. Make a treaty of cession. Give up these lands and go over beyond the great Father of Waters."

Several of men grunted their approval. With tears in their eyes, they gathered around The Ridge and grasped his hand with respect. "We will follow you to the strange land in the west," they promised.

Boudinot then made a short address to the gathering. "I desire to make this treaty but I know I take my life in my hand when we make and sign this treaty. You, my friends, can then cross the great river but Tom Foreman and his people will put us across the dread river of death. We can die but the great Cherokee Nation will be saved. They will not be annihilated; they can live. Oh, what is a man worth who will not dare to die for his people? Who is there here that would not perish if this great nation may be saved?"

On Tuesday evening, December 29, 1835, the committee of twenty met with Schermerhorn in the parlor of Boudinot's large, two-story, frame home in New Echota. Smoking their pipes in silence, the Cherokee sat around the hearth as the treaty was read once more by candlelight. It was now time to sign the document. On behalf of the United States, Schermerhorn signed in bold letters. No one from the Cherokee delegation volunteered to be the first to sign. Finally, one by one they signed. Nine were literate in English and signed their names. Eleven made their mark as the clock ticked toward midnight. As he made his mark, Major Ridge said softly, "I have signed my death warrant."

CHAPTER 24

BETRAYAL IN THE SENATE

His stomach in knots, Ross crushed the papers in his hand and slumped into a chair. Outside, the cold, February wind moaned, driving sleet and snow against the thin walls of Mrs. Arguelle's Boarding House. Smoke belched from the coal burning stove and hung in the room like a thin fog. Ross waved his friend to a seat in the scantily furnished room.

"Who gave this to you, Jesse?"

"Major Ridge himself. Schermerhorn, Boudinot, and your brother, Andrew, are at the Indian Queen. The Ridge desperately wants us to join him and endorse the treaty."

Ross sighed and shook his head. "We are the only duly authorized delegation from our nation. We will not unite with the Ridge Party and sign their treaty. No, to that we could never give our consent." He leaned back and looked into the broad, serene face of his colleague. Rev. Jesse Bushyhead was the first Cherokee to be ordained by the Baptist missionary, Evan Jones, and the first Cherokee to head his own church. "Wouldn't the old red-head rather be back with his mission work instead of battling politicians in Washington?"

A gentle smile creased the face of Bushyhead. All his life he had been teased about his hair, an inheritance from his grandfather, the English Captain John Stuart. "We Cherokee never make the distinction between religious or political vocations. I will serve my people and my Lord where needed. Right now, I think I'm needed most here."

"Your support is valued more than you know," said Ross. "You say the Commissioner of Indian Affairs no longer recognizes us as the delegated authority from the Cherokees?"

Bushyhead nodded. "He says Jackson will not recognize us because our constitution called for an election in 1832 and one was not held. It's my guess that he feels no need to deal with us since he has a treaty with the Ridge Party."

"All is lost then," Ross sighed, "if the agreements of a few, who arrogate to themselves the power to deal with the rights and liberties, and the future destiny of the Cherokee Nation, are recognized by the Federal government." He spread the crumpled treaty from The Ridge on the table and pressed out the wrinkles. "This is what Jackson has longed for. At last, in spite of all my efforts, he and his minions have succeeded in driving a wedge between our people."

Bushyhead rose and placed his hands over those of Ross. "Look at me, my friend. This is not the John Ross I've known all my life. The John Ross I know has never com-promised and has never quit. All is not lost. The senators who will vote on this treaty are men of conscience. The message you must make them hear is that there is no right way to do a wrong thing."

*   *   *   *

Ross smiled and nodded as he made his way across the crowded, noisy room filled with silken gowns and thrusting bosoms. With the convening of the 24th Congress in December of 1835, the social season in Washington had come to life. Margaret Bayard Smith, leader of Washington society, was noted for her efforts to secure European nobility, ambassadors, and other prominent individuals for her parties. Thus, Ross, leader of the Cherokees, found himself this cold February night of 1836, an invitee to the home of the Smiths. He had learned earlier that a seven o'clock invitation really meant supper at midnight and that the "great folks" came by degree: Senators and Representatives arrived at parties about nine; cabinet members came about ten, and higher ups came at eleven. It was a recognized fact that, in their way, wives of eminent politicians in Washington exerted considerable influence on the political process. This was particularly true of Mrs. Smith.

Ross threaded his way to where a morose Clay sat alone stirring brown sugar into his whiskey.

"My sincere condolence on the loss of your daughter, Mr. Clay."

"Your kinds words are appreciated, Chief Ross. Please sit." He waved to a chair. "Losing Anne was a shocking catastrophe. I could not function; I could not stop weeping. Of all our children, she was the most like me. Her loss made for a sad Christmas." Clay drained his glass and reached for the decanter. "But tell me, Ross, how is your family?"

"Everyone is fine. On my way here I stopped off in Salem to see my daughter, Jane. I have her enrolled at the Moravian Female Academy there."

They sat in silence listening to the chamber music being played by a black quartet. Across the room Ross watched a gray-haired figure, tall, gaunt, and stooped. "I see Senator Calhoun is here alone."

Clay paused to sniff a pinch of fine maccaboy. "Yes, his wife, Floride, refuses to live in Washington as long as Peggy Eaton is here. She can't suffer the woman."

"And where is Mrs. Clay?"

"Back home in Kentucky, running the farm and taking care of Anne's seven children." Clay hesitated then added with a guilty smile, "My wife can't tolerate my obsession with politics."

Ross then posed a question he had been wanting to ask. "What are the chances that the Senate will defeat the proposed treaty of removal?"

"Why are you opposing it? Don't you know it's for your own good?" A wicked smile spread over Clay's thin lips.

"I'm sure it is for our own good," Ross replied in kind, "I see sales by your government of our land will set an all-time high this year."

Clay sobered. "I shouldn't joke, Chief Ross, not when your people are threatened. The margin is slim but we should be able to defeat it. Webster, Calhoun, and I will lead the fight against it. Hugh Lawson White is on Jackson's shit list because White is running against Van Buren for the presidency...so White should oppose the treaty."

"White has given us his promise that he will oppose it," said Ross.

Clay frowned and sipped his drink. "I should caution you, Chief Ross, that in Washington politics nothing is ever certain. There is so much on the Senate agenda right now...war with France, the Texas issue, the debate over expunging the censure of Jackson...with elections coming up this fall, any kind of deals are possible."

"What are the chances of war with France?" asked Ross.

Clay chuckled. "Little to none, my friend. The old bastard snorts war but Jackson will not spend twenty million on a war just to gain five million, which he claims France owes us. You don't see any military or naval build-up, do you?"

"How about Mexico?"

Clay ran his long fingers through thinning, gray hair. "Mexico is a powder keg. Jackson wants Texas so bad he can taste it. He fears Great Britain will gain control there. Beyond that, he knows that Mexico is a major source of gold for this country, a source hard currency people don't want to lose. Jackson's friend in Texas, Sam Houston, keeps nudging us to annex them, but until Texas and Mexico work out their problems, I don't want our country to get involved in a war."

"I understand our friend Crockett went to Texas last November. I'd feel guilty if anything happened to him."

"Why should you feel guilty," Clay snorted, "Crockett is a grown man."

"Crockett lost his seat in the House because he opposed Jackson's policy toward the Cherokee."

"Well, as I said, Crockett can take care of himself. I'd damn sure hate to be the Mexican that tangles with him."

"It is rumored that you will run for the presidency, Senator Clay."

A twisted smile spread across Clay's thin lips. "There's plenty of candidates, Mr. Ross. You have Van Buren of New York…the hand-picked puppet who will jump at Jackson's command. You have Daniel Webster from Massachusetts…but that Yankee can't carry the south. There's Hugh Lawson White from Tennessee…who I don't think is a true Whig…and William Henry Harrison from Indiana Territory…no, this is not the time for me to run."

"Who do you think might win?" Ross asked.

The Kentuckian shook his head. "Anything can happen, Mr. Ross. It is a mistake to presume the public is well informed on any given subject."

"Knowing that you have long coveted that office, I just assumed you would run."

Clay let out a long sigh and crossed his bony legs. "No, I won't run. I'm tired…wore out. I've been rode hard and put away wet too many times. I'd gladly leave the Senate and return to the comfort and peace at Ashland but for one thing…the slavery issue. It is my sworn duty to see to it that my country is not torn apart.

*   *   *   *

Angry puffs of smoke rose from the president's pipe. His hands trembled as he laid the April 6 copy of the Charleston Courier on his desk. Tapping the front page with his finger, he vented his anger. "Godammit, Blair, this is not good news, not good at all. Events have moved too far, too fast. Good Americans were massacred at some place called the Alamo."

"They knew the risks," was Blair's laconic reply.

"By the eternal, Americans have the right to move where they want to move."

"The Mexicans probably don't share your sentiments."

Jackson ran his fingers through his stiff, gray hair. "I feel like Texas is slipping away. Declaring her independence was brash and premature. Is Houston getting us into a war with Mexico?"

"We won't know until we receive the next dispatch from him."

Jackson sighed, put aside his pipe and painfully rose from his chair. Opening a south window he breathed in the warm air. Outside the snow-white petals on dogwood trees glistened in the sun and the redbud trees where showing pink. "You know, Blair, days like these make me long for The Hermitage, watching horse races and cock fights. Sometimes the burdens of the presidency are too much for one man." After a moment, he turned to Blair. "This Alamo thing will set off a firestorm with the public demanding revenge. John Quincy Adams will claim it is just a ruse to extend slavery into Texas."

Blair nodded. "He will say you are the one courting war with Mexico."

Jackson shook his head. "The public will be howling for war, bygod, but what they don't know is that we ain't prepared for war with Mexico…not in the least. Old Fuss and Feathers Scott is sucking up all our money trying to whip the Seminoles in Florida…and I can't even persuade Congress to cough up enough money to reinforce General Gaines at Nacogdoches." He left the window and shuffled wearily back to his desk. "None of this bodes good for Van Buren's election."

"I'm still putting my money on him," said Blair.

"By the eternal, if you don't want to lose your money, you'd better use The Globe to good effect. But don't let your newspaper get the Texas thing tangled up with the slavery issue. I still want Texas but it must be done without stirring up the abolitionists."

*   *   *   *

During the next few weeks Ross worked feverishly contacting individual senators. On March 8 he sent a lengthy memorial to the senate detailing the illegitimate events to which the Cherokees had been subjected. Annexed to the memorial were over seventy documents which supported his claims.

Ross contacted Calhoun, counting on his hatred for Jackson to be stronger than his antipathy for the Cherokees. The tall, gaunt South Carolinian assured Ross of his opposition to the treaty of removal.

The St. Charles Hotel, located at 3rd Street and Pennsylvania, had housed some of Washington's great: Jackson, Clay, Calhoun, Webster, and Van Buren. Since senators had no office space, much business was conducted in local hotels and taverns. Ross found Webster there. Dressed in frock coat and tight pantaloons, the aloof and austere Webster was dining alone. From beneath bushy eyebrows, his dark, penetrating eyes assessed a haggard Ross.

"From your appearance, Chief Ross, I'd say you needed a good drink. May I pour one for you?"

Ross shook his head and slumped into a chair.

"Then you won't mind if I freshen mine. As our good friend, Chief Justice Marshall used to say, wine is the elixir of life, capable of prolonging your days on this earth."

"I miss the old gentleman just as I miss the wise counsel of Mr. Wirt," said Ross.

"As do I. Both good friends, both good Federalists." Webster finished off a piece of chicken, leaned back in his chair, and studied Ross. "I presume you are concerned about the upcoming vote on the removal treaty."

Ross nodded. "I've talked with every senator who would listen to me, including Clay and Calhoun. They pledge me their support and I wanted to assure myself of yours."

"Senator Calhoun...now there's a man, the ablest one in the Senate. I have high regard for him. You can count on his word."

"And Clay?"

Webster shifted in his chair and crossed his long blucher boots. "Clay and I belong to the same party. Our political ideas are often in harmony...but the fact is, he is no lawyer. He is great before juries, but he is not suited by training or education to speak before the Supreme Court. He is a statesman, a politician of the first rank, and a superb orator...but he is no reasoner."

"Does that mean you doubt him on the treaty issue?"

A slight frown furrowed Webster's broad brow. "Men are nothing, Chief Ross, but principles are everything. The Whigs are worn out and exhausted trying to win justice for the Indians. The Jackson Democrats, no matter where they come from, have no concern for Indian rights. In this case, Clay will stand on principle."

A pause for a sip of wine and Webster added plaintively, "In past elections, I have supported Clay in his bid for the presidency. But he has never reciprocated in my efforts for that high office. I must frankly admit, I do not like the man."

Ross sat silently, assessing Webster's comments. "And how goes your campaign for the presidency, Senator?"

Webster refilled his glass then settled back in his chair. "As I grow older, I rely more and more on the food of the Greek and Roman gods to get me through the day. Now, as to the campaign…" A wry smile formed on his lips. "Chief Ross, I was born in the rocky hill country of New Hampshire. My family was as poor as the soil we tilled. For some reason, my father, Ebenezer, picked me out of all his sons and saw to it that I had an education. He wanted me to have a public career that was denied him. I have worked diligently to be worthy of his trust. When the good Whigs of Massachusetts nominated me for the presidency, I felt I had near reached the pinnacle of my career. But I must tell you, my friend, that feeling of ebullience has now so far vanished that I have considered withdrawing from the presidential race and resigning from congress."

Ross, deeply puzzled, interrupted. "But, Senator, how can that be…?"

"I am a practical man, Ross. Jackson has set himself up as co-equal with the Supreme Court in the interpretation of the Constitution. If the opinions of the President be maintained, there is the end of all law and judicial authority. He has nominated Roger B. Taney to succeed Chief Justice Marshall. I openly stood in opposition to that nomination. When Taney was approved by the Senate, I knew I would now face a court totally out of sympathy to my Federalist views."

Webster signaled for the barmaid to bring more wine before continuing. "For me to count on any voter support from the south or west would be foolhardy. None of those slave owners will trust a Yankee who is already on record saying it is not fit that the land of the Pilgrims should bear the shame of slavery any longer."

If Webster knew that Ross was a slave owner, he didn't acknowledge it. "Slavery has poisoned our commerce, soiled our constitution, and divided our government so greatly that I tremble for the future of our country." Webster paused and smiled at Ross. "Forgive this soliloquy, but I cannot anticipate any glory for me in this place…and without glory, life is not worth possessing."

✳   ✳   ✳   ✳

The morning of Wednesday, May 18, 1836 found William Shorey Coodey, nephew of John Ross, crowded into the domed gallery of the recently remodeled senate chamber. Today, the heated and bitter debates over the Treaty of New Echota that had begun in the Senate on March 7, would be brought to a close. In their rooms at the Indian Queen, Ross and his party nervously awaited the outcome.

To Coodey's left, arrayed in colorful gowns, with carefully coifed hair, sat the perfumed ladies of Washington City and their escorts. Because crowds would jam the Senate floor to hear Clay or Webster, making it almost impossible to get around, by act of the Senate, a third of the gallery had been set aside for the ladies.

Below, on the Senate floor, seated in a high, leather-backed chair, the balding vice-president patiently waited for the Senate to come to order. To his right and left Van Buren was framed by arching, wine-colored drapes which were clutched at the top by a massive, bronze eagle. Above all this hung a portrait of George Washington.

As the Senate proceeded to consider the resolution for ratification of the Cherokee Treaty of Removal, Henry Clay summoned all his oratorical skills in a last valiant effort to reject it. Debate ended, the fate of the Cherokee was now at the mercy of the Senate.

Van Buren, one of the most skillful politicians ever to grace Washington, was not unmindful of the many, strong, religious groups that opposed the treaty, even in his home state of New York. He was also aware that he needed the support of the southern states if he were to have any chance of winning the upcoming presidential election. The division was so close, he might have to cast the deciding vote.

The loyal Jacksonian cleared his throat. "It has been moved that the Senate do advise and consent to the ratification of the treaty between the United States of America and the Cherokee Indians concluded at New Echota, the twenty-ninth of December, one thousand eight hundred and thirty five. The clerk will please call the roll."

The whole number in the Senate was forty-eight; four were absent. For the treaty to be approved a favorable vote of two-thirds of the members present was needed. Coodey, his throat dry, his heart beating rapidly, kept a tally as the states voted. As the votes mounted he was surprised and disturbed to note the number of "yeas" coming from the northern states. New Hampshire and New York were voting in favor of the treaty, but Massachusetts, both senators from Vermont, and Rhode Island opposed it. The vote from Connecticut was split.

Clay, Calhoun, and Webster boldly voted no. When Senator Goldsborough of Maryland voted "yea", a thunderous scowl formed on Webster's brow. Goldsborough had broken his promise. And when Senator Hugh Lawson White of Tennessee voted "yea", Coodey felt the ground slip away beneath him. White had assured the Cherokee delegation that the treaty would be defeated. How could White be party to such betrayal? He lost track of the count.

With voting concluded, a quiet settled over the Senate as Van Buren called upon the clerk to announce the results. The final count stood at 29 yeas and 15 nays.

And thus it was done. On May 18, 1836, by the thinnest of margins, one vote, the Senate had decided that thousands of Cherokees were to be evicted from their ancestral homes and driven beyond the Mississippi!

CHAPTER 25

THE LAST HOPE

The tall, wizened figure stood looking out the south window, sucking on his pipe. Below, his gardener, Jemmy Maher, busily tended the two acre, southeast flower beds. Through the branches of two old weeping willow trees that stood by the gate, Jackson could see boat traffic moving up the Potomac toward Georgetown.

"Boys, it will soon be time to go home…and I'm ready. By the eternal, I did what I said I would do. I paid off the national debt, I killed the national bank, and we finally have the power to remove all Indians west of the Mississippi. Eight year's work has wore me so that I'm too damned weak to stand." With that, he shuffled back to his rocking chair.

"We may have the authority," ventured Secretary of War, Cass, "but our generals don't seem to have the power. The Seminoles continue to baffle Scott and now the Creeks in south Georgia are raising hell."

"Scott," Jackson snorted. "Old Fuss and Feathers couldn't find his ass with both hands much less find those Seminoles. I could teach him a thing or two about fighting Indians."

"Well, in fact, the worst in Florida does seem to be over. Why not reassign Scott to Georgia and let him quell the Creeks led by that crazy Neamathla?"

Jackson nodded. "See that it's done, Cass. And, while you're at it, I want you to send someone to see that the Schermerhorn treaty with the Cherokee is carried out. I want someone who is a match for Ross. I don't trust that bastard."

"General John Wool is available," Cass suggested.

Jackson rocked in his chair and nodded his assent. "And Hanks, I want you to accompany the general. With your knowledge of the Cherokee, you can render valuable assistance to Wool."

"I'm sorry, Mr. President, I cannot accept that assignment."

Jackson grunted. "Be serious, Hanks. This will give you field experience; you'll be in command of troops. It's a great opportunity for your military future."

"I am serious, Mr. President. I cannot accept any assignment that involves removal of the Cherokee people."

Jackson ceased his rocking and fixed an icy gaze on Hanks. "What'n hell's name is wrong with you, boy? Have you lost your mind?"

Hanks cleared his throat. "Mr. President, you and I go back a long way. I've known you since the Battle of Horseshoe Bend. Had the Cherokees not saved your ass that day, you would not be sitting where you are today. But you have forgotten that. Instead of rendering gratitude, your hand has ever been against the Indian…"

"Now hold on, boy. Everything I've done in this administration has been for the welfare of the aborigines."

Hanks snorted. "No one believes that, sir, least of all yourself. What you did promoted the interest of land speculators. You congratulate yourself for having paid off the debts of this nation but you won't acknowledge that you did so through the sale of lands taken from the Indians."

Froth formed around the corners of Jackson's mouth. "Watch your tongue, boy. You don't know a damned thing about how government works."

"But you do know how it works, don't you, Mr. President? No one knows better how to evade the laws of this nation. You know how to skirt around Supreme Court decisions; you know how to ignore legitimate treaties and secure fraudulent ones through disreputable men of the cloth. You've used every deceptive trick in the deck to secure removal of the Indians and now you are playing the only card you have left…the army." Breathing hard, Hanks removed the belt holding his sword and laid them on Jackson's desk. "By the name of the ever-living God, I'll have no part of it. You have my resignation from the army effective immediately."

Trembling with rage, Jackson struggled to his feet and shook a bony finger at Hanks. "In the past any man who addressed me so would have faced me on the field of honor. As Commander in Chief I could have you courtmartialed…" A spasm of coughing rent his frail body. He wiped blood from his lips. "but I owe

THE LAST HOPE   273

you for saving my life at Horseshoe Bend. That debt is now cancelled. Get the hell out of my office. If we ever meet again, I'll shoot you on sight."

*   *   *   *

On a small knoll, from beneath the shade of a huge cedar tree, Ross looked on as Tennessee volunteers labored in the hot September sun constructing a stockade in the vale below. Trees from the surrounding hills were being felled, split with wedges, sharpened on one end, and set in the red clay picket fashion. Inside the stockade, rows of log pens, about sixteen feet square and crudely roofed, were built. Cherokees destined for removal were to be held here at the Old Cherokee Agency at Calhoun on the Hiwassee River. Ross knew that similar stockades were being constructed at Ross's Landing and at Gunter's Landing.

Ross glanced at the sun then nudged his horse toward home. Tonight he was hosting General John Ellis Wool, the man charged with Cherokee removal.

With Lewis Ross presiding, the diners crowded around the kitchen table in the tiny hut for a meal of well-cooked roast beef, kidney beans boiled in meat, hominy, and fried bread. As was the Cherokee custom, neither Ross or his wife, Quatie, sat down to eat with the company. The food was considered to be provided for guests.

"I apologize for the fare, General," said Ross, "the heat and drouth this summer severely damaged our crops."

"Chief Ross, I am a guest at your table…a guest charged with the task of removing you and your people…and yet you apologize?"

Ross smiled. "General, perhaps my motives are self-serving. My people are in the dark regarding the true state of their affairs. I have called a council meeting for the fifteenth to inform them."

"But you are forbidden to hold any such meetings."

"This will be a peaceful, informational meeting. The Ridges and their friends have been invited, and I hope it will suit your convenience to afford us the pleasure of your visit to this council."

Wool reflected for a moment. "I'm sure the President would not approve. Perhaps no good will come of it…and much evil may be possible…but I will accede providing I have the opportunity to address your council."

On Saturday, October 15, 1836 when the Council of the Cherokee Nation met at Red Clay, a military guard of the United States Army was stationed around the grounds.

"Ah, General Wool. Just the man I'm looking for. I'm Wilson Lumpkin, one of the commissioners appointed by President Jackson to execute the removal treaty. If I do say so myself, I have contributed more than any one man in bringing this treaty into existence."

Wool replied with a cool nod. "My pleasure, sir."

"This council ought never to have been permitted. No good can come of it. Ross is still engaged in plans for mischief."

"It was my decision, Mr. Lumpkin."

"I must say, general, I'm somewhat mortified that you have seen fit to throw a military guard around Ross and his ilk. The deference you have shown them I consider humiliating to our government."

"Mr. Lumpkin, I've been a soldier since 1812. In all my years of service, I've never brought embarrassment upon my country."

"Oh, I never intended to imply such, general, "responded a flustered Lumpkin. "The power of the sword is committed to your hand and I am so happy that you are here. A great portion of our citizens are liable to the massacres of the Indians at any moment."

Wool snorted. "Mr. Lumpkin, look at these poor creatures; old men, women, and children. You never saw a more docile, dejected group. No, I don't think you need fear a massacre."

"Don't be deceived by the guile of Ross, General Wool. He is not to be believed or trusted. You and I are here to enforce a treaty. Ross's statement that the treaty was made contrary to the will of the Cherokee people is entitled to no respect or consideration whatsoever. In truth, nineteen-twentieths of the Cherokee are too ignorant and depraved to entitle their opinions to any weight or consideration. I could have executed this treaty myself if I could have had sole control."

"An interesting observation, Mr. Lumpkin."

"Another thing, if you find any Creek hiding out here with the Cherokee, arrest them. And if you find any Cherokee engaged in harboring, concealing, or preventing the apprehension and delivery of such Creeks, arrest them to. No food or clothing are to be furnished to any Indian who refuses to yield to the provisions of this treaty."

Wool leveled a steely gaze at Lumpkin. "Commissioner, I have my orders. I will enforce the treaty. As to your recommendations, I'll reserve the right of judging whether they will be acquiesced in or not. Now, if you'll excuse me…"

Around the council house Cherokees by the hundreds knelt as the Rev. Evan Jones opened the meeting in prayer in Cherokee. Ross then introduced General Wool and invited him to offer comments.

"All of you know why I am here," Wool began. "I am here to enforce the treaty between your people and my government. Let no one mistake it; I will enforce the treaty. I notice that you are short of food and your children cry from hunger. They shiver in the cold. As soon as you enroll to emigrate, I am authorized to provide provisions; food and blankets. Consider carefully. You really have no alternative."

In spite of Wool's comments, the General Council passed a resolution declaring the New Echota pact null and void and unenforceable. Another resolution was passed sending Ross and delegates back to Washington, but they were instructed to first proceed to the Cherokees west of the Mississippi so that the two groups might act in concert to overturn the treaty.

*   *   *   *

How long he had been asleep he could not tell. The fireplace had enveloped him in a downy warmth, lulling him into a deep slumber of exhaustion. Tension had fallen away and aching muscles relaxed as the cold was driven out of his rain-soaked body. He had fought the final, muddy miles to Sequoyah's cabin on Skin Bayou through penetrating rain, wind, and snow. As he slowly opened his eyes, he saw his socks steaming as they dried before the fire. He stirred and removed the blanket his host had draped around his shoulders.

"You press your luck in this November weather, Little John. A spring chicken you're not."

Ross smiled at his host. "For one who has seen over sixty winters, aren't you the one to talk." He stood and stretched. "My mission is too urgent to wait for fair weather."

Sequoyah nodded. "We've heard. The whites can't wait to pick your bones."

"Before you two get into politics, sit and eat." Sequoyah's Sally was a strong-willed wife. "It ain't much and it ain't fancy but it'll stick to your ribs."

As they ate, Ross glanced around the one-room cabin of hand-hewn logs. It was sparsely furnished: a bed covered with Sally's patch-work quilt, an iron-bound wooden chest, a spinning wheel, iron cooking pots hanging at the fireplace, some handmade chairs, and the small table at which they sat.

"When we were forced to leave Illinois Bayou in '29, everything we brought was on a pack horse," explained Sequoyah. "We had to leave behind harness, salt kettles, a whip saw, a spinning wheel, household pots and our ducks and chickens. Sally tried to sell them to a white family with no luck. Why pay for something they knew they would get free."

"The same is happening in Georgia," said Ross. "The whites had to get you out of the way so that Arkansas could be admitted as a state. Which reinforces my argument that if the federal government cannot guarantee our existence in Tennessee and Georgia, it cannot and will not guarantee it anywhere west of the Mississippi. I had hoped we would get a better deal if the Whigs had won in November, but no such luck. The new president, Van Buren, won't dare cross a man who put him in office."

Sequoyah's face crinkled in a smile. "Little John, it matters not which party is elected, the aim of the white man is always the same…to get our land. Now, tell me, what else of interest is happening back east. We get little news out here."

"Well, let's see…President Madison died last June…Harriett Gold Boudinot passed away last August…and Sam Houston was sworn in as president of Texas last October…"

"Well, I'll swan," said Sally. "I'm so sorry to hear about Harriett. She was such a wonderful lady. What happened?"

"She endured considerable suffering. She died shortly after one o'clock in the morning last August 15th. Mr. and Mrs. Northrup, who had come for a visit with their daughter, Sarah, John Ridge's wife, were at her bedside. So were Sally Ridge and her parents, Major and Susanna…as was Elias, of course. They buried her on the little hill west of New Echota."

"How is Elias taking her death?"

"I don't know," admitted Ross. "I haven't see him for some months."

"Not even to offer him your condolence?" pressed Sally.

"No, Sally. Elias and the Ridges are considered traitors to our people."

"Don't be too harsh with him," Sequoyah suggested gently. "He is only doing what he thinks is right. Elias is convinced that the whites will never accept us as equals. Everything I have seen supports his stance."

"But most of us have not given up the fight," Ross responded. "That's why I was sent here. We need your help in our fight; we need the help of all Cherokees here in the west. If we can unite in our struggle, with a strong petition, we still have a chance of Congress overturning the treaty signed at New Echota."

Sequoyah nodded. "Chief John Jolly will call the council into session. We will meet, we will sign the petition, and my signature will head the list."

On December 8 the legislature of the western Cherokees met. Troubled by their recent forced removal from Arkansas, they found common cause with their eastern brethren. But, there was considerable concern that the land assigned to them would be inadequate to comfortably accommodate all the eastern Cherokees should they be removed to it. After several days of quiet deliberations, the Council passed a resolution opposing the "instrument purporting to be a treaty" and appointed a delegation to accompany Ross to Washington. A few days later the party boarded a steamboat at Ft. Smith. Bad weather and ice on the Ohio River delayed their passage and compelled them to travel the Tennessee River route.

Ross arrived at his home near Red Clay in a state of exhaustion. His hopes of resting up before starting for Washington were shattered when a note from his brother, Lewis, warning of his imminent arrest by General Wool's troops if he remained at home. After one night in his own bed, Ross left for Knoxville. Upon arriving he found that road conditions were so deplorable that stage travel was impossible. After purchasing horses, he and his party set off for Washington. They made a stopover in Salem, North Carolina where Ross was reunited with his daughter, Jane, and where the party was warmly received by the sympathetic Moravians. With improved roads, they made it by stage to Washington by February 9th.

Ross lost no time in informing Secretary of War Benjamin Butler of the delegate's arrival and soliciting an interview with Andrew Jackson. An impassioned memorial, signed by members of the western and eastern delegations, was submitted to the Senate and House of Representatives on February 22nd. The memorial was laid on the table.

On the 24th Butler informed them that an interview with President Jackson was not possible, as Jackson did not recognize Ross's party as official representatives of the Cherokee. Undaunted, Ross decided to wait upon the new administration.

*   *   *   *

Dawn broke on March 4, 1837 on a warm and cloudless Washington; a perfect day for an inauguration. At noon two bareheaded figures emerged from the White House into the bright sunshine; one tall, erect, with a shock of white hair. The other, balding and half a head shorter. A weak and ailing president was assisted to his seat in the handsome carriage. Against his doctor's advice, Jackson was determined to attend the inauguration of his chosen, Martin Van Buren.

The elegant phaeton, constructed of oak from the original timber of the frigate, Constitution, had been made in Amherst, Massachusetts and was presented to Jackson by sixty of his admirers. It had one seat, holding two persons, and a high box for the driver in front. The grain of the unpainted wood gleamed with a coat of varnish. A panel on either side featured a representation of "Old Ironsides" under full sail. The phaeton was drawn by General Jackson's four iron-gray carriage horses.

Van Buren, who had spent the night at the White House, seated himself beside Jackson. Led by a small detachment of volunteer mounted dragoons, they made their way through a dense throng of people. Delegates of Cherokee and Pottowatamie Indians were on hand. Beds were at a premium. Hundreds slept in the market house on bundles of hay. Some affluent Bostonians had passed the night in the shaving chairs of a barber shop.

On the east portico of the capital, where a wooden platform had been erected, Jackson witnessed the glorious scene of his political protégé, once rejected by the Senate, being sworn in by his choice for Chief Justice, Roger B. Taney. Taney himself was under attack by the Senate. Clay and Webster were onlookers; Calhoun absented himself.

At noon on March 6, a weak, thin, and weary Jackson bade goodbye to Van Buren at the White House door, climbed into his coach at the north portico and began the thirty day journey to The Hermitage.

*   *   *   *

Through the chilly, morning mist Major Ridge gazed for the last time upon the land he loved so dearly, seemingly unaware of the bedlam that swept around him. Here at Ross's Landing, four hundred and sixty-six members of the Treaty Party were being loaded onto a flotilla of eleven flatboats. So filled with his own misery, the Major ignored the sobs and moans of his people as they settled themselves among the bushels of cornmeal, barrels of flour, and bacon stowed on board. Not a few came docilely, nursing splitting headaches from drowning their sorrows in too much whiskey the night before.

The Major turned and embraced his daughter. Adding to his distress, the dark, charming Cherokee beauty, the pride of his life, would not be departing with him. She had married a young Georgia lawyer named George W. Paschal.

"Goodbye, father. Take care of yourself," said Sally. Overcome with emotion, The Major could only nod his head. She kissed him, walked down the gangplank, mounted her spirited horse, and rode off with her husband.

On March 3, 1837, with the passengers exposed to the wind and cold, the little fleet of open boats cast off for the lands beyond the Mississippi.

*   *   *   *

On the 16th of March the new president, Martin Van Buren, extended his hand and motioned Ross to a chair. "I apologize for the delay in seeing you, Chief Ross, but the transfer from one administration to another sometimes results in turmoil. I hope you understand."

Ross nodded. "Of course, Mr. President. I would not intrude upon your busy schedule except the matter at hand cannot wait. Sir, in your heart you know the Schermerhorn treaty is morally wrong. It is my wish to settle all difficulties by amicable treaty on perfectly reasonable terms. One word from you, Sir, is now enough to save the expense and the inevitable danger which might result from enforcing the treaty. You hold in your hands the equal scales of justice and the power to enforce decisions. All we are asking for is a hearing."

Small, dapper in dress and courtly in manner, Van Buren seated himself. After a colored servant served coffee, he turned and said, "Let me apologize again for the messy remodeling going on. Now, tell me your pressing concerns, Mr. Ross."

"Mr. President, as we speak General Wool is constructing stockades in which to hold my people like cattle...all because of the New Echota Treaty which was never authorized by the Cherokee people. I propose that new negotiations be initiated between my people and the United States government to settle all these issues."

Van Buren brushed the graying tufts of auburn hair that stood out on each side of his balding head. "In what way are the Western Cherokees concerned with these matters?"

"Sir, they fear that should it again become the interest of the United States to remove Cherokees, as it now seems to be with us, and were the president to fail in negotiating a treaty through the proper authorities of the Cherokee Nation, he might resort to the expediency of again picking some individuals among the Cherokee, who assume to themselves the title of chiefs or headmen, and enter into a treaty with them."

Van Buren cupped his chin and thoughtfully stroked it with his fingers. "What you say is of uncommon interest, Mr. Ross. I'll certainly make sure someone looks into the matter."

Realizing the conversation with the inscrutable Van Buren was leading no where, Ross stood to take his leave. Speaking bluntly, he said, "Mr. President, the Cherokee Nation never authorized that spurious compact. They never conferred upon the individuals who signed it any authority to give it their assent. We have never recognized its validity and never can. I leave you with something to think about; what would be the action of your government if the Cherokees do not remove at the expiration of the two year limit?"

Shaken by the prospect, Van Buren promised to get back in touch with Ross in the near future.

A few days later, on March 24th, Ross met with the new Secretary of War. He knew the South Carolinian by reputation. Joel Poinsett was a well-traveled diplomat and statesman. During the nullification crisis he had been the leader of the Unionist Party of South Carolina, thus winning the heart of Jackson. Van Buren had called him from retirement to head up the war department. Ross was not surprised by the reception he received from Poinsett.

The secretary sadly shook his head. "I'm sorry, Chief Ross. The president regards himself bound to carry into effect all the stipulations of the document in question. He does not feel that he can overturn a treaty passed by the Senate. Personally, I do not feel that Van Buren would ever consent to undo anything done by his good friend, Andrew Jackson."

After a brief conversation, Ross stood to depart. "I thank you for your courtesies, Mr. Poinsett. But I must remind you, the ratification of the treaty by your Senate has not impaired our rights. It was the act of one party alone. We shall continue to resist."

*　　*　　*　　*

Clay cocked his boot upon the table and leaned back in his chair, whiskey in hand. Ross had called upon him at Mrs. Handy's boarding house at the corner of Louisiana Avenue and West Sixth Street, a half dozen blocks from the capitol. "I'm not at all surprised at your disappointment in meeting the president. We call him the Mistletoe Politician…he feeds off the life sap of Old Hickory. He is a real enigma…never reveals his true position…he thinks the purpose of language is to obfuscate, not clarify."

"That would seem to mark him as the perfect politician," Ross responded.

Clay laughed. "Van Buren cannot afford to be candid with you, Mr. Ross. He has a great tendency to avoid personal collisions. Let me acquaint you with some facts regarding the current financial crisis of our nation. Due to overproduction, demand and prices for cotton have hit bottom. British investors are withdrawing their capital by the millions. Any available investment capital from the Old Lady of Threadneedle Street will carry interest rates of twenty-five percent or more. Because President Jackson decided that all public lands must be paid for by gold or silver, speculators do not have the money to buy new land nor pay their debts on previous purchases. Banks by the hundreds are closing. Let me be frank with you, Mr. Ross. The treasury is bare. Where my government will find the five million to pay the Cherokee under the Treaty of New Echota is beyond me."

"All the more reason the treaty should be abandoned."

Clay sighed. "I would be deceiving you, my friend, if I offered you hope that the treaty will be reviewed. With the nation in such a financial crisis, the treaty will receive no more attention than a fart in a whirlwind."

*   *   *   *

By the end of May Ross was back in Red Clay calling for a General Council meeting for July 31. To Wilson Lumpkin, who was keeping an eye on Ross, this was cause for his arrest. When General Wool showed up at Red Clay, Ross assumed that he would be put in custody. He was in for a great surprise.

"I wanted you to hear it from me,"said Wool. "I have asked to be relieved of my assignment. The whole scene since I have been in your country has been nothing but a heartrendering one. Everywhere I see white men, hovering like vultures, ready to pounce upon your people and strip them of everything they have.

"I have tried to reason with your people, in vain, as they almost universally oppose the treaty. I have tried to provide food to the hungry but they refuse to accept the offer of provisions for themselves and their families for fear that it would indicate their agreement with the false treaty. Some of them are living on roots and sap from trees. They say the will die before they will leave this country. I salute your people, Chief Ross, for the strength of their convictions. If it were in my power, I would remove your people so that they would never be corrupted by the whites. Disrespect for other races seems to be one of the most deeply rooted sins of my people."

"And I, sir, have nothing but admiration for the character you have exhibited in your stay with us," Ross replied.

"Colonel William Lindsay will replace me. He will, of course, insist upon enforcing the treaty."

*   *   *   *

Ross stretched his arms wide and soaked in the warmth of the sun now burning through the morning mist at Red Clay. He watched as his people, in a peaceful, pastoral scene, dipped water from the blue waters of the limestone spring and moved back to their campfires located at the edge of the arcadian forest. Waking children laughed as they began another day of play. How innocent they were of the life-changing crisis pressing upon them. To the east of the council house, in a grove of oak trees, the elder chiefs were smoking their pipes and talking with the Rev. Evan Jones and Jesse Bushyhead.

The rattle of an approaching stagecoach ended Ross's reverie. As it neared, the driver yelled "whoa", pulled back the reins, and stomped on the brake pole with his right foot, bringing the conveyance to a halt. Two men emerged from the coach, one young, the other middle-aged and toting a heavy valise.

The young man extended his hand to Ross in greeting. "Chief Ross? I'm John Mason, Jr. I have been sent here by my government as a special emissary. And this gentleman is George William Featherstonehaugh, a visitor from England. I hope you do not object to my inviting him along."

"No objection whatsoever," replied Ross as he shook hands with Featherstonehaugh. "And what brings you all the way from England, sir?"

"I'm, a naturalist, Chief Ross. I have come to America to collect samples of native mineral deposits."

"Mr. Ross." It was Mason interrupting. "As I told you, I am a special emissary from the federal government. I need to speak to your people. I'm asking your permission to address them."

"In due time, Mr. Mason. Colonel Lindsay has already informed me of your coming and I assured him that we would receive any communication you may wish to deliver on behalf of President Van Buren."

Featherstonehaugh looked about in amazement. "I've been told by frontiersmen that it's impossible to civilize Indians but these people are well dressed and they speak English better than some whites I've met hereabouts."

Ross chuckled. "Come along, sir. Let's have some breakfast then there's someone here you should meet."

Featherstonehaugh's jaw dropped when he was introduced to Rev. Jones. "By jove, you are an Englishman, sir. I can tell by your accent."

"Quite close. I was born in Wales," responded Jones.

"It's the likes of Rev. Jones that helped my people make the strides you've noticed," Ross grinned. "I say that even though he is a Baptist."

"A Baptist?" Featherstonehaugh repeated.

"As a youngster I was a member of the Anglican Church," explained Jones. "When I married I became a Methodist. In '21 we came to Philadelphia to join some Welch relatives. That's when I joined the Baptists. And, in that capacity, I now invite you to join us. I have a sermon to deliver."

Featherstonehaugh followed to the council house. He stood outside watching the great numbers who had assembled. He listened as Evans read out verses from the Bible in English which Bushyhead, in his deep, sonorous voice, rendered into Cherokee. At the end of every verse he emitted a deep grunting sound which reminded Featherstonehaugh of the hard breathing of a man chopping down trees. He listened as the group sang from hymnals printed in the Cherokee language. He sized up Evans as a man of sense and experience, not even ignorant of Hebrew.

On August 7 Mason delivered his prepared statement to the Cherokee. While he stood under a stand near the council house, about two thousand Cherokee listened quietly in the pouring rain.

"The President is very powerful," said Mason, "but his power is guided by justice and his first wish is for the safety and happiness of the Cherokees. Listen not to those who tell you to oppose the benevolent design of the government. They speak with a forked tongue and their bad advice will lead you to inevitable ruin."

The address made little impression. When Mason finished the Cherokee returned to the council house to prepare resolutions against the New Echota Treaty and appoint another delegation to return to Washington. In their last desperate concession, they were prepared to yield to Georgia all the land the Nation held in that state. In return for this sacrifice of almost one-third of their remaining land, they would ask President Van Buren to allow the Cherokee to remain on its land in the other three states.

Before John Ross and a delegation of seven other Cherokee men left for Washington, Ross, at the request of the United States government, appointed Jesse Bushyhead to go to Florida to persuade the Seminoles to end their war of resistance against removal. By so doing, he hoped to win a favorable response from Van Buren.

On September 12, 1837 the Ross deputation set out for the long, weary ride to Washington; by horseback to Salem, North Carolina then by stage to the capitol.

In late September a small number of prominent Cherokees, including John Ridge, his wife and children, John's sister, Sally, and her new husband, George Paschal, left for the west in carriages. Also in the company were Elias Boudinot and his new wife, Delight Sargent, a teacher from the Brainerd Mission. Before he left, Ridge wrote to Wilson Lumpkin thanking him for the humanity which he had manifested to Ridge's people.

"In the history of the Nation, if there is a page assigned to my name and that of our house, I know not what will be said. Foul representations have been made by our opponents as to our motives and we have passed thru the ordeal of awakened prejudices of the ignorant portion of our people. If we have merits to be seen and adjudged we leave them to the consideration of an enlightened world and to our God."

*   *   *   *

From where he sat, Ross could not tell whether Adams was sneering with contempt or wearing a fiendish smile of exaltation. Bedlam engulfed the House with delegates from the South standing, flushed with anger and clinched fists, roaring 'Order! Order! Order!

Bald head thrust forward, eyes flashing, Adams stood facing his antagonists. Because of lifelong problems with hemorrhoids, he preferred standing to sitting. "Am I gagged? Am I gagged? Am I forbidden to speak for the people whom I represent?" he stormed.

Speaker James Polk rapped his gavel, cast a cold look toward Adams, and said the gentleman from Massachusetts was not gagged.

"I have several memorials against the annexation of Texas to present, and a petition, with fifty thousand signatures, praying for the abolition of slavery in the District of Columbia. As I have observed before, the resolution adopted by this House laying all such petitions on the table is unconstitutional and, consequently, null and void. The right of citizens to petition their government is guaranteed by the constitution. I do not feel bound by that resolution anymore than I would feel bound to submit to physical force."

Polk interposed. "It is not in order to speak disrespectfully of the action of this House."

"I am much obliged to the Speaker for not having stopped me before," Adams wryly replied. "I assert that it is a principle that it is our duty not only to receive petitions but to consider them as well. Laying petitions on the table without reading them has created a great deal of excitement throughout our country."

Representative Henry A. Wise of Virginia rose to his feet. "Mr. Speaker, I move to lay on the table the petition submitted by the venerable gentleman from Massachusetts." His motion quickly passed, 135 to 70.

Adams held the floor, ignoring the reference to his age. "I have several other petitions from Massachusetts and Pennsylvania on the same subject, Mr. Speaker."

Wise sprang from his seat. "Mr. Speaker, has the petition been received? If not, I raise the question of reception. I consider the petition as ridicule of this House."

Polk responded, "No, the petition has not yet been received."

"Then I raise the question of reception," said an impatient Wise.

"I deny, Mr. Speaker, that the petition is the least bit disrespectful of the House," Adams maintained.

"Aren't many of your petitions against the annexation of Texas signed by women?" asked Benjamin Howard of Maryland. "I always feel regret when petitions thus signed are presented to this House relating to political matters. I think that those females have a sufficient field for the exercise of their influence in the discharge of their duties to their fathers, their husbands, their children, and cheering the domestic circle. I feel sorrow at this departure from their proper sphere."

Adams shot a withering glance at Howard. "And the right to petition, according to the gentleman from Maryland, is to be denied women because they have no right to vote? Mr. Speaker, I demand the yeas and nays on the question of reception."

The House resoundingly defeated the question of reception 177 to 24.

Adams stubbornly held the floor. "Mr. Speaker, since the House has refused to receive, will the motion to refer be entered into the journal?

"No, it will not," replied Polk, "since the petition is still in the possession of the gentleman from Massachusetts."

"If it is in order, Mr. Speaker, I move the printing of the petition so that the House might see what they refused to receive."

"Such a motion is not in order," said Polk.

"Then I request that it be entered upon the journal that I have made the motion to print," Adams persisted.

"That motion, too, is out of order," Polk snapped. "Considering the hour of the day, the House stands adjourned."

Ross waited for Adams as the hunched, pudgy man gathered up his papers. "It seems your strongest efforts went for naught," he said.

Adams cracked a tight smile. "All mortals have a duty to aim for perfection with God's help, Mr. Ross. This fight is just beginning."

"You are to be admired for controlling your temper in such struggles."

"Heaven has given to every human being the power of controlling his passions, and if he neglects or loses it, the fault is his own, and he must be answerable for it," Adams replied.

As they walked out the doors of the capitol building into the January chill, they halted for a procession of thirty slaves, chained and handcuffed, together with twenty women and children, to pass.

"What have these people done that they should be chained and driven? What crime have they committed?" asked Adams. They walked down Pennsylvania Avenue in silence. "As a slave-holder, I suspect you prefer not to discuss the question. Why do the gentlemen of the South not discuss it? Do they fear the argument? If not, why do they refuse to enter into it? If they are so firm, so confident, why will they not speak? Show us the blessing of the institution of slavery."

"I must confess, Mr. Adams, I have been so deeply immersed in the fate of my people that I have not considered the plight of the blacks."

"As a Methodist, Mr. Ross, you need to give serious thought to the matter. The question of slavery is convulsing my Congregational Church in Massachusetts; it is deeply agitating the Methodists, and it has already completed a schism in the Presbyterians. We have some preachers of the gospel who are taxing their ingenuity to prove that the Bible sanctions slavery. Such preachers might just as well call our extermination of the Indians an obedience to Divine commands."

"Which brings us to the topic I wish to discuss," said Ross. "When will the Cherokee memorial be taken up by the House and what is your considered judgement as to what will happen?"

With his coat collar turned up against the cold wind blowing in from the Potomac, Adams shuffled a few steps in silence. "I cannot predict, Mr. Ross, what the House will do. It would be improper for me to create false hope. It is true, the slave states covet your good cotton lands, but the money marketers in the northern states…it is they who finance their evil practices. Too many in our Congress now serve an army of speculators whose only loyalty is to their own profit margins."

At Brown's Hotel, where Ross was staying, Adams, white-haired and bent, wiped his red and watery eyes with hands shaking with palsy. He would trudge on a few more blocks to his home in the 1300 block of F Street. "You are a good man, Mr. Ross. Instead of turning to violence, as the Seminoles have done, you put your trust in our laws and fought your battles through the courts and the halls of Congress. You were, unfortunately, betrayed by lesser men."

*   *   *   *

On Monday, January 22, 1838, Ross had barely located a seat in the House gallery before Representative Horace Everett of Vermont moved that the House take up the memorial from the Cherokee Nation. "I have no desire to debate the treaty; I merely want to move it to the Committee on Indian Affairs."

George Owens of Georgia rose to object. "I see no need to take up the memorial. A treaty has already been concluded. I call for yeas and nays on the motion." After calling for the yeas and nays, the House determined to consider the memorial, yeas 86, nays 83.

"I now move," said Everett, "to refer this memorial to the Committee on Indian Affairs with instructions 'to report the facts in the case',"

In a weary tone Charles Haynes of Georgia rose to say, "Mr. Speaker, I move to table the whole subject. Why waste time on a matter that has already been acted upon?"

At this point, Henry A. Wise of Virginia rose to inquire, "Mr. Chairman, would it be in order to call for a reading of the memorial?"

"It would not," replied Polk, "since a motion to table has been made."

"Then how can the House vote with understanding on a subject it has never heard read?"

Ignoring Wise, Polk called for the yeas and nays. The motion to table the memorial was decided in the negative, yeas 93, nays 94.

Hearing the results, Haynes sprang to his feet. "If gentlemen wish to have a Cherokee war, I believe we should have it here and now rather than defer it to later pro-ceedings. I move the indefinite postponement of the whole subject."

Horace Everett calmly replied. "I am unwilling to go into a discussion of a matter before the facts of the case have been reported on. But, if it must be discussed, I will take this occasion to say a few remarks. Considering the magnitude of this issue, I find it sur-prising that motions are made to table so to prevent the hearing of petitions. The question is of importance, not only as it relates to the rights of the Cherokee, but so far as it relates to the character of the American government. If our government believes that a valid treaty was made, let it produce the evidence."

Here Chairman Polk announced that the hour had arrived for proceeding to the special order of the day. The subject under discussion was ordered to lie over.

Ross bowed his head, clasped his hands and slumped over in his chair. The dark cloud and threatening storm which had been gathering over his native land now seemed about to erupt with all its horrible consequences. How mysterious was the will of Provi-dence in the fate of mortal man. Was it time to give up? After a time he stood and shook off his despair. No. He must not quit...never. There was still the Senate and it had not yet acted upon the memorial.

*   *   *   *

On the same day, newly elected senator from Georgia, Wilson Lumpkin, made his last contribution to Cherokee removal. "At this moment, sir, nothing hinders the consum-mation of this treaty with the Cherokee people but the opposition of John Ross and his associates. The treaty has been made and ratified according to the forms of our constitution. The time stipulated for their removal is in May next; and when the time arrives, go they must. No power can abrogate or overturn this treaty.

"I now move the adoption of the following resolution: Whereas, a memorial, accompanied by various other documents, of a delegation of the Cherokee Nation of Indians, remonstrating against the validity of the Treaty of New Echota of 1835, has been printed by order of the House of Representatives, and whereas said memorial and documents not only call into the question the validity of such treaty, but greatly derogate the character, and impugn the motives of those individuals of the Cherokee Nation who negotiated and signed said treaty on the part of the nation: And whereas, Elias Boudinot, late editor of the Chero-kee Phoenix, and one of the principal agents of the Cherokee Nation who negoti-ated and signed said treaty, has written a reply to the various allegations set forth in the memorial referred to: therefore, be it resolved that fifteen hundred copies of the reply of Mr. Boudinot be published for the use of the Senate."

The resolution was adopted.

*   *   *   *

"You must admit, Boudinot's letter makes a convincing case. Many in Con-gress will believe it." Clay kicked back in his chair and curled his long fingers around a tumbler of whiskey."

"Boudinot is an embittered man who has no belief that the white man and Indian can ever co-exist," Ross replied. "Lumpkin's publishing of Boudinot's slanderous remarks will only add confusion to the Senate's discussion."

"And you are wondering what the Senate will do with your memorial."

"Exactly. We have been denied interviews with either the President or Secre-tary of War, Poinsett. Poinsett sends a note telling us that the president considers the Treaty of New Echota to be the law of the land which the Congress requires him to execute and, therefore, no negotiations can be opened. I am now con-vinced that Van Buren is unwilling to take the responsibility upon himself of doing away with that which has been done by General Jackson. If there is to be any reprieve for my people, it must come from the Congress."

"My friend, I have been too long in politics to predict what the final outcome will be. I do know that each Senator will vote his own interests."

"And the Senate leadership...Calhoun, Webster...where lie their interests?"

Clay left his chair, refilled his tumbler, and walked over to the window. Outside the flowers of May were nodding in the warm breeze. A pack of dogs barked at a cow that had strayed down Pennsylvania Avenue.

"Ambition has a blinding effect," mused Clay, "and I think Webster's case is shocking proof of that. He has his eye on the presidency two years down the road. He is a spellbinding orator but he lacks the charisma to attract voters. He will oppose annexa-tion of Texas as he will oppose anything that expands slavery. On other issues he will hedge his bets. He will do nothing to alienate the mon-eyed interests of the north." He turned to Ross. "Yes, he will support your cause in the Senate...to a degree. He will not risk his career. Remember too, he is a great land speculator."

"And Calhoun?"

Clay's facial muscles visibly tightened. "That sonuvabitch Calhoun is a traitor to the Whigs. No one could have expected his support of Van Buren's treasury solution."

"But will he stand by the Cherokees? Will he demand a review of the treaty?"

Clay dropped his head and stared into the whiskey swirling in his glass. "You have to understand Calhoun's thinking. He is a strong advocate of slavery. As he sees it, for the survival of the South, slavery must expand and so he will demand the annexation of Texas as slave territory. To him, there is no difference between expanding slave territory in Georgia or Texas."

"You're saying he will no longer stand by the Cherokee."

"Hell, Calhoun never really supported the Cherokee. He used your cause as a weapon against Jackson. He and Jackson hate each other's guts."

"I suspected as much all along."

"Calhoun figures northern business will support slavery so long as slavery profits northern business. He calculates that the North cannot afford to let the abolitionists over-throw slavery. Profits, not principle, Calhoun believes, is the keystone to Northern policy." Clay sighed. "Unfortunately, my friend, on this issue I'm afraid he is correct."

*   *   *   *

A cloudy, cold, and rainy dawn broke over Washington on the morning of May 22. Somewhere a barking dog was sent yelping as a disturbed sleeper discharged his pistol. Ross rose, dressed and went down for breakfast. Later in the morning, his mood matching the weather, he made his way up muddy Pennsylvania Avenue, past the St. Charles Hotel, to the capitol and the Senate chambers. This Tuesday morning the Senate received a message from President Van Buren, delivered by his son and private secretary, Abraham Van Buren. The message consisted of a letter the Secretary of War, Joel Poinsett, had addressed to John Ross and the Cherokee delegation. "Where the rights and just expectations of sovereign states are involved," Poinsett said, "it is deemed inexpedient, without their consent, to change any stipulations which affect them in a solemn treaty…the government of the United States could not agree to any change in the New Echota Treaty without the consent of the states whose rights were involved."

Poinsett went on to say that if the Cherokee Nation desired to be in charge of their emigration, their wishes could be complied with. Necessary escort and protection during the removal would be provided by the United States. This final communication on the matter, containing the most liberal terms the Executive can grant, is the final determination of the government.

When Abraham Van Buren finished reading the message, Senator William A. King of Georgia rose. "I cannot but regret that such a paper as this has been laid before the Senate. It appears to me that the delegates of the states immediately affected should have been consulted prior to this letter." He looked toward the gallery where Ross sat. "I would observe that there is no evidence that the Cherokee delegation has shown any disposition to accept the terms proposed by the Secretary of War."

An agitated Clement Clay of Alabama took the floor. "Firmness and energy, with adherence to the terms of the treaty, is the only course to prevent war and bloodshed. This temporizing policy is not the way to preserve respect of the Indians. I have been informed that there have been several recent murders perpetuated on our citizens by these misguided Indians, excited no doubt, by the delusion held out to them by their leading men here at the seat of the government. I have told the Secretary frequently that the most dangerous consequences would ensue if the treaty was not carried into effect.

"What induced the Secretary to falter in carrying into execution a treaty already passed?" Swinging about, Abraham Clay pointed his finger toward Ross. "What prompts this pretended Cherokee delegation? It's money. Money due to the nations are to be disposed for the benefit of the tribe. John Ross and his associates would have the money paid directly to them. Their goal is to gain control of the money, not for the benefit of the tribe, but for their own enrichment."

A flush of anger crept up Ross's neck. How many times before had these lies been peddled in the halls of Congress.

"I must express my regret that this paper was not approved by gentlemen representing the states concerned." It was Webster at his soothing best. "There is a strong and growing feeling in the country that a great wrong is being done to the Cherokee by the Treaty of New Echota. I will not enter into a discussion of that now but we have here a communication from the Executive, requesting action of Congress. I think the proper course is to refer the matter to the appropriate committee. I therefore move that it be referred to the Committee on Indian Affairs."

The gentlemen of the South would have no part of that. Felix Grundy of Tennessee, who had blatantly made known his desire not only to add the Floridas to the South but the Canadas to the north, spoke with a tone of disgust.

"I thought the vote of the Senate had settled forever the question of the validity of this treaty. With regard to consulting the states interested, the state of Tennessee could not be consulted for her legislature will not be in session until a year from next October. The legislature of that state, at its last session, under the faith of the existing treaty, and believing that it was to be carried into effect unaltered in any of its provisions, has provided for the sale of all the lands within the Indian boundary. All the legislation of my state will be set aside if this treaty is not carried into effect. To let the Indians remain where they are is out of the question."

Events were causing Grundy to reveal his true motives, thought Ross. Tennessee, as well as the United States, were banking on the sale of Cherokee lands to redeem their debts.

Senator Lumpkin of Georgia joined the melee. "Evil has been, and more will be, brought upon the Cherokee by Ross and his associates unless the Indians are removed at once."

Lumpkin's colleague, Senator Alfred Cuthbert of Alabama, snorted in indignation. "May I point out that tomorrow is the day appointed for the execution of the treaty. Yet it was proposed by Secretary Poinsett that the state of Georgia, six or seven hundred miles away, be consulted for the purposes of changing a treaty that is to go into effect tomorrow."

Webster again attempted to calm the waters. "I am persuaded that those who know me, know that no personal or political gains caused me to refer this matter to committee. It is my wish to treat these Indians with justice and kindness, and to convince the people of these United States that it is our determination to do so. Many excellent and worthy men have it on their conscience that some great wrong has been done to the Cherokees by the Treaty of New Echota. For this reason, everything should be done to disabuse them of this impression."

Senator Cuthbert rose to respond. "Speaking of justice and kindness, where are the Indian tribes which once covered the territory of Massachusetts? Where slumbered the consciences of the people of Massachusetts when these tribes were exterminated? Indeed, sir, butchered! Are their consciences to be aroused now? Who were these men of conscience? Are they the men of tender conscience who would now let loose all the horrors of abolition in the Southern states? God of heaven! How are terms abused! Conscience! Merciful God! For men to talk of conscience while their course leads to violence and bloodshed!"

Webster sat silent, glowering.

Cuthbert continued. "For two years Georgia has passively yielded and suspended the operation of her laws under the full belief that this treaty would be faithfully carried into effect. I will vote for laying this communication from Secretary Poinsett, not to be taken up again."

Webster rose in defense. "It seems I stand on peculiar ground. Here is a communication from the President, deemed by him important enough to be considered by the Senate. If there is anything in that document which could draw forth such strong ejaculations from the Senator from Alabama, let him direct his ire against the source from which it emanated. My mere object when I moved to refer it was that it receive the respectful attention the importance of the subject demands."

The senior senator from South Carolina now weighed in. "I am not prepared to say whether there is any practicable plan that can be devised to satisfy all parties, but I think that a reference of the subject to the proper committee is certainly in order. It is important, however, that the emigration of the Cherokee begin at once in good faith and progress as fast as circumstances will allow."

The years of Calhoun's hypocritical dealings with the Cherokee were now clearly revealed to Ross. Calhoun had one object in mind…protect slavery and the south.

Cuthbert, determined to have the final word, responded. "If there had been a fair attempt on the part of Mr. Ross to avoid difficulties, I have no doubt we could have done so. But, instead, he has remained here creating prejudice and foment for his own selfish and ambitious reasons."

Since no motion was necessary to lay the paper on the table, the documents then, by general consent, laid on the table. With that, Ross's hopes for relief from the Senate vanished.

In the House of Representatives a bill which would allow additional compensation to the Cherokees for lands ceded, provided they ceased opposition to the Treaty of 1835, was submitted by Rep. John Bell of Tennessee, Chairman of the House Committee on Indian Affairs.

In a surprise move, Henry A. Wise, a strong state's rights man, took the floor to soundly condemn the treaty. "This treaty is a fraud perpetuated by Parson Schermerhorn and Agent Curry. The Cherokee had no voice in the compact made between Georgia and the United States in 1802 and, therefore, it has no binding upon the third party. The state of Georgia should be compelled to abide by action of the Federal Government. She should be castigated if she refuses to obey the laws of the general government. I say that as a state's rights man. A state is bound to obedience and can be coerced if it refuses. This treaty was brought about by improper means, by the use of whiskey, and by the withholding of annuity. It is a minority treaty."

Stunned by this attack from a fellow southerner, the spellbinder from Georgia, Rep. George Washington Bonaparte Towns, unleashed a defense. "Castigate? Castigate for what? Georgia had not disobeyed any laws. Quite the opposite; Georgia is on the side of the law. By adhering to the compact, Georgia is on the side of the law. I deprecate, with much severity, the use of such a term as that of castigating a state."

"Your state has declared, "replied Wise, "that unless the treaty is carried out Georgia will take her rights in her own hands. Your governor Gilmer has threatened that if President Van Buren extends the Cherokees more time for removal, a direct collision between the authorities of your state and the General Government will ensue."

"The House," Towns interrupted, "is not a treaty-making power. Therefore, we should not got into an examination of this treaty with a view to its revocation. It is a valid treaty. The whole difficulty, and the only difficulty, has grown out of John Ross, who produced it for his own personal benefit; for he has shown himself, by his own admissions in his letters to the Secretary of War, to be purchasable at a price. So far from Ross being actuated by a regard for the interests of his people, or a love of his country, he is impelled solely by a love of lucre; and if enough is given him, if he is bribed high enough, we will consent to any treaty."

Wise regained the floor. "I say again, the pretended treaty is no treaty. Schermerhorn made a treaty with only a small portion of the Cherokees who were not properly authorized. I have documents here to prove that less than seventy of the nation, consisting of eighteen thousand souls, agreed to the treaty. The people did not feel bound to attend a council which was summoned by Mr. Schermerhorn, who is not a chief in their nation. If the gentlemen from Georgia do not know this, they ought to know, and would if they would look at the documents."

Wise was interrupted with a question; did the treaty not offer the Indians better lands?

"That question is not pertinent," responded Wise. "The question is, whether a treaty exists at all. I have in hand here a report from General Wool in which he states that the Cherokees have refused to accept rations from the United States for fear they might compromise themselves in relation to the treaty and that they prefer to live on sap from the trees and roots rather than accept rations.

"I find it extraordinary that the authority of John Ross should be unquestioned by his nation if he is as the gentleman from Georgia has described him. If Ross is so corrupt, why has he not accepted the many attempts to bribe him? Much abuse has been heaped upon him but John Ross could not change his course; he could not change the feelings of his nation if he would." The House erupted with southern gentlemen clamoring for recognition. In the bedlam that ensued, the House was adjourned. With adjournment, the last hope for congressional review of the treaty was dead.

CHAPTER 26

NO BALM IN GILEAD

"Too bad you don't drink, my friend. I find the spirits exhilarating when I'm rejoicing and I find them comforting when I'm downcast. Right now, you need some comfort."

Ross remained silent as Webster poured himself another drink. Peering out beneath his shaggy eyebrows, with loosened tongue, he rumbled on. "You have fought your battles on the high ground of moral principles expecting your opponents to do the same. My dear fellow, don't you realize that the cause of the Cherokee was doomed from the start? Can't you see that your people are nothing more than a pawn on the chessboard of national politics who must be sacrificed for the nation's good?

"Hear me out. This confession brings pain to your ears and pain to my lips. To bring this nation into existence, it was essential that the south be a part of it. In securing the south, the bitter pill of slavery also had to be accepted. Now, today, we find that if we are to hold this nation together, the south must be appeased by permitting it to expand slavery into new territory. It is simply easier for Congress to remove your people than to face the prospects of a nation divided by civil war. Jefferson and Adams avoided the issue in their lifetimes. How much longer we can close our eyes to the dark cloud looming larger each day, I cannot tell."

With a sad smile, Ross reached for his hat and extended his hand to Webster. "As long as there are men of conscience, I will continue to battle on the high ground of principle. I must return now to my nation to assist General Scott in the removal of my people."

*   *   *   *

On a grassy knoll, under the shade of a large cedar tree, Ross dismounted his horse. Two years ago, on this very hill, he had assured General Wool that there would be no need for stockades to house the Cherokee. Then, it was inconceivable that the government of the United States would forcibly remove his people. Now, as he watched, a squad of Georgia militia herded a string of some two hundred men, women, and children into the already overcrowded enclosures. The shouts and curses of the militia were clearly audible as the last of the aged and ailing Cherokee were forced through the gates. Red dust swirled in the dale below as the helpless company sought to find shelter from the blistering July sun.

As Ross mopped his brow, two horsemen approached from the west. As they neared he recognized the Rev. Daniel Butrick and a weathered Tom Hanks. They dismounted and joined Ross in the shade of the cedar. Overjoyed to see Hanks, Ross asked," Where have you been all these months? When you left Washington you dropped out of sight."

"It's a long story. I've spent some time with the Cherokee in Texas and some with the Cherokee beyond the Arkansas. Set a place for me at your table tonight and I'll give you a full account." He turned and looked down at the imprisoned below. "That's the damnedest sight I've ever seen. How many are in that hell hole?"

"There are some eight thousand souls penned up there." The shoulders of the fifty year old Massachusetts ministers sagged. His words came out between sobs. "Since I first came to Brainerd over twenty years ago, I have labored among these people, preaching the love and mercy of God to those who follow Him. I preached that the best way to save their country was to become civilized…become Christians. They have done no wrong to merit any part of this evil. How can they believe now? Is there no balm in Gilead?"

Ross clamped a calming hand on the minister's shoulder. "Reverend Butrick, if there is anyone to blame, it is I. As their principal chief, I let my people fall into this fate."

Hanks snorted. "If you two will stop all the breast-beating, maybe we can offer some help to those poor devils."

"How so?" asked Ross. "Butrick is permitted to preach and offer prayers, which is more than I can do. I have no authority over those militia."

"Well, bygod, maybe I do." Hanks reached into one of his saddlebags and brought out a wrinkled military jacket with captain rank clearly showing.

"What are you doing? You are no longer in the military," said Ross.

"We know that…they don't"

The guards warily eyed the three as they dismounted at the stockade gate. As Ross entered the stockade, a gaunt warrior struggled to his feet and took Ross by the hand. Through parched lips, his voice barely above a whisper, he said, "My chief, I knew you would come."

"John McPherson? Is that you?"

"Yes, it's me," he croaked. "Could you get us some water? We haven't had a drink all day. Some of these folk are in bad shape."

Hanks turned to one of the guard. "Get these people some water…right now."

"Can't give me orders…ye ain't my boss."

In an instant the guard was staring at the muzzle of a pistol. "Get some water, you scummy sonovabitch or I'll be your personal firing squad," hissed Hanks.

As the cowed guard hurried to comply, Hanks turned to a moaning woman. "I think she is in labor," said Rev. Butrick.

"You mean she's having a baby here and now?"

Butrick nodded and knelt beside the woman. "She needs help right away. She's hemorrhaging."

"Is there a doctor here?" Hanks asked the returning guard.

"Yes, sir. I'll fetch him."

In a few minutes a disheveled man arrived and introduced himself as Dr. Phineas Grant.

"Doctor, this woman needs help immediately. She's having a baby," said Hanks.

Grant looked at the woman and shook his head. "You've got the wrong guy. I know nothing of delivering babies."

"The hell you don't. You're a doctor, ain't you?"

"I make no pretensions to the knowledge of medicine. I'm a dentist," Grant replied indifferently.

"A goddamned toothpuller…trifling with the lives of these people. Get the hell outta here," Hanks raged.

"If you men will move aside, maybe we can help." Hanks turned to see a young girl and three matronly Cherokees. As the young girl knelt to assist the woman in labor, the others held up blankets to form a screen from the leering soldiers watching on the hillside.

Noticing bare feet, Rev. Butrick asked, "McPherson, where are your boots?"

"Didn't have time to get 'em on, preacher. Was settin' down for supper when the soldiers barged in. Jabbed me with a bayonet and shoved us outta the house. We left with what we had on. Couldn't wait until we were out of sight before white trash was stripping the house and driving off my hogs and cows. They took my horses and made us walk for two days to get here. That's what happened to most of us."

"I see several families here without their menfolk," observed Butrick.

"Yep. Genrul Scott is holding these women hoping to force the men to come in and surrender."

Ross turned away in anger. Down the hill he could see women holding up blankets to shield other women from view while they were relieving themselves. The smell of human excrement hung in the dusty air. There were no sanitary facilities in sight. No food, no water, no bedding. From the crude, crowded log shelters he could hear spasms of coughing from the sick and elderly and the wailing of babies. Here and there in the crowd he recognized cultured and educated women, now bewildered by their wretchedness, numbly brushing away flies. Torn suddenly and savagely from comfortable homes, they now found themselves impoverished, exposed to the elements, housed like pigs in a sty.

"Come on," said Ross. "I've got to see Scott. Something has to be done about these conditions."

Walking back to their horses, they stopped by the woman in labor. "How is she?" asked Hanks.

The lithe, young woman who had taken charge, faced Hanks coldly. "She's dead. The child lives...for now."

Dirty dress, black, stringy, hair, flashing green eyes, bloody hands from assisting the delivery...yet, there was something about the defiant young girl that stirred Hanks.

Ross sighed. "Alright, get some shovels from the guards." He looked up the slope to the huge cedar tree. "Bury her up there."

Back in the saddle, they rode down the hill, crossed the Hiwassee on Walker's Ferry, passed Camp Cass and dismounted at the home of Lewis Ross in Charleston.

After Rev. Butrick asked the blessing, they ate supper in silence by candlelight. Hanks broke the silence. "Any of you remember Duwali?"

"Yes, I remember The Bowl," replied Ross. "He and Doublehead sold some Cherokee land without authorization. Major Ridge killed Doublehead; Duwali fled to the west to save his hide."

"I visited him in Texas. He is caught between the Mexicans and Houston's Texans. Both Benito Ramirez and Houston promised them land in return for Cherokee support. As long as Houston is in a position to protect them, they will be alright. But, considering that they are located on some of the best cotton land in Texas, my guess is they will be forced out before long. Americans are flooding into the Red River country. So, forget any thoughts you might retain of moving to Texas."

Ross nodded in agreement.

"I then visited the Old Settlers," Hanks continued, "and members of the Treaty Party around Ft. Gibson. I must tell you, they are not thrilled at the thought of your coming. They realize they will be outnumbered and fear that you will take control."

"Be that as it may, we are destined to come," Ross stated grimly. "When the strong arm of power is raised against the weak and defenseless, the force of argument must fail. We no longer have a choice. As Thucydides once said, the strong do what they can; the weak suffer what they must."

"I also stopped over in Nashville," Hanks continued. "Heard that Jackson was thinking of joining the church. The old bastard has much to repent. I guess he wants to go to heaven."

Ross reflected for a moment. "If Jackson wants to go to heaven, who's to stop him?"

"Chief Ross," said Butrick, "I do not wish to trouble you with trivia but, if it please you, we, my wife Elizabeth and I, would like to accompany you to the west."

Ross stared at Butrick for a moment. "The road will be long, the hardships many, but if you wish to be part of our exodus, then come."

Barking dogs announced the arrival of a visitor. As Hanks raised the wooden latch, the Rev. Evan Jones stumbled across the threshold. With the help of Hanks, he collapsed into a chair. Beads of sweat on Jones's brow glistened in the warm candlelight.

"The man is burning up with fever," said Butrick. "Get some water."

Hanks reached into the wooden bucket and handed Jones the gourd dipper. "You're in bad shape, parson. Drink this."

With shaking hands, Jones drank, handed the dipper back to Hanks and wiped his mouth with the back of his hand. "I'm in good shape," he said, "compared to those in camps. They are dying there…fifteen, sixteen a day. Chief Ross, you must put a stop to this disaster."

"The Senate of the United States, with their eyes wide open, ratified the treaty that put us in this plight," Ross replied bitterly. "But, I will see General Scott tomorrow and try to delay our departure. With this heat and drought the Tennessee River is too low for boats; grass has dried up and so have wells and springs."

"Then I must go with you."

"Reverend Jones, you are in no condition to go anywhere."

Jones stood and faced Ross, his eyes glittering from fever. "I have seen Cherokee women, in order to secure food for their children, succumb to drink pressed upon them by guards. Once they are drunk, they are raped. Who knows how many of our young, Christian ladies have been so debauched? The guard commanders take no notice when I complain. I must confront General Scott with what I have seen with my own eyes. This is the work of war in a time of peace. Such depravity must end."

After a moment Ross nodded and solemnly replied. "Yes…yes, you will accompany me."

"It is also my sad duty to inform you," said Jones, "our friends, Jesse Bushyhead and Rev. Stephen Foreman, and their families, are being held as prisoners in the camp at Candy's Creek."

"So much gratitude for Bushyhead's peace efforts with the Seminole," observed Ross.

It was not a long walk from the home of Lewis Ross to Fort Cass where General Scott was now quartered. The fifty-two year old Virginian rose to his height of six feet, four inches and greeted Ross and his party.

"It's good to see you again, Chief Ross. You will be pleased to hear that your request has been granted. You are no longer under the control of the army. The whole business of the emigration of your people will be placed in the hands of the Cherokee. I don't need to tell you, the army is happy to be relieved of such responsibilities. Our efforts to remove your people have been less than satisfactory. The burden now moves from my shoulders to yours. But I must emphasize…all your people must be on the trail no later than September 1."

CHAPTER 27

THE EXODUS

Loud voices woke Hanks from a troubled sleep. He opened the door from his bunkroom to the kitchen and found Ross and Butrick in heated discussion.

Ross put down his pen beside a stack of papers on the kitchen table. "Reverend Butrick,"he said impatiently, "I've got thousands of people to move. I'm trying to locate mules, wagons, and supplies. I don't have time to discuss this woman."

It was then that Hanks noticed the young woman, who had served as midwife at the stockade, standing with Butrick. She was fingering a silver amulet hanging from her neck. In Hank's sleepy mind visions of the Battle of Horseshoe Bend came forward...a screaming child he had rescued from a burning hut...the amulet he had left with her.

Butrick threw up his hands in protest. "But Chief Ross, she is a Creek and Lumpkin said that Creeks must be surrendered."

"Lumpkin has no authority here. We are no longer under the army's control."

"But," Butrick persisted, "she is not a member of any family. She is not even married."

"What's that got to do with anything?"

"Chief, if we take this young, unwed lass along, there will be nothing but trouble with the young bucks. I will not be responsible for lack of morals in our group. She needs to be married or left behind."

Hanks yawned. "Then I'll marry her."

Three pairs of eyes locked on Hanks with astonishment and disbelief.

Butrick sniffed. "This is no occasion for levity."

The woman's green eyes flashed defiance. "I don't want to marry you. I can take care of myself."

Hanks grinned mischievously. "You marry me or you get left behind to the Georgia boys."

Like a trapped animal, panic and bewilderment flashed across her face.

"Why are you doing this?" Butrick asked.

Hanks gestured toward the outside. "Listen to those drunks. You want to leave her to the rabble out there?"

Flustered, Butrick paused then looked to the woman. "Miss, are you willing to…uh…to marry this man?"

She hesitated. Then, with fists clinched, she looked up at Hanks, then nodded numbly.

"Very well," Butrick rolled his eyes upward in despair and reached for a bible. "It might help, miss, if we knew your name."

"Tiva"

"Tiva? No last name?"

"No, just Tiva."

The ceremony was brief and stark, devoid even of a sealing kiss.

As Butrick closed his bible, Ross spoke up. "Tiva, this is my brother's house. Since Tom and I have some work to do, why don't you take the comfort of a bedroom upstairs."

Hanks and Ross worked well into the night forming travel detachments by families and towns.

The rains had not come. Water in the Tennessee was so low that the steamboats could not operate. The planned departure of more than 13,000 emigrants by September first had been ruled out. They would have to go overland and follow the route B.B. Cannon established the year before.

Ross yawned, glanced at the clock on the mantel, and ran fingers through his graying hair. "Scott insists that each detachment contain at least a thousand souls. I have finally arranged with him for 645 wagons and teams, and 5000 riding horses. That means each wagon must haul provisions and possessions for 20 people, plus space for the very young, the sick and the elderly. Most will have to walk."

Hanks snorted. "And Scott says the exercise will be beneficial. Let that pompous ass try walking 800 miles in 80 days."

Ross moved on. "Scott approved, reluctantly, sixteen cents per day per person for rations. Brother Lewis is already at work contracting for food and supplies along the way."

Hanks walked to the stove and refilled his coffee cup. "From what I hear, General Scott caught all kinds of hell from whites who had hoped to procure the privilege of supplying us en route."

Ross nodded. "Even Andrew Jackson blew his top. He may be old and feeble but he can't contain his hatred for me. Most conveniently forget that all these costs for our removal are being deducted from what the government owes us."

Hanks stood to stretch and looked out the window into the night. Lights winked from a thousand campfires. For ten square miles stretching south toward the town of Cleveland, the Cherokee huddled, awaiting their fate. Driven from comfortable homes, they now lived in tents, lean-tos, and bark shelters. Here and there, a wail of a child was drowned out by the raucous sound of drunken brawlers. "Death hangs over this camp, Hanks said. "If we don't get a break in the weather and get these people moving, there is a good chance that winter will catch us on the trail."

Ross stood and joined him at the window. "It may be a choice of dying here in these camps or dying on the trail," he murmured. "I wake in the gray of dawn feeling hopeless, enduring the misery of the damned. My weakness was in trusting the government to honor its laws. God forgive me but I want to wreak vengeance upon those Judas's who betrayed us. In the history of the United States government, this toxic stain will never be removed."

Hanks glanced at Ross and quietly replied, "It all depends upon who writes the history."

$$*\qquad*\qquad*\qquad*$$

Entering the bedroom, Hanks found Tiva standing, clothed in a dirty, blood-stained dress, her hands behind her. Light from a candle on the chiffonier cast a warm glow on her face.

"It's late," he said awkwardly. "I thought you would be in bed."

"I will not sleep with you," she snapped.

Hanks tugged off his boots. "Tiva, you are safe here. No one is going to harm you." He stretched out on the bed without undressing. "I should have had one of the servants draw you bath. Tomorrow we will find you a new dress."

"I'm sorry I don't come up to your standards," she replied sarcastically.

"When was the last time you slept in a walnut four-poster with a canopy, a featherbed and real sheets? Lewis Ross knows how to live." As an afterthought he added, "There's a chamber pot under the bed. I'll step outside if you need to use it." Exhausted, he fell asleep as his head hit the pillow.

For a time the young woman studied the sleeping figure with suspicion, trying to untangle her thoughts. Bitter experiences with white soldiers had filled her heart with hatred and distrust. She knew with certainty that her future could be no worse with this man than it would be if she remained here. But why was this stranger concerned with her safety? What would her future be now that she belonged to him? Unable to make sense of it all, she lifted her skirt and slipped the knife she had been holding behind her back into the sheath strapped to her leg. Quietly, she lay down beside the sleeping Hanks. Later, in the cool of the night, she snuggled close to his body warmth.

*   *   *   *

As the sun rose, Butrick pulled the blanket away from a body. Vacant eyes stared upward. Bloody hands held blue entrails that spilled from the slit stomach. "This was Smoke...always a trouble maker. He and his drunken companions were playing cards last night. They got into an argument. You see the results."

Ross nodded and covered his nose with a handkerchief. "Scott's soldiers are doing a lousy job of keeping whiskey peddlers out of the camps," he said grimly.

Butrick removed another blanket, this one covering the bodies of a man and a woman. "This young man was on a drunken frolic. He went to his sister to borrow some money for more whiskey. When she refused, he stabbed her to death. Two of his brothers, enraged at the death of their sister, beat him to death with clubs." Butrick stood erect and motioned toward a row of bodies wrapped in blankets. "These other ten are children and old people. The children died of dysentery, whooping cough, and chicken pox; the old folks died of ague, pneumonia...and broken hearts. We are losing 12 to 15 every day in these camps. I sometimes wonder if it isn't deliberate murder."

"Bury them on the hill beneath the cedars," said Ross, "but keep the blankets."

*   *   *   *

On September 28 a downpour drenched the Cherokee. The drought was broken. General Scott pressured the Cherokee saying they must all be on the trail before another moon or he would refuse to issue rations.

October 1, 1838, dawned clear and crisp. The first detachment of emigrants under Cherokee control prepared to embark from Rattlesnake Springs. A line of 60 wagons, and a party of 1,090 souls, led by Captain John Benge and his assistant, George Lowrey, waited in the pines. They were equipped with only 83 tents.

The group was silent as Hanks helped Ross up on the tailgate of a wagon. In a voice that betrayed the sadness of his heart, he said, "We are now about to take our final and farewell of our native land. It is with sorrow that we are forced by the authority of the white man to quit the scenes of our childhood, our tree-shaded homes, the cooling spring, the graves of our fathers. Our homes and livestock are stolen and robbed from us in open daylight in view of hundreds. Why? Because they know we are in a defenseless situation.

"Our Council has determined that our system of government will remain intact. It has also resolved that the title of the Cherokee people to their lands is the most ancient, pure, and absolute known to man; its date is beyond the reach of human record. The free consent of the Cherokee people is indispensable to a valid transfer of the title to this land. We have never given such consent. It follows that the original title and ownership of these lands still rests in the Cherokee Nation, unimpaired and absolute. It cannot be dissolved by the expulsion of our Nation by the power of the United States Government."

The forty-eight year old Ross then removed his hat and spoke a prayer in the Cherokee tongue wishing the party God's guidance. At noon, amid flowing tears and final hugs, a bugle gave the signal to move out. Going Snake, a venerable chief whose hair was white from more than eighty winters, mounted his favorite pony and led the way in silence. In wagons loaded with blankets, tools, cooking utensils, and fodder for the horses, the aged, sick, and very young were crowded in. Behind the wagons, young mothers with newborn babes in arms, women old and gnarled with heavy packs on their backs, and some black slaves, took up the order of march. At that very moment a low sound of distant thunder rumbled across a cloudless sky.

A detachment of 748 men, women, and children started three days later under the leadership of Ross's brother-in-law, Elijah Hicks. Only a few of the poorly clad people in this group even had wagon covers to protect them from the weather. At the head of the column rode the ancient White Path. Though failing in health, he refused accommodation in the wagons.

At random intervals as quickly as wagons and teams could be assembled and provisioned, detachments took to the trail during the rest of the month and into November.

As Ross would lead the last detachment, he remained behind with his family packing and boxing Cherokee records. These documents, dating back to 1808, contained their first written laws and correspondence between the Cherokee Nation and all the Presidents of the United States from Washington to Van Buren. He also received by riders reports from early detachments on what the later groups could expect.

On Thursday, November 1, 1838 Hanks was set to leave with the detachment led by Richard Taylor. The fifty-year-old leader was a highly respected veteran of the Battle of Horseshoe Bend.

Hanks was assigned to the Light Horse Guard. As an outrider it was his task to assist any with trouble and keep the wagons moving.

Tiva had volunteered to drive one of the wagons. Perched on the spring seat of a worn, weather-beaten wagon, purchased from a local white farmer at an exorbitant price, one of the few with canvas cover, she sported sturdy shoes, a new deerskin dress, and a buffalo robe that Hanks had purchased for her in Lewis Ross's store. In the weeks she had been married to Hanks, he had not touched her. His winning smile, sense of humor, and protective manner had lowered her fears. At times, in fact, she wished for more from Hanks than courtesy.

John McPherson and his woman, Mary Quaqua, drove the wagon behind Tiva. Their marital status was a source of constant dyspepsia for Rev. Butrick but the fact that John and Mary had adopted the babe born in the stockade assuaged his conscience somewhat. Nettie Haxton, a buxom, black nanny, with a new baby of her own, would also breastfeed the waif.

Two miles north of Rattlesnake Springs, the wagons crossed to the north side of the Hiwassee River at a ferry above Gunstocker Creek. For two days they followed a muddy road along the river for twenty miles to where it joined the Tennessee at John Blythes's Ferry. Here they made camp with others who were waiting to be ferried across the river. Corn meal, bacon, and salt pork were issued to families and corn and fodder were issued for the teams of horses, mules, and oxen. Whites, eager to make their last profits, rolled in a barrel of whiskey ensuring that no one would have a peaceful night's sleep.

*   *   *   *

In the early morning the wagons left camp beneath the huge live oaks trees and made their way through deep sand to the foot of Walden's Ridge. Here at the tollgate the emigrants first encountered the fleecing and gouging they would meet along the way. After paying the white gatekeeper forty dollars, each wagon was charged thirty-seven and a half cents and each horse passed for six and a quarter cents to cross the ridge.

Behind them were the ferry and their homeland. While the teams were given a breather before assaulting the steep, two-mile climb, Hanks rode up and down the train making sure all was in readiness. He stopped at Tiva's wagon.

"You may need to use the whip on this climb," he instructed. "It will be a rough and rocky stretch. Give the horses a loose rein, take your time and keep plenty of space between you and the wagon ahead."

Tiva nodded and gave him a reassuring smile.

Half way up the ridge, the horse's withers were covered with foamy lather. Breathing hard, they slipped and strained to gain footing on the rocky surface. Tiva clucked encouragement to them. Suddenly, the horse on the right plunged forward and fell to his knees; the horse on the left reared and neighed in panic. The wagon started to roll back down the hill dragging the horses entangled in their harness. Tiva let out a scream of terror. Hanks rode alongside and held out his arms. "Jump, Tiva, jump!" In desperation she made the leap and wrapped her arms tightly around him.

Another outrider hurled himself off his horse onto the wagon and pushed hard on the brake pole. McPherson, seeing what was happening, dismounted his wagon, grabbed a large boulder and placed it behind a wheel. The runaway wagon swayed and came to a shuddering stop just ahead of McPherson's team.

Tiva, shivering with terror, clung to Hanks. He gently pried away her arms and let her to the ground. Upon inspection he found that the single tree on the right, weak and rotten, had snapped leaving only one horse hitched to the wagon. After untangling the harness and trace chains, he led the horses to the top of the ridge and returned to the wagon with another team and a borrowed single tree.

By one o'clock in the afternoon the entire train was at the summit of Walden's Ridge. Worn out from getting up the mountain, they went into camp near a white settler called Ragsdale for the rest of the day.

To add some variety to their meal of salt pork and corn mush, Hanks purchased some tomatoes, apples and a pumpkin from Ragsdale. Since the first contingent passed through Ragsdale's place, the price of apples had gone up from six cents a dozen to fifty cents. As they were finishing their meal, Mary Qua qua ambled over from her wagon. "Could we borrow your pot and skillet? We were driven out so quickly we had no time to bring our cooking vessels."

As the sun set early on this November day, Hanks stood at the top of Walden's Ridge looking back across the Tennessee. Nearby the brilliant colors of autumn were captured in the gold of the hickory, the rusty brown of the oaks, and the red of sumac growing out of the layered rocks. In the distance the mountains thrust their smoky blue peaks above the smothering fog. Wrapped in a shawl to ward off the evening chill, Tiva quietly joined him. "What are you thinking, Tom?"

"Take a last look, Tiva. When we crossed that river, we forever left our homeland. It was our Red Sea. Ahead of us lies the wilderness. God only knows how many of us will survive the journey."

That night, as they bedded down in the hay in their wagon, Tiva pressed close to Hanks and drew the buffalo robe over them.

*   *   *   *

Chilled to the bone in the cold rain, Tiva guided the wagon along the muddy, deeply rutted road. The other poorly clad outcasts plodded mutely along for eleven and a half miles to a wet camp at Morgan Springs.

Dawn broke clear and crisp. From the ridge where Hanks stood, a spectacular view of the Sequatchie Valley lay below. Today they would have to descend a steep, winding, narrow road that led across the Sequatchie River into Pikesville. Hanks went down the line checking the brake pole and brake pads on each wagon. On the lead wagon he hooked a short chain to a spoke in a rear wagon wheel then to the wagon box. To prevent wear on the iron wheel tires, he affixed a wooden drag shoe on the bottom of the wheel, which was also chained to the wagon box. In effect, the wagons would be skidded down the steep, slick, mountain trail.

Hanks rode back and forth watching the wagons as they slipped and slid down the muddy mountainside. As the wagon driven by Little Mouse went by, he noticed the driver was nodding. Before Hanks could shout a warning, the right rear wheel struck a jutting limestone boulder. In an instant, spokes splintered and the wheel collapsed. The wagon tipped and rolled down the steep incline. Women, children, and provisions sprawled from the wagon box, scattering among the trees and rocks. The horses whinnied in terror and struggled against the pull.

Hanks quickly dismounted and slid down the hill. The wife of Little Mouse lay still, spread-eagled on the ground. A quick examination showed that her neck was broken. Nearby, under the broken wagon box, was their crushed baby. Over to one side lay Little Mouse, his brains splashed against a rock. In death his hand was holding a broken whiskey bottle.

Safely down the steep mountain road, the detachment went into camp on the outskirts of the frontier town of Pikesville. Earlier detachments had made camp at the same place.

Hanks rose from the smoky fire. "Tiva, this wood is wet. Keep an eye on the fire so it doesn't go out. I'm going to help Rev. Butrick bury the dead."

The Pikesville settlement, like most frontier towns, had little that was pleasant or agreeable: a muddy street flanked by a few rough-hewn houses, a land office, and a tavern. A crudely painted Justice of the Peace sign hung over one hut. Here a boisterous crowd had gathered to watch as one terrified man was lashed thirty-nine times on his bare back after which his head and hands were thrust into holes in a wooden pillory and secured. To whoops of encouragement, one local proceeded to nail the victim's ears to the pillory as another came up with a red-hot poker. Through screams of agony an H was branded on one cheek of the hapless fellow and a T on the other.

A bystander, recognizing Hanks as a stranger, chortled, "That's what a horse thief gets 'round here."

Just then Rev. Butrick pushed his way to the pillory and cried out, "In the name of God, I command you to stop this cruelty."

Quiet fell over the crowd. Then a beefy fellow stepped forward and grabbed Butrick by his lapels, lifting him off his feet. "Who the hell are you, stranger?"

"I'm Reverend Butrick," he wheezed, "a minister of the gospel and I condemn what you are doing!"

"Holy shit! Boys, we got ourselves a preacher...come to save our souls from hell. You wouldn't be traveling with them gut eaters, would you?"

"I'm traveling with the Cherokees," gasped Butrick, "we want nothing more than to bury our dead in your cemetery."

The man sneered with disdain. "It'll be a cold day in hell before I let you bury any redskins in a white man's cemetery. Now, get the hell outta my sight." With that he heaved Butrick back into the crowd.

At that moment a drunken, burly fellow stepped forward and smashed a whiskey jug against the head of Butrick's assailant. "Clem, "he said, "you're going to hell for sure if you don't show more respect for a man of the cloth."

Clem scrambled to his feet, trying to clear his head. "Alright, Fector, you've been asking for it." With a roar he charged, his ham fists swinging. As they kicked, gouged eyes, bit ears, and clawed at each other, the crowd cheered them on. Hanks grabbed Butrick and thrust him through the distracted onlookers. "You've done enough good here for one day, Reverend. Let's get out of here."

*   *   *   *

Backwoods citizens of the town learned early how to exploit the Cherokee emigrants passing through. Now they came out, prowling the camp, stealing, trading, and seeking female companionship in exchange for food or a sip from the whiskey jug.

Tiva, kneeling by the fire, had succeeded in fanning it into flames. Her blood ran cold at the sound of the voice behind her.

"I'll be goddamned...it's my little Creek cunt or my name ain't Junior Brill. Back for more ain't ya?"

Tiva looked over her shoulder at the drunken, leering figure. Her hand slipped beneath her skirt.

As Brill lunged toward her, Tiva, in fluid motion, came out of her crouch, sidestepped and swung her right hand to the man's mid-section. With a cry of surprise, he stumbled forward and fell facedown into the fire. As the stench of burning hair and flesh filled the air, Tiva hugged herself tightly and shivered.

"What the hell...?" Hanks rushed up, pulled the man from the fire rolling him over on his back. Skin pealed off the blackened face. It was burned beyond recognition. Protruding from his chest was the hilt of a small knife. Throwing a quick quizzical glance at Tiva, he quickly removed the weapon.

A crowd soon gathered. "It was an accident," said Hanks, putting his arm around a trembling Tiva.. "This fellow fell into the fire...musta been drunk."

With mumbles and looks of suspicion, Pikesville townsmen dragged away the corpse. In a gesture of generosity, Rev. Butrick offered to conduct the last rites.

They lay silently, bedded down in the wagon box, listening to the cold rain beat against the canvas. "Want to talk about it, Tiva?" Hanks asked.

Through quiet sobs, she whispered, "He raped me."

"When?"

"When we were penned up in the stockade. I went to the river for water...he was one of the guards...he followed me..."

"Do you know who he was?"

"His name was Brill...Junior Brill."

Hanks sat upright. Scenes of a battleground raced across his memory and the desecration of a beautiful woman.

"What is it, Tom? What's the matter?"

"Tiva, how much do you remember about the fight at Horseshoe Bend?"

Tiva sat up beside Hanks. "Not much. I was only three or four at the time. Both my mother and father were killed there. I remember that someone pulled me out of a burning house. I don't remember much else. I was taken in and raised by another Creek family."

"Where did you get the amulet that you wear around your neck?"

"I don't know, Tom. I've always had it. Why do you ask?"

Hanks inhaled deep then let it out. There was no way he could describe to Tiva how her mother had been so profanely violated by Brill. "Yes, your mother was killed at Horseshoe Bend; I'm not so sure about your father. I think your father was Menawa. He fought in the battle but his body was never found...so he may still be alive."

"How do you know about such things?" Tiva asked.

"I was there. I saw your mother on the battlefield. And," he slowly added, "I am the one who pulled you out of the burning house...and I gave you that amulet." He put his arm around her and pulled her close. "If it's any comfort, Tiva, you avenged your mother today."

*   *   *   *

The rough, frontier town of Pikesville lay in the open Sequatchie Valley of gently rolling hills. Isolated by Walden's Ridge to the east and the Cumberland Mountains to the west, there was no easy way in nor out.

Reverend Butrick, and his wife Elizabeth, in their four-passenger carryall, drove by Hank's wagon. "Let us remove these children of Israel as quickly as possible from this vale of Sodom," said Butrick. "I've never encountered a place so exceedingly wicked."

"You go on ahead, Reverend. We have five, steep miles ahead of us. Because of that, I'm going to double up the teams on a wagon. It will take more time to gain the top but it won't kill off the horses."

At the end of the day, all wagons had successfully reached the top. After a move of only five miles, they made camp in the woods. Next morning, Thursday, November 8, they awoke to wagons covered with snow.

For the next two days the wagons jolted through frozen ruts across the Cumberland Plateau. His pony, exhaling steamy plumes in the icy air, Hanks rode alone with his thoughts. His fears of being caught on the trail by a cruel winter had been realized and the journey had just begun. Looking at his burdened people plodding barefoot through the snow, he wondered how they could possibly survive what lay ahead. They had been promised shoes and blankets in Nashville but that goal was over a week away.

He marveled at his feelings toward Tiva. Orphaned as a young lad, he had grown up with no family ties, relying upon his own wits to survive. He treasured his early, fatherly friendship with Ross but he was never comfortable with his military service under Calhoun, and then Jackson. It was good to be back with his own people. Tiva filled a void in his life that Hanks never knew existed. He was in love...and he loved the feeling.

Across the Cumberland, through Mt. Crest, and Spenser, and then, with feet numb and lips blue with cold, the emigrants made a steep descent into camp along the Collins River. Saturday and Sunday, November 10th and 11th, women attended to washing clothes, the men to getting wood, shoeing horses, and mending wagons. Jed Haxton and other slaves built large brush fires to thaw the ground so graves could be dug for the dead and the dying. On the Sabbath a large crowd of locals, starved for diversion, gathered with the Cherokee as Reverend Butrick preached. Using I Timothy 4:8 as his text, he exhorted his listeners to endure the present privations with hope for a better tomorrow.

Some of the Cherokee had no confidence in Butrick and his god. An outbreak of measles among the children turned them to their shaman. These Adawehi, physicians and priests, and skilled in the secrets of medicine and religion, led the children to a purifying plunge in the icy waters of the Collins River. The immediate results were gratifying...but an hour or so later they began to shiver and shake...and die.

Detachment leader, Richard Taylor, sensing the growing anger and feelings of hopelessness in his group, called a council meeting of the elders. There was little he could say to raise their morale. Many were making this journey in poverty because the United States government did not pay them due compensation before they left their country. A few openly advocated abandoning the removal, return to the mountains and take their chances.

Hard Mush, a chief and son of the wealthy war chief, John Watts, made their case.

"Brothers, when the white man first came to our country, we gave him land and kindled fire to make him comfortable. But when the white man had warmed himself by our fires, and filled himself with our hominy, he became very large. His foot covered the mountains, the plains and valleys. Then he became our Great Father. I love my red children, he said, but you must move a little farther west lest by accident I step upon you. He pushed us beyond the Oconee and the Ocmulgee. He made another talk. He said much but it all meant, move a little farther; you are too near to me. I have heard many talks from our Great Father and they all ended the same. Now he says, go beyond the great waters. It is a pleasant country. There is game; there you may remain while the grass grows and the rivers run. It shall be yours forever. Brothers, will not our Great Father come there also?"

"Eda-ditlu-nutsi…brothers, we, sons of the same mother"…Taylor sat silently contemplating the words of Hard Mush. He lifted his head. "Brothers, what you have heard is true. But I cannot offer you false hope. Our homes, our farm-lands…all are taken. Even if the whites permitted it, we could not return to our mountains and survive. We have no choice. We must endure the unendurable, press on, and hope the Great Spirit smiles upon us beyond the big waters."

The unending march continued. Into mud and manure, through biting cold rain and cutting winds they pressed on across the Cumberland River into Kentucky. Hunger clawed at their stomachs when food and supplies failed to appear where they were expected. Bare feet cut with ice and rocks left bloody footprints in the snow. Camp grounds of earlier detachments were cemeteries…salt pork and cornmeal…gaunt faces gray with fatigue…mother's milk drying up…no time nor energy to dig graves…dig a slit trench and cover them up. Not a blade of grass left for the horses to eat. Butrick prayed to his God…why had the storms, the elements, conspired to afflict these people?

Near Hopkinsville, Kentucky they came upon a slab of wood and a pole flying a white flag. Here was a shrine to White Path. Sickness and hardships of the trail had finally felled the seventy-five year old warrior who had fought so hard against removal.

On Friday, December 14, Hanks wearily leaned against his horse and watched as Taylor's detachment straggled into Berry's Ferry on the Ohio River. Thin and gaunt from lack of food, with only filthy rags to deflect the cold, and many with bare feet, these children of nature mutely endured. Barely halfway to their destination, the eighty-day estimate for the entire journey long ago discarded. Hanks choked down bitter bile of anger. As he walked to the waterfront where the ferry was tied up he noticed a big draft horse in a corral walking in circles.

"Something wrong with that horse?" he asked the boatman.

"Mister, if you'da spent your life walking in circles, you'd act the same way." The boatman spewed a stream of tobacco juice into the air, and jerked his thumb toward the ferry. "See that turntable? Made of oak, but it's damned near wore out with horses walking round and round turning that capstan. Put horses on land after years of working these boats and they just keep goin' in circles."

Tom extended his hand. "Forgot to introduce myself. Name's Hanks. Was wondering how soon we can get these wagons across tomorrow?"

"Baxter's the name. I own this ferry. Getting across right now is chancy. The old Ohio is running high, 'bout five miles an hour, with chunks of ice and trees that could send us to hell in a hurry. But, come sunup, we'll give it a try."

Early the next morning the detachment started crossing the Ohio River to Willard's Landing. Two big draft horses walking round and round a turntable, winding the ropes that pulled the boat across to Golconda, Illinois and back, was a slow process. The horses and turntable took up so much room that only two wagons could be transported each trip. About half of the wagons made it across that day. They went to a place designated for camping, about a mile and a half from the river. Rev. Butrick was gathering wood for fires and preparations were being made for supper when a local white man approached and ordered the emigrants to move on. Leaving fire and wood, teams were harnessed and the group moved down the road to another site. Tents were set up, wood was gathered, fires were made and Mrs. Butrick was preparing tea when the land owner appeared and declared that the Cherokees were not permitted to cut and burn any wood on his place. Rev. Butrick protested to no avail. It was now nearly dark but the detachment, now quite tired and hungry, moved further down the road to a site on public land.

Taylor and Hanks leaned against a wagon wheel out of the wind and studied a crude map. "It is less than sixty miles across the southern tip of Illinois, from here at Golconda on the Ohio River to the eastern bank of the Mississippi River," said Taylor. "The group of Cherokees led by B. B. Cannon last year took only eight days to get through Illinois, from Willard's Landing to Green's Ferry at Moccasin Springs."

"But he had less than three hundred in his group; we have a thousand." Hanks responded. "He was six weeks earlier. Here we are in mid-December. Locals tell me it's the worst winter they've ever seen. It will take us a bit longer to make the crossing than Cannon."

A despondent Taylor shook his head. "Our people are not prepared for this weather. Their clothing is not adequate and they are underfed. God only knows how many will make it."

Their discussion was interrupted as a group of local men came up. "My name is Potter," said their apparent spokesman. "We found one of your old men dead down by the river. We buried him for you so we'll hafta charge you thirty-nine dollars for the coffin and service."

Taylor bristled. "I have no old man missing. Perhaps he belonged to another detachment. In any case, I am under no obligation to pay any charges for him."

"I'm sorry to see you take that stand," said another man stepping forward. "I'm Sheriff Tate. I'm afraid you'll have to come with us."

Hanks accompanied Taylor and the locals to a small hamlet called Vienna. There, after some debate the justice of the peace reluctantly conceded that there was no evidence against Taylor and he was released.

Hanks returned to his wagon to find Tiva holding a baby. "What's this?" he asked. "Where's Nettie?"

"While you were with Taylor, Nettie and Jed brought the baby to me. They said now that they were in the free state of Illinois, they would no longer be slaves. They fled with their baby."

"Damn their hides. They knew we had no way to feed this child. They left a baby to starve."

Winter had come early with devastating effects. Without warning, Taylor's detachment was caught in a blast of frigid air from the north. The narrow, swampy road across southern Illinois wound through a dense forest of beech trees. Weakened horses strained to pull the wagons through the slush and black muck. Frequently wagons wheels dropped into potholes axle deep forcing equally weakened men to lift a wagon out of the hole. Like ghosts, the exhausted Indians trudged silently through the blizzard. They had no escape from the cold and wet. They bedded down at night under wagons with nothing between them and the cold ground but a single blanket. Newborn babies, expelled from the warmth of their mother's womb, were greeted with piercing cold. They did not survive the night…and neither did the unattended mothers. Then pneumonia struck ravaging the weak and aged. Corpses were stuffed into wagons along with the living as there was neither time nor energy for burials.

On Christmas Day Rev. Butrick's carryall hit a pothole, the linch pin came out of the fore axletree, the wheel came off and broke against the frozen ground. For the next six miles he and his wife struggled to the house of a settler who claimed to be a wagon maker. They were welcomed to spend the night with the family as the sixty-year old wagon maker set out to retrieve the carryall. He returned just before nightfall in a high state of intoxication. A horrified Butrick offered to lead family worship then found that none of the family could read or write. The following morning, in a repaired carryall, he left with a lowered opinion of the citizens of Illinois.

About a mile down the road he found the detachment encamped. There Taylor greeted him. "Might as well make camp, Reverend. We ain't going anyplace. Two detachments now at the Mississippi are stopped by floating ice and Hildebrand's detachment was stopped by the same means on the Ohio River. One detachment is four miles this side of the Mississippi, one sixteen miles this side, one eighteen miles, and one three miles behind us. There are eight thousand souls in those detachments, Reverend. There is sickness or death in every tent. Ask your god," he said bitterly, "for what crime is this nation doomed to perpetual death. Why this unheard of suffering?"

Butrick placed his hand on Taylor's shoulder. "I understand how you must feel. Though we have been distressed on every side, yet we have not been destroyed. Take comfort in God."

"There is no comfort in this, Reverend. My people are starving...freezing. We've got to kill some of our mules to feed them."

"As Job was tested by God, so are you now being tested. Rely on your faith, do not turn away. God will comfort you."

Taylor turned away with a snort. "Job was not responsible for a thousand people. Would it not be of greater comfort if God had not allowed all this to happen in the first place?"

On January 21, 1839, after remaining in camp for two weeks, Taylor's detachment moved on. They passed through the settlement of Jonesborough and finally, on Friday, January 25, after forty-one days spent in crossing sixty miles, and almost three months on the trail, the exhausted group arrived at Willard Landing on the east bank of the Mississippi River. There they buried their dead. Among those laid to rest in the cold ground was an unnamed baby born in the stockades.

A canvass tarp stretched between two wagons gave little protection from the driving rain, sleet and snow. A worn and haggard Taylor addressed the council. "Cut your rations in half. Our suppliers left enough food to last one detachment for two or three days. Now we have five detachments here waiting to cross. With the ice clogging the river, we have no idea when Green's Ferry will be able to operate. Our only hope right now is that Lewis Ross can make it to St. Louis and back in time with supplies."

In the night Hanks held a shivering Tiva close. A snake of doubt slithered into his head keeping him from sleep. Hundreds of his people were sick and dying, weakened by disease, exhaustion, and depression. Penned up in wagons or stretched upon the ground with only a blanket to keep out the January blast, how many of them could survive? Just across the river was food, medicine, and help but it might as well be a thousand miles away. The river was frozen solid far out from the banks. In the center of the stream ice chunks, big as houses, created a fearful noise night and day as they crashed and ground against each other. There would be no celebrated crossing of the river Jordan. An internal rage built within Hanks against those who had made him hostage now to the icy grip of the mighty, indifferent Mississippi.

CHAPTER 28

TSALI

The general eased his ponderous frame into the chair, an unlit cigar clamped between his teeth. "I have no desire, Chief Ross, to hunt your people down like dogs, but someone must pay for these crimes."

Ross sat impassively, listening.

The general continued. "Two soldiers of the 1ˢᵗ Dragoons, by the name of Perry and Martin, were killed while bringing in some of your friends from Qualla Town. Our national honor will not stand for that. The individuals guilty of this unprovoked outrage must be shot down."

"Have you any idea who was responsible?"

"Rumors are that it was some fellow by the name of Charley…Tsali, I think you call him. Frankly, Chief Ross, I'm weary of chasing your people. My soldiers are needed elsewhere. I would appreciate your help in finding those responsible for these crimes, and bring them to justice,"

"If the rumors are true, and Tsali is involved, will he be tried by a military court or…?"

Scott lunged to his feet and strode to the window. Outside an icy rain slashed against the house. "There will be no trial," Scott replied grimly. "If Tsali is guilty, he, and all who gave aid to him, must be shot. Furthermore, he will be executed by his own people."

"Those are hard terms, General Scott. I cannot agree with them."

Scott turned on his heel to face Ross. "Your agreement is not required. All you need do is ask yourself, is it better that one or two people pay for this crime or several hundred of your people?"

*   *   *   *

Ross aimlessly prodded the coals then returned the poker to its rack. "It pains me, James, that you have to take on this responsibility but I have no choice. I must remain here and get the remainder of the detachments ready for the trail."

"Not to worry, father," James grinned. "The oldest son should be able to take some load off your shoulders."

Ross leaned back in his rocking chair and looked at his handsome, twenty-four year old son, James McDonald Ross.

"Your confidence is to be admired, James, but this could be a dangerous mission. General Scott's demands are extremely harsh. Once Tsali's followers find out what they are, they may not give him up…if you do find him. There could be bloodshed."

"I promise, I'll be careful. But tell me, why is Scott so angry with Tsali?"

"I can only tell you what I've heard," Ross replied. "A few hundred of our people, the Oconaluftee Cherokees, refuse to surrender to Scott and are hiding out in the Great Smoky Mountains on the border between North Carolina and Tennessee. One day some of Scott's soldiers captured Tsali, his wife, two sons, a brother and started marching them to the stockade at Calhoun. One of the soldiers struck Tsali's wife with a horsewhip for stopping to care for her infant. In order to make better time, Lt. A.J. Smith, who was in charge, ordered one of his men to dismount and give his horse to Tsali's wife and baby. As she mounted, the horse bolted. Her foot caught in the stirrup forcing her to drop the infant. The baby sustained a fractured skull and died. Farther down the trail, an angry Tsali gave instructions in Cherokee to his family. On a signal, Tsali jumped one soldier, took away his gun and killed him with the bayonet. His brother also grappled with another soldier and killed him. On horseback, Lt. Smith got away. Tsali and his family then fled back into the mountains."

"Can't say as how I blame Tsali," James said.

"My word doesn't carry much weight with the Cherokee on the Oconaluftee. They have disregarded my pleas as well as those of Scott. They are mostly full-bloods who are highly opposed to removal. None of them showed up for the Treaty of New Echota. They live under a chief called Utsala. He won't be easy to convince."

"Well, father, if he won't listen to you, then who?"

Ross stood and stretched. "Scott is sending William Holland Thomas along with members of the 4th Infantry. Thomas is a lifelong friend of those people, he speaks Cherokee, and Utsala trusts him. You will go with Thomas and, on my behalf, try to persuade Tsali. Now, let's get to bed. You've got to be up early."

*   *   *   *

For twelve days the commander of the 4th Infantry, Colonel William S. Foster, led his regiment as they threaded their way through the narrow, heavily timbered valleys and up icy streams, looking for fugitives. Late one afternoon they came upon an encampment of a hundred or so Indians. Foster turned to James Ross. "Tell them I want to speak to their headman."

In answer to Ross's words, a gaunt and elderly man stepped forward. "I am Euchella," he said in a quavering voice. "I am the chief. We have worked hard to be good people. Why do you hunt us like animals?"

Ross replied. "We do not wish to harm you. We are looking for Tsali. Do you know where he is hiding?"

Euchella squinted through watery eyes. "Tsali was my neighbor. He is my friend. The white soldiers have hunted him like a deer. I will not betray him."

"If you know where he is," Ross insisted, "it would be best for you that you tell us."

"My wife and child starved to death here. With my own hands I buried them at midnight. What more can the white soldiers do to me?"

Ross pointed to Colonel Foster. "This man can order his soldiers to take you across the father of waters. Euchella, do not commit your people to such a fate."

Impatient with the discussion, Colonel Foster broke in. "If he will tell us where Tsali is, he and his people can stay here in these mountains. I give my word."

Euchella studied the face of Ross for several moments. Then, dropping his head he spoke in a low voice. "I know the man with you...Thomas. He can be trusted. You, son of a chief who betrayed us, I cannot trust. I will tell you where Tsali is but only Thomas may go to him."

*　　*　　*　　*

Tsali emerged from his cave, a smile creasing his wrinkled face. As he embraced William Holland Thomas he murmured, "It is so good to see you Will Usdi…it has been too long since I smoked the pipe with my friend."

In a voice choked with emotion, Thomas replied. "It is good to see you too. It has been a long time since anyone addressed me as Little Will."

Holding him at arm length, Tsali looked at Thomas's troubled face and in a sympathetic tone said, "Do not fret, my friend. I know why you are here."

Thomas nodded and wiped his eyes. "General Scott has ordered you to surrender."

"I am prepared to do so."

"Your sons must surrender also."

Tsali dropped his hands and stepped back. "I will take my punishment. But General Scott cannot chastise my sons for obeying my command."

"I'm sorry, Tsali, but General Scott gives no quarter on this matter. They must surrender with you."

Tsali hesitated.

Thomas continued. "Colonel Foster has promised that if you surrender, the rest of your people can live at peace in these mountains."

For a long moment, Tsali was silent. His shoulders slumped. With a deep sigh he said, "It is better that a few should die than all."

*　　*　　*　　*

The November sun was almost at its zenith when Colonel Foster signaled with his hand and the riders came to a stop. Three men were waiting beneath a huge sycamore tree that stood on the banks of the Tuckasegee River. Foster dismounted and shook hands with the trio. James Ross heard Foster ask, "Is this the place?"

Ross looked at Tsali, a question in his eyes.

Tsali, nodded and said quietly. "Yes, this is the place. This is where we killed the soldiers."

Foster walked toward Tsali. "You have been duly recognized by Lieutenant Smith as the ones who killed his men here. This is where you will be shot."

"But," blustered Ross, "don't these men get a fair trial? Your laws require that."

Foster scoffed. "Lawyers deal in legalities; I'm a soldier. I follow orders." He turned to Tsali. "You may choose among your friends to carry out the sentence."

Tsali quietly dismounted. "I am an old man. I am not afraid to die, but, I beg you, spare my sons."

"I have no discretion in the matter…General Scott's orders," Foster replied.

"Surely you won't execute this one," Ross protested. "He's just a child."

The colonel turned to Tsali's youngest. "What is your name?"

"Wasituni," the lad replied.

"Wasituni means Washington," Ross injected. "He is only fourteen."

Foster grunted. "Alright. He lives. He can tell his people what happens to those who oppose the United States Army." He turned to Tsali. "You…you have the privilege of choosing your own executioners. Do it now."

Tsali walked slowly among the band of warriors who had accompanied him. Most avoided his eyes, not wanting to be chosen. Stopping in front of Euchella, Tsali placed hands on his shoulders. "We have shared many trials together in this life, my friend. Do this last favor for me."

Euchella swallowed hard and nodded.

Tsali chose six of his closest friends; two executioners for himself, two for his brother, and two for his eldest son. He held his son for a long time in a tight embrace, then, with tears in his eyes, he turned to Will Thomas. "Take care of our people," he said. A weeping Thomas nodded silently.

Foster placed the three near the white trunk of the sycamore tree, facing the firing squad. Refusing a blindfold, Tsali picked up a large leaf from the ground, fastened it to his shirt over his heart, then signaled to Euchella.

James Ross turned away as the shots rang out.

CHAPTER 29

A DEATH
IN LITTLE ROCK

On Wednesday, December 5, 1838 the last detachment departed the Cherokee Agency. The small party of 231 souls, led by John Drew, included John Ross, his family, and slaves.

Thomas N. Clark, Ross's agent in Nashville, had purchased for Ross two horses and a carriage for $625, and horses and a baggage hack to haul tribal documents. Clark also hired two free blacks to serve as drivers for two dollars a day. He advised Ross to take the river route as the winter was severe and supplies in Missouri were scarce.

Ignoring Clark's advice, Ross set forth with 18 horses and oxen to transport 31 of his family, kinfolk and slaves to the west. Worry about his immediate family, along with the immense responsibilities for the total emigration, weighted the shoulders of Ross. His wife, Quatie, was ill; his son James McDonald was in a state of depression following the execution of Tsali. His son, Allen, now twenty-one, and his seventeen year-old daughter Jane helped out with the care of their younger brothers, Silas, only nine, and George, who was eight.

In short order Drew's detachment caught up with and joined the 1,600 member company of Peter Hildebrand at the Tennessee River. By the time they had reached Paducah, Kentucky, Quatie's illness had worsened into pneumonia.

Here Ross abandoned the idea of travel by land and took his family aboard the steamboat Victoria.

The vessel creaked and rolled as it changed course, dodging chunks of floating ice as it made its way down the Mississippi. Sitting beside Quatie's bed, in a smoky stateroom, an exhausted Ross slumped in his chair, listening to her labored breathing. He struggled to stay awake but the warmth of the room and the drumming of the engine soon lulled him into deep slumber. Quatie's cough awakened him.

"I'm glad you were able to get some sleep, John," she said with a wan smile. "I've worried so about you...you've carried the burden for so long..."

"You are not to worry," he replied as he tucked the quilt around her thin body.

Quatie lay back on her pillow and sighed. "I remember the first time you left me to go to Washington City with Major Ridge."

"Ridge was my friend then; now he is my sworn enemy. Best that I had never been involved...I've failed...the good world we once knew now lies in ashes."

"Hush, John. You have not failed. Under the circumstances, no one could have done more for our people."

"But I have failed, Quatie. When I first got involved I didn't believe failure was a remote possibility. The United States Congress was made up of honorable men; their government was bound by treaties with the Cherokee. Nothing could go wrong." He heaved a deep sigh and covered his face with his hands. "How wrong...Oh! How wrong I was. My people are divided into warring camps and we are now all exiles in the wilderness."

$$* \qquad * \qquad * \qquad *$$

Ross waited impatiently as the Victoria slowed to a crawl and inched its way through keelboats, flatboats, and steamboats, toward the crowded waterfront at Arkansas Post. Space was made for them when a huge steamboat, with cotton stacked ten bales high on its deck, backed into the stream and headed down the Arkansas River for a few miles where it joined the Mississippi and then on down to New Orleans. After the Victoria was secured, Ross was first off the boat. Quatie's condition was worsening; he must find a doctor...and any mail that might be awaiting.

Leaving the waterfront, he crossed the frozen mud of Front Street and made his way against a cold northwest wind down Main Street, past offices filled by lawyers, land speculators, and merchants, all thriving on trade in land, cotton, and slaves.

"You'll likely find the doctor," one of the locals informed him, "at the tavern. Jus keep on goin' down this street. You'll see it cross from the brickyard. Ya can't miss it."

At the tavern a surly bartender pointed through the smoky haze. "That be Dr. Spettles at the billiard table."

"Dr. Spettles?" At Ross's question a lanky, bleary-eyed man swayed and turned to face him.

"I'm Doc Spettles. Doctor Adam Spettles. What kin I do fer ya?"

"My name is Ross; John Ross. My wife is very ill, doctor. Pneumonia, I think. Can you help her?"

Spettles leaned on his cue stick. "Stranger round here, aintcha? I provide service for cash only."

"That's no problem, doctor. She is on the Victoria. Can you see her there?"

Spettles considered Ross for a moment. "Did you say your name was Ross? I knew a Ross once. Can't 'member where."

"It was at the Battle of Big Bend...your father saved the life of Sam Houston."

"Well, I'll be damned," Spettles grinned. Turning to his well-dressed companion, he said, "Colonel Notrebe, meet John Ross...he's some kinda chief or somethin'."

Notrebe extended his hand. "I see that you are quite agitated, Mr. Ross. How serious is the condition of your wife?"

"It's quite urgent, sir."

Notrebe looked at Spettles and sighed. "Give me a little time, Mr. Ross," he whispered. "I'll get some coffee down the doc. As you can see, he is in no condition to see a patient."

*   *   *   *

Notrebe pushed back from the table and flicked ash off his cigar as his servant filled his glass with port. "Spettles isn't a bad doctor...when he's sober."

Ross nodded. "His father had the same problem at the Battle of Horseshoe Bend. If I had to put soldiers back together...well, I guess I'd take to drink too. But Adam has a strange way with patients."

"He won't tolerate anyone looking over his shoulder when he is with a patient. He excludes everyone."

"I thank you, Mr. Notrebe, for this sumptuous dinner. Now, I must be getting back to Quatie."

"Don't hurry your meal. I'll have a carriage take you back to the waterfront when you are ready." Notrebe stood, stretched and looked at Ross. "Many of your people have already passed through here so I'm quite aware of their problems. But you…you are a man of substance and intelligence. Why must you subject yourself to such deprivations?"

Ross, surprised, placed his fork down. "Things are not going well with my people in the new lands. The old settlers resent them. Someone must place things in order and that is my responsibility."

Notrebe puffed a ring of smoke into the air. "Mr. Ross, this is a land of opportunity. When I left Napolean's army and came to this place in 1811 I had practically nothing. I started with a dry goods store then I saw the opportunities in cotton. Arkansas Post is the center of cotton production. I now own about 8,000 acres worked by 71 slaves. I own a cotton gin and a considerable share in the local bank. There is considerable profit in slave trade. I just sold a couple of good looking breeders for sixteen hundred apiece."

Ross smiled. "My brother, Lewis, recently purchased five hundred slaves in Georgia and is now bringing them to our new lands."

Notrebe nodded in satisfaction. "Obviously, your brother is an astute business man. You could rebuild your fortune here. The south is going to need people like you and me."

"I understand what you are saying, Mr. Notrebe, and I appreciate your offer. But my people wish to avoid entanglement in north-south disputes. We hope we can do so in our new lands."

Notrebe chuckled and picked up a copy of the Arkansas Democrat Gazette and pointed to a story on the front page. "The Twenty-sixth Congress has adopted a rule prohibiting the discussion of slavery. It cannot avoid the issue and neither can you. As long as you are a slave owner you will never escape condemnation by the northern abolitionists. Come now. The carriage is waiting for you."

*   *   *   *

All the bleeding and ministrations done by Dr. Spettles to defeat pneumonia was to no avail. On February 1, 1839 Quatie Ross died at Little Rock, Arkansas

A cold, north wind whipped up old snow and crystals of ice. It blew across the Arkansas River as the shivering Ross family huddled around a shallow pit that had been chipped out of the frozen ground on the south side of the river. There was a brief eulogy and a reading of Quatie's favorite scriptures. Behind the family stood the weeping and moaning household slaves.

Without benefit of body washing, or anointing with bear's oil, Quatie, dressed in her finest, was hurriedly laid to rest in the new Mount Holly cemetery, her body encased in a cargo box which was donated by a sympathetic trader.

CHAPTER 30

TROUBLE IN CANAAN

In the warm, sticky heat of April, the general mopped his broad, receding brow and nodded briskly towards a chair. Looking down his aquiline nose he said, "Have a seat, Mr. Ross and welcome to your new home."

"Not by our choice, General Arbuckle."

"Nor by mine," Arbuckle responded defensively. "It was not my doing that brought about the resettlement of the Indians here on the frontier but it is my sworn duty to maintain peace among you people. I will tolerate no violence in my command here at Ft. Gibson."

"I did not come here to discuss violence, General Arbuckle. I watched the last detachment of my people arrive here a few days ago. They were a people in despair; worn out from 154 days of travel, ill and emaciated from lack of food. Before we left we had fully discussed the subject of subsistence provisions with General Scott. The Cherokee people have been taught to expect that justice and protection would be extended to them through the commanding general in this hemisphere. Upon arrival we find the contractors, hired by the United States government, are providing rotten meat unfit to eat. We cannot hunt as our guns were taken from us east of the Mississippi. We have no axes with which to build cabins."

Arbuckle heaving a big sigh, rose and pointed to a map hanging on the wall behind his desk. "Mr. Ross, I have been commander of Ft. Gibson since I founded it in 1824. I am responsible for territory extending from the Grand

River here, to the Red River on the south. Mexican agents from Texas are encouraging Indians to revolt against the whites. I'm trying to keep from being drawn into the struggle between Mexico and that damned Houston and his Texans. This frontier could explode. I am trying to keep peace with the Osage who consider you intruders." Arbuckle turned to Ross with a flinty glare. "Now, with the arrival of your people, there is restlessness among the Old Settlers and the Ridge Party. They fear that you plan to take over."

"Those fears will be allayed, General Arbuckle. Two governments cannot and ought not to exist in the Cherokee Nation. Therefore, a general council meeting of our people will be held on June 3 at Takatoka, or Double Springs as you call it. You are welcome to attend."

With a sigh of weariness Arbuckle sat down. "Too many issues press upon me, Mr. Ross, but I will try to attend. I will refer your complaint regarding food to Montfort Stokes, the resident federal agent here at Ft. Gibson."

*   *   *   *

On June 3, 1839, the sun rose and dried the morning dew at Takatoka. Cold, clear waters bubbled from the springs and flowed over rust colored sandstone forming Double Springs Creek. Overhead, hawks spiraled lazily on an unseen, rising current. Meadowlarks warbled in the short grass while young, red squirrels, frolicking in the oak trees, paused to watch as people emerged from thick timbers into the clearing. Here, about four miles northwest of Tahlequah, families and small groups of Cherokee began to assemble at the springs.

By June 10 some 6,000 of them had gathered with much visiting between the Old Settlers and the new arrivals. About eleven o'clock a horn was blown. No attention was paid to the summons. With a hot breeze blowing from the south, the smoking, talking, and lounging under the shade of the sycamore trees went on. At three in the afternoon another signal was given and the people slowly assembled and prepared for business. Three chiefs, John Brown, John Rogers, and John Looney, all suspicious of John Ross's motives, represented the Old Settlers.

In a spirit of unity, Ross addressed the delegates. "Although many of us have for a series of years past been separated, yet, we have not and cannot lose sight of the fact that we are all of the household of the Cherokee family and of one blood. Let us kindle our social fire and take measures for cementing our reunion as a nation by establishing a government suited to the conditions and wants of the whole people. The late emigrants, being compelled by the strong arm of power to come here, though constituting a large majority, have no desire to require anything that is not just and satisfactory to the whole people. Let us never forget this self-evident truth, that a House divided against itself cannot stand. United we stand and divided we fall."

Suspicious of Ross's intent, the Western chiefs huffily removed their people to another site on the council grounds

On June 14 Major Ridge, his son, John Ridge, Elias Boudinot, and Stand Watie, all of the Treaty Party, rode into the council grounds at Double Springs. Sensing the intense hostility against them, after a hurried conference with the Old Settlers, they departed.

Later that day, as the sun slanted over the oak-covered hills, John Brown, first chief of the Old Settlers, replied. "We take pleasure to state distinctly, that we too desire to see the Eastern and Western Cherokees become reunited and again live as one people. As to that matter, it is believed by our council that the two people have already been united. We have made you welcome as partakers of all the existing laws in this country.

"We respect your wishes for your original laws to be brought here and to have full force in this nation. But such an admission would be entirely repugnant to our people. To admit two distinct laws or governments in the same country, and for the government of the same people, is something never known to be admitted in any country."

Six days of fruitless haggling followed. On June 20th Chief Brown dissolved the council. Later that night Ross and George Lowrey mulled over the setbacks of the day. "I feel regret and surprise at Brown's response. I thought we were reaching unity."

"Perhaps we were," Lowrey replied, "until the Ridge Party rode into camp. There is great anger among our people as they suspect the Ridges, and your brother, Andrew, are trying to break up this council. I greatly fear that some of our young bucks may no longer respect your forbearance toward the signers of the treaty. They may invoke the blood law."

A weary Ross pressed his fingers against his eyelids and massaged his temples. "I pray that you are wrong about that George. Such action would create a chasm between our people that might never be bridged. But I'll admit, any attempt of the Old Settlers, a small majority, to enforce their will over a great majority, appears to me to be a course so repugnant to reason and propriety, that it cannot fail but to arouse hostility.

"But it is important that we unite for the purpose of settling our accounts with the United States. We can adjourn for now, let heads cool, and call for another meeting of both parties later."

*   *   *   *

Roosters were crowing as the first rays of dawn streaked the sky on Saturday, June 22, while twenty-five horsemen stealthy approached John Ridge's large, clapboard home at Honey Creek and surrounded it. Three men broke down the front door, forced their way into the house and found Ridge in bed. One placed a pistol against the head of Ridge, pulled the trigger, but the gun misfired. Sarah screamed as the men dragged her struggling husband from his bed into the yard. The children, now awakened, joined their wailing mother who was barred by riflemen at the front door. Horrified, they watched as two men held their father by the arms while a third repeatedly plunged a knife into Ridge's body. Then, with a lethal swipe, the executioner slashed his jugular vein. As a final act of dese-cration, the bleeding body was thrown into the air. When it struck the earth, each assassin stamped on it as they marched over it single file, mounted their horses and quickly departed.

Sarah ran to the side of her husband using her night cap to staunch the flow of blood. He struggled to raise himself on his elbow and reached for her. Blood gushed from his mouth and throat as he made a garbled attempt to speak his last words.

*   *   *   *

On the same morning, a second band of horsemen, some thirty strong, arrived at Park Hill and hid in a thick stand of timber. They watched silently, focused on the mission home of Samuel Worcester where Elias Boudinot and his wife, Delight Sargent, were living. After breakfast, Boudinot kissed his wife goodbye then walked east about a quarter mile where he was building his new home. Using a sledge and wedge, he was splitting shingles from a slab of oak when three Cherokees approached. Wiping the sweat from his brow, Boudinot greeted them.

"Si-yu'. What can I do for you gentlemen?"

"We are in need of medicine," one of the men stated. "We thought you could secure it from the white preacher."

"Well, let's go ask him," said Boudinot. He laid aside his sledge and started up the sandy lane toward Worcester's house. He had not taken many steps when one of the men, following close behind, swung a knife high and buried it in Boudinot's back. His shriek of pain was cut short as the others rained blows of his head with war hatchets, crushing his skull. The deed done, the assailants left Boudinot bleeding in the dust, and fled to where their cohorts waited on horseback.

Worcester had witnessed the attack from his house. He and Delight rushed to Boudinot's aid but to no avail. For a few minutes the victim struggled in agony then breathed his last.

Stunned with grief, Worcester and Delight knelt and wept. "They have cut off my right hand", he said.

*   *   *   *

After spending the night with his friend, Ambrose Harnage at Cincinnati, Arkansas, Major Ridge and his slave, Peter, proceeded south on Line Road which paralleled the border between Arkansas and Indian Territory. Lush greenery hugged both sides of the road. The hot, June air was perfumed with wild flowers, blossoms from wild plums, and grapevines. About ten o'clock they paused at Graystone Creek so the horses could drink. Ridge removed his hat and mopped his broad brow with a kerchief. Peter dismounted, went a few steps upstream from the horses, and cupped the cool, clear water to his mouth. At that moment, a blast of rifles was heard. Peter threw himself flat on the stream bank and turned toward his owner. Major Ridge had slumped in his saddle. As his horse reared in panic, his body toppled to the ground, blood flowing freely from multiple gunshot wounds. Peter jumped upon his horse and kicked it into a dead run for the settlement of Dutch Mills, about two miles south.

From the small rise where they had lain in the brush to ambush, a dozen assassins rose and looked down on the body of Ridge. One named Bird, the son of Doublehead, spoke. "An eye for an eye, a tooth for a tooth. A-ya', I, myself, have killed the killer of my father."

*   *   *   *

Late afternoon on June 22 a clamor outside his house disturbed Ross as he worked at his desk preparing for another meeting on unifying the Cherokee. Opening the door he saw a horde of armed men surrounding the house. His twenty-two year old son, Allen, rushed in. Breathless he blurted, "They're dead...they've been killed!"

"Who's dead?" Ross demanded.

"The Ridges...and Boudinot. Some of the others got away."

Stunned, Ross groped for a chair. "Who killed them, Allen? And why are all these men outside?"

"They are here to protect you. Word is that Stand Watie is out to kill you. He thinks you are responsible for his brother's death."

Ross ran his fingers through his thick, now graying, hair, struggling to take it all in. "You say Boudinot is dead?"

Allen nodded.

Lunging out of his chair Ross opened the door to where Tom Hanks was standing guard, his Kentucky rifle cradled in his arms. "Tom," Ross said, "ride over to Boudinot's and make sure that Delight and the children are alright."

Ross closed the door and slowly came back to his chair. Jaw muscles twitching, a deep scowl on his brow, he fixed dark eyes on his son. "Allen, tell me about these killings. How did you know so soon? Were you a party to them in any way?"

Allen swallowed hard but spoke defiantly. "Yes, father, I was. We invoked the Cherokee blood law. If the Ridge Party had not sold out to Jackson, we would not have lost our homes in Georgia and thousands of our people would not have endured such misery and death on the trail coming to this country. They would not now be hungry and destitute in this place. When we saw how your efforts to unify the Cherokee were disrupted by the Ridges, we felt there would be no peace and harmony as long as they were alive."

"I see," said Ross. "You mentioned that some got away. Who got away?"

"Stand Watie, John Bell, George Adair, and some others."

"And my brother, Andrew?"

"He was not on the list, father."

The quiet was broken only by the squeak of Ross's rocking chair. "Allen, did you pull the trigger on any of these killings?"

"No, father. Those chosen to carry out justice drew numbers out of a hat. When it came my turn to draw, I was refused. They told me that my job was to stay near you and see that you got no word of their plans, and that's what I did."

Ross ceased rocking, leveling his gaze at his son. "Allen, I am saddened and deeply angered. Did you never stop to consider the consequences of what you were doing? You have brought about a division that may never be closed. You may have brought civil war to our people."

*   *   *   *

"You can't forever hide your pain in work, Little John. You need something more."

Without looking up from his work, Ross asked, "And just what do I need, Sequoyah?"

"A woman." Sequoyah leaned forward and tapped the sketch on Ross's desk. "You may call these the plans for the Peoples'House', but if I were you, I'd make room for a woman in it."

Ross hesitated, placed his pencil down, and looked at a smiling face of seasoned mahogany, deeply furrowed from weather and time. "My friend, if I needed counsel on matrimony, no one could top your experience. After all, a man in his sixties who has had five wives and twenty children should know what he is talking about."

Sequoyah leaned back in his chair, puffing contentedly on his pipe. "And I would have more if permitted by Asgaya-Galun-lati'. I love the feel and smell of a woman. I love the look in women's eyes when I satisfy them. Why The Man Above denies the sweetest nectar to the aged is beyond me. But you...you are only fifty. There are still sons in your loins."

Ross sighed and ran fingers through his hair. Through the window he could see glistening black bodies sweating in the heat as slaves constructed his new home near Park Hill Creek. Outside, hundreds of men were still on guard. "Sequoyah, Stand Watie is out to kill me, General Arbuckle wants to arrest me, and you want to counsel me on women. What is really on your mind?"

With a toothless grin Sequoyah tapped his long-stemmed pipe against the arm of his chair, spilling ashes on his calico shirt. "You are not the only one, Little John, who seeks unity among our people. Before we dispersed at Double Springs, Jesse Bushyhead and I managed to get both factions to agree to another meeting at the Illinois Council Grounds on July first. I believe I can bring the Old Settlers to the table."

Ross's eyebrows lifted in surprise. "But what about John Brown and John Rogers? Have they agreed...?"

Sequoyah raised his hand to silence Ross. "Leave Brown and Rogers to me"

Quickly taking in what he had just heard, Ross spoke with urgency. "Sequoyah, if you can secure agreement from the Old Settlers, we can stay the hand of violence, we can stop the effusion of Cherokee blood, and we can restore tranquillity among our people."

Sequoyah reached for his cane and struggled to his feet. "I can use my influence with the Old Settlers. The Treaty Party is another matter. They are bent on revenge. For now, they are gathered at Fort Gibson under the protection of General Arbuckle." As he limped toward the door, he turned, grinned, pointed his cane toward Ross's desk, and said, "Remember, make room for a woman in the People's House."

*　　　*　　　*　　　*

Located on Tahlequah Creek, a mile from where it joined the Illinois River, the Illinois Council Ground was sheltered by two sides of hills running east and west. In this valley, under a hot sun, over two thousand Cherokees gathered on July 1, 1839 in another attempt at unity.

"I do not see Chiefs Brown, Looney, or Rogers in attendance," Ross observed. "It seems your powers of persuasion are limited."

Sequoyah sighed. "Those three are still at Fort Gibson. I'll try once more to change their minds."

As one of the presidents of the convention, he immediately wrote a letter, in his own syllabary, urging their attendance. "We, the old settlers, are here in council with the late emigrants, and we want you to come up without delay, that we may talk matters over like friends and brothers…We have no doubt but we can have all things amicably and satisfactorily settled."

A few days later Brown and Rogers replied, declining the request to meet at the Illinois Council Ground and announcing that they had called for a meeting on July 22 at the old Tahlontuskey Council House at the mouth of the Illinois River. "We affectionately call upon our Eastern Cherokees," they added, "to stop the further effusion of Cherokee blood and abstain from any further acts calculated to disturb the peace and security of the Cherokee people…"

John Looney of the Western Cherokee, realizing the futility of further opposition, had joined with Ross.

On July 7 the convention issued a decree granting full pardons and amnesty to members of the Treaty Party if they disavowed their threats and pledged to conduct themselves as good and peaceable members of the community. However, they were barred from holding public office within the Cherokee Nation for at least five years. Those who refused to accept the terms of the convention remained liable to the pains and penalties of outlawry. Pardons were also extended to those accused of killing the members of the Ridge Party.

On July 12 an act of union was adopted between the Old Settlers and the late emigrants by which the two parties declared "one body politic, under the style and title of the Cherokee Nation."

*   *   *   *

Enraged, the general rose from his desk, kicking over his chair in the process. "This decree is totally unacceptable. Ross's attempt to punish those who refuse his amnesty will ignite the fires of hell. I will not tolerate his insolence."

"I, nor none of my friends, will endure such humiliation from Ross, General Arbuckle," said Stand Watie. "Ross should be placed in shackles. I urge you to employ the military and put an end to such high-handed tactics."

Arbuckle mopped sweat from his brow with a handkerchief. The heat and humidity of July along the river was debilitating. "I wish I had the authority to remove Ross. His actions have scared the hell out of the whites. They fear they might be caught in the middle of a civil war."

Worry showed on Watie's broad, furrowed brow. "As hard as we are oppressed, and flagrant as our injuries, I value Cherokee blood too highly to engage in the horrors of a civil war. I condemn the actions of Ross but I seriously deprecate a civil war, General. It would result in the total destruction of our nation. I feel our only alternative is to solemnly and directly appeal to the government of the United States."

*   *   *   *

A southern wind, blowing strong and hot on July 16, shook Ross's carriage as he paused on the east hill overlooking Fort Gibson. Twenty-nine heavily armed mounted men accompanied him. Tired of his meddling and misrepresentations, it was time to confront General Arbuckle.

In a show of hospitality, Arbuckle provided the delegates with drinks of cold water and tried to make them comfortable in his crowded quarters. He mopped sweat from his brow and fidgeted with his tight, military collar before coming to the point.

"I am much displeased that your actions of July 12 do not conform with my wishes. Your Act of Union, which purports to grant amnesty to members of the Ridge Party, is humiliating and unacceptable."

"The world is large," Ross calmly replied. "If any of our people refuse to abide by Cherokee laws, they can leave us. But if they remain in our country, being a part of our people, they must come under our laws."

"Do you not realize that your actions could bring about a civil war among your people?" Arbuckle demanded.

"We cannot admit that our actions have produced these difficulties. General, if I may be so blunt, it is you who talks up a civil war. We do not apprehend any danger of civil war in this country and no set of men in Christendom would more deeply deplore such a state of things than we would. The only war we are interested in waging is a war of reason."

Refusing to bend, Arbuckle fired back. "Isn't it true that you have been guilty of stirring up the Creeks and other tribes. Settlers by the dozens have fled in fear to the state of Arkansas."

Ross blandly replied. "I am surprised that your apprehensions of hostilities were so strong as to call for the issue of arms and ammunition to white settlers. It is true that we have found it necessary to keep other tribes apprised of the true nature of things. The interests of the red men are the same and we seek to hold each other by the hand."

Unaccustomed to defiance, Arbuckles's face reddened. "My patience is not inexhaustible, Mr. Ross. Have you any plans to bring to justice those who murdered the Ridges and Boudinot or will I have to do so? You should know that I have received instructions from the War Department to arrest and bring to trial those murderers."

Leaning forward and leveling his dark eyes at Arbuckle, Ross replied. "It is well known to you, sir, that we are not in this country by our own procurement but in conformity with the mandate of the United States Government. The loss of property and loss of life have saddened the hearts of my people. Many parents are childless and many children are orphans. Their wounded and bleeding hearts cannot suddenly be healed. And yet, for the sake of peace all has been borne in silence.

"I am wholly at a loss to conjecture by what right or sound policy the Cherokee people are to be deprived of the exercise of their own legitimate authority over acts of one Indian against another. As to the matter of exercising justice and punishment, it is a business which belongs exclusively to the Cherokee people. No other person has a right to dictate the course we shall pursue. I am impelled to protest any further interference on your part in these local political affairs. I know my duty to my own people and our obligations to the United States and I shall not shrink from the performance of them. If perchance, it should please you to overstep the proper bounds of official propriety to indulge in invective or decide questions not at all within the scope of your duties, it will not change my course. The matters of union within our people is exclusively our own. It is not considered that your approval is required to legalize the transactions. In these, General Arbuckle, you have no jurisdiction."

CHAPTER 31

MAY AND DECEMBER

On November 15, 1839 John Ross and his delegation left the Cherokee Nation to counter claims by representatives from the Treaty Party and the Old Settlers Party who were already in Washington DC. Ross took time to travel to New Jersey where he placed his ten-year-old son, Silas, in the Lawrenceville Classical and Commercial High School. The all-male school housed about sixty boys. Founded in 1810 and modeled after the British boarding schools, it was considered to be one of the most prestigious secondary schools in the nation. After making proper arrangements for his son, Ross journeyed on to Washington where he joined the other delegates at Fuller's Hotel.

Desiring to obtain an update on affairs in the capitol city, he walked over to Brown's Hotel where he was told Henry Clay would be. Inside he found a loud, inebriated Clay in a smoke-filled room drinking with his friends. Rapidly pacing, one fist pounding the air, the ends of his swallow-tail coat swishing back and forth, whiskey in his glass sloshing onto the floor, Clay coarsely proclaimed, "Those fuckin' sonsabitches in Harrisburg did me in…Who is most responsible for the Whig Party? Who has fought its battles? Me! The Whig Party is nothing without me…but the afterbirth of humanity in Harrisburg, Thaddeus Stevens and Thurlow Weed, deny me the nomination for president. I had the South tied up but Georgia, South Carolina, Arkansas and Tennessee don't even show up at the convention. My friends are not worth the powder and lead it would take to blow them to hell!"

Those in the room sat in disbelief, stunned at such a show of vulgar profanity from their political idol. Suddenly, Clay calmed down, his anger changing to self-pity. "It is a diabolical intrigue, which has betrayed me. I am the most unfortunate man in the history of parties; always run by my friends when sure to be defeated, and now betrayed for a nomination when I would be sure of election." Looking up, he added. "I apologize for my gross behavior to the men of the cloth I see here…and to my friend Chief John Ross. My words must have shocked you."

With Ross in tow, Clay crossed to the south side of Pennsylvania Avenue to his boarding house. Stench from the nearby Chesapeake and Ohio Canal hung in the air. Pouring himself a glass of whiskey, he waved Ross to a chair. "I'm sorry for the outburst, my friend. What brings you to Washington?"

"There are three delegations of Cherokees here vying for recognition by your government. The bar to the Executive door has been bolted. Because of General Arbuckle's reports, Secretary of War Poinsett suspects me of being a party to the murder of the Ridges and will not meet with our delegation even though we represent four-fifths of the Cherokees. Since he will not pay any annuities to us, I don't see how we can remain in Washington."

Clay lowered his lanky, sixty-two year old body into a chair and took another sip from his glass. "I'm sorry I won't be able to afford you much help. Losing the nomination to that old fart William Henry Harrison will diminish my influence here in Washington." Clay emptied his glass then looked to Ross. "If the Executive door is closed, I'd suggest you take your case to the legislative branch. Congress is hardly enthralled with Van Buren and you have a good friend in John Bell of Tennessee who heads the Committee on Indian Affairs. With the election in the air, the nation in a financial depression, and with the annexation of Texas heating up, you may not get much attention…but that's your best bet."

Following Clay's advice, Ross and his delegates spent the next few days compiling a petition to Congress describing, at length, their repeated, peaceful efforts to bring about an acceptable government among the Cherokees and refuting gross misinformation which General Arbuckle had reported to Washington. In the memorial, which they submitted on February 28, they were critical of Secretary of War, Joel Poinsett, but were careful to downplay the subject of forced removal.

While awaiting action from the House Committee on Indian Affairs, Ross enjoyed the social scene in Washington. He made his way through heavy snow to the White House where Van Buren was presiding over the annual Christmas dinner. As the guests assembled in the parlor, the President moved through the crowd endeavored to restore good feeling. When the dinner was ready the large folding doors leading to the dining room were thrown open. Ross stared with awe at the damask window curtains, sparkling chandeliers and candelabra, large, gold-framed mirrors, tabletops of Italian marble, imperial carpets, satin-covered chairs, and the glint of silverware. Seated toward the head of the table, near the president, were Dolly Madison, the widow of Alexander Hamilton, Elizabeth, and ex-president John Quincy Adams. At the foot of the table Ross was seated next to Henry Clay.

"From log house to White House," Ross commented. "Must be quite a transition for Harrison to make."

"Bullshit," laughed Clay. "That old bastard has never lived in a log house. He has a fine home in Ohio and he certainly ain't poor."

"He's sixty-seven years old. Do you believe he can win?"

Clay reached for a pinch of snuff then pensively responded. "I feel cheated of an office for which I am far better qualified than any of those nominated. I felt certain that my time for the presidency had come. But, to answer your question, yes, Harrison can win…if he handles the slavery issue with skill. Southerners keep blowing out the moral lights by following Calhoun's declaration that slavery is a good, positive thing. Although I do own slaves and I understand the intense anxiety of my fellow slaveholders, I consider slavery a curse; a curse to the master and a grievous wrong to the slave. The South speaks too frequently, and with too much levity, of a separation of the union. If Harrison is to carry any votes in the South, he must tiptoe around this issue."

When the dinner was over, and carpets were rolled back for dancing, Ross found a quiet nook where he could sit and observe. Deep in thought he was barely aware as a woman seated herself beside him.

"Chief Ross?"

Roused from his reverie, Ross politely stood. Before him sat a strikingly beautiful woman. "Yes, I'm Chief Ross. What can I do for you?"

"Please sit down, Mr. Ross. It isn't a matter of what you can do for me; it is what I can do for you."

Ross sat. "Do I know you…Miss…?"

"Yes, you do know me. I'm Kate Brill. When you brought me to Washington I was a very young girl."

Ross stared in amazement at the mature, fashionably dressed woman sitting beside him. "You've done well, Kate. The last time I saw you…"

She placed her hand on his. "The last time you saw me I was a servant girl. Life has been good to me since then. I want to repay you for your kindness."

"Kate," Ross stammered, "I don't need repayment..."

"You and your friends are about to be evicted from your hotel, you don't have money to get home, and the federal government isn't giving you the time of day."

"But how...?"

"I doesn't matter how I know. I have very good connections to high places in this town."

"But where would you get the money...?"

"It's a long story. When my brother, Virgil, got cheated out of his gold mine by Obadiah Speeks, I left here and went back to Georgia. Speeks failed to find the vein of gold that Virgil knew was there. So when Speeks gave up, I managed to get the mine back."

"How did you manage that?"

Kate smiled coquettishly. "Never mind how I did it. A woman has her ways. Anyway, Virgil and I developed the mine and I came back to Washington with a small fortune. I now own a profitable business on Marble Street."

"Marble Street! Isn't that the...?" Ross slowly shook his head. "I can't take money from you Kate..."

"You won't embarrass me, Mr. Ross. You were going to say the red light district of Washington." She slid a small leather bag across the table. "Take it. It's clean money well earned."

Ross leaned back in his chair. Not only was he enchanted with this beauty; he was captured by her frankness. It had been a long time since he was this close to a beautiful woman, so close he could smell her perfume. "You still call yourself Kate Brill. Does that mean you never married?"

"No, Chief Ross, I never married." She hesitated. "but I do have a grown son...I named him Houston...Houston Brill."

*   *   *   *

Late in August, 1840, Ross left Washington and headed home, overland to New Orleans, then by steamer up the Mississippi and the Arkansas Rivers to a settlement called Van Buren, Arkansas. He was bitter at Arbuckle for sabotaging his efforts with the United States Government and depressed that he would have to report a complete failure to his people upon returning to Tahlequah. His only consolation; the House Committee on Indian Affairs had sided with the Ross Party. In fact, the committee findings were so critical of Van Buren and the War Department that the House would not permit the report to be published. John

Bell, a member of the committee, had so informed Ross and on July 20, 1840, Bell leaked the information to the press.

*   *   *   *

On Monday, October 28, Ross rode the five miles from his residence to the council grounds in Tahlequah, arriving about noon. After tying his horse to a tree, many Cherokees quietly came up to shake the hand of their chief. Ross could see the fear in their eyes as word about his mission in Washington had already spread.

After about an hour of visiting, Ross took his place in the Council Chamber, which was merely an open air shed with a roof sustained by log uprights. Rev. Jesse Bushyhead, the Chief Justice of the Cherokee Nation, accompanied him. Members of the council took their seats on split logs, each log holding a dozen or so members. With both men standing, a sober Ross then read his message in English, which was, sentence by sentence, translated by Bushyhead. "Had our true position been understood in Washington," Ross said, "I should have been enabled to present you a less discouraging report from your delegation. But, as it is, I am compelled to announce their entire failure to gain any objects of their mission. The War Department refuses to recognize us as the legitimate Cherokee government and thus will not pay our annuities."

Ross nervously cleared his throat. "I hope for, and expect, a change of policy in the United States government regarding our affairs. I will therefore hope that you men will continue to be patient and to place every confidence in the honesty and honor of the government and people of the United States. The more difficult our position, the more honor we shall merit in deporting ourselves with prudence. May your labors for the public good merit the smile from Heaven!"

An uncomfortable silence hung over the council as Bushyhead finished his translation. Faith in Ross remained strong but the dire poverty of the Cherokee made any delay of relief a luxury. The silence was broken when a tall, gaunt John McPherson rose from his seat at the rear of the council.

"No disrespect intended, Chief Ross, but I can't wait for a smile from heaven. My family is starving. I can't hunt deer because the soldiers took away our guns. I can't build a log shelter for want of an axe. I can't put seed into the ground without a hoe. When the soldiers herded us out of our homes, we had no time to bring anything with us. To survive we have had to fall back on the wisdom of our elders who taught us how to hunt with bows and arrows and make snares to catch small game. We cook in clay pots. We eat with wooden spoons. We have no shoes or coats to cover us from the cold. How many more of us must die of star-vation? No, Chief Ross, I cannot accept your plea for more patience. If you can-not secure us relief from the United States government, then maybe we will have to look to someone else."

McPherson's implied threat was not lost on Ross. He was acutely aware of continuing efforts by members of the Treaty Party, and some of the Old Settlers, to undermine the existing Cherokee government. The six grown, mixed-blood sons of James Starr, in revenge for the slaying of the Ridges and Boudinot, were engaged in house burnings, horse stealing, and even murder...anything to expose the weakness of the new government.

Late in December Ross learned that William Henry Harrison had been elected president of the United States. With renewed hope for better treatment by a new administration, and with the blessings of the National Council, he, along with David Vann and John Benge, left for Washington on February 1, 1841.

Before arriving at the capitol, Ross detoured to New Jersey and the Lawrenceville high school to visit his son, Silas.

*   *   *   *

She was a girl now becoming a woman. Even in her plain, gray and white-trimmed dress, her young body taunted the longing eyes of men. Flashing dark eyes, full lips with an inviting smile, and glistening black hair cascading around her shoulders...As Ross held open the door for her entry into the build-ing, he felt a pagan urge and stood tongue-tied as a school boy.

Acknowledging his courtesy with a nod, she smiled teasingly. "It would seem thee is late to matriculate in this school, sir."

In an attempt at repartee, Ross answered. "I'm here to visit my son, but what excuse is there for a beautiful female to be here at a boy's school?"

Boldly stepping forward, the young lass offered her hand. "I'm Mary Brian Stapler and this is my sister, Sarah. Would thee mind assisting with my coat?"

Ross bowed to the older, and plainer, sister.

"To answer thy question," Mary continued, "our temporary excursion into the world of men is to visit a friend of the family. My school is the Moravian Female Academy in Bethlehem, Pennsylvania."

"We have long welcomed Moravian missionaries among my people," said Ross.

"And who would thy people be?" she teased.

Flustered by her nearness, he replied. "Excuse my poor manners, Miss Stapler. I'm John Ross, principal chief of the Cherokee Nation."

"Thy fame precedes thee, Chief Ross. We know of thee and the remarkable Cherokee people through our friend, Thomas McKenney."

Basking in her captivating smile, Ross struggled to regain his composure. "I, too, claim McKenney as an old friend."

His appointment with the school's head master was announced before he could say more.

In the stagecoach bound for Washington City, he settled back, bundled up against the cold but warmed by his fantasies of a young, dark-haired lass.

✳   ✳   ✳   ✳

On February 8, 1841 a physically exhausted William Henry Harrison arrived in a rainy and snowy Washington on the Baltimore and Ohio Railroad. On Thursday, March 4, Ross stood with thousands as the General, seated on a white horse, and wearing a plain frock coat, made his way from his rooms at the National Hotel up Pennsylvania Avenue, bowing and waving his top hat to the people. Floats of log cabins, militia companies, and veterans of the War of 1812 under flying banners, escorted him. For a fleeting moment Ross thought of another inauguration in 1829 and another general riding a white horse. At half-past twelve o'clock a procession led the president from the Senate chambers to the eastern front of the capitol where there was a platform some fifteen feet high, constructed for the occasion. Under overcast skies with a chilling wind blowing from the northeast, the tall, thin, careworn old Virginian stood bareheaded without coat or gloves and clearly delivered his inauguration speech for the best part of an hour and a half. He then turned to Chief Justice Taney and, with Bible in hand, repeated the oath required.

A few days after the inauguration, Secretary of War, John bell arranged a meeting between Ross and the new executive. President Harrison, though fighting a head cold, was magnanimous in promising equitable indemnification of Cherokee claims. Ross left the meeting with a surge of confidence. But all was not going well with Harrison. When he did not make his usual appearances at two churches on the Sabbath, public speculation began about the seriousness of his condition. Dr. Thomas Miller was summoned. The President was bled, cupped with hot metal cups to create blisters, given doses of calomel, laudanum, castor oil, and powders. Shots of warm whiskey were given him at regular intervals.

On Sunday, April 4, one month after the inauguration, Ross awoke to the shocking news that Harrison had died of pneumonia at half past twelve o'clock that morning.

Being the first president to die in office, there was no established form for official mourning and funerals. It was clear, however, that the death of a President called for formal ceremony, symbolism suitable to the dignity of the state.

Ross and his friend Thomas McKenney, crowded into a packed East Room of the White House where Harrison's mahogany coffin rested on a temporary catafalque which was covered with gold lace and over it was thrown a velvet pall with a deep golden fringe. On this lay the sword of Justice and the sword of State, surmounted by the scroll of the Constitution, bound together by a funeral wreath, formed of yew and cypress. Around the coffin stood in a circle the new President, John Tyler, the venerable ex-President John Quincy Adams, Secretary of State Daniel Webster, and other members of the cabinet. The Rev. William Hawley, pastor of St. John's Church, performed the Episcopal service.

At the conclusion of the service, the mahogany coffin was placed inside a larger walnut coffin, which fit into a monumental third coffin of lead. As the coffin was placed in a large funeral car, drawn by six white horses, and moved toward the Congressional Burial Grounds, Ross nervously posed a question to McKenney. "Can I trust Tyler to carry out the measures contemplated by General Harrison?"

McKenney shrugged. "Tyler is a question mark. After the inauguration, he was so disgusted with the powerless position of vice-president that he left Washington and went home to his estate in Williamsburg. When he was brought back after Harrison's death, the Cabinet thought he should be styled as acting President. Tyler would have none of that. Since Chief Justice Taney was out of town, he summoned Chief Justice William Cranch, of the Supreme Court of the District of Columbia. In the parlor of Brown's Indian Queen Hotel, Tyler took the oath of office administered to preceding presidents. He may be a problem that the Whigs don't need."

Ross shook his head in despair. "Does your government ever deal with questions of substance, or is it always a game of politics?"

McKenney chuckled. "In Washington, politics is the only substance. And, since it will take some weeks for Tyler to settle in, your problems will receive no attention in the immediate future. Why not take a break and come with me? I have some business to attend in Bethlehem."

Intrigued by the possibility of seeing a saucy young maiden, who attended the Moravian Female Academy in Bethlehem, Ross quickly assented.

*   *   *   *

Outside of earshot, but within visual scrutiny of elder sister Sarah, Ross and Mary Stapler sat beneath the shade of a red maple and talked. He listened as she told him of her Quaker faith, her family, of her wealthy, adoring father and of her life in school. Mesmerized by the play of filtered sunlight on her raven hair, he lost focus as she chattered on. Silently, his eyes took her all in, wondering how those moist lips would feel against his, how she would respond to his caressing her firm, rounded breasts, how she would respond if he bedded her? Now he felt a flush of shame. How could a man of fifty years be so physically stirred by this innocent child of sixteen?

"John, art thou listening to me?"

Fearing Mary had read his thoughts, he replied lamely. "Yes, I was just dwelling on your Quaker faith. You didn't mention the marriage ceremony."

With a quizzical smile she replied. "There isn't much of a ceremony in a Quaker wedding. In fact, it is very simple. At a meeting of the Friends, parents of the bride and groom are seated on a front bench. The bride then takes the bridegroom's arm, walks down the aisle, and the couple proceeds to take their seats between their parents. After a few minutes silence, the bride and groom rise, and take each other by the right hand. The man says first: "In the presence of the Lord and this assembly, I take thee, and here he says the woman's name, to be my wife, promising with divine assistance to be unto thee a loving and faithful husband until death shall separate us." The same words are repeated by the woman. Then they sit down as man and wife. A marriage certificate is then signed by the contracting parties and the woman now assumes the name of her husband. The whole subject is closed at the next Monthly Meeting when the committee appointed to have oversight of the marriage reports that the marriage was accomplished in accordance with the good order of Friends." With a flirtatious smile, she looked at Ross. "And why doest thou ask such questions, John?"

*   *   *   *

Back in Washington, Ross quickly made an appointment with John Quincy Adams who had just been appointed as Chairman of the Committee on Indian Affairs. At the Adams home in the 1300 block of F Street, Ross made his plea. "We come with weak hands. We have been at the seat of your government since last February but no definite result has come about. We have been unable to secure a meeting with President Tyler.

The seventy-four year old statesman listened sympathetically. Beads of sweat, brought on by the August heat, formed on his baldpate. "You mean His Accidency," he replied scornfully. "That slave breeder of mediocre talents was never elected president. He is one in which I have utter distrust."

"Be that as it may, Mr. Adams, he holds our fate in his hands. We are concerned that he carry out the promises of President Harrison."

Adams frowned and patted his forehead with a kerchief. "Mr. Ross," he replied in his high pitched twang, "I admire the determined commitment you have shown over the years on behalf of your people. Without a doubt, you were victimized by Andrew Jackson. For him, justice was whatever agreed with his thinking. You have been victims of fraudulent treaties and brutal force, but, I regret to say, I cannot help you. I have asked to be excused from serving as chairman of the committee because it is so scandal ridden. Your complaints of delay and neglect from Mr. Bell are legitimate and I promise to speak to him on your behalf. However," he paused to wipe his watery eyes, "do not get your expectations too high. Thanks to your friend, Sam Houston, his urging of annexing Texas has us facing again the prospect of war with Mexico. Congress and the Cabinet are in revolt against the President regarding the banking bill. Therefore, nothing of consequence is likely to occur during Tyler's administration."

The predictions of Adams were realized when, on September 11 at half past twelve o'clock, all of Tyler's cabinet members, with the exception of Webster, started handing in their resignations.

On Monday, September 13, Ross paid a last visit to the House of Representatives hoping for some recognition and support. Instead, in a House with tempers on edge, he witnessed a fistfight between Henry A. Wise of Virginia and his long time enemy, Edward Stanly, a Whig congressman from North Carolina. With the Speaker crying at the extent of his voice, "Order—Order—Order," the House almost erupted into a full-blown brawl. Shaking his head in despair, Ross left the House. Before leaving, he stopped to observe, what they called a magnetic telegraph, being exhibited in the capitol building by a Samuel F.B. Morse.

His last stop was to say goodbye to his old friend, John Howard Payne, who was leaving for his newly acquired post as United States Consul in Tunis. He would never again see his trusted friend alive.

Ross left Washington on a hot and dusty stage heading to Cumberland, Maryland where he connected with the heavily traveled National Road, which would take him on to Wheeling, Virginia. Steamboat passage would carry him to Fort Smith.

Ross held two letters in hand. One, from President Tyler, was filled with profuse promises to secure justice and, at a future date, to negotiate a new treaty with the Cherokee. With a shrug of resignation, Ross stuffed this letter into his inner coat pocket. The other, hinting a scent of lavender, was a penned note from Mary Brian Stapler. Ross slumped into his seat, reread the letter and, in a primal place deep within, engaged in a struggle with the sweet sickness of being in love. Without question, his heart was irresistibly fixed on the fair Quaker miss but his head fought back. Was it total foolishness for a man in his mid-fifties to covet a girl who was thirty years younger? Could the lass really love a man old enough to be her father? Dare he reveal his love and risk the hurt of rejection? Was this merely a flirtatious affair for her?

Quatie was an experienced woman when he married her, a widow with a young child. In bed he had matured under her tutelage and she had borne him several children. How would the chaste and youthful Mary Brian, perhaps innocent even in thought of sexual intercourse, respond to his lust?

Mary was the youngest daughter of John Stapler, a devout Quaker and a wealthy merchant in Wilmington, Delaware. She had been raised in affluence with all the advantages that money could obtain and had attended the best schools in Pennsylvania. For Ross the question of highest magnitude, that ultimately could not be avoided, was how would Mary's father react when he, Ross, revealed the situation and sought his blessing.

By the time he arrived home at Park Hill, his mind was made up.

CHAPTER 32

A QUAKER DISMISSED

It was evident that Ross was pleased with the work as he showed Sequoyah through the house under construction. Everything spoke of quality materials from the one and a half-inch thick, tongue and groove, yellow pine flooring to the heavy, hand-cut mortise and tenon beams in the rafters. In some of the unfinished areas slave craftsmen were plastering over hand-split lathing with a mixture of limestone, sand, water, and animal hair. Unpacked boxes of Wedgwood china, silverware, and Waterford crystal sat unopened here and there.

On the north side of the white painted house four two-storied columns supported a portico which over hung the entrance doors. These opened into a large living room and parlor furnished with walnut and mahogany furniture from Philadelphia. The south side featured a spacious, sunny room with a long, polished dining table. A kitchen adjoined. Fireplaces were located on the east and west ends of the house. A wide stairway led to the bedrooms upstairs. One such bedroom housed a large rosewood bed, with a six-foot headboard. A matching dresser, with a white, marble top, oval mirror, and oil lamp stood on the opposite wall. Something caught Sequoyah's eye.

"What the hell is that?" he asked, pointing to a small, box-like fixture at the foot of the bed.

Ross reddened. "That is what the French call a pot de chambre."

"I don't care what you call it. What's it for?"

An embarrassed Ross raised the lid of the box revealing a chamber pot. "If one has to go at night," he explained, "you use this. It contains water so that you can flush it into a holding tank below. The servants can empty it in the morning. It's the latest thing."

For a moment Sequoyah looked at Ross in disbelief then broke up with laughter.

Wiping tears from his eyes with his thumb, he quipped, "I see a woman coming to this house."

"I'm working on it," Ross confessed.

They walked outside and gazed at a thousand apple trees greening up in the warm, March sun of 1842. For a moment Sequoyah was silent, standing in his conventional hunting shirt trimmed with red fringe and a red shawl twisted around his head as a turban. "Tsan-Usdi, there is something I must tell you."

Ross listened expectantly.

"Many years ago, even before I came to this side of the Great Waters, some of our people moved west. They are now living in Mexican territory. I must go find them and bring them home for I fear a great war will soon break out between Mexico and the United States."

"What you say about a war is probably true. But you don't even know where these people are. Mexico is a large country. You will be groping in the dark. Besides, that is a job for a young man," Ross stated. "Let your son, Tessee, go."

"Tessee will go with me. I have persuaded The Worm and six others to accompany me. I will be safe," he assured Ross.

"When do you plan to leave?" asked Ross.

"I will depart this summer, soon as we can afford supplies and horses."

"Then I will not be here to see you off. I leave for Washington at the end of this month. I pray God's protection for you."

✳   ✳   ✳   ✳

During the last week of March 1842 Ross left for Washington. With him were his youngest son, George, who he would enroll in the Lawrenceville Classical and Commercial High School, and his sixteen-year-old niece, Eliza Jane Ross, who he hoped to enroll in the Moravian Female Seminary at Bethlehem, Pennsylvania, not coincidentally, the same school Mary Brian Stapler attended.

As the steamboat moved downriver, and the children slept, Ross reread the letter from the previous September in which President Tyler had promised him that justice for the Cherokee would be done. How many trips had he made to Washington in recent years when he had come away with high hopes that were subsequently dashed because congress or the administration had failed to keep promises made? Painful as it was to admit, it seemed to Ross, in matters where the Cherokee were concerned, that the United States government always relegated them to a low level of significance. The question gnawed at him: would it be the same this time?

As Ross journeyed toward Washington, a tired and frayed Henry Clay stood in a hushed and tense Senate chamber. Virtually everyone in the city knew what he was about to say. At half past one o'clock on Thursday, March 31, 1842, the formal business of the day being completed, Clay rose to address the Senate.

"My friends, the time has arrived for this old coon to retire from public service and return to my private affairs. If a Roman soldier could claim title to discharge after thirty years of service, surely, I, who have served a much longer period, may justly claim mine. So allow me," he said with a tremulous voice, "to announce, formally and officially, my retirement from the Senate of the United States. I first entered this honorable body in December of 1805, nearly forty years ago. From that time to the present, I have been engaged in the service of my country. History, if she deigns to notice me, and posterity, will be the best, truest and most impartial judges; and to them I defer for a decision upon their value."

Clay's eyes filled with tears as he continued. "Now, in retiring as I am about to do from the Senate, I beg leave to express my heartfelt wishes that all the great and patriotic objects for which it is instituted, may be accomplished, and the destiny designed for it by the framers of the Constitution may be fulfilled. May the most precious blessings of Heaven rest upon the heads of the whole Senate, and every member of it; and when they shall retire to the bosoms of their respective constituencies, may they all meet that most joyous and grateful of all human rewards, the exclamation of their countrymen, "well done thou good and faithful servants."

"Mr. President, and Messieurs Senators, I bid you, one and all, a long, a last, a friendly farewell."

Most everyone in the chamber was weeping. No one could conceive the Congress without the presence of Henry Clay. As the senators crowded around Clay to shake his hand and bid him goodbye, he spoke to each one. As he finally broke free and started to leave, he noticed the gray eminence, John C. Calhoun, standing alone at a distance. Clay walked over to him and the two old enemies embraced in silence.

The warm memories of time spent with Mary Brian Stapler were rudely crowded out shortly after Ross arrived in Washington. He was stunned to learn of Clay's departure. He also learned that he would have to deal with President Tyler's new Secretary of War, John C. Spencer, since his friend, John Bell, along with other cabinet members, had submitted their resignations last September. For any information on Washington politics that could be trusted, he turned to the crotchety, seventy-five year old representative in the House, John Quincy Adams.

When Ross arrived unannounced at 1333 F Street NW, Congressman Adams and his wife, Louisa, were just finishing lunch with their guests. Adams introduced them as Mr. and Mrs. Charles Dickens from Great Britain. "Mr. Dickens," Adams added, "is the greatest writer of our time. He has the literary fame I shall never gain."

Leaving Louisa and Mrs. Dickens to their tea, Adams led Ross and Dickens into his book-laden library. "Welcome to the most precious portion of my estate," said Adams, waving toward his books. "My time is never tedious when I have my books around me."

Seated comfortably and lifting a glass of amber-colored Madeira, Adams turned to Ross. "Worry not about our friend, Henry Clay. That Old Coon has not given up politics. At this very moment he is home in Kentucky preparing to run for the presidency in '44."

"And what of President Tyler and his new Secretary of War?" Ross asked.

"I know nothing of Spencer. You already know of my contempt for Tyler. As Plato once said, 'In simple matters, like shoe making, we think only a specially trained person will serve our purpose. But in politics we presume that everyone who knows how to get votes knows how to administer a city or state.' And, unguided by knowledge, the people are a multitude without order."

Ross smiled. "I believe your comments would fit Jackson as well as Tyler."

"Jackson!" Adams spat, his undying hatred for his successor in the White House clearly evident. "Just as with Tyler, Jackson's petty, partisanship made sensible compromise unattainable. Jackson applied force as the ultimate proof of superiority. He confused power with virtue and wielded power without understanding. I fear the same will happen with Tyler and his desire to annex Texas and that will put us into a war with Mexico."

"Mr. Dickens," said Ross," I read in the newspapers that Great Britain has an interest in Texas."

The young man nodded and stroked his beard. "Yes, Lord Aberdeen of the Foreign Office has agreed to guarantee a Texan loan if the Lone Star Republic will abolish slavery."

Adams butted in. "This is part of Sam Houston's strategy to secure annexation of Texas, playing England against the United States. The prospect of Texas becoming a refuge for fugitive slaves from the south has alarmed the South to the point of panic."

Dickens picked up where he had been interrupted. "My country desires, and is constantly exerting herself to procure, the abolition of slavery throughout the world."

"And that has roused Calhoun to call for immediate annexation," Adams pursued. "My daily fight in the House is against slave holders, those befoulers of the nation's sacred freedoms. One hundred members of the House own slaves; four fifths of whom would crucify me if their votes could erect the cross."

*   *   *   *

It became increasingly obvious that the Tyler administration had greater priorities than Cherokee problems. Tyler, consumed with the annexation of Texas, turned the negotiations of a new treaty over to his new, and uninformed, Secretary of War. Ross engaged in futile sparring with Secretary of War Spencer throughout the summer of 1842. Ross wanted indemnity for Cherokee losses, a guarantee of their lands, and a permanent basis for the political relations between them and the people of the United States. Each report Spencer required from Ross was returned with demands for greater details. The offers extended by Spencer were so far short of wishes and expectations that, in frustration, Ross terminated the negotiations. In August he sent a note to Spencer saying, "If we have unwittingly been induced to expect too much, to infer what was never intended, then we must take a respectful leave of the Honorable Secretary and the President and return immediately to our nation."

Stopping over in Philadelphia in late September, Ross addressed a letter to David Greene, Secretary of American Board of Commissioners for Foreign Missions, ordering a new printing press with English and Cherokee characters.

Back in Tahlequah, on November 14th he apologized for delivering his annual message to the nation a month late. A disheartened council listened to Ross's report of another failure in Washington. Before adjourning they voted not to send Ross back to Washington in 1843.

When Ross finished gathering up his papers only Tom Hanks was standing by. He cradled his Kentucky rifle in his arms. A pistol was jammed under his belt.

"That report will not help your prospects for re-election," he said.

"You don't have to be so cheerful about it," Ross smiled ruefully.

"You got fucked by Spencer in Washington and your enemies here will exploit that to the hilt."

"I know," Ross nodded and looked at Hanks. "Why are you carrying all that hardware?"

"Need I remind you that the Starr brothers have you high on their kill list? They have been murdering, burning, and pillaging as if they had a god given right."

"Better look out for yourself, Tom. You are now a husband and a father."

"Chief Ross, you cannot ignore these outlaws. They will most certainly kill us unless we kill them first. They have no intention of letting you succeed. They won't let missionaries do their work. Trade is disrupted. Our roads are unsafe. The Starrs have spread panic among whites who live along the Arkansas border telling them that a major Indian uprising is in the works."

Ross paused, noting the urgency in Hank's voice. "Alright, Tom. By all means, let's reassure Governor Yell, and his people in Arkansas, that their fears of an Indian uprising are ridiculous."

*   *   *   *

On June 24, 1843 Ross addressed representatives from twenty-one Indian tribes assembled at Tahlequah. "Brothers, you have smoked the pipe of peace and taken the hand of friendship around this great council fire. Our hearts rejoice in the goodness of our Creator in having thus united the heart and hand of the red man in peace.

"For it is in peace only that our women and children can enjoy happiness and increase in numbers. By peace our condition has been improved in the pursuit of civilized life. Brothers, it is for renewing and perpetuating for ever the old fire and pipe of peace that you have been invited to attend this council."

For a month the delegates, seated on crude benches under a large open shed, worked in the summer heat to establish tribal boundaries, secure the extradition of wanted criminals, and compacts of peace and mutual support. The only item that upset the observing federal agents present was a pledge by the tribes never to cede to the United States any part of their present territory!

With some of his popularity restored with this successful convention, Ross now faced the August election for principal chief. The chief issue in the campaign was Ross's failure to obtain any financial settlement with the United States government, and hence any per capita money. His running mate for assistant chief was George Lowrey. In an overwhelming victory Ross polled nearly two-thirds of the ballots cast, winning over two Old Settler candidates, Joseph Vann and W.S. Adair by a majority of nearly nine hundred votes.

On August 9, a day after the election, Hanks stopped by Ross's new home, Rose Cottage. Ross, seated at his plain mahogany desk, waved Hanks to a chair.

"If I ever saw bad news, you look it," said Ross.

"It's bad news and it ain't funny. Yesterday, your election superintendents in the Saline District were attacked while making out election returns. Isaac Bushyhead was stabbed to death. David Vann was beaten within an inch of his life. Elijah Hicks also got roughed up. I warned you such could happen."

Ross sat in stunned silence for a moment. "These are rough times for the Bushyhead family." He looked at Hanks. "Do you know who did it?"

"Done in plain daylight in front of a crowd of people. George West killed Bushyhead. His father, Jacob and his brother, John, beat up Vann. Jacob West is a white man married to a Cherokee."

"If he married into our tribe, he is subject to our laws. Find him and bring him in, along with his sons."

*   *   *   *

For his part in the murder, John West was given one hundred lashes. His brother George had escaped and taken refuge across the line in Arkansas.

After trial by a jury, comprised of twelve Cherokee men, Jacob West was sentenced to die. On Saturday, October 21, Jacob West, sitting on a kitchen chair, was hauled by a mule-drawn wagon to a huge oak tree just south of Tahlequah. A coffin was also in the wagon. A large crowd followed. At precisely twelve o'clock, West was asked to stand upon the chair. With his last words steaming in the frosty air, West protested that as a white man, he was not subject to Cherokee jurisdiction. The High Sheriff secured a rope to a limb of the tree and adjusted the knot of the rope alongside West's neck. As the sheriff jumped from the wagon to the ground, a whip was laid on the mules. The chair toppled over and West was left twisting in the air.

The blood bath in the Cherokee Nation had just begun!

*   *   *   *

Ross sat quietly struggling to maintain control as the new Secretary of War, William Wilkins ranted on at him and the small Cherokee delegation. "You say you want a new treaty. You already have a treaty which you do not honor."

"The treaty to which you refer was not signed by any authorized party," Ross protested. "It is a fraudulent piece of paper."

"Mr. Ross, you demand a fair and just indemnity be made to your nation for all land east of the Mississippi. That fraudulent piece of paper, as you call it, has already cost my government over six million dollars. You have been further enriched by the grant of a vast territory where you now reside. We have kept our agreement with your people."

"A grant of land for which we hold no secure title," Ross rejoined.

"Allow me to correct you," said Wilkins. "In conformity with the Treaty of 1835 a patent was made out and sent to Indian Territory on the 18th of July 1839. You declined to accept it. The offer still remains although I'm uncertain as to whom it should extend, to your party, to the Old Settlers, or to the Treaty Party."

"I am not representing a party, sir. I am representing the entire Cherokee Nation."

"So you say, Mr. Ross, but many complaints have come to me from many of your people alleging that they are unable to enjoy their liberty, property, or live in safety. The Old Settlers claim that the Act of Union superseded their government without their authorization. There are even allegations that you have misappropriated funds due to the Cherokee people.

"I shall submit to the President, and ask his instruction to send into your nation a commission of officers to inquire into and ascertain the true and exact extent of the dis-content and spirit of hostility which prevails amongst your people to enable us to decide how far it may be necessary for this government to interfere and adopt such measures as may be calculated to keep down domestic strife. They will determine the oppression, the resistance, and the violence directed toward the minority. We must know if the discontent among the Old Settlers and the Treaty Party is of such extent and intensity that it precludes their living together peaceably under the same government as the Ross Party."

Flushed with anger, Ross replied. "What you are proposing is, in our judgement, a violation of the rights of the Cherokees. Your comments represent an extreme departure from the promises held out to us by the President of the United States in his letter to us of 20th September 1841. All the proposals heretofore submitted to you by us, and now I assume rejected, were drawn from the authority of that letter and in strict con-formity to its promises. It would be a ridiculous farce if the Government of the United States can, upon an ex parte statement, interpose its authority and actually excite and keep alive "domestic strife". If the commission were to be charged with any inquiries regarding the division or separation of our people, we would most solemnly protest against it as a violation of our treaties with the United States. We see no necessity for such a commission.

"As to the Treaty of 1835 to which you refer; we submitted to a necessity which we could neither control nor resist. Nor can we say that the termination of these negotiations is satisfactory. We did hope that the time had arrived when the "new sun" would dawn upon the Cherokee Nation. But we are mistaken."

*   *   *   *

In the heat and humidity of July, Ross walked dejectedly from the War Department building back to Fuller's Hotel with his nephew, William P. Ross, where they had been staying since April. William was a recent graduate of Princeton University and had accompanied his uncle as secretary for the delegation.

"All the time and resources we've invested here in Washington did not result in a profitable introduction for you into politics," Ross sighed.

*   *   *   *

A current issue of The Globe newspaper made it evident to Ross that official Washington was in turmoil over annexation of Texas. "Texas or Disunion" was a toast he frequently heard in the hotel bars. For John C. Calhoun, Tyler's new secretary of state, annexation of Texas was a life and death issue for slavery and the South. A treaty required the two-thirds vote of the Senate, which Calhoun knew he could not achieve. A joint resolution required a simple majority of both houses of Congress. This was the mode he utilized to effect annexation.

Wary of war with Mexico, and dividing the nation, Whig presidential candidates, Henry Clay and Martin Van Buren, issued statements opposing annexation. Democrat candidate, James K. Polk, with the strong support from fellow Tennesseean, Andrew Jackson, who had tried to buy Texas during his presidency, was for it.

Ross put aside the paper. Matters pertaining to the Cherokee were of little interest in Washington. Frustrated, lonely, and in need of affection, he quickly packed and caught the cars from Washington to Baltimore, then by stage on to Wilmington, Delaware, home of Mary Brian Stapler.

*   *   *   *

Ross was enchanted by the beauty of the girl-woman and their surroundings as they sat in the shade of a clump of willows, the clear Brandywine River flowing at their feet. Monarch butterflies flitted from wild roses to yarrow; noisy grasshoppers contested with the buzz of cicadas in the July heat.

"Esteemed Uncle, aren't you taken by the beauty of my favorite place? I anticipated much pleasure in showing thee all the beauties which my pen has failed to convey to you."

Ross winced. Esteemed Uncle, a term Mary had applied to him early in their correspondence, reminded him of the vast span of age difference between them. Her nearness to him generated a heat and a hunger which he tried to sublimate, yet he managed to reply, "No, I can think of no other place so graced with beauty and pleasantness."

Mary flushed with pleasure at his words. She knew he wanted her.

"Mary, does the great difference in our ages not concern you?"

"Heart to heart knows nothing of age," she teased. "Thee tarried so long in Washington I feared thee had forgotten me."

Could he really fathom this Quaker Venus who had cast such a spell over him? "I have not, nor could I ever forget you," confessed Ross. "You are ever in my thoughts and I agonize when I am away from you."

Mary pensively plucked the petals from a wild rose. "Dear friend, could I induce thee to bid adieu to the far west and abide more safely in these parts?"

Ross stood and turned away. He had long known, in spite of his passion for this girl, what the answer to such a question must be. He also knew his answer might well put an end to a future he so desperately desired, but answer he must. "Mary, you could induce me to do most anything, but you must know, I can never desert my people."

"Then must I compete with those dark-eyed maidens, with their graceful charms, seated in a circular wigwam, carpeted with soft buffalo skins?" she teased.

Such female behavior puzzled and annoyed Ross. Was she playing him for a fool? He turned to face her, placing both hands on her shoulders. He wanted to shake her and make her silly head realize how powerful his passion was for her. He wanted an end to pretense and playing games. "Be serious, Mary. I cannot stand the temporizing policy of the fairer sex who are wont to adopt a cunning, coquettish negotiation that robs a confiding man of his only heart. When I'm around you, I become tongue-tied…it's as if I'm standing betwixt two fires of discipline and desire. I can't make the pretty speeches I want to say, but, God help me, I love you." He dropped his hands, hung his head, and said quietly, "But you are not obligated to reciprocate. Let your hand and heart go together and never surrender them until capitulated with love."

Mary threw herself into his arms. Body against body, sensations she had never experienced before flowed through her body. "John, I have already capitulated. Can't you see that?"

Ross pushed her away, took her face between his hands, and looked fervently into her eyes. "Oh, Mary, are you really sure? Are you really, really sure?"

"Yes, John. I've been sure since I first met you." Still quivering with excitement, she added, "Please talk with father soon."

Ross held her close and crushed his lips against hers. Away down the path alongside the Brandywine, sister Sarah smiled and turned away.

*   *   *   *

Quaker John Stapler sat stunned as he reread the letter that had just arrived with the morning mail.

Boston, Massachusetts
August 14, 1844

My Dear Sir,

For the surprise which this Note, will no doubt give you, I hope you will pardon me, especially, when I tell you that, I am deeply interested and most fervently attached to your beloved Daughter Mary; and that, with your consent, I should be happy to be united to her in Marriage. Did I not believe it will be in my power to confer upon her the ordinary comforts and happiness of this life, I should certainly never wantonly be instrumental in bringing about any change in her situation, calculated to render her condition less happy than it is at present. You will therefore, be pleased to receive this my petition for the hand of your Dear Mary! I shall await your response at Howard's Hotel in the city of New York & I hope you will do me the favor to send it there without delay. I am Dr. Sir, very respectfully, you obt. Servt.

Jno Ross

It took a few moments for the impact of the letter's contents to sink in, then Stapler looked across the room at his daughter. Clearing his throat he said, "Mary, is there something between thee and John Ross that I should know about?"

Mary paused with her sewing, eyes downcast, cheeks aflame. "I saw his letter to you. I think I know what it's about."

"I can't believe thou hast deceived thy father, Mary. How long has this been going on?"

"I would not deceive thee, father, had I been sure I was not deceiving myself about my esteemed uncle."

"Esteemed uncle? Thou think of John Ross as thy uncle?"

"Oh no, father. T'was merely a form of address that..." Mary dropped her sewing and clasped her hands. "T'was merely a way to cloak my true feelings. One's heart must be protected from rejection," she floundered.

"And I suppose thy sister, Sarah, knew all about this?"

Mary nodded. A tear trickled down her cheek.

"My child, hast thou considered the disparity of age between thee and Ross? I'm fifty-five and he can't be a day younger than I."

Again Mary nodded. "Yes, father, we have considered it. It is a matter of great concern to Mr. Ross but not to me."

"There are many young bucks near your age in our meeting house. I see them cast their eyes in thy direction. So why Ross?"

Mary smiled wistfully. "The young men seem so childish. Mr. Ross...John...is so gentle and wise...we can talk forever...about everything."

"Doest thou ever talk about slavery? Thou knowest how Quakers feel about slavery and thou knowest that Mr. Ross is a slave owner."

Mary lowered her head. "No, father, we have not discussed slavery."

"And what about the matter of religion, Mary? Have thee and Mr. Ross considered that if thee marry outside the Quaker faith, thee will be dismissed from the church?"

Mary silently nodded as tears trickled down her cheeks.

Stapler stood, clasped hands behind his back and walked to the window, away from his daughter. He spoke, haltingly. "Mary, thy mother passed away when thee were only four years old. It fell to me to raise thee alone but, in truth, thy sister, Sarah, took the place of thy mother. Consequently, thee knows little about expectations in marriage...or the passions of men. Nor does thy sister. Therefore, as thy father, I am naturally concerned about thy protection...and thy happiness.

I do not object to John Ross personally. He strikes me as a fine fellow. But for reasons we have discussed, this seems to me an unacceptable alliance."

Mary stood erect, wiped the tears from her eyes, and spoke with a firm voice. "Whither thou goest I will go, and where you lodge I will lodge; your people shall be my people, and your God my God."

Stapler shook his head in disbelief. He recognized that she was quoting from the Book of Ruth in the Bible. Seeing the look on his daughter's face, and hearing the determination in her voice, he knew this was a matter on which he must concede.

* * * *

On September 3, 1844 the New York Tribune issued the following society news:

"...John Ross, the celebrated Cherokee Chief, was married in the President's parlor of the Hartwell's Washington House Hotel in Philadelphia last night September 2, 1844, to Miss Mary B. Stapler of Wilmington, Delaware. He is about 55, and she is only 18 years of age; she is a very beautiful girl and highly accomplished...Her father was formerly a highly respected Quaker merchant of this city.

She was given away by her brother and attended by her sister and a niece of John Ross as bridesmaids. He had collected several of his daughters and nephews from boarding schools in New Jersey to be present at the wedding; and after the ceremony a family party of 20 of the Ross's (all half-breed Indians) sat down to a most sumptuous banquet.... Ross is considered to be worth half a million dollars. He proposes to sojourn with his beautiful bride at this excellent hotel for a short time, after which he goes straight to his wild home in the South Western prairies."

The ceremony was conducted by Reverend Orson Douglass of the Mariner's Church. Mary had been dismissed from the Quaker Church.

CHAPTER 33

ON THE PRECIPICE

The new Mrs. Ross slowly awakened to low, September sunrays streaming in through the window. Stretching luxuriously, she listened to the New York City street noise outside the honeymoon suite of the Globe Hotel and let her thoughts retrace the rapid and dramatic changes she had experienced in the last four days.

She had lain in bed on her wedding night not knowing what to expect. Awkward and unsure, she felt a moment of panic in the dark as John slowly removed her nightgown, for no one, certainly not a man, had ever seen her naked. Panic quickly gave way to sensations of pleasure as her charged body yielded to John's gentle kisses. How could something so enjoyable not be a sin? Yet, God had commanded that a wife submit to her husband so, perhaps, it wasn't sinful. As John moved on her, she felt a twinge of pain in her soft, swollen cleft, a part of her body she had given little consideration to in her young life, then gave in to rhythmic hot surges that swept through her eager body. Afterward, as John dropped into deep slumber, she smiled in awe at what had transpired. No longer was she a little girl; she was now a woman.

In Philadelphia Mary ordered some furniture to be delivered to the home in Park Hill she had not yet seen. By September 12 she, her sister, Sarah, and John were back in Lawrenceville, New Jersey to check on the health of Ross's niece, Jane Ross. Assured of her health they journeyed on to Baltimore. Ross desired to be in Tahlequah before the annual Cherokee Council ended so on Thursday, September 19th, as Mary said goodbye to all she had known in her first eighteen years of life, they caught the cars for Cumberland, Maryland. A riot of autumn color opened up as the train crossed the Potomac River at Harper's Ferry, curved north toward the Pennsylvania border, then, at a cut in the Allegheny Mountains, the tracks turned southwest to follow the river. At Wheeling, Virginia a steamboat would convey them to her new home in the West.

Days later the weary travelers disembarked at Van Buren, Arkansas. The small river city was crowded with those heading for the free land in Texas. Ross was met by a coach and six, heavily armed, mounted riders. A white-haired Negro with a toothy smile assisted Mary and her sister, Sarah, into the carriage. "Ah, m Moses, ma'am. Welcome to our fambly."

Noting that Mary was visibly disturbed at seeing armed men, Ross testily hissed to Hanks, "What's going on? Why did you have to show up with a small army?"

"Didn't want your young bride to become a widow too soon, John. In case you don't know it, your ass is on the line. The Starr brothers have sworn to get you," Hanks quietly responded.

As they neared Rose Cottage, down the long driveway lined with bushes whose roses had wilted from the frosts of early November, Mary wondered about all the horses tied to the hitching rack in front and the rough-looking, armed men scattered around the house. She turned to question John. For the past few weeks of their married life, he had been relaxed and smiling. Now she saw an unfamiliar face with cold eyes squinting from a stern mask. Fear stuck in her throat.

Inside the house, Ross turned Mary over to the servants while he retreated to his study. Waiting for him was a very agitated Baptist missionary, Evan Jones.

"I am in a desperate plight, Chief Ross. I need your advice."

"For whatever it's worth, you are welcome to it."

Jones took a deep breath and began. "The Baptist Foreign Mission Board has learned from the abolitionists that Rev. Jesse Bushyhead owns slaves. If it forces Bushyhead to resign as a missionary it will provoke a storm among the Cherokees and the Southern Baptists. On the other hand, if they ignore the charge, it will provoke a storm among the Northern Baptists. The Board has requested that I report on the matter." He lifted his hands, palms up. "What am I to do?"

Ross thoughtfully rubbed the stubble on his chin. "I can see your dilemma. Bushyhead is your close friend and invaluable assistant in translating the Bible. He is also one of the most popular and influential leaders in the Cherokee Nation. To expel him from Christian fellowship would be unthinkable. To suggest that he free his slaves will cause a tremendous upheaval among the rest of us who own slaves. If I lost my fifty slaves, this plantation could not function."

"I fear," said Jones, "the slavery issue will split the Baptists along sectional lines. If that happens, other denominations will split and then the whole Christian community will be sectionalized. If Christianity cannot hold this nation together, what will prevent a civil war?"

Jones continued to stall the Baptist Board. His dilemma was solved on July 17, 1844 when the Rev. Jesse Bushyhead suddenly developed a serious case of bilious fever and died.

*　　*　　*　　*

Inside the carpeted home Mary was overwhelmed by a bevy of fawning, black maid-servants all too eager to guide their new mistress through the house elegantly furnished with cane bottomed chairs, Boston rocking chairs, a mahogany sofa, and a highly-polished Chickering piano. At this juncture a small, soft-spoken woman took over and shooed the maid-servants back to their duties.

"Ah'm Zipporah," she smiled at Mary, "Massa Ross done tole me to look after you."

"Why thank you, Zipporah. What a lovely name. It's from the Bible, isn't it...the wife of Moses?"

"Yas'm. Massa Ross thought he needed a Zipporah since he already had a Moses so he bought me."

"Zipporah," Mary stammered, "I was brought up Quaker. I am not comfortable with the buying and selling of people."

Zipporah patted Mary on the arm. "Don't fret, Chile. Out here you have a lot to get comferble with. Now, lemme show you the rest of the house."

As she was led outside to the kitchen area, Mary inquired, "Zipporah, are you married to the man who drove the carriage?"

"Yas'm...fer almost thirty years. Moses is a Christian man...after Massa Ross bought me, he'd have nothin' to do with me till we jumped over the broom stick and said the words with a preacher man."

In back of the house Zepporah pointed out the stables, slave quarters, blacksmith shop, carpenter shop, and smoke house. Suddenly Mary froze. Before her a black man, stripped to the waist, with ropes on each wrist, was tied to an oak tree. The flesh on his bare back was raw and bloody. "Zipporah", she gasped, "who is that?"

"Dat's Black Fish. He done runaway to Webber Falls to find his woman. Dese days young nigger boys run 'round smokin', drinkin' whiskey and grievin' de Lord and their mamas. Doan' know what this world is comin' to."

"What happened to him?"

"He got a whippin'. Massa Ross don't like runaways."

Mary faltered. "Zipporah, please get me to my room. I'm going to be ill."

Zipporah cracked a toothless grin. Signs of pregnancy were not unknown to her.

*   *   *   *

That night a very subdued Mary presided over a dinner such as she had never experienced. Smelly fur trappers from the northwest swapping stories with cigar-smoking traders from Chouteau's post, a Moravian minister from New Springplace chatting with Evan Jones of the Baptist mission, a few blanket Indians, and a couple of soldiers from Fort Gibson ranged round the long table, attacking platters of greasy pork and slabs of beef, bowls piled high with boiled potatoes, and boats of redeye gravy. Talk was of war with Mexico and the recent killings done by the Starr gang. For Mary the Brandywine River and Wilmington, Delaware now seemed so far away.

*   *   *   *

As Ross entered Washington City in April, 1845, he was struck by how little the place had changed since his first arrival in 1815. The pretensions of the capital building were belied by spasmodic attempts to pave the streets with gravel, ash, or bricks. Loose planks flopped in the mud serving as sidewalks. Sewage drained along the roadways and pigs, geese, and cattle wandered among the garbage heaped in the streets. Shanties, pigsties, cowsheds and hencoops lined Pennsylvania Avenue along with boarding houses, hotels and markets. If this place had ever held any allure for Ross, it was long gone.

He had left Mary, heavy with child, and her sister, Sarah, in Wilmington with their father. Leaving them at Park Hill, exposed to the Starr gang, was an unacceptable risk.

His age and his resentment of the constant bickering with elements of the Old Settlers and Treaty Party, who were already in Washington, left him in a foul mood. Yet, the Inquiry Commission of Jones, Mason, and Butler had finished its hearings with the malcontents at Tahlonteeskee, and, from what he had heard, the commission findings were favorable to the Ross Party. But he also knew that the new president, Polk, was a protégé of Andrew Jackson and only God knew what he would do with the report.

He found that Henry Clay, narrowly defeated by James Polk, had gone home to lick his wounds in Kentucky. Many in Washington were astounded that a dark horse, a third-rate politician from Tennessee, a nobody, had defeated the greatest statesman in the nation.

Calhoun was restoring his health at his home at Fort Hill, South Carolina. Massachusetts had returned the sixty-three year old Webster to the Senate where he took his seat on March 4, 1845 with the inauguration of President Polk. Ross had missed the heated debates of January when his old friend, John Quincy Adams, warned that if Texas were admitted to the union by a joint resolution of Congress, it would leave the Constitution a monstrous rag. With Congress no longer in session, Adams had retreated to New England.

Andrew Jackson passed away on June 8, at the age of seventy-eight, bemoaning the fact that he had not hanged Calhoun "as high as Haman." When Adams heard of the death, his epitaph for his old enemy was blunt: "Jackson was a hero, a murderer, an adulterer who in the last days of his life belied and slandered me before the world."

$$* \qquad * \qquad * \qquad *$$

Ross knew that Ezekiel Starr, a leader in the Treaty Party, was already in Washington seeking to have the new president divide the Cherokee Nation, and financial allocations, proportionate to numbers. To prevent this disaster, Ross needed to gain the ear of President Polk. To gain access to President Polk, Ross had to go through the new Secretary of War, William L. Marcy. But this sixty-year old former United States Senator and three term governor of New York, was not eager to accommodate anyone. Ross waited during the hot, humid days of Washington before he secured a meeting with Marcy the early part of August.

Heavily built and awkward in movements, few regarded Marcy as an amiable man. When Ross walked into his office in the War Department Building, the heavily jowled man, seated behind a desk, reached into his snuffbox and nodded indifferently toward a chair. Waiving formalities, Marcy picked up a piece of paper from his desk and thrust it toward Ross.

"I have here," rumbled Marcy, "a letter from Wilson Lumpkin of Georgia in which he raises serious questions regarding your character."

Ross flushed with anger. Not only had Marcy ignored common courtesy, but had issued an insult in his first remarks.

"I know Mr.Lumpkin very well," Ross replied crisply. "Anything he might have written to you about me I'm sure is not complimentary."

Marcy took another pinch of snuff. "Mr. Lumpkin suggests that accounts allotted to you for schools, allowed by the War Department, will not bear scrutiny. President Polk expects strict accounting of these funds, Mr. Ross. He desires to know how much has been expended, how much is in the balance, how much has been invested, and the amount of income from the investments."

Ross's first impulse was to state that the Cherokees were perfectly capable of managing their own finances. But, to give offense to Polk's administration could tip the balance regarding the division of the Cherokee Nation in the wrong direction. He managed to calmly reply. "You should know, Mr. Marcy, that we now have in successful operation eighteen common schools in several districts of our Nation. To accurately respond to the president's questions I'd have to consult records at home."

Marcy leaned his bulk back in his chair, his gaze penetrating under heavy brows. "In that case, Mr. Ross, annuity payments to your people will be suspended until the president's demands are met."

For the remainder of the year, Marcy kept Ross dangling. Each financial report submitted by Ross was returned with requests for greater details. "Obviously," thought Ross, "these were stalling tactics."

His gloom deepened in December after receiving a letter from his daughter, Jane, in which she reported that on the night of November 1, seven men, led by Tom Starr and his brothers, had burned her home to the ground at Park Hill. On Sunday morning, November 9 Tom Hanks, accompanied by 31 men, rode up to the home of James Starr. At sunrise gunfire erupted and James died from a bullet through his heart. His sons, Tom and Washington, severely wounded, fled across the Arkansas line to the town of Evansville. Five days later, Thomas Watie, Stand's brother, was slain. Such disorder would not bode well for Ross's cause. But official Washington had its mind on other matters. Throughout the city southerners were boldly crying "Texas or Disunion" and others were threatening a war with England over Oregon country with their "Fifty-four forty or fight" slogan.

With the start of the Twenty-ninth Congress, Ross visited the House of Representatives on December 2. Anticipating the president's speech, the corridors were filled with land speculators. The Clerk, Benjamin Brown French, read to Congress the first message of President Polk. He not only came out strong for the annexation of Texas but Polk announced an American claim to all of Oregon. It was also clear to all that he had another major goal, the acquisition of California. It was evident to Ross that Polk's hunger for Texas was propelled by the desire of slave owners, would-be slave owners, and the prodding of Andrew Jackson, to extend the realm of slavery.

On December 10 Senator Dixon Lewis of Alabama introduced a bill for the admission of Texas to the Union as a state. Ross's anxiety rose as he heard the drumbeat of "manifest destiny" and saw his nation, which held no legitimate title to its territory, being surrounded by states becoming a part of the Union.

On Saturday night, December 20, Ross joined Daniel Webster for dinner in the new National Hotel, now a draw for the curious because of its private bathtubs and Mr. Morse's machine that made the wires talk.

"Consider compromise with the Treaty Party," Webster counseled between sips of Madeira, "or you might lose it all. President Polk will, no doubt, support the Treaty Party, which was endorsed by his old hero, General Jackson."

"But Senator," Ross argued, "a division of our country would heap deplorable calamities on our people and end in the utter ruin and destruction of our nation."

"Well, as I live and breathe…" Webster put down his wineglass. Ross followed the direction of Webster's gaze. Entering the room was a stooped, hollow-chested man with gray hair hanging in masses from his neck and temples. "My god, it's Calhoun," said Webster as he rose to escort the aged South Carolinian to his table.

"I thought you had retired to your ease at Fort Hill for good," said Webster as he helped Calhoun remove his black cloak.

The old senator emitted a deep cough into his kerchief. "One cannot live at ease on one's farm, not with high costs and mounting debts. With cotton futures what they are, even survival is questionable for me and every farm in the South."

"It would be my pleasure to extend a loan to an old friend," offered Webster.

Calhoun seated himself and shook his gray mane in declining the offer.

Trying to make light of an embarrassing moment, Webster laughed. "At least let me buy you a drink." He snapped his fingers at a waiter. "Bring the senator a glass of his favorite claret." Turning back to Calhoun, he asked. "Now, tell me, what brings you back to Washington?"

"I would never have considered returning to public life," answered Calhoun as he tucked a pinch of snuff under his lower lip, "but I am quite concerned over President Polk's recklessness. By his insistence on 54/40 in the Oregon territory, I have a deep conviction that he is risking war with England. Why should I, a

South Carolina cotton planter, wish to shed blood in a fight against my best customer?"

"And why should I, a senator from the north, risk war with Mexico just to expand slavery into Texas?" Webster teased.

With a tremulous hand, Calhoun returned his wineglass to the table. He smiled ruefully. "Yes, I noticed that you did not stand with me on that issue. Rest assured, there will be no war with Mexico over Texas."

"I understand the president is ready to send General Zachary Taylor to the Rio Grande. If he does so, Mexico could interpret that as an invasion. But back to the Oregon question—don't you realize that if Oregon ever becomes a member of the Union it will come in as a free state? Just what is your resolution for this predicament?" Webster inquired.

Calhoun stifled a tubercular cough before answering. "I can only say this. When this question comes before the Senate, I shall make a proposal that will let Polk escape his political dilemma and one that will, I believe, be acceptable to the English Parliament."

Calhoun, who had shown a studied indifference to the presence of Ross during his conversation with Webster, now turned and said. "I suppose, Chief Ross, that you are still trying to wheedle money from the United States government?"

Ross smiled at his old adversary. "Senator, we are after nothing more than the fulfillment of your government's promises."

As Calhoun rose to depart, he managed a sardonic grin. "Considering all that Polk has on his mind right now, and with this nation having a public debt of six or seven million dollars, I wish you good fortune."

*   *   *   *

As weeks passed, the irony of Calhoun's wish became ever more evident to Ross as he was unable to obtain an appointment with President Polk. When he learned of General Arbuckle's intervention on the side of the Treaty Party, he fired off a testy note of protest to the President, reminding him that the Ross delegation was the only authorized representative of the Cherokee Nation now in Washington.

To add to his discouragement, Ross found that the topic of war with Mexico over Texas or a war with England over the Oregon Territory dominated conversation in every hotel, saloon, and the halls of Congress. Concern over Cherokee matters did not exist in official Washington.

*   *   *   *

Great expectations had people assembling around the doors of the Capitol before eight in the morning. By noon the passages were clogged with a mass of hot and sweaty humanity. Female flesh, the swirl of silks and satins, and the seductive odor of perfume filled the galleries. Ross had no interest in the Oregon matter, but the lack of amusements made Congress a place of public entertainment. He was seated in the Senate gallery on March 16, 1846 when Calhoun rose in the stifling hot room to address the Oregon issue, knowing that his opposition to the President was putting his political future at risk.

As was his custom, Calhoun began quietly, stating that there need be no war. "I know," he said, "that in the existing state of the world wars are necessary. The most sacred regard for justice, and the most cautious policy, cannot always prevent them. When war must come, I appeal to my past history to prove that I shall not be found among those who falter.

"I regard peace as a positive good and war as a positive evil. I shall ever cling to peace, so long as it can be preserved consistently with safety and honor. But there need be no war. The question can still be compromised on the basis of the forty-ninth parallel. North of there, none of our citizens are settled. Morally we have no right to more. Establish that line and we give our citizens in Oregon peace and security."

When the perspiring, exhausted old senator finally sat down, his colleagues swarmed about him, hands outstretched, congratulating him. Even the staunchest 54:40 advocates praised him for presenting a face-saving solution for President Polk to defuse a war with England.

For a morose Ross, the speech held little interest or relevance for his problems. What he could see was the United States, like a boa constrictor, gradually encircling the Cherokee Nation.

With little notice, on March 25 Ross was summoned to meet with President Polk. As he entered the president's office upstairs in the White House, a thin, narrow-faced man, seated behind his desk, impatiently waved Ross to a chair. Ross noted a middle-aged woman seated nearby. Since the president made no effort to introduce her, Ross assumed she was the president's wife. He had heard politicians complain of her constant presence while they were discussing matters of state with the president.

From a twist of homegrown tobacco Polk bit off a chew. "Mr. Ross, I don't have much time for trivial matters, so let's get to it. Complaints from members of the Treaty Party state that no one can consider himself safe in the Cherokee Nation because of your hostility. General Arbuckle reports many murders in your nation with little effort from you to apprehend the guilty parties."

"I feel it to be my duty, sir" Ross replied, "to attribute to General Arbuckle, more than to any other man, the blame and responsibility for the present state of things. He is doubtless a well-intentioned, but a deeply prejudiced and disappointed man. All of his acts and conversations have had a direct and powerful tendency to defeat the work of reconciliation."

Polk gave Ross a jaundiced glare and aimed a stream of juice at the spittoon. "Other complaints indicate that there has been avarice and gross misuse of funds by your government."

"Not very presidential," thought Ross, but he remained calm. "Mr. President, your Secretary of War has denied us access to the complaints so we know not how to respond."

Sensing his failure to intimidate Ross, Polk charged. "It has been asserted that the Major Ridge was killed on the orders of your government."

"Blatantly false. Major Ridge forfeited his life under an existing law of the nation; a law voted for and carried through by Ridge himself. Mr. President, Jones, Mason, and Butler addressed all those complaints and issued a favorable report in our favor. We would appeal to that report and to the unfulfilled promises made by President Tyler."

"You should be aware, Mr. Ross, that promises made by previous administrations are not binding on subsequent ones, nor are the findings of Jones, Mason, and Butler."

Ross ignored the condescending remark. "Yes, in my years of dealing with your government, I've come to expect that."

Polk, uncertain for a moment on how to respond, hurried on. "My government is currently facing momentous problems with Mexico and England. I'm sorry, but I cannot devote the time you desire to these tribal matters. I'll make my recommendations to Congress in the near future."

On April 13 Ross was stunned by the nature of the president's recommendations. In a letter addressed to both the Senate and House of Representatives, Polk announced his determination to divide the Cherokees politically and geographically. "I am satisfied," he said, "that there is no probability that the different bands or parties into which it is divided can ever again live together in peace and harmony—It will be perceived that internal feuds still exist which call for the prompt intervention of the Government of the United States—several unprovoked murders have been committed by the stronger upon the weaker party of the tribe, which will probably remain unpunished by the Indian authorities; and there is reason to apprehend that similar outrages will continue to be perpetrated unless restrained by the authorities of the United States—I submit to Congress the propriety of dividing the country which they at present occupy as a means of preserving the weaker party from massacre and total extermination—and equitably distributing the annuities among the parties according to their respective claims and numbers."

Depressed and angry, Ross sat in his room contemplating his next course of action. Throughout his life as principal chief of the Cherokee, he had struggled to maintain unity of the Nation, knowing that division made them weaker and prey to outside interests. Even after Congress passed the removal act, he had stood firm. When the Ridge Party signed the Treaty of New Echota he had held the majority of his people together. Now, with his back to the wall, and feeling that Polk was not fully acquainted with the facts, he would once again appeal to Congress. As much as he hated the 1835 Treaty of New Echota, he feverishly set to work drawing up an exhaustive memorial, addressed to both houses of Congress, that showed Polk's recommendations to be in direct violation of that treaty. He also pointed to the findings of the Commission of 1844, by Jones, Mason, and Butler, and their conclusion "that the old settlers and treaty party enjoy, under the act of union and the constitution of the Cherokee Nation, liberty, property, and life, in as much security as the rest of the Cherokees."

Circumstances again betrayed Ross. On Saturday, the ninth of May, just a week after Ross had submitted the memorial to Congress, Washington learned that Mexican and American troops had skirmished along the eastern bank of the Rio Grande River. Polk exuberantly proclaimed, "War exists…notwithstanding all our efforts to avoid it…by the act of Mexico herself. Congress need not declare war at all but merely recognize the existence of the war."

Gloomy and concerned that his memorial would be shunted aside, Ross sat in the Senate gallery on Monday, May 11 as the clerk, French, read the president's call to war, "to repel the invasion and avenge the honor of the United States Army."

A haggard and tremulous Calhoun rose in response. "There must not be war; there cannot be war," he pleaded. "A border incident is not a war. War should not be waged for territory but for honor. War with Mexico could mean the intervention of England and perhaps loss of the entire Oregon country. I cannot accept the president's request to recognize a state of war. By our constitution, only Congress can make war. Not the President of the United States! It would set a precedent which would enable all future Presidents to bring about a state of things in which Congress shall be forced to declare war however opposed to its own conviction. It would divert the warmaking power from Congress to the President. The doctrine is monstrous."

Calhoun's burning eyes swept the Senate, his whole body trembling. "During the discussions for the annexation of Texas, I promised Mexico an honest negotiation on the most liberal and satisfactory terms. The proposed Rio Grande boundary is nearly a hundred miles from any territory which America can justly claim. To claim this land would include people whose language, religion, and culture are alien to our own. I know not whether there is a friend to stand by me, but sooner than vote for that preamble, I would plunge a dagger through my heart."

Calhoun's passionate plea stopped nothing. His colleagues shouted him down. Even his southern worshipers—all were for war! Thirty years had passed since the United States had been at war. Now, there was no fear, only the prospect of victory and the fulfillment of political objectives. On May 13 Polk signed the declaration of war.

*   *   *   *

Resolved to prevent the destruction of his nation, a determined Ross made his way through the hot and muggy streets of Washington filled with exuberant crowds celebrating the declaration of war. He now realized that to preserve the unity of his nation a compromise had to be made with the Treaty Party. He must secure a lawyer to serve as a go-between, an intermediary. He would find his man at the White House where a party was planned for the evening in honor of Dolly Madison's birthday.

Ross watched as the President himself went to the north portico to assist Dolly from the tattered old carriage in which she had been driven in state for one block. Now in her late seventies, Dolly tried to hide the unkindness of time with powder, rouge, and dangling, artificial hair. Her husky, exuberant laugh filled the air in the Blue Room as she greeted old favorites: John C. Calhoun, Daniel Webster, and the new senator from Texas, Sam Houston.

"Where is that Kentucky rogue, Henry Clay?" she joked suggestively. "Not down on Marble Avenue, I trust."

"Remarkable woman, isn't she?"

Though spoken in Cherokee, Ross recognized the voice—Sam Houston.

Ross turned and looked up at a tall, bronzed giant draped in an Indian blanket and wearing a broad-brimmed white hat. "Where there is free whiskey, there you will find Sam Houston," he laughed. "Yes, Mrs. Madison is a remarkable woman. I remember what a charming lady she was when I met her on my first visit to Washington City back in 1816."

"Speaking of beautiful women, what ever became of Diana Rogers?" Houston asked hesitantly.

"I thought you knew…the woman you deserted died of pneumonia back in 1838."

"No, I didn't know." Houston's eyes misted over. "I've thought of her often." He cleared his throat. "Come, let's get a drink. Mrs. Polk won't allow dancing or serve good whiskey so we will have to settle for table wine."

With his glass in hand, Houston looked around the room at his fellow senators: Martin Van Buren, Thomas Hart Benton, Daniel Webster, and John C. Calhoun. "I wonder what Calhoun thinks of me now," he mused. "Years ago he humiliated me. Now he must recognize me as an equal."

"Calhoun can't disregard the fact that you brought Texas into the Union, but the person who would be most proud of your exploits would be General Jackson."

A winsome young girl approaching caught Houston's attention. He nodded in response to Ross. "Too bad that he didn't live to see this day."

"Would you be the famous Sam Houston?" cooed the young girl.

"Houston, yes; famous, no! I don't believe I've had the pleasure…"

The girl smiled flirtatiously and tossed her long finger curls of chestnut brown. "I'm Joanna Rucker, Mrs. Polk's niece. These are my friends, Representative Jefferson Davis from Mississippi and his bride, Varina."

"Sir," said Davis, extending his hand. Houston shook hands with the tall, slender man with a soldierly bearing, and glanced at his bride who looked to be half Davis's age.

"I'm honored," said Houston. "What can I do for you?"

Joanna boldly tapped her fan on Houston's shoulder. "We need a foursome for a game of whist, and I chose you."

Houston smiled and bowed. "How can I resist? Chief Ross, I hope you will excuse me."

For a time Ross milled aimlessly about the room, silently sizing up the men he knew to be reputable lawyers when he was arrested by a hand on his arm. Turning, he gazed into the smiling face of Kate Brill.

"You seem to be looking for someone, Chief Ross."

"Kate…Kate Brill…so good to see you again…" Her sudden appearance and directness flustered Ross.

"Chief Ross, may I present my son, Houston Brill." Shaking hands with the young man, Ross noted that he had inherited Kate's fair skin and blonde hair. His height and facial features left little doubt in Ross's mind as to his sire.

"I'm aware of your predicament," said Kate, "so let's sit down and talk."

"Kate, you baffle me. How did you know I was in trouble?"

"There's very little that goes on in this town that I don't know about. I also know you are looking for an attorney, that's why I brought along my son...he is a lawyer."

Looking at the young barrister, Ross hesitated. "The Treaty Party has employed seasoned attorneys...Amos Kendall and..."

"My opponents have been fooled by my youth," said Brill, "It works to my advantage. I can deliver for you."

Something about the confident manner, caused Ross to yield. "Feelings between my people, the Treaty Party, and the Old Settlers, are too raw for face to face meetings. I need a person who can persuade them to come together and petition for a neutral commission to settle our differences. You will be that person."

Brill nodded. "Assuming I can accomplish that, who appoints the neutral commission?"

"President Polk must be persuaded to appoint such. That also is part of your assignment."

*   *   *   *

Brill had done his work well. In the still, mucky heat on the morning of June 27 three uneasy, sweaty groups assembled in Ross's room at the Fuller Hotel. The Old Settlers were represented by John Brown, William Dutch and Richard Drew. John Bell, George Adair, and Stand Watie would speak for the Treaty Party. Ross's party included David Vann, Stephen Foreman, William S. Coodey, and Richard Taylor.

Ross was the first to speak. "We are not enemies." He paused then repeated. "We are not enemies. Yes, we have disagreed, violently so, even to the point of bloodshed. But we are kin. We are brothers. But if we, the hope of our people, cannot recognize our true enemies, those who have taken our lands, those who would divide and destroy us, then our people have no hope."

Ross mopped his brow and continued. "I have labored my entire adult life on behalf of my people. President Polk's recommendation that the Cherokee Nation be divided, if approved by Congress, will weaken us to the point that ultimately we will be devoured bite by bite at the leisure of the United States. Surely, that is too horrible for any of us to contemplate. That is why I beseech you to join with me and petition the president to appoint an independent commission that will study and resolve our differences once and for all. I give you my pledge, I will abide by their recommendations."

In the quiet that followed, Stand Watie stood, his broad brow wrinkled with concern. "All of you here know that I have no love for John Ross. In days past I would have gladly buried my knife in his heart for the killing of my brothers. Nevertheless, I have abstained from excesses willing to suffer wrong rather than be the aggressor. You also know that I have desired no reconciliation with the Ross Party and that I have argued for a division of the Cherokee Nation. But my heart has changed. Ross is right. For the sake of our people and any hope for their future, we must remain united. I will sign the petition to the president and put my trust in a neutral commission."

During the stifling heat of July the three-man commission appointed by Polk hammered out an agreement suitable to all factions. On August 7, three days before it adjourned, the Senate approved the new treaty by a margin of one vote.

On August 13, 1846 the three delegations gathered in President Polk's office to sign the treaty as approved by Congress. Twenty signatures were affixed to the agreement, animosities were renounced, and hands were clasped. Ross and Watie, tense and wary, pressed palms. Harmony was restored…for now.

CHAPTER 34

A STORM
IN THE SENATE

Long plumes of smoke and a din of bells filled the terminal at New Jersey Avenue and C Street N.W. where John Ross prepared to board the train to Baltimore.

Ross kissed Kate and extended his hand to her son. "Houston Brill, I'll forever be in your debt. For once I can leave Washington with a sense of something accomplished."

"Just call me Hugh, Mr. Ross. Two Houstons in Washington at the same time are too much."

"Sam is a life-long friend of mine, but you are the Houston I will look to in the future to keep me informed of the activities here and to look out for Cherokee interests. In my many years of dealing with this government, I've found that they are long on promises but short on delivering."

"It will be my pleasure to serve a man of such distinction," smiled Brill.

"Distinction? No. I'm getting old, I'm tired, and my health isn't at its best. I'm looking forward to peace within the Cherokee family and getting home to take my ease."

With that Ross boarded the Baltimore and Ohio ending his long, tiring stay in Washington City.

*   *   *   *

"It was the most damnable land grab I've ever seen pulled off," grumbled Hanks. "That fucker, Polk, has taken more than 500,000 square miles of territory from Mexico and added it to the United States. Then he had the brass to offer a hundred million to Spain for Cuba. Andrew Jackson would be most proud."

Ross put aside the letter he had received from Hugh Brill describing how John Quincy Adams had died at age 80 on a sofa in the Speaker's private chamber on February 23, 1848.

"You don't sound too proud of whipping the Mexicans," he said.

Hanks snorted. "They fought Zach Taylor like hell at Buena Vista. That's where I took my second hit. But many of them were raw, untrained recruits, poorly equipped…and not too keen about fighting for Santa Anna. I didn't think it was a fair fight."

Ross looked up with interest. "I didn't know you had been wounded twice, Tom."

Hanks smiled sheepishly. "The first was at Matamoros. The Mexican army was on the south side of the Rio Grande, we were on the north. But our presence did not keep those beautiful Mexican damsels from swimming nude in the river. They smiled and waved so some of us stripped and decided to join them. That's when the Mexican guards opened fire. A bullet creased my ass so for a few days I rode mostly in the stirrups." Hanks paused. "You tell my wife, Tiva, about this and you are a dead man."

Ross laughed. "I take that threat very seriously. You got a bullet and Zach Taylor got the presidency. Such are the fortunes of war."

Rising from his desk he walked over to the window. Through a light, January snow sifting down on Park Hill he could see a horseman approaching through the slush at breakneck speed. He hurried to the door as the rider dismounted.

"Gold!" croaked the rider. "They've discovered gold in California." He thrust a newspaper into Ross's hands. He opened the Cherokee Advocate to read, "The whole valley of Sacramento may be said to be one vast deposit of gold, the metal lying in more or less abundance…"

Ross crumpled the paper in his fist. "When news of this gets out, you will see Dahlonega all over again. This time our men will rush to California and most will return poorer but wiser. Man's lust for gold far exceeds his lust for women."

"I might debate that point," grinned Hanks, "if I were younger."

*   *   *   *

Gold fever struck Tahlequah as it did neighboring communities. Within days a company was formed with nothing in mind but the gold fields of California. Unfortunately, no one in the group had an inkling of how to get there nor the requirements necessary for the trip.

On April 21 the Cherokee group rendezvoused at the Grand Saline with another group of one hundred and thirteen men who called themselves the Fayetteville Gold Mining Company. The Grand Saline, a long used crossing of the Neosho River, was an important source of salt. On the east side of the river was the grand, brick home of Lewis Ross who operated the salt works. He also owned a store which supplied the needs of the men.

Darkening clouds, carried along by a soft, southern wind, gave the threat of rain. Lewis Ross, standing on the porch of his store, was patiently trying to answer questions from the impatient travelers. "I cannot tell you how much you will need for the journey. I can only tell you what it will cost. Flour is two dollars a hundred pounds; bacon is five cents a pound, coffee is twelve cents a pound, and corn is thirty-five cents a bushel…" He broke off talk as a party of twenty men rode up. A muscular young man dismounted. Golden hair farmed an open, bronzed face in which penetrating, blue eyes were set.

Approaching Lewis Ross he extended his hand. "I'm Green Russell from Georgia. Me and my friends are heading for California but we would like to camp here for the night."

Lewis shook hands and peered at Green. "I'm Lewis Ross and I welcome you. Might I ask, what part of Georgia do you hail from?"

"Dahlonega, sir."

"Would you be related to a gold miner by the name of James Russell?"

"James Russell, God rest his soul, was my father."

Lewis's dark eyes squinted. "Have you any recollection of what happened at Dahlonega?"

"Yes, sir, I do. I was just a lad of eight when gold was discovered in the Cherokee Nation but I know how they got fucked out of their gold. They couldn't even mine their own land."

"Mr. Russell, you seem quite familiar with the Cherokee."

"So I am, Mr. Ross. My wife, Susan, she's part Cherokee."

Lewis leaned back and eyed Russell from head to toe. "So…you are hankering for California?"

"Yes, sir. The best mining has played out in Georgia. The gold pickin's ain't worth the sweat."

"Then, I take it you know something about mining for gold."

"Done it all my life, Mr. Ross, and I'm pretty good at it if I do say so myself."

Lewis turned to the crowd which had been hanging on every word. "Men, you heard him. This here feller, Green Russell, can tell you all you need to know about mining for gold in California."

*   *   *   *

Ross tossed the paper aside and snorted. "This California gold rush…never expected it to affect me one way or the other but it has cost me the editor of the Advocate and now my son-in-law wants to join him."

Mary, warm and fresh from her bath and smelling of lilacs, stood behind his chair and massaged his temples. "Don't fret so, John. We have plenty of room and your daughter will be no trouble at all."

"Of course Jane will be no trouble. It's just that I cannot understand a man who would abandon his family to go chasing after rainbows."

Mary brushed her fingers through his hair. "The children are all asleep, John. Why don't you come to bed?"

"I must finish my report to the general council," he replied, the sweet aroma of lilacs making it difficult for him to concentrate. "We are facing serious problems."

"John, you are giving too much of yourself to the council. No one really appreciates that."

"Where my people are concerned, no appreciation of my efforts is necessary to sustain me."

Insistent, Mary slid around his chair and seated herself on his lap. As she did so, her bathrobe fell open. The lamp cast a golden glow on her full, voluptuous breasts.

His pulse quickening, Ross reached to touch her nipples which rose to meet his fingers. "Well, my little Quaker girl, you have my undivided attention."

"I'm no longer a little girl," she panted. "In case you haven't noticed, I'm a grown up woman…and a woman has needs."

With a gentle tug, Ross slipped the robe off her shoulders. "Well, I guess the council report will just have to wait."

*   *   *   *

Seated in the twenty by twenty log house, newly erected for the National Council, Ross drew his coat closer against the early October chill. Wet, oak logs sputtered and spit in the brick chimney that was not drawing well, sending smoke into the crowded room. Seated facing him were the mixed-blood, slave owners, who were eager for change and progress, after the fashion of the whites. Alongside them sat the full-bloods whose distaste for slavery was well known. But, as long as they were left to themselves, and had food for their families, they tolerated the leadership provided by the mixed-blood elite.

Never comfortable speaking in Cherokee, Ross gave his report in English with the Rev. Stephen Foreman translating. First on his list was the national debt.

"In making the Treaty of 1846 we incurred debt of over one hundred thousand dollars by the employment of council and law agents to bring about settlement of some of the long delayed claims against the government of the United States. The credit, the honor, and all the best interests of our people demand that provision be made for payment of that debt with the least possible delay.

"I propose that we retrocede to the United States the eight hundred thousand acres in the northeastern part of the Cherokee Nation, known as the Neutral Lands. Missourians are already encroaching upon these lands. If we can sell the Neutral Lands for eight hundred thousand dollars, we can pay off our debts and avoid conflicts with white settlers."

"But what if the United States is not interested in buying the land?" The question came from full-blood John McPherson.

"I have instructed Houston Brill, our council in Washington, to advance the idea," Ross replied.

"If he can't sell the idea to Washington, then what?" McPherson persisted.

Ross hesitated. "Then I would recommend that the National Council levy a small tax…say five percent of the amount each individual receives from the United States according to the Treaty of 1846. Our debts would be liquidated and we could maintain our Male and Female Seminaries."

"I would resist such taxation," McPherson replied. "Your seminaries, your copies of Mount Holyoke College and the Boston Latin Schools serve the elite few. Since it opened in 1851 the Female Seminary had been nothing but a ladies' finishing school for the rich to make your daughters eligible to become wives of wealthy men. We full-bloods benefit little from these schools and we make up two-thirds of the whole nation."

A rumble of assent rose from the assembly. There would be no taxes! Ross quietly folded his papers. He had learned that acculturation would take place at different rates among different groups of his people.

*   *   *   *

Under the burning sun John McPherson followed his single mule and plow as he prepared a patch for fall planting. He could plow deeper in the prairie soil if he had two mules but that was something he could not afford. This dry and rocky soil could not compare with the rich bottomlands he had plowed in Georgia. But fate had placed him here on the east bank of the Grand River between Fort Gibson and Union Mission. He had built his log cabin near a small stream, where water was easy to fetch, just north of where Sam Houston's Wigwam Neosho had stood. To the east stood low, oak covered hills that provided wood for his fire; to the west was a well-beaten trail called the Texas Road, so named because many land seekers from Missouri followed it to Texas and because, recently, droves of cattle were being driven on the trail from Texas to the railhead in Joplin, Missouri.

McPherson paused at the end of the row to rest his mule. Removing his broad brimmed hat, he mopped sweat from his brow. His needs were few. Considering the erratic weather, he had a fair crop of corn now tasseling out. Pumpkins and crowder peas grew between the rows of corn. He had a few hogs running loose in the woods that he would slaughter come fall. Yes, there would be enough corn for his own use and ample fodder for the mule. Why the white man chose to kill himself off in the struggle to gain more possessions was something McPherson could not understand. In fact, there was no good reason for him to stay out in the blazing sun when there was a shady, vine-covered porch waiting. He unhitched his mule.

The sun was turning orange in the west when McPherson was awakened from napping in a rocking chair on his porch by a frenzy of barking from his dogs. Through the billowing dust McPherson saw a herd of longhorn cattle making straight for his cornfield. Grabbing his hat and the closest implement at hand, he rushed to head off certain disaster. He yelled and poked at the cattle but there was no stopping the onslaught. Corn, peas, and pumpkins were trampled under hoof as the hungry herd surged forward. Out of the maelstrom of dust a rider appeared. He lashed McPherson across the face with a leather whip and shouted "Get outta the way, you fuckin' redskin!" Without thinking, McPherson hurled the implement in his hand. The rider fell at his feet. Two tines of the pitchfork had pierced his throat and protruded from the back of his neck.

*   *   *   *

"The Supreme Court of the Cherokee Nation acquitted McPherson," Hanks reported. "They saw it as a case of self-defense but a United States marshal from Ft. Smith has taken him into custody. Says he must stand trial there."

Ross scowled and eased his aging body into a chair. "That is contrary to all treaties signed with the United States government. I have no great love for McPherson, but if we permit his trial to take place in a federal court, it will be a fatal blow to our sovereignty. It will seriously undermine our claims to independence if marshals can enter our country and arrest our citizens for any alleged offence. I will notify Houston Brill to be prepared to carry this case all the way to the United States Supreme Court if necessary."

*   *   *   *

Hill's boarding house stood a block east of the capitol building. In 1814 the three-storied, brick structure had served as home for Congress during the grim days following the burning of Washington by the British. It was here, on March 31, 1850, in a late spring snowstorm, that the greatest son of South Carolina, John C. Calhoun, died at age sixty-eight.

Clay and Webster led the Senate in the customary eulogies to the deceased but Benton refused to join them. "Calhoun died with treason in his heart and on his lips. I cannot abide such," said Benton.

As Houston Brill left his room at the boarding house on a bright April morning, doubt and uncertainty went with him. Could anyone imagine the Senate without Calhoun? With him gone, who would keep the South united and, and at the same time, cool the hotheaded slaveholders who feverishly demanded accommodation or secession? And with Congress totally occupied with the question of slavery in the newly acquired territory from Mexico, how could he succeed in carrying out the charges laid on him by John Ross. No one in the government showed the least interest in retrocession of the Neutral Lands. Unless the federal government purchased the land from the Cherokee, there would be no way Ross could pay off the national debt. And how could he, a largely untested, young lawyer, win the case for John McPherson when he had never argued before the Supreme Court?

If he had to buttonhole senators, he must go where they were. Putting aside his doubts, Brill entered the packed Senate gallery. Looking down he could see Sam Houston, the new senator from Texas, wearing a broad hat and wrapped in an Indian blanket, whittling away on a stick. The rotund senator from Missouri, Thomas Hart Benton, was at his desk apparently reading a book.

Since January the question of whether slavery would be admitted in the newly acquired territories had produced heated debate in the Senate. On January 29 Henry Clay had introduced a plan in which California would be admitted to the union as a state without any mention of slavery. For the territories of Utah and New Mexico Clay would allow the residents to decide the question of slavery for themselves. The seventy-three year old Clay called his plan a compromise that would save the country.

Jefferson Davis, a thirty-nine year old, wealthy cotton planter and Senator from Mississippi, rose in rebuttal. Heatedly he stated, "I see no compromise at all in this proposal. The South cedes all and gets nothing in return. The North has inflicted a wrong on the South which will involve us in total ruin. This so-called compromise is a fraud on the South and is unconstitutional."

Brill watched the unfolding drama. The aging Clay, dressed in a black suit and a high white collar that reached to his ears, rose wearily to his feet. "Mr. Chairman, the question is whether the Senate will maintain its power, whether it will maintain its dignity, and whether it will maintain its consistency. I call for the yeas and nays on the question."

Senator Benton objected immediately. "Sir, the motion of the honorable Senator from Kentucky is a motion to overrule the rules of the Senate; to trample the rules of the Senate underfoot for the purpose of stifling debate; for the purpose of cutting off amendments."

At this point, Senator Henry S. Foote joined the fray. Brill had heard of the homely little man's violent reputation. Foote had been shot down in four duels and had attacked in the Senate aisles another senator from Pennsylvania. He also knew that Foote regarded Benton as a traitor to the South.

Baiting Benton, Foote spoke to his colleagues. "We all know that the late Senator from South Carolina, John C. Calhoun, is the author of the South's position, and that position declares that Congress has no right to interfere with slavery in the states. Those of us who were associated with and sanction that position are charged with being agitators. In our presence here today, that position is denounced by a gentleman long denominated the oldest member of the Senate..."

The screech of a chair being pushed back stopped Foote mid-sentence. As the hulking Benton moved down the aisle in fury, Foote drew a pistol and aimed at Benton as he retreated toward the Vice President's chair. Like the shaggy buffaloes that ranged in his state, Benton surged forward. In a moment the Senate was in an uproar with calls for "Order, Order". The dignity and decorum of the Senate deteriorated. Senators seized Benton's frock-coat for a moment before he shook them off. "Let him fire," he shouted. "Stand out of the way. Let the assassin fire. I have no pistol. I disdain to carry arms. I never quarrel, gentlemen. But sometimes I fight and when I fight, a funeral follows. Stand out of the way and let the little bastard fire!"

Several senators surrounded both Benton and Foote. One took Foote's pistol and locked in away. Both men were persuaded to return to their seats.

Blandly, Clay intoned, "I hope that order will be preserved."

Still steaming Benton rose in his place. "We are not getting off in this easily. A pistol has been brought here to assassinate me…"

Foote protested. "I brought it here to defend myself."

"Nothing of the sort, sir," Benton retorted. "It is a false imputation. I carry no pistol and no assassin has a right to draw a pistol on me."

Several senators spoke out, "Order! Order!"

"It is a mere pretext of the assassin," said Benton. "Will the Senate take notice of it or shall I be forced to take notice of it by going and getting a weapon myself?"

To quiet Benton, the chair quickly stated that he would establish a committee of seven to investigate the affair. After the Senate adjourned for the day, Benton remained at his desk scribbling notes.

"I trust I'm not disturbing you, Senator Benton."

Without looking up, Benton continued writing. "This day will be an unforgettable one in the history of this Senate," he said, "which I firmly intend to write when I retire." Then, putting aside his pencil, he looked up warily. "Who are you, boy?"

"My name is Brill, sir…Houston Brill. I am an attorney employed by the Cherokee."

"And what concern would that be with me?"

"Sir, you represent the state of Missouri. Large numbers of settlers from your state are moving into the Neutral Lands of the Cherokee. If you could persuade your government to purchase those lands, it would be to the benefit of both parties…it might head off any conflicts."

Benton leaned back in his chair and smiled. "My boy, up to 1840 the United States have paid the Indians about ninety million dollars for land purchases. That is near six times what we gave the great Napoleon for Louisiana…the whole of it. There will be no more payments to the Cherokees for land!"

Benton heaved his bulk from his chair and poked Brill's chest with a stubby finger. "You have much to learn about politics and poker, my boy. You are holding a weak hand and you are not good at bluffing. The American settlers will go where they please. Sure, the Indians need to be protected but they must not be allowed to stand in the way of progress." He gathered up his papers and started to leave. He paused, and turned to Brill. "My boy, consider getting another client. The Cherokees are so broke they won't be able to pay your fee."

*   *   *   *

As the date for the McPherson trial neared, Brill was assailed with doubts. Since his attempts to have the United States purchase the Neutral Lands had failed, the Cherokee faced financial bankruptcy. Pangs of anxiety ratcheted up in his mind knowing that if he did not succeed in the Supreme Court, he would have failed Ross completely. Neither would he measure up to his mother's expectations.

At high noon, on Tuesday, June 29, 1852, as Brill plodded through the crowd toward his boarding house, church bells began slowly tolling. Someone on the street shouted, "Henry Clay is dead!"

That afternoon President Millard Fillmore issued an executive order closing all federal offices for the rest of the day. Work on the Washington monument and the transformation of the Mall from pasture to national park ceased. The capitol went into mourning.

On the first day of July Brill joined the long procession to honor Clay who lay in state in the rotunda of the capitol, the first person accorded that honor in American history. A chaplain extolled the virtues of Clay. "A great mind, a great heart, a great orator, a great career, have been consigned to history." But in Brill's mind the name of Henry Clay would at any time and in any part of the Union create more sensation than any other.

There was a lull in the bitter political discussions following Clay's death. There were the customary receptions at the White House, and hops in the hotels, but few large social parties were given.

For weeks Brill remained cloistered in his hot, stuffy room reading material from John Ross. He pored over copies of treaties made between the Cherokee and the United States, making copious notes. To the Treaty of New Echota he applied special scrutiny.

The sticky heat of Washington summer gradually turned to autumn. During those weeks, over drinks with fellow lawyers, Brill actively probed for information on Roger B. Taney. These talks revealed that Taney, a voracious cigar smoker, was born into an aristocratic tobacco family in Maryland. A slave owner, and an avid supporter of Andrew Jackson, the president had appointed him chief justice in 1836. That piece of knowledge raised Brill's suspicion that Taney would be friendly to any Indian cause.

On a bright, sunny Monday, October 25, 1852, Brill made his way toward the Supreme Court chambers on the ground floor of the Senate wing of the capitol building. Feeling that his preparations for the McPherson case were complete, he mustered his courage for the trial. As he approached the capitol, he met Benjamin B. French, former Chief Clerk of the House of Representatives.

"There will be no government business today," the New Englander announced. "Word has just come over the wires that Daniel Webster died yesterday at his home in Marshfield. President Fillmore has ordered that all flags be lowered and declared a thirty-day mourning period."

Stunned by the news, Brill stood silent.

"The funeral will be in Boston this coming Friday," French added, "then he will be laid to rest in Marshfield. The age of statesmen seems to have gone by, and that of upstarts, striving to be great without the first germ of intellectual greatness within them, has taken its place."

With a sober nod, Brill turned toward his boarding house then stopped. "Calhoun, then Clay, and now Webster. Who will save the nation in this time of crisis?"

"I don't know," French replied. "I have no desire to end slavery in the South but I will fight to save the Union."

*   *   *   *

Brill stood as the justices in their black, silk robes filed into the dimly lit room led by the tall, narrow-faced Chief Justice. Taney took his seat in the center as his colleagues sat to his right and left in the order of their appointment, the oldest judge on his right hand, the next on his left. They sat in a row on the straight dais raised a foot or two above the rest of the floor. The light from deep windows behind them fell upon the shoulders of their robes and on top of their heads leaving their faces in shadow. For some odd reason it registered in Brill's mind that Taney was wearing trousers instead of the traditional knee breeches.

Once seated the black haired Taney looked down at Brill and nodded.

With his heart pounding, and in a voice he did not recognize as his own, Brill began. "Mr. Chief Justice and members of the court, under Article 6, section 2, of the United States constitution, all treaties made…under the authority of the United States shall be the supreme law of the land. Treaties are made between sovereign nations. With that in mind, let me call your attention to Article 5 of the Treaty of New Echota, signed on December 29, 1835 in Georgia. This treaty was signed by General William Carroll and John F. Schermerhorn on the part of the United States and the chiefs, headmen, and people of the Cherokee tribe of Indians. Article 5 clearly states, and I quote, 'The United States agree that the land herein guaranteed to the Cherokees shall never, without their consent, be included within the limits or jurisdiction of any State or Territory. The United States also agree to secure to them the right to make and carry into effect such laws as they deem necessary, provided they shall not be inconsistent with the Constitution of the United States…'"

As he spoke, confidence surged through Brill. "Clearly the alleged crimes of John McPherson fall within the jurisdiction of Cherokee laws and not those of Arkansas. Based on all the treaties signed between the United States and the Cherokees, the federal government has limited jurisdiction. It has never been questioned that the Cherokees had the right to make and enforce their own laws."

In the limited time accorded him, Brill concluded, "If the laws of the United States may be extended over the Cherokee in this particular case, why may it not be done in all cases? And surely, if the United States may enact such laws, they have the right to administer and execute them. This monstrous pretension in mandating its criminal laws over the Cherokee Nation is without precedent and without legal basis. Enactment of such laws would signal the demise of an essential attribute of Cherokee sovereignty. If this can be done, surely all the residue of less important powers may be in the same manner arrogated and the right to prescribe all the laws, and to appoint judges to administer, and officers to execute them. What is the limitation of this power?"

In a few days Taney rendered his decision. Using his power to decide what to decide, he ignored constitutional issues altogether. Looking down his long, aquiline nose he delivered his ruling. "Indians," he said, "have never been acknowledged or treated as independent nations by the European Courts nor regarded as the owners of the territories they respectively occupied. The Europeans who came to North America treated the continent as vacant and claimed it for themselves. It is too firmly and clearly established to admit to dispute," he continued, "that the Indian tribes residing within the territorial limits of the United States are subject to their authority and when the country occupied by them is not within the limits of one of the states, Congress may, by law, punish any offence committed there..."

Stunned, Brill tried to grasp the implications of the ruling. By Taney's decision the status of the Cherokee Nation was being unilaterally and forever altered.

*   *   *   *

His weary body sagged into a chair as Ross handed Brill's report to Hanks. "It appears that Chief Justice Taney has reinvented history. He is asserting that the federal government has always had unlimited power over us. His ruling will justify deeper federal encroachments into our sovereignty."

"The old bastard is also inventing law," replied Hanks. "If consent is not a viable doctrine, then why the hell have we made hundreds of treaties with the feds? He folded the papers and handed them back to Ross. "This report wasn't an easy one for Brill to write. I suppose we have no more need for his services now."

"On the contrary," said Ross. "I still have hopes of reselling the neutral lands to the government. We need eyes and ears in Washington so I'll keep Brill on."

With the barking of dogs outside, Old Moses entered the room. "Der's some mean lookin' men want to see you, Chief Ross."

The mean lookin' men that Ross met at the front door consisted of a dozen or more of dust-covered, mounted men led by a weasel-face wearing a badge.

"Y'er dogs ain't too friendly," said Weasel-Face.

Hanks, his instincts taking control, "We like 'em that way. Too many horse thieves around."

Weasel-Face shot a disdainful glance at Hanks then turned back to Ross. "My name is Shively...Otis Shively, federal marshal out of Ft. Smith. We are looking for John McPherson...understand he might be in these parts."

"Since your government doesn't see fit for us to punish whites for crimes, you'd render a greater service if you cleaned up some of the white trash that moved in here," snapped Hanks.

Ignoring him Shively pursued his quest. "Our warrant is for McPherson."

Ross shook his head. "Can't help you, marshal. The last we heard, you had John in jail at Ft. Smith."

Shively snorted. "That sunuvabitch beat the hell out of a jailer, him and a nig-ger slave, and got away. Thought maybe he might have come to ground here."

As the posse rode away, Ross turned to Hanks with a worried frown. "This is just the beginning of it. After Taney's ruling, the feds will try to ride rough-shod over us."

✳   ✳   ✳   ✳

After the moon had set, blackness ruled. Gray owls, and other hunters of the night, were briefly exposed by sheet lightning in the west. Hanks was awakened from a deep slumber by a tapping sound. With Colt revolver in hand he moved to the door.

"Who's there?" he asked.

"McPherson...John McPherson," came a whispered reply. "Let me in."

Hanks opened the door. "What the hell...?"

McPherson stepped quickly inside and closed the door.

"What the hell are you doing here?" asked Hanks as he lit a kerosene lamp. "Don't you know you are being hunted by every marshal in the territory?"

"There's one less hunting me now. Shively was gunned down yesterday in Tahlequah. Don't know who did the shootin' but someone spread the word that it was me."

Hanks gazed at the weather-beaten old man. "You look like hell...are you hungry?"

"I could use some grub."

Over a plate of cold pinto beans and a chunk of corn bread McPherson looked at Hanks. "What do you think I ought to do...turn myself in at the federal court in Ft. Smith?"

"Hell no," Hanks snorted. "That's the last thing you want to do. Remember, you beat up a jailer and escaped. You could be as innocent of killing Shively as the virgin Mary but they'd hang you just the same, as they would any Indian sus-pected of killing a U.S. marshal."

McPherson sopped his tin plate with the last piece of bread. "Then I have no choice but to take to the hills."

"That's the call I'd make," said Hanks. "They'll never catch an old coon like you in the brush."

"Then I'd best be on my way, 'fore sunup." McPherson looked up on the wall. "I need another gun. Would you mind selling me that long-barreled Kentucky rifle?"

Hanks shook his head. "Too much sentiment tied up in Old Bess. We go back as far as Horseshoe Bend. But I'll do even better. I'll give you my Colt repeating rifle. Its eight shots might make things even in a fight."

McPherson draped his blanket over his shoulders, pushed on his battered hat, and reached out to Hanks with callused hands. "Look out for Mary Quaqua for me." A firm handshake then he and his rifle were swallowed up in the darkness.

*   *   *   *

At the end of each day Ross closed his eyes and leaned back in his chair listening to Mary render several selections on her pianoforte. Annie, now a gracious young lady of 14, sat on the piano bench with her mother. John Jr., age 12, was engrossed in a magazine. Tonight, as Mary finished her last selection, she noted John was completely immersed in a newspaper.

"What, no compliments from my favorite audience tonight?" she teased.

"I'm sorry, my dear. There's more disturbing news in the Advocate. It seems the candidate for governor of the Kansas Territory feels that Indian treaties with the United States constitute no obstacles to white expansion onto our lands." He laid the paper aside. "Furthermore, the state of Massachusetts is sponsoring Free Soil settlers to move into the territory. Douglas's so-called popular sovereignty will cause blood to flow between them and the Missourians…it's just a matter of time." He rose from his chair; "The troubles could spill over into our nation. I'd better get a letter off to Brill. He needs to increase his efforts to sell the Neutral Lands."

"I understand Ft. Smith now has a telegraph office." Mary stifled a cough with her linen kerchief. "A wire would be much faster than a letter."

Mary smothered another cough as she left for her bedroom.

*   *   *   *

Brill re-read the telegram and stuffed it in his coat pocket. Ross was unaware of the hostility building daily in the halls of Congress. Some congressmen, Brill had noted, were carrying pistols for protection. Nevertheless, he had a job to do.

He found Senator Sam Houston from Texas lounging on the east side of the capitol, where steps had yet to be built, smoking a cigar and taking in the bright, morning sun of May.

"I'm looking for the Chairman of the Committee on Territories," said Brill.

Under the shade of his broad-brimmed hat, Houston peered up at the young man. "That would be Douglas...Stephen A."

"Is he the one they call the Little Giant?"

"Giant prick if you ask me," Houston snorted. "You'll find him on the Senate floor, kissin' any ass that will further his agenda."

As Brill departed, Houston's eyes followed. There was something hauntingly familiar about the lad...reminding him of someone out of his past.

Brill did find Douglas, leaning his stout, five foot four body against the rear wall of the Senate chamber...his breath exuding whiskey and his body the sweat of tension.

"Senator Douglas?"

"Shhh!" said Douglas, placing his finger to his lips. "I want to hear this sunuv-abitch."

Brill looked at the tall man in the well of the Senate. Immaculately dressed in a light sack coat and white pantaloons, he was speaking with wild gestures. "Who is he?"

Douglas scowled. "Sumner...Charles Sumner of Massachusetts. Now shush!"

It took only a few moments for Brill to realize that Sumner was denouncing something called The Crime Against Kansas. With clenched fists and waving arms he lashed out at everything and everyone supportive of slavery. "Douglas, the author of this loathsome act, a noisome, squat, and nameless animal, has filled this Senate chamber with an offensive smell. The Senator from Illinois is the squire of slavery, its very Sancho Panza, ready to do all its humiliating offices."

"That damned fool will get himself killed by some other damned fool," Douglas hissed under his breath. "He has a maggot in his brain."

Next Sumner turned his insulting words to Senator Andrew Pickens Butler from South Carolina, whose seat was unoccupied.

"The Senator from South Carolina overflows with rage at the simple suggestion that Kansas has applied for admission as a free state. He heaps incoherent phrases and spews spit in his speech upon her representatives and then upon her people. There is no possible deviation from truth which he has not made. This Don Quixote has chosen a mistress to whom he has made his vows, and who, though polluted in the sight of the world, is chaste in his sight...and I mean the harlot, slavery."

"The insensitive bastard," breathed Douglas. "He hesitates not to attack an absent, sixty-year old man who has suffered a stroke."

"Were the whole history of South Carolina blotted out of existence," stormed Sumner, "civilization might lose, I do not say how little, but surely less than it has already gained by the example of Kansas against oppression. Ah, Sir, I tell the senator that Kansas, welcomed as a free state, will be a ministering angel to the Republic when South Carolina, in the cloak of darkness which she hugs, lies howling."

As Sumner finished, Douglas growled audibly, "No wonder his brief marriage did not last. His young wife could not stand living with God."

"Senator Douglas," said Brill, "I have an issue which requires serious and immediate..."

Douglas brushed him aside, calling over his shoulder. "See me in another day or two. I've got to answer that sunuvabitch."

On May 22 Brill was back in the Senate chamber. Although the senate had adjourned for the day, he saw Douglas still at his desk. As Brill started down the aisle, two, tall, young men, carrying canes, hurried past him. To his astonishment, one of the young men viciously struck with his cane the head of a seated senator. As the brutal flailing continued, the bleeding senator lurched from his desk, ripping its screws from the floor. Brill then recognized the senator as Sumner. Watching the attack, the other young man stood with folded arms, preventing senators from interfering. None of the senators present, including Douglas, made a move to stop the murderous assault. When the attacker finally backed away, his cane shattered, he was congratulated by some of the senators.

"Perhaps, Senator," said Brill, "in view of what has happened, it would be better for us to discuss business at a later time."

"Tut, tut, my boy," responded a jovial Douglas, "I thought the contentious son of a bitch deserved to be taught a lesson. Now tell me, what can I do for you?"

"But first...you tell me...who were those two young men and why did they attack Sumner?"

"The one doing the whacking was Preston Brooks...nephew of Senator Butler. The other was Laurence Keitt, Preston's friend. As you can see, it ain't safe to insult southern honor."

"My request," explained Brill, "has nothing to do with southern honor. As Senate Chairman of the Committee on Territories, you are in a position to expedite repurchase of the Neutral Lands held by the Cherokee. It would greatly reduce their financial stress and it would legally open the lands to white settlers."

Douglas's face clouded immediately. He fixed his dark blue eyes on Brill. "What's legality got to do with it? Those Indians don't own the land. Any Indian control of land between Missouri and the Rockies would be a travesty. How are we to develop, cherish, and protect our immense interests and possessions on the Pacific shores with a vast wilderness 1500 miles in breadth, filled with hostile savages, and cutting off all direct communications. Removing that Indian barrier, along with the filthy and vile Mormons, and establishing white government will bring a tide of emigration and civilization to the west. I'm sorry, young fella, you are wasting my time."

*   *   *   *

"This is another insult to my people!" Ross fumed. "It shows the greatest contempt for us as human beings!"

"Maybe that's how your slaves feel toward you. You have grown rich on their sweat and toil but what have they to show for it?"

Ross turned toward his friend, Rev. Jones. "Evan, I treat my slaves well as long as they do what they are supposed to do." He shook a newspaper at Jones. "When President Buchanan is quoted in the Arkansas Gazette as saying that the days of Cherokee sovereignty are numbered and that it is only a matter of time before Indian Territory is incorporated into the Union…that is a blatant breech of faith."

"What else would you expect of Buchanan? He is a captive of the southern slave-holders."

"It's more than Buchanan. It's Congress too…they have added two counties to Kansas Territory by taking land from the Cherokee Nation…clearly a violation of our solemn treaties with the United States and a great threat to our sovereignty."

The old Welshman steadied himself as he rose from his chair. "I'm seventy-one years old. I've preached the word of the Lord to your people for forty years. From the time of Andrew Jackson, your people have been weakened. John, you delude yourself. The Cherokees have no sovereignty."

"If I believed that, my entire life would be meaningless." Ross clenched the newspaper in his fist. "No, as long as God gives me strength, I will not surrender. Old and weak though I may be, once again I will go to Washington to carry on the fight."

"Then I wish you well," said Jones, making his way to the door.

"One more thing, Reverend, before you go." Ross hesitated. "A rift, a dangerous one, is developing among my people. I understand you are leading a group called the Keetoowah Society."

Jones swallowed and thrust out his chin. "Yes, I am. The full-bloods despise slavery and so do I. We are committed to opposing it."

Ross sighed. "I've always suspected that you were an abolitionist at heart. Your departure from religion into politics has caused the mixed-bloods slave owners to form a society of their own, the Knights of the Golden Circle. The Keetoowahs support the North; the Knights are sympathetic to the South. This produces antagonism among my people which we do not need. I would like for the Cherokees to remain neutral."

"John," Jones spoke defensively, "You do not realize the tremendous pressure I have endured from the Baptist Board back east. They have insisted that I expel slave owners from the church. I stalled and stalled, knowing what an uproar expulsion would create. When the Board threatened to withhold funds, which is the power of life or death over our mission churches, I had to do something. Instead of expelling slave-holding members, I gave them letters of dismission. I may dislike slavery, but I dislike hurting my brethren even more."

Ross's eyebrows lifted. "A letter of dismission is nothing more than a grant from a pastor to a member in good standing to join another church of the same denomination. There are no other Baptist churches nearby for them to join. They would have to stay in their same church."

"I know," smiled Jones.

The humor of it caused Ross to chuckle. "You are a wily one. Samuel Worcester was right when he called your procedure improper."

"Worcester, God rest his soul, and I did not agree on a lot of things. I thought his Biblical translations were too intellectual, too hair splitting. He thought my translations too loose. We Baptists do not believe in a 'learned ministry' so much as a 'spirit-filled ministry'."

"And your spirit will lead you to continue support of the Keetoowahs?"

Jones nodded. "My conscience will permit no acceptance of slavery."

"That's difficult for me to understand," said Ross as he reached for the Bible on his desk. "Show me anywhere in this book it says slave ownership is a bar to church membership. Even St. Paul, in his letter to Philemon, does not condemn him for owning the slave Onesimus. How, then, can you condemn slave holders when they are guilty of no sin?"

"I hold to a higher requirement," smiled Jones. "The Golden Rule...do unto others as you would have them do unto you. Would you, by choice, be a slave?"

Ross shrugged and opened the door for the preacher. "It seems our politicians are becoming more religious every day and our religious more political. Take care, my friend. I cannot protect you from your own indiscretion. You could be expelled from the Cherokee Nation."

CHAPTER 35

DANGER AND DEATH

In early February, 1860, with Kansas in open warfare, Ross, with his wife, Mary, their two children, Annie and John, Jr., and sister-in-law, Sarah, boarded the steamboat, Leon, at Van Buren, Arkansas to begin the long journey to Washington, DC. The children, whose world had been limited to Park Hill and Tahlequah, watched with wide-eyed wonder as the steamboat made its way down the Arkansas River. At Memphis they transferred to a wooden, nine by fifty passenger car. Smoke from the coal-burning stove and soot and ash from the locomotive, kept Mary in distress. At night her passage to the toilet was lit by two candles at the end of the car. By day her stomach was assaulted with hurried meals at brief stops at railway eating-houses. The train inched its way to Corinth, Mississippi, across northern Alabama, then northeast to Chattanooga. There Mary rested for a few days while Ross took his children across the state line to Rossville, Georgia to visit his old home place. Reboarding the train they proceeded northeast to Bristol, Tennessee, and across Virginia.

In late February they reached Wilmington, Delaware where Ross deposited Mary and the children with her relatives. He gave her firm instructions to consult with a doctor about her persistent cough. When Ross returned to Washington alone he was met at the station by Houston Brill.

"I wasn't aware that I should have come equipped for combat," Ross commented on noting the pistol Brill was wearing.

"Don't laugh. Since John Brown's raid, this town has become an armed camp," replied Brill as he assisted the seventy-year old Ross into the carriage. "Most Congressmen are carrying."

"How is your mother these days?" inquired Ross.

"Fine…oh…just fine."

When the carriage stopped at the corner of Pennsylvania Avenue and 14th Street NW., Ross gingerly stepped down onto the new brick sidewalk and looked up at the impressive structure. "I've been away from Washington too long. I don't recognize this building."

"It's the Willard Hotel," Brill explained, "the most popular one in the city. It was built about 1850."

Inside they found the parlor blue with cigar smoke and chattering women wearing low-cut evening gowns. Most of the men were featuring the latest Washington craze, mustaches.

Later, as they were consuming a sumptuous dinner of fried oysters and steak with onions, Brill, finishing his third brandy, looked across the table at Ross. "You know, don't you?"

"Know what?"

"About my mother…what she does for a living?"

Ross paused, fork in hand. "Suspicions, maybe…nothing definite."

With a dismissive wave, Brill continued. "I lied to you. Mother is quite ill; in fact, she is dying."

Ross wiped his lips with a napkin and spoke quietly, "I'm so sorry, Hugh. I didn't know. It's been fourteen years…"

In a broken voice, almost a sob, Brill blurted, "You can't live that life and escape the consequences." Recovering quickly, he said in a hushed tone, "Sorry, I just found out recently."

From a nearby table a whiskey-fueled shout went up, "Lincoln inaugurated as president? Never!"

"Let's get out of here," Brill suggested, "the South is in full voice about the coming political conventions."

Outside, they strolled toward the White House along the north side of Pennsylvania Avenue. An unsavory smell of sewage and offal from the many privies and the old city canal hung in the air. Pigs nosed impertinently through the slop and garbage dumped in the street. On the south side of the avenue was an agglomeration of sheds and dingy shacks.

"Not much change since I first brought your mother here in 1814," Ross observed."

"From an incestuous home life to a life in prostitution. It took little time for her to realize what lonely men here wanted and were willing to pay for it," Brill mused. "Our time together was limited. She managed to keep me away from her and Washington. I was sent to boarding school when I was very young, then later to the Lawrenceville High School. Following that, it was William and Mary law school. For a time I thought the separations were arranged because she had no love for me. Later, I found it was because she did not want me to learn of her...her profession."

"How did you find out?" asked Ross.

"Let's turn back," said Brill lifting his collar up against the February air. "It's getting dark" They walked along in silence. "I found out purely by accident. I came home from school unexpectedly. Mother was not in our hotel room. The clerk gave me an address on Marble Avenue and said I would find her there. A lovely brunette...with long, raven black hair and flashing green eyes answered my knock."

"Welcome," she said, extending her hand. "You must be new...not one of our regulars."

"I'm looking for..."

"I know what you are looking for," she smiled. "Come on in. Would you like a drink before or after?"

"Look, miss," I said, "there must be some mistake."

She laughed and her gown slipped off her beautiful, mahogany shoulders "My name is Darcy. What's yours?"

"My name is Houston."

Well," she teased, "you may look like Sam Houston but I know for certain, you ain't him."

"No! Not Sam Houston. I'm Houston Brill."

"Oh! Kate has been keeping secrets. If you are a relative, the first one is on the house."

"I'm not just a relative; I'm her son."

She smiled, put an arm around me and led me to a bed. "In that case, I'll take care of you personally."

I pulled back. "No, really, I'm just looking for my mother."

"You're too big to be a mamma's boy," she cooed, shedding her gauzy gown altogether. "This is your first time, isn't it?"

Palms out, Ross held up his hands. "Hugh, stop. Say no more. This is too personal."

"Yes, it is, but you need to know why the rift with my mother. She caught Darcy and me in bed. After that Mother sorta went crazy knowing that I had found out about her life. Since then, we have hardly spoken."

"From your comments, Darcy seems to have made quite an impression on you. What happened to her?"

"Mother fired her on the spot. No one knows it, but I've provided for Darcy ever since. I can't stand the thought of another man touching that beautiful body." They walked on in silence. "How do you reconcile your thoughts?" Brill asked. "Admiration for my mother on the one hand for her toughness and success and all that she gave me. On the other hand shame and humiliation for what she was."

Back at the Willard, Brill ordered another brandy. "Don't drink hotel water," he advised Ross. "People have died from it"

Turning his back to the bar and looking at people milling about under gas lit chandeliers, Brill observed. "Though mother had money, which she claimed came from Georgia gold, she was never accepted by Washington society. Pick at random any of these fancies in here and odds are they owed her money. She carried great clout in this town."

"But," said Ross, "not enough clout to secure our goals."

Brill placed his glass on the bar and looked squarely at Ross. "I'm the one responsible, not my mother. I'm the one who failed you. I failed in reselling the Neutral Lands to the government and I failed in the Supreme Court with McPherson's case."

"Hugh, I'm not blaming you for any of that," Ross protested. "I've been out of Washington for fourteen years. My old contacts, Clay, Webster, Wirt, and Marshall are gone…all dead. Sam Houston has gone home to Texas. You are the only one who can get me a meeting with Buchanan! It's urgent that I see him. The existence of my people is at stake."

"Don't raise your hopes too high," cautioned Brill. "Buchanan is a chip from the Andrew Jackson block. Are you aware that he has encouraged Congress to subvert Indian treaties and claims of sovereignty by passing a law that would transform your nation into a territory, and then into a state?"

✳   ✳   ✳   ✳

Ross fidgeted impatiently waiting for his turn to see the president. The cane-bottom chairs in the outer room were filled with politicians eager to gain the president's ear. China spittoons were well splattered along the walls. Sparse, worn-looking, and smelling of cigars, the east hall was as crowded and noisy as a hotel lobby.

When Ross entered the Oval Office a tall, pale, silver-haired Buchanan greeted him. With a wave of his hand the President guided Ross to a seat on an ornately carved, fully gilded, and upholstered sofa.

Head cocked to one side, Buchanan squinted at his visitor. "My apologies, Mr. Ross, for keeping you waiting. As you very well know, these are troublesome times. The hanging of John Brown has created considerable excitement throughout the nation. I'm trying to spread oil upon the waters."

"I appreciate your predicament, Mr. President. I shall not add to your problems."

Buchanan retreated behind his desk and fingered the starched white choker around his neck. "Now, my dear sir, in what way may I be of service to you?"

"Mr. President, we Cherokee have, for many months, solicited your government to repurchase the tract of land commonly called the Neutral Land. It belongs to the Cherokee Nation but white citizens of the United States are trespassing upon it with impunity. In fact, it was recently included within the territorial limits of Kansas. It would greatly relieve our distress if your government would purchase that land."

Buchanan reached inside the humidor on his desk and selected a cigar. Lighting it, he leaned back in his chair and stared at the ceiling. "There is a tide in the affairs of men...I am caught in a tide; you are also caught in a tide."

"Which, taken at the flood, leads on to fortune...to complete your citation of Shakespeare," Ross responded. "Surely you do not imply that one is helpless in a tide?"

Buchanan blew a ring of smoke. "Helpless? Perhaps. I am a victim of my time. What can I, as president of these United States, do to stop the tide of war that will surely sweep over this nation? Am I Moses? Can I hold up my staff and stop the settlers from moving west?"

"Mr. President, as the chief executive, sworn to uphold the laws of your government, you could preserve our sacred rights; you could enforce solemn treaties between your country and mine."

Buchanan squinted with his one good blue eye. "Mr. Ross, I'm told you are an educated man. Surely, you realize that your posturing about Indian sovereignty is a joke. I suspect you also know that your days of recalcitrance against progress are numbered."

What Ross did now clearly realize that here was a worn-out, frightened, old man who was tired of being president and had decided to do absolutely nothing during the remainder of his term. He would not extend protection to the Chero-kee. He would let the next president inherit the wind.

"Mr. President," said Ross, rising to his feet, "thank you for your time. There is nothing more for us to discuss."

* * * *

"It will be a waste, Mr. Ross," Brill opined. "Democratic members of Con-gress are dispersed to the nominating convention in Charleston, South Carolina. Their attention is fixed on whether the north or south will control the party and secure the nomination for the presidency. The Republicans are focused on their convention in Chicago."

"My main concern is preservation of the Cherokee people, not slavery nor the presidency."

"This nation is about to come apart at the seams; do you really think the Cherokees will get the time of day in Congress?"

Ross heatedly responded. "What you say may be true but circumstances com-pel me to try. I'm submitting a memorial to Congress protesting their creation of the Territory of Kansas and including therein a part of the Cherokee lands. I need to know, my people need to know, this whole country needs to know if there is a shred of honor to be found in this Congress!"

* * * *

Douglas, sweating from the June heat, leaned back in his rocker and took another sip of whiskey. "As I've already told your lawyer, Mr. Ross, I will not stand in the way of America's progress. The west will be settled."

"But Senator," Ross demurred, "The good people of these United States, who love their country, their union, and their constitution, have nominated you as a candidate for the presidency. They expect you to abide by the constitution which includes honoring treaties made in good faith between your government and the Cherokee Nation."

Before Douglas could respond, his servant entered with a calling card in hand. Glancing at the card the senator sat upright, sloshing whiskey on the floor. "Jef-ferson Davis? Why is that goddamned bastard calling on me?"

Turning to his bride, he said, "Adele, please leave the room while I take care of some unpleasant business."

The servant opened the door and Davis entered. Standing bony and erect, he fixed his one good eye on Douglas. "I have a proposition to make. Will you hear me out?"

Douglas, attempting to appear civil, motioned Davis to a chair. "If the Democrats stay split and run two candidates for president, the Black Republicans will win the election. In that event, the south will secede. That is a stance I have long advocated. But I love this Union and, if possible, I want to save her."

Douglas nodded. "On that we can agree."

"I have a plan," Davis continued. "It calls for you, Breckinridge, and Bell to agree to withdraw and unite behind a compromise candidate, a Democrat that is acceptable to the south, to run against Lincoln. Bell and Breckinridge have agreed to withdraw if you will."

"The plan is totally impractical," Douglas bristled. "Why the goddamned hell should I withdraw when I'm the best candidate to bring this nation together?

"I ask you to think about it," countered Davis.

"Hell, I don't need to think about it. The South has ruled the Democratic Party for years and we northern Democrats have followed like country cousins. If I withdraw, all my friends will go over to Lincoln. I won the nomination fairly and I will not unite with the vandals who will not maintain the Constitution and preserve the Union. I mean to crush the disunion wing of this party once and for all."

Davis stood to take his leave. "If you do not unite," he cautioned, "you may not have a country to rule over."

Closing the door, Douglas reseated himself and poured another glass of whiskey. "That traitorous turd," he fumed. "With Davis it's either rule or ruin. I think we should treat all attempts to break up the Union as Old Hickory treated the nullifiers in 1832."

Ross eased his rheumatic body out of his chair. "I too must be running along, Senator Douglas. I thank you for listening to my plight."

"I wish we faced better times, Mr. Ross, for your people and mine. A violent storm is gathering over this land. My country is facing the greatest danger in its history."

At the door Ross turned to reply, "So is mine, Senator. So is mine."

CHAPTER 36

WAR AND PEACE

As the members gathered in the council house in Tahlequah on a crisp, October 4th morning in 1860, Ross watched in contemplation. How many times in the past thirty some years had he faced this assembly trying to achieve harmony, preserve national unity, and advance their economy? And why, just when the goal seemed within reach, did some disruptive crisis emerge? He realized that even as the United States teetered on the brink of civil war, there remained dangerous fractures within his own people. The deep wounds created by the Treaty of New Echota were only thinly concealed by scar tissue from the reconciliation of 1846. Now, divided sympathies for the North abolitionists and South slaveholders threatened again to violently rend his people.

Failed crops, due to drought and excessive heat this past summer, left many of the Cherokees in a state of destitution. The failing health of his dear wife, Mary, added to his woes. And how long, at age seventy, with deteriorating health, could he continue to carry the load of leadership?

With whitened head, and furrowed brow, in a slow cadence he delivered unwelcome news to the Council. "Our delegation to Washington City, requested that the federal government appoint a commission to negotiate a new treaty with us. To this request, there was no reply. A memorial was submitted to Congress, praying that the Government would repurchase the Neutral Land or strike that portion of the land from the territory of Kansas. The injury done to that tract of land by trespassers is considerable. To date no action has been taken by the Congress."

From under shaggy eyebrows, Ross looked at the silent Council members, wondering how his next remarks would be received. "It is a cause of deep regret that the subject of slavery has become paramount to all other considerations in opposite sections of the United States and is producing so much harsh recrimination and alienation among those bound together by the glories of an unequalled history and the sacred ties of one blood.

"Slavery has existed among the Cherokees for many years and is recognized by them as legal; and they have no wish or purpose to disturb or agitate it. Agitation in regard to it can be productive of good to no one."

Speaking with more firmness, Ross concluded. "Our locality and institutions ally us with the South, while to the North we are indebted for a defense of our rights in the past. Our political relations are with the Government of the United States. Our duty is to remain neutral, stand by our rights, allow no interference in our internal affairs from any source, comply with our treaty obligations, and rely upon the Union for justice and protection."

A solemn Stand Watie then stood and addressed the Council. "It is well known that Chief Ross and I have a long history of disagreement." With a sweep of his hand toward council members, he stated, "Many of us here feel that it is folly to think that we Cherokee can remain neutral, not with the systematic efforts of the northern missionaries to abolitionize our nation. Their efforts, if successful, would ruin our economy."

"Beware of any extremism," cautioned Ross, "Remember, our income is greatly dependent upon the trust funds administered by the federal government."

"And," countered Watie, "remember that most of those funds are invested in the South. In case of conflict, we would lose all if the North were to win."

"Then let us steer a course of neutrality," Ross suggested, "and mind our own affairs."

Watie shook his head in disagreement. "With Arkansas on our east border and Texas on our south, both being slave-holding states, there is no way they will permit us the façade of neutrality." A rumble of assent followed his remarks.

Noting high tension in the air, and wishing to avoid a showdown that might get out of hand, Ross calmly stated, "As yet, there is no conflict between the North and South. For now, let us postpone any action that might jeopardize our relations with either."

*   *   *   *

Tom Hanks stood before the fireplace thawing out after riding four miles from Tahlequah to Ross's home in Park Hill to bring him news of Lincoln's election on November 6.

"I see no cause for jubilation," Ross mused. "We can only wait to see what action the southern states take."

Hanks rubbed his hands before the fire. "Rumors are that John Jones, Evan's son, has gone to Springfield to meet with Lincoln."

"That's true," Ross affirmed, "he is seeking appointment as the next federal agent to the Cherokees."

"Don't want to appear cynical," Hanks laughed, "but do you really think Watie's group would accept an abolitionist as an agent? Surely not, after running him out of this nation."

"True, but it would be a pleasant change to have an agent friendly to the cause of the Cherokee."

*   *   *   *

January 10, 1861 dawned cold, just above freezing. Maintaining his efforts to keep Ross informed of developments in Washington, attorney Brill sat in the Senate gallery. With paneled walls and mahogany desks, the new chamber, in use for only two years, was a fitting arena as a haggard Jefferson Davis took the floor. Although Mississippi had voted to secede from the Union the previous day, their senator still retained his seat.

"My friends," Davis began, "I am sure I feel no hostility to you, Senators from the North. I am sure there is not one of you, whatever sharp discussion there may have been between us, to whom I cannot now say, in the presence of my God, I wish you well. I am probably making my last argument before this august body.

"Mississippi secedes, not in hostility to others, not to injure any section of the country; but from the high and solemn motive of defending and protecting the rights we inherited, and which it is our sacred duty to transmit to our children.

"Our perfidious President Buchanan takes the position that the federal government possesses no power to hold the Union together, but he simultaneously denies the constitutionality of secession. His breach of promises to South Carolina regarding the dangerous situation in Charleston harbor has brought that state and the federal government almost to the point of conflict.

"The intransigence of the Republican Party and its ignorance of the South and southern politics has brought us to this brink. They have fatally misjudged when they deem secession as a mere passing political mood. Instead, something fundamental is at stake. Republicans have forced upon the South a choice it does not wish to make; the destruction of our community independence or the destruction of the Union which our Fathers made. Separation has now become inevitable; two confederacies will now exist. The critical issue is, how best to effect that separation. My fervent wish is for peace but if peaceful separation is not permitted, then it becomes an issue from which we will not shrink; for, between oppression and freedom, between the maintenance of right and submission to power, we will invoke the God of battles, and meet our fate, whatever it may be." His gaze swept his Republican antagonists. "I leave the case in your hands."

*   *   *   *

"The North thought it was just another South Carolina temper tantrum until it seceded. The Republicans received another cold dose of reality when Florida, Alabama, Georgia and Louisiana followed. Mark my word, there will be others. This is no time for us to dilly-dally...no time for indecision."

Ross, still wondering why this unexpected visit from Watie, responded, "There is no indecision. I have plainly stated that the Cherokee would remain neutral."

"I hear that you have received a letter from the governor of Arkansas?"

"Apparently you have already been in contact with Governor Rector," Ross replied tartly. "If so, you already know that I have assured him, and the people of Arkansas, of our desire to remain neutral in case of a white man's war. While I told him that we have treaties that bind us to the United States, our institutions, locality, and natural sympathies are unequivocally with the slave-holding states."

Watie nodded. "Arkansas will secede. It is merely a matter of time. With all the Indian tribes along its western border, Rector feels that Arkansas is the most exposed state in the Union. He will not make a move until he knows on whose side we stand."

"Then he has nothing to fear from the Cherokees."

Watie looked directly at Ross. "But what about Kansas and those abolitionists right on our northern border? What is to keep them from attacking us? Nothing. Because the United States is withdrawing its troops."

"And your solution is?"

Watie breathed a heavy sigh and walked over to a window. "That's why I came to see you. My solution is this: we, who are in favor of the Confederacy, must form military companies of Home Guards for the purpose of defending ourselves in case of invasion from the North. The state authorities in Little Rock have already taken possession of the arsenal there. They will supply the guns. My hope is that you would concur with the idea."

Ross replied indignantly. "Stand Watie, you know very well I could never consent to that. First, it would be a palpable violation of my position as a neutral; second, it would place in our midst organized companies not authorized by our laws and in violation of our treaty with the United States. It would be an instrument of stirring up domestic strife by offending and arousing the non-slave holders to form their own armed companies. No, I will not permit it. It would not serve my people well."

Watie shrugged his shoulders in finality, picked up his hat and moved toward the door. Coldly speaking he addressed Ross. "We have long disagreed upon what serves our people well. You jealously guard your power, believing what is good for Ross is good for the Cherokee. For that the Cherokee people have suffered greatly. If you continue to have your way, the Cherokees will lose all the advantages that would accompany a treaty with the South. My party will no longer be slaves to your tyranny."

*   *   *   *

By the time Brill located him at the Willard Hotel, Douglas was well into his cups and loudly expounding to Benjamin Brown French. "Lincoln, that silent sphinx of Springfield, knows nothing of the South. He is fundamentally ignorant of his southern political foes. He has not got out of Springfield, Sir. He does not know that he is President-elect of the United States. He does not see that the shadow he casts is any bigger now than it was last year." He paused and waved for another drink.

"By god," he continued, "I campaigned in every state, from Maine to New Orleans, something that no other candidate for the presidency has ever done. I never intend to give up hope of saving this nation so long as there is a ray left. If only those jackass Republicans would have accepted Crittenden's compromise. Damn! His speech was magnificent...never heard such applause in the Senate!"

"Being out of town, I missed his speech. What did he say?" Brill quizzed.

"In essence," said French, "the restoration of the Missouri Compromise was the keystone of his talk. Had his proposal been adopted, land acquired in the

Louisiana Purchase would have been divided along the 36/30 latitude with slavery prohibited north of that line. The South will accept nothing less but Lincoln has instructed the Republicans to entertain no proposition for a compromise in regard to the extension of slavery."

"Is Lincoln aware of the severity of the situation?" Brill asked.

"His silence may be fatal," Douglas moaned. "The Union is at the mercy of the President-elect, even before the inauguration. Sirs, this ship of state is without a rudder. Buchanan, damn his soul, realized the gravity of the situation too late. His plan for a constitutional convention to work out a compromise is conspicuously unrealistic.

"South Carolina," intoned French, "has already seceded. If she could do so alone, I think it would be the best thing possible. Getting rid of an insignificant, nigger-ridden state, whose main endeavor seems that of breaking up our Federal Union, sets well with me."

"No! no! no!" Douglas replied, stumbling over his words to challenge French. "Better that all platforms be scattered to the winds; better that every public man and politician in America be consigned to political martyrdom; better that all political organizations be broken up, than that the Union be destroyed and the country plunged into civil war."

"Don't get me wrong," French retorted, "I am an ultra Union man; I am for concession and conciliation. But I believe that if the Republicans had undertaken, with all their ingenuity, to make a plan to drive the South into revolution and disunion, they could have devised no better course."

"Chief Ross is concerned," said Brill, "that this crisis could turn into a civil war. Is that likely to happen?"

Douglas shook his head and in slurred speech replied, "Don't know, but if the Southern States do attempt to secede, I am in favor of their having just so many slaves and just so much slave territory as they can hold at the point of a bayonet and no more."

*   *   *   *

. Outside the rains of early June poured down, reviving drooping corn and freeing the slaves from field work for the day. On this hot and humid day Ross rubbed his rheumatic hip joints and shuffled from the window to his favorite chair. "The guns of Fort Sumter astound me. I thought South Carolina would huff and puff, as she has done in the past, then the whole slavery matter would blow over." He shook his grizzly head in disbelief. "Now it appears that the hot heads will have their civil war."

"You've done all you can do," Hanks assured him. "The Cherokee will be alright if your proclamation of neutrality is respected."

Ross wearily shook his head. "Sad to say, I fear it will not be. Kansas is now a free state on our north border and we have Arkansas, a slave-holding state on our east. With Arkansas seceding I feel our situation has become almost untenable. We are caught in the middle and inextricably enmeshed in the political intrigues of the whites."

"S'cuse me, Chief Ross, there's some gennelmen here to see you." It was soft-spoken Moses interrupting.

Taking their rain slickers, he ushered in two men. The first, a huge, bear-like man of at least three hundred pounds, with curly hair falling to his shoulders and a long, full beard, effusively introduced himself. "Albert Pike, sir, special agent to the Cherokee, appointed by the Confederacy. It's good to meet a fellow Mason." Pointing to his companion, "And this is General Ben McCulloch, Confederate commissioner to the Indians."

Ross shook hands with both and waved them toward some chairs. Pike, seeing none that fit him, chose the horsehide couch. After amenities over coffee, the white-haired McCulloch got to the object of their visit.

"Chief Ross, the Choctaws, Chickasaws, and all the other major Indian nations have signed treaties of alliance with the Confederacy; only the Cherokees remain on the fence. Everything considered, your rightful place is with the South."

"I mean no offense, General McCulloch, but our rightful place is to be neutral and I hope we may be permitted to remain so. We desire to do nothing that will impair our rights or to disturb the cordial friendship between ourselves and our white brothers."

"You insist that you must abide with the treaties you have made with the United States," McCulloch pursued.

"That is correct, sir."

"Last month Mr. Lincoln issued a proclamation that the federal government would offer your people protection. To my knowledge, Chief Ross, all federal troops have been withdrawn from this area, which leaves no one to protect the Cherokee from foreign intervention. It appears that the treaties have been abandoned."

"Not by the Cherokee, General McCulloch. We have never broken a treaty."

"And we respect you for that," McCulloch continued. "The Confederacy can provide your people with protection. We would like to organize your people, that is, those who favor our side, into military companies as Home Guards, for the purpose defending you in case of invasion from the north."

Ross shook his head. "I must respectfully decline your request, general. To organize such companies would not only violate our neutrality stance, it would be an open invitation for the Union supporters in Kansas to invade."

McCulloch heaved an impatient sigh. "Chief Ross, I understand the Cherokee Nation is heavily in debt. Has the federal government delivered the annuity now due you?"

Ross answered with a sardonic smile. "You know very well that it has not. The agent in Kansas, who has the annuity, does not feel it safe for him to venture here."

"I'm puzzled, Chief Ross. Without that money, you cannot manage your affairs and the likelihood of your receiving it is marginal because there are no federal troops nearby. Neutrality seems impossible for the Cherokee. If I were you, I'd give serious consideration to a change in alliances."

"It has been my experience," Ross replied, "that a comparison of Northern and Southern philanthropy in their dealing with Indians reveals little difference, but we have every cause for friendship with the South. At the same time, we have no reason to make war on the United States."

*   *   *   *

"They seemed to have a very knowledgeable understanding of our predicament," Hanks observed.

Ross smiled, "Indeed they do, except Pike is unaware that I have not attended a Masonic meeting in years."

"It is also evident that they have been in close communication with Stand Watie."

Ross thoughtfully gnawed at his lower lip. "Much of what McCulloch said is true. We have received no support from Lincoln, the Union seems weak, and we may never see our annuities. Has my ego, as Watie has implied, ignored the real desires of my countrymen?"

"Watie never had any inclination to be neutral. With Confederate support, his Home Guard grows stronger day by day," Hanks observed. "Soon he may have too much support."

Ross caught the implied threat to his position. He realized his influence was being eroded by events over which he had no control. "Before that happens, we must take preemptive action, else we will have a civil war within a Civil War."

✳   ✳   ✳   ✳

War had finally come and he was glad. It was time to end the endless, degrading hypocrisy of pretension with Ross. For too long he had controlled and misled the Cherokee. Ross could have accepted the inevitability of removal, signed the Treaty of New Echota, and moved west in peace and comfort. His failure to do so had brought unnecessary misery and endless conflict to his people. Although disposed to eloquent pleas for unity, Ross's actions, in control of Cherokee annuities and appointment of officials, all but ignored the Ridge faction. His face flushed with anger as Watie recalled the brutal murder of his brother, Elias, and the subsequent denials of complicity from Ross.

Under blazing heat of an August sun, the Confederate colonel pulled his horse aside and watched a regiment of a thousand Cherokee march single file through the parched dust of southwest Missouri. Without tents, blankets, many barefoot, and armed only with old muskets and shotguns, these men and boys had cast their lot with Watie and the South. Somewhere ahead of them they would contest the Union army for control of this state.

Squinting against the sun, he saw at the end of the marching line a horseman rapidly approaching. The rider was none other than his nephew, Elias C. Boudinot.

He removed his broad-brimmed hat and wiped a shirt sleeve across his brow. Watie nodded in greeting. "You've rode that horse too hard in this heat."

"You're needed back home," Boudinot gasped, "Ross has called for a tribal council. We don't know what he's up to."

Watie scratched the stubble on his chin. "Nor do I. Ross never does anything that ain't to his advantage."

"There's rumors that he plans to raise a regiment and place them under John Drew's command."

"Old Drew...huh!" Watie's brow wrinkled with concern.

"Know him?"

"Yeah, he led the last detachment of Ross's party back in '38...married Ross's niece."

"Well, you can count on Ross appointing those he controls."

"He picked a good time to raise a regiment while my men are out of the territory. And which side will that regiment be?"

"Best you head for home, Uncle Stand, and find out."

"Not a good time to leave my regiment...but you're right." Watie glanced up at the sun. "If I leave now, I should make it home in a couple of days."

"Make me a major, like I want, and I'll take over the regiment," Elias grinned.

Watie reached over and placed his hand on his nephew's shoulder. "After losing her husband, your mother would skin me alive if I let anything happen to you. What you can do, my boy, is overtake that column...tell 'em to make camp near Wilson's Creek...plenty of water there and some farms nearby...corn should be ready for eatin'. General McCulloch will take command when he gets there."

*   *   *   *

On August 21, 1861 over four thousand Cherokee males, at Ross's request, gathered at Tahlequah. Stand Watie and some fifty of his armed followers were among them. Full bloods and half-breeds were camped in tents, covered wagons, or under the brush along the stream that ran near the capitol grounds. Smoke from campfires, flies, and stench from horse dung filled the hot wind blowing from the south. Fifteen cooks were employed preparing beef to feed the crowd.

Ross reflected upon what had brought them here. Violent incidents had taken place recently between the pro-slavery and anti-slavery Cherokees. President Lincoln had failed to come to their aid. Federal troops had been withdrawn and the area was controlled by Confederate forces, including a regiment headed by Stand Watie. Union Indian agents had left. Missionaries who were northern adherents, including his close friend, Evan Jones, had departed under duress. Other Indian tribes had already allied themselves with the South. The Cherokees stood alone. Anxious and troubled at heart, once again the old chief would try to save his people.

The crowd pressed close to hear as Ross stood on a wooden platform under the shade of a huge oak. Speaking through an interpreter he began. "You need not be told, that evil times have befallen the great government with which we have been connected. Rent by dissensions, its component parts stand in hostile array. Already they have engaged in deadly conflicts. The Cherokee will be concerned with the results. Your authorities have directed their attention in deciding the course to be pursued by the Cherokee Nation in the conflict between the whites, to whom she is equally bound in peace and friendship...I felt it to be my duty to advise the Cherokee people to remain neutral and issued a proclamation last May to that effect…The great object with me has been to have the Cherokee people harmonious and united…Union is strength, dissension is weakness, misery ruin! In time of peace together! In time of war, if war must come, fight together. As brothers live; as brothers die…When your nationality ceases here, it will live nowhere else. When these homes are lost, you will find no others like them."

Ross paused and took a deep breath. The consequences of his final remarks could be greeted with acclaim, or they could be catastrophic. "The state of Arkansas on our border, and the Indian Nations about us, have severed their connection with the United States and joined the Confederate States. Our general interest is inseparable from theirs and it is not desirable that we stand alone. And in view of all the circumstances of our situation, I say to you frankly, that, in my opinion, the time has now arrived when you should signify your consent for the authorization of the Nation to adopt preliminary steps for an alliance with the Confederate States upon terms honorable and advantageous to the Cherokee Nation."

Silence prevailed. No words of hostility or agreement were expressed. The crowd dispersed to fill up on beef and quietly discuss their future. When they reassembled, a series of resolutions were passed, the last stating "reposing full confidence in the authorities of the Cherokee Nation, we submit to their wisdom the management of all questions which affect our interests growing out of the exigencies of the relation between the United and Confederate States of America and which may render an alliance on our part with the latter States expedient and desirable."

*　　　*　　　*　　　*

In his newly constructed two-story log house on Brush Creek, Watie sat at the kitchen table with his friend William Penn Adair, and his brother-in-law John Bell. When a black servant finished refilling their china coffee cups, an enraged Bell spoke.

"With Albert Pike making a treaty with Ross, our hands are tied and our mouths are shut. It puts our destiny in the hands of Ross, a man who already has more power than we can bear."

"That's right," Adair joined in. "By making that alliance with the Confederacy, Ross will have political dominance. His pin party, the Keetoowahs, must be broken up."

"He is also trying to gain military dominance by organizing a regiment under Drew," Bell added. "Most officers in the regiment are related to Ross."

A grim Watie drained his cup and wiped his mouth. "Gentlemen, as he has always done, Ross is doing whatever it takes to maintain his power. After the battle at Bull Run, and our victory at Wilson's Creek, the writing was on the wall. The South will prevail and he wants to be on the winning side. The only reason he made treaty with Pike was to keep control of this nation, but I can assure you, Ross's true sympathies are with the North."

"There is no honor in politics," Adair observed.

"If I'm right," Watie responded, "if Ross is a turncoat, then God have mercy on his soul for surely I shall have none."

*   *   *   *

Ross turned his backside to the fireplace and rubbed his buttocks. "It goes against my grain, General Pike, to have our boys fight outside Indian Territory. Our treaty with the Confederacy prohibits such."

"I completely agree with you," the bearded one replied, "it was a promise I made to you but it is now a promise I cannot keep. The new commanding general, a fellow named Van Dorn, has issued orders. He wants us to tie down Union troops in Missouri so they can't be sent back east to reinforce Grant."

"Why Van Dorn?" Hanks asked. "We've got you, Price, and McCulloch. How many generals do we need?"

"Price and McCulloch don't get along. You can't fight a war when they aren't even on speaking terms."

Ross nodded with understanding. "Drew and Watie aren't too cozy either."

"Jefferson Davis thinks his old friend from Mississippi can solve the problem. But, from what I've heard, Van Dorn is too reckless and impulsive for my liking."

Seeing the hesitation of Ross, Hanks spoke up. "If you don't agree to sending troops, Watie's crowd will have your head."

"Alright," Ross sighed, "but I do wish our men were better equipped. Their muskets are so old and they have no uniforms. Jefferson Davis has let us down."

"May I suggest, Chief Ross, that, for the sake of morale, you accompany the Cherokee regiment for a ways. It might help the feelings of those who resent having to fight outside Indian Territory." Pike turned to Hanks. "Would you care to come along?"

Hanks smiled. "Sorry, General Pike. I don't like the color of your uniforms."

With cold winds gusting out of the northwest, on a morning in late February 1862, Colonel John Drew's regiment took up the line of march from Park Hill towards Fayetteville, Arkansas. At the head, in a carriage, rode the bewhiskered Pike, decked out in feathers, leggins, and beaded moccasins. With him was John Ross in frock coat and stovepipe hat. The Indians, mostly full bloods, followed in a long, straggling line, many mounted, some trudging on foot. Twelve miles east of Park Hill, the cold seeping into his rheumatic joints, Ross turned back.

*   *   *   *

"The defeat of the Confederates at Pea Ridge casts a different light on everything. Pike has retreated to Texas. There is no force to withstand an invasion of the Federal Army. The funds of our nation, and all its public records are unprotected." An agitated Ross drank a solution of soda and water hoping it would relieve pain in his chest.

"Such are the fortunes of war," was Hank's laconic reply. "You bet on the wrong horse."

"I had no choice. I did what I had to do. Lincoln would not save us; now Jefferson Davis has broken his promises."

"You ain't the only one upset. The governor of Arkansas is so mad at Davis he's threatening to secede from the Confederacy."

"He's got his problems," grumbled Ross, "I've got mine."

"You've got choice now. You can order up Cherokees to fight for the Confederacy, or you can agree to meet with Colonel Weer."

"I have no intention of enlisting more young men for the Confederacy; neither do I plan to meet with the Union Colonel."

"Surely, you don't consider yourself still bound by treaty to the rebels!"

"I don't enter into treaties lightly," Ross responded testily.

"Look," Hanks reasoned, "Weer knows you were forced into a treaty with the South. Evan Jones has made that plain to him. You're mostly concerned about Watie."

Ross nodded in acknowledgement. "Watie hates my guts. If he believes I sold out to the Union, he and his renegades will wreak havoc among my family and friends. I won't hand him an excuse for doing that."

Preoccupied with matters at hand, Ross was unaware that on July 5 an act of Congress nullified all previous treaties with the Indians.

Knowing that the Union forces were advancing, Ross made no effort to flee. On a blazing hot July 27, 1862 Colonel William F. Cloud and a force of fifteen hundred Union troops rode into Park Hill. He was unopposed by Drew's regiment which had been guarding the Cherokee seat of government. John Ross was arrested and became, technically, a prisoner of war. During the next week he and his relatives packed their personal items, Cherokee records, a treasury of a large sum of gold, and some Confederate money.

Early morning on August 3, Ross, in his carriage with his ailing wife, Mary, Annie and John Jr., and thirty-two of his close relatives in wagons and on horseback, prepared to leave Park Hill under the escort of Colonel Cloud. A gray haired, toothless Moses, and his wife Zipporah, stood by. With tears streaming down his weathered cheeks, Moses said his farewell. "Ah'm too old Massa Ross...too old to travel...too old to be of service. Zipporah and me...we will die here."

Unable to speak, Ross hugged the old man.

"What Moses said...guess that goes for me too."

Misty eyed, Ross reached out both hands to Hanks, his friend of fifty years, a boy he had first met at the Battle of Horseshoe Bend, then a companion and confidant most of his life. "Take good care of yourself and take care of Rose Cottage. I'll write when we reach Ft. Leavenworth."

*   *   *   *

From his home nearby in Park Hill, the Reverend Stephen Foreman, a loyal Watie man, watched the departure. He quickly recorded his thoughts. "As I contended from the very outset, Ross's alliance with the Confederacy and then his surrender to the Union Army at the first opportunity, was part of a well-thought-out plot. He played a game with Pike. His arranged arrest was designed to conceal his duplicity. He has taken thousands of dollars from the Cherokee treasury, which he will use, no doubt, to pay his expenses in Washington and to educate his children in expensive Eastern schools." He immediately dispatched the letter to Watie.

*   *   *   *

On August 12, when Ross's entourage arrived, the streets of infant Leavenworth, Kansas were churned into dust by the coming and going of wagons. Teamsters, walking alongside the loaded vehicles, cursed and cracked their whips over their oxen.

"These are the freighters of Russell, Majors, and Waddell." Explained Colonel Cloud. "They are under contract to the army."

Along the street Ross saw a blacksmith shop, a lumberyard, a wagon repair shop, outfitting and grocery stores, and a meat processing plant, all under the sign of Russell, Majors, and Waddell. There was also a stagecoach station advertising a passenger fare of $125 to the gold fields of Colorado.

Colonel Cloud steered the procession to the infirmary, where the road-weary Mrs. Ross was left in the care of a doctor. Cloud then lead Ross to a long, white building, which he called The Rookery. Here, in the living quarters for the soldiers, he was welcomed by the commander of Ft. Leavenworth, General James Blunt.

*   *   *   *

As the sun sank low in the west, a breeze skimmed over the broad waters and cooled the men standing on the high bluff overlooking the Missouri River. The newly minted brigadier gently stroked his beard. "I don't harbor any doubt, Chief Ross, that you are a man of candor and a loyal Union supporter. Rev. Jones has convinced me, but you must convince Washington of that. My advice is, go to Washington and gain the ear of President Lincoln. Convince him to send more support. Thousands of your people have taken refuge here in Kansas. Around Ft. Scott they are without shelter, without shoes and blankets. They are starving and dying of disease. I have given them what little I can spare. They need to return to their homes, plant crops, and feed themselves."

"If they returned", argued Ross, "Watie's men would exact horrible reprisals upon all they consider traitors. They will not be safe until you control the territory."

In the gathering dusk they walked across the grassy square to Blunt's quarters. "I intend to mount an expedition against Watie this fall," said the general, "in the spring at the latest. For the sake of your suffering people, it is urgent that you get on to Washington. You must talk with the President. I will give you an honorable parole for that purpose."

One month later, to the day, Ross sat down with President Lincoln.

*   *   *   *

Before going to Washington, Ross ensconced his family in a house at 708 Washington Square in Philadelphia, a house Mary had inherited from the Stapler family. Here his ailing wife could live in comfort with daughter, Annie, sister Sarah, and receive the best of medical care available.

His fifteen-year-old son, John Jr., was placed in a boys' academy at Nazareth, Pennsylvania. Sired when his father was in his mid fifties, and accustomed to his father's absences from home, the two had never formed close attachments. In saying an awkward goodbye, Ross admonished his son. "What has sustained me all my life is this belief: put your shoulder to the wheel and remember it is the long and steady pull after all that achieves in life the most."

Ross was met by Hugh Brill at the Baltimore and Ohio Railway Station, located three blocks north of the capitol at New Jersey Avenue and North C Street. Hurriedly loading Ross with his baggage, Brill said, "Let's get the hell out of here before they confiscate this horse and carriage."

Hearing the note of alarm in his friend's voice, Ross asked, "What's going on?"

Brill urged the horse on with a whip. "Last week the Union took a hell of a beating at Manassas from the rebels. For over a week the wounded have been brought in. This town has been transformed into a hospital. Sick and wounded soldiers are everywhere; in hotels, private homes, schools, seminaries, even in warehouses. Along with them came the rich, their slaves, and ragged stragglers fleeing in panic. This town is scared stiff."

They passed an empty passenger car sitting on the street railway that ran down Pennsylvania Avenue. Brill pointed, "Not a horse to draw the cars. After what the army took, you can't get a cab in this town."

He deposited Ross at the Willard Hotel then rushed off to hide his horse and carriage. Inside Ross found that most of the waiters had enlisted and the dining room was now staffed by Negroes. At the bar he listened as drunken West Point officers sneered at the government and bragged about running Republicans out of town and putting the army in power.

On the morning of September 12 Ross made his way on foot from Willard's Hotel to the White House. After mounting the steps to the second floor, he paused until an ache in his chest subsided. As he rested a flushed, ruddy-faced man emerged for Lincoln's office muttering "McClellan should be shot."

At nine o'clock he was ushered into the President's office at the east end of the upstairs hall. The room was still flavored by the cigars that Buchanan had habitually smoked. From a black, haircloth covered chair placed near the window, a tall, gaunt Lincoln rose to greet his visitor. "You will please excuse the housekeeping," he said, waving to the Cabinet table cluttered with maps, books, and documents, "we haven't had much time for sleep lately."

"I fully understand, Mr. President. I'm sorry to hear of your loss at Manassas."

Even though exhausted, Lincoln could not repress his propensity for jokes. "Mr. Ross, if to be the head of hell is as hard as what I have to undergo here, I could find it in my heart to pity Satan himself."

Seating himself, he picked up a letter and turned to Ross. "General Blunt affirms your loyalty to the Union, but I understand your treaty of alliance with the Confederacy is still in effect. Is this a Janus-like situation?"

"Certainly not, Mr. President. For the preservation of their country, and their very existence, the Cherokees were forced to negotiate a treaty with the Confederate States. We had no other alternative."

The president's grunt gave no indication that he was swayed. "And what is it that you need from me, Mr. Ross?"

"Sir, we would like the enforcement of those treaties of friendship and alliance that bind us to the United States. We desire ample military protection for life and property. We have maintained good faith with you."

"Up to a late period."

Noting the skepticism in the president's voice, Ross responded defensively. "Sir, I have three sons serving in the Union Army. One of my sons, James, and two of my nephews have been captured by the guerrilla bands and I know not their fate."

Apparently Lincoln's mind was elsewhere. "Mr. Ross," he said, "I am a man with a multitude of cares. I would be pleased if you would reduce your concerns to writing and submit them to me."

*   *   *   *

Surrounded by the quiet elegance of the Quaker house, Ross sat watching the green gardens of Philadelphia soak up a late September rain. As his manservant replenished the coffee in his china cup, Ross spoke to his guest.

"I have fulfilled the request of President Lincoln and I submitted a petition to the Secretary of War, Stanton. I've heard nothing from either."

"For god's sake, Mr. Ross, they are probably still reeling from Antietam Creek. The Union suffered over twelve thousand dead or wounded in that battle."

"And they call the Indians uncivilized."

"Face reality, Mr. Ross, as long as this war goes on, the Cherokee problems will be a mere pimple on the president's ass."

Ross placed his cup on the walnut end table. "I've observed politics for many years, Mr. Brill. Experience shows that those who ask for little tend to be accorded nothing. In Washington our problems have always been a pimple on someone's ass. But my people are also casualties of this white man's war and I will insist that they be recognized as such."

Ross rose from his straight-backed chair as the doctor came downstairs from Mary's room. "How is she?"

The doctor fiddled with his glasses. "She shows a great strength of spirit," he said.

"But is there anything that you can do for her physical strength?"

"For congestion of the lungs, the very best you can do, Mr. Ross, is give her bed rest. She should be up and around in a few days." The doctor hesitated at the door. "I'm sorry, but I will not be able to attend your wife in the future. My country requires my immediate service."

*   *   *   *

Tiva looked up from her knitting at her scowling husband. "Is it good news or bad?"

"It's a letter from a William P. Dole," Hanks answered. "He is Lincoln's Commissioner of Indian Affairs. Apparently, he and Ross have become friends."

"What else?"

"He wants me to investigate the conditions of the Cherokee refugees in Kansas. He suspects fraud among those who have contracted with the federal government to provide food for the displaced."

"So do it. We could use the money."

Hanks was not surprised at the outspoken manner of his wife. "Tiva, you forget that Watie's men are still out there. I can't leave you and the boys here alone."

"When everyone went north with Weer, we knew we were taking a chance but we decided to stay. If Watie wants to raid us, one man won't stop him." She put aside her knitting. "We have a roof over us and a warm bed. We have chickens in the pen and cured hams in the smokehouse. Those in Kansas have nothing!"

"Tiva, Watie knows that Ross and I are close friends. If he finds us, God only knows what he will do."

*   *   *   *

According to Dole's orders, Hanks should be in uniform. Instead, he rode against the north wind bundled in civilian garb. At night he would take shelter in an abandoned cabin, turn his horse loose in a deserted corral, or hobble it to feed in a weed-grown field. Raiding parties, both North and South, had left the Cherokee Nation stripped and barren. The few souls who dared remain he avoided not knowing their allegiance.

Four days after leaving his home near Tahlequah, Hanks approached Ft. Scott. Guided by the smell of smoke and the stench of human excrement, he rode onward through deep snow. At the edge of timber bordering the Marmaton River, he reined in his horse to watch a man digging away at the snow with brush and bare hands. When a small area was cleared of snow, the man removed his sheepskin coat and then his shirt, revealing prominent ribs and bony shoulders. Ignoring Hanks, he picked up a small bundle, wrapped it gently in his shirt before placing it on the frozen ground. Hair prickled on Hank's neck. With distended belly and skin shrunken so tightly around its skull, the form was barely recognizable as a baby. Donning his coat the man sat about digging stones out of the snow and stacking them over the tiny body.

As the man finished his melancholy task, Hanks dismounted his horse, dug some cured ham out of a saddlebag, sliced off a slab and handed it to the man.

"Dysentery?"

The man shook his head. "Starvation. My wife died…no one nurse the baby."

Visions of Teva and the removal stockade at the Calhoun Agency flashed through Hank's mind. "Was there no doctor to help you?" he asked.

"No doctor. Wife get sick soon after baby come. Too weak…no food."

"No food?"

"Yeah, some food. But too many weevils in wheat and corn…many maggots in meat. Soldiers won't eat…give to us."

"Who are the agents that provide your supplies?" Hanks asked.

"Biggers and Brill…I think."

At the name of Brill, another bell rang in Hank's mind. He mounted his horse and kneed it toward the sour smelling camp. Riding slowly through the bends of the river, he estimated some six thousand Cherokee, and some Creek, were strung out along its banks. These were refugees from warm homes and good farms…refugees who feared Waite. For their shelter he could see a threadbare tent here and there, some lean-tos formed from planks or brush, or merely a blan-

ket spread under a cedar tree. To keep from freezing, many were standing around
the open fires that were kept going night and day. The lucky ones had a blanket.
The wail of infants and the deep coughs of the elderly harked back to death on
the long trail.

There was no semblance of sanitation. During their long weeks of encampment, well-worn trails led back into the nearby trees where thousands had defe-
cated. Hanks now nudged his horse east toward the nearby settlement of Fort
Scott.

Fort Scott was located on the south side of the Marmaton River, a crossing on
the Fort Gibson-Fort Leavenworth Road. It was now the supply center for the
Union Army of the west.

Outside a rough-sided warehouse bearing the name of "Biggers and Brill—
Indian Agents" he hitched his horse. Entering the front office, Hanks was enveloped by warmth. Two men sat around a coal burning, potbelly stove sharing a
bottle. A tall, lanky one arose, adjusting glasses over his crossed eyes.

"Yessir! What kin I do fer ye, stranger?" Hanks noted the tall one's Adams
apple bob up and down in his skinny neck.

"Hear tell you're looking for teamsters. I need a job."

The tall one looked to the portly one still seated by the stove. "Gettin' a little
long in the tooth for that work, aintcha?" It was the portly one.

"No more that you, sir."

The portly one grunted. "Any experience?"

"Drove some for Russell, Majors, and Waddell up at Ft. Leavenworth."

"Big outfit." Suspicious, Portly asked, "How come you left? With the war on
everybody needs help."

"They said something about ethics."

A chuckle started in portly's chest. Looking up at Hanks he laughed. "Ethics?
Hell, boy, you just got caught in the cookie jar."

Portly struggled up from his chair. "Name's Brill...Virgil Brill. Maybe we can
use a man with your experience."

Brill? Could this be one of the brothers he had witnessed counting and cutting
the noses off Creeks at the Battle of Horseshoe Bend? Hanks thought it best not
to ask.

Tall and lanky introduced himself as Clyde Biggers. "Most just call me Four
Eyes," he laughed, adjusting his glasses.

*   *   *   *

"You'll find Roe's Fork 'bout ten miles south of here," Virgil directed. "Injuns camped there are expecting this corn. Just follow the smell. You won't have any trouble finding 'em"

"This manifest says they are due ten barrels of shelled corn," noted Hanks. "These barrels are full of corn on the cob."

"What difference does that make?" scoffed Virgil. "They can keep warm sleeping in the shucks and wipe their ass with the cobs."

The difference, Hanks knew, was that the Indians would have half the amount of food needed and Virgil would collect from the federals twice the amount he was due.

That afternoon, his delivery made, Hanks reported to the agent's office. As he was about to enter, an army officer, obviously angry, stormed out the door.

"Goddamned army...pokes its nose in everyone's affairs," growled Virgil. "Wants to send the Injuns home...says the good citizens of Kansas are tired of them. Hell, that would ruin our business."

Day after day, Hanks curried favor with the agents, all the while collecting evidence of fraud. To charge an Indian three or four times the value of a purchase was small potatoes. When he had no money at all, Virgil was all too willing to advance goods by accepting deeds to farmland as security. That the Indian had affixed an X to a legal document he did not understand, and knowing the Indian would never be able to pay off his debt, were of no concern to Biggers and Brill.

Hanks awaited orders as he looked over a small herd of emaciated cattle. "I'll swear, that old steer with the broken horn looks just like one I delivered the other day."

Virgil laughed, "If'n the Injuns don't get around to killing their beef, some of the steers drift back here where they've been fed. They get sold two or three times." He checked his notebook. "Let's see now...fifty steers at four hundred pounds each...drive them to the Cherokees camped at Drywood...just a few miles south of here."

By Hank's count, the steers were half in number and weighed half Virgil's estimate. Without collecting his pay, he delivered the cattle to the graveyard of starving Indians, then pointed his horse toward home.

Numb from riding through the November nights, Hanks neared his home at dawn. Seeing a column of smoke rising in the early light, he spurred his horse onward. Breaking out of the timber into a clearing, he breathed a sigh of relief;

his house was still standing. He was greeted by his two teen-age sons, Joshua and Caleb, both armed and standing guard. Inside he found Teva trying to comfort Jane Nave, the daughter of John Ross.

Wiping away tears, Jane tried to compose herself. "It was Stand Waite," she said, "the devil incarnate. He and his men killed all the armed PINS in Tahlequah then burned the council house. He burned Rose Cottage to the ground. I think it was because he hated my father so. They took everything that could be worn by men, women, and children, every article of bedding and blankets; they took all the livestock and some slaves. Watie captured Daniel Hicks and John A. Ross and then he came to our place." Jane shuddering involuntarily and continued. "My husband, Andy, refused to surrender to Watie. When he tried to escape, Dick Fields shot him in the back with a double-barreled shotgun." Jane paused to compose herself. "I expected every minute to see my child dragged out of the house. I sent up an inward prayer, Lord help me. We were spared."

After a time of silence, Hanks spoke up. "Jane, you cannot remain here. I will make arrangements and send you back to Philadelphia. Your father would want it so. I also have a paper for him which you can convey."

*   *   *   *

On a sunny Sabbath, excited to be back among her faith, Mary Ross and daughter, Annie, attended services at a Quaker meeting house. John, although registered as a Methodist, was never a devoted member. As he and Evan Jones walked slowly down the quiet, brick footpath on Sixth Street in Philadelphia, the war was ever present. "My family," remarked Jones, "has been made to drink the cup of sorrow. Who would think that this conflict would reach into Lawrence, Kansas? My eldest son, Samuel, a good and God-fearing man, was shot down by William Quantrill's barbarians, along with another one hundred eighty seven men and boys...anyone old enough to carry a gun; then he burns the town."

"From the report I got from Hanks, he and Watie seem to be of the same ilk, destroyers," Ross responded.

"No, not quite. Watie believes in the cause, that's why he wears the Confederate Uniform. Quantrill wears the same uniform but he holds no allegiance to either North or South. The war merely gives him an excuse to do what he loves best...kill and plunder."

Ross nodded in agreement. "Both are responsible for afflicting the Cherokee Nation with desperation. You recently came from there and have firsthand information regarding their plight. Even though Lincoln feels the Indian question can wait while he settles the war, we must insist upon an early meeting with him."

Jones smiled. "John, if any one could win heaven by a life-long devotion to the good of his people, you most certainly would. At age seventy-five, I may not be able to give you much more than moral support, but I am most honored to be the only non-Cherokee ever appointed as an official delegate."

"With your seventy-five years, and my sixty-six," laughed Ross, "no one has more experience than we."

They stopped to gaze at Independence Hall. "Can you believe," mused Ross, "that within those walls some of the most profound and honorable words relating to the government of man were composed…'that no one man is born with a natural right to control any other man'…and yet the heirs to those words would control and subject the Indians to such a low status.

On Monday, February 15, 1864 Ross and Evan Jones arrived for an appointment with Lincoln. Union victories at Gettysburg and Vicksburg were reflected in a more relaxed president. Hoping to capitalize on what he sensed as a more receptive ear, the aging Ross gathered strength to make his appeal.

"Mr. President, the Cherokees, prior to the rebellion, were the most numerous, intelligent, wealthy, and influential tribe. When the rebellion came, we steadily resisted the efforts of the rebels who would have us abandon our allegiance to the Federal government. When the United States forces withdrew from all the forts on the frontier, and the means of communicating with your government were cut off, we were finally compelled to enter into a treaty with the rebel authorities. Since the Cherokee Council has renounced that treaty and reaffirmed our allegiance to the United States, we are asking that treaties with your government be fulfilled."

Lincoln leaned back in his chair and extended his long legs. "You gentlemen realize that the Sioux uprising in Minnesota has our people riled up. Finding sympathetic ears for Indians among the congressmen might not be easy."

"Mr. President," Ross protested, "the Cherokees have had no part in the Minnesota problem. In our weakness, it would be folly to think otherwise. During the vicissitudes of this war, my people have been visited by direct calamities. They have been robbed, plundered, and murdered; their homes have been destroyed, their fields laid waste, their property seized and destroyed. They have been reduced to the most abject poverty, suffering and distress. We beg respectfully that you provide military security for the Cherokee Nation."

For a time Lincoln sat silent. In the midst of death and destruction of a civil war using white soldiers for an Indian cause would not receive popular support.

He temporized. "Mr. Ross, I am not entirely ignorant of these affairs and I am not unsympathetic to the plight of your people. I will request that Dole, the Commissioner of Indian Affairs, address these issues without delay."

When weeks passed with no relief from the Lincoln administration, Ross and Jones turned to the general public for charitable donations. An article on the desperate plight of the Cherokees was written and sent to newspapers in New York and Philadelphia. Moravians, Quakers, and other benevolent groups promised help. Ross achieved a small victory when Edwin M. Stanton, Secretary of War, promised to pay the freight and safe passage for all packages for Cherokee relief.

Unwilling to sit idle, in June Ross sent a memorial to the Senate and House of Representatives restating the information he had placed before Lincoln in February. No action was forthcoming.

In August he finally received some good news. Stanton informed him that his son, James, was alive but being kept captive by the rebels near Tyler, Texas.

Ross continued to receive news from relatives at Ft. Gibson of the constant raids and pillaging of Watie's men. In late September Ross received devastating information that the supply trains, with relief for the Cherokees huddled around Ft. Gibson, were captured by Watie at Cabin Creek.

Tired from effort and weary with age, in November he went home to Philadelphia for a rest. Even so, he could not forget that his nation was still surrounded by danger. On the seventh he sent a note to Lincoln urging him to keep Union forces at Ft. Gibson in order to protect the Cherokee from Watie. He received no response.

November 8, 1864, a dark and rainy Election Day, Lincoln restlessly prowled the White House, unable to settle down to work. He plodded through the rain to the telegraph office in the War Department where he anxiously awaited the verdict of voters. By midnight, he was assured of a second term.

Ross stood at his window in Willard's Hotel on a February morning with Hugh Brill watching the steady procession of rebel prisoners of war coming into Washington. "With the fall of Atlanta, Savannah, and Charleston," he mused, "it seems nothing but good news is coming to Lincoln in '65."

Brill demurred. "Lincoln doesn't see it that way. I've visited congress in the last few days and the Republicans are bitterly divided over his reconstruction plans for the South. The radicals are fiercely at odds with Lincoln and his stand that 'we must not sully victory with harshness.'"

"Congress seems oblivious to reconstruction needs in the Cherokee Nation," Ross grunted. "I am determined that they shall not ignore our plight. I sent another memorial to the House and Senate. I also had a pleasant visit with the

Secretary of War. Mr. Seward seems to be a gentleman of his word. He promised to bring up the matter of Cherokee affairs in a cabinet meeting."

Brill gazed fondly upon the old Scottish warrior. "I admire your doggedness, Chief Ross. Over the years you have gained few victories from the federal government. How you have managed to sustain yourself is beyond my comprehension."

Ross rubbed the ache in his chest and moved to a chair. "To cease my efforts, Hugh, would mean ultimately the dissolution of my people. Congress will achieve that goal if the current Senate bill passes that calls for the consolidation of all Indian tribes, and the establishment of civil government, in Indian Territory. I must contest that bill with all my might."

"But how do we do so with no champions, no allies, in Congress?" Brill wondered.

On April 8, 1865 Congress was in a state of celebration. Lee had surrendered to Grant at Appomattox. The long, bloody national ordeal was over!

*   *   *   *

As inauguration day approached, special trains roared in on the Baltimore and Ohio tracks bringing avid visitors to Washington. Foggy and muddy streets were alive with people in search of rooms. At the Willard, as with other hotels, cots and mattresses were placed in halls and parlors. The four hundred and fifty registered houses of prostitution, offering female companionship, were unblushingly indulged in.

Dawn of March 4 broke with lowering clouds and rain. "Portentous," Ross thought, "of sorrows and weeping in the land." He had joined the great multitude that assembled at the capitol to witness the second inauguration of Lincoln. At high noon, as a worn and underweight Lincoln appeared on the east portico, the clouds cleared, the rain ceased, and the sun shone brightly. Ross listened as Lincoln spoke. The estimated fifty thousand citizens heard a magnanimous speech instead of a citation of wartime victories they might have expected. His address completed, the president turned to Chief Justice Salmon Chase who administered the oath of office.

Ross stayed in Washington for the remainder of March and the first week of April contending with patronizing federal bureaucrats over Cherokee issues. He then hurried to Philadelphia to be with his ailing Mary. It was there that he received the devastating news of Lincoln's assassination and death on April 15.

When Annie left her mother's bedside, she found her father in the living room slumped into his favorite chair. Running her fingers through his stiff and graying hair, she tried to lift his spirits. "Do not torture yourself so, father. Who can fathom the purposes of God."

Ross gazed at his twenty-year-old daughter. She had the same grace and beauty as her mother. Taking her hand, he drew her to his side.

"I was not thinking of Lincoln, Annie. Selfishly, I was thinking of myself and what a terrible father I have been."

"Not so, father. How can you say that?"

"I have spent far too much time away from you and your mother. I have put tribal business ahead of family." Ross paused and looked questioningly at his daughter. "Would you think ill of me if I had to leave again...soon?"

"But why, father?"

"All the progress I may have been with Lincoln is now for naught. I must start over with a new president who I do not know. There are men in Congress who would make the Cherokee Nation a territory under federal control. I must return to Washington."

Annie bit her lip and nodded her understanding.

"You and sister Sarah can look after your mother. If you need me, wire me in Washington and I will return as quickly as possible."

Ross received the wire at Willard's Hotel in Washington. On a hot summer day, his wife of twenty-one years passed away on July 20, 1865 of lung congestion. Supported by the arms of his son, John Jr., and his daughter, Annie, the shattered old man watched as the body of his beloved forty-year old wife was lowered into the ground of the Stapler family plot in the Wilmington-Brandywine Cemetery in Delaware, not far from where he had courted her as a young girl. He was to be given little time for mourning.

*   *   *   *

With little notice, Ross learned that Senator James Harlan of Kansas, newly appointed Secretary of Interior by President Andrew Johnson, had designated six commissioners to go to Ft. Smith and sign articles of peace with five major tribes. Deliberations were to begin on Friday, September 8.

Ross stood in the bow trying to catch a cooling breeze in the late heat of August 31 as the Iron City steamed up the Arkansas River, a few miles below Webber Falls. The war was over but he knew that bitter hatred and factional quarrels within the Cherokee family would not soon be forgotten. Since the Treaty of New Echota they had been politically divided; Watie now led one faction, Ross the other. Trust between the two did not exist. Their nation was economically devastated; livestock was gone, either captured by rebels or stolen by whites. Cabins were burned, fences were gone for firewood, and fields had returned to weeds. As he basked in the last rays of the setting sun, Ross questioned whether he could put into place those noble thoughts expressed by Lincoln, "with malice toward none; with charity for all...do all which may achieve and cherish a just and lasting peace among ourselves." Would God give him the strength, and the time, to achieve his lifelong goal...unity of the Cherokee?

Fort Smith was buzzing with activity. Federal troops were being demobilized; Confederate soldiers were being paroled, and lively bidding was going on at public auctions of surplus army property. Horses and mules from government stables were in high demand from farmers who wanted to get back to work.

Cooley inspected the rooms that officers at Fort Smith had set aside in the post buildings for the commission council chambers. He was impatient for the talks to begin. It was time to put an end to the illusion that Indians were sovereign nations; time to brush them aside so that progress could move ahead. There was coal and timber in this land and grass for cattle. And there were railroads needing rights of way. If he were successful in these meetings, land speculators and railroad owners would surely be appreciative. Success would bring with it the highest approbation by James Harlan, Secretary of the Interior.

The first meeting of the Fort Smith Council began at ten o'clock with an invocation delivered by a Baptist minister, the Reverend Lewis Downing, in the Cherokee tongue. Although only the Union Indians were present, Chairman Dennis Cooley lost no time in presenting the general terms of treaties that should be made. Slavery was to be abolished, the Indian nation would be formed into territorial status with white officials to manage it, railroad builders would be given rights of way, and, since they were rebels, as punishment, they would have to forfeit land.

Smith Christie, who had served as acting chief of the Cherokee in the absence of Ross, responded. "Mr. Cooley, we beg leave respectfully to say that we have not the proper authority to make a treaty, or to enter into any agreement of any kind with the United States, or with any Indian tribes. We had supposed that we were summoned here to make peace with the secessionists. This is the first notice that we have been given of the actual purpose of this council. We must have time for deliberation."

"The Watie Party will not arrive until the eleventh," Cooley hurried on. "Our business must not be delayed. Brothers, we have been instructed by the President to negotiate a treaty, or treaties with any or all of the nations or tribes. Because you have by your own acts made treaties with the enemies of the United States, you have forfeited all rights to annuities, lands, and protection by the United States." He then proceeded to read the list of tribes who had made treaties with the rebel government. Then looking at the dismayed Cherokees, he concluded. "All these nations and tribes forfeited and lost all their rights to annuities and lands. You are left without any treaty whatsoever, or treaty obligation for protection by the United States."

A rumble of dissent arose from the Cherokee delegation. Almost as an ultimatum Cooley pressed on. "We, as representatives of the President, are empowered to enter into new treaties with the proper delegates of the tribes located within the so-called Indian Territory. These are the stipulations of said treaty."

"Chairman Cooley," Smith Christie replied, "we are no more authorized to make treaties than we were before."

"If you are waiting for authority from Chief Ross," Cooley snapped, "forget it. We believe him still at heart an enemy of the United States and disposed to breed discord among you. We do not feel he represents the will or wishes of the loyal Cherokees. He is not recognized by this commission as chief of the Cherokee."

"But we do recognize him as such," Christie defiantly replied. "We draw our authority from our people who voice their opinion through our General Council."

John Ross arrived at Fort Smith on the fourteenth. The next afternoon, as he took his seat among the Cherokee delegation, Cooley stood and read a villainous attack on the aged chief. "Whereas, John Ross, an educated Cherokee, formerly chief of the nation, became the emissary of the states in rebellion...and induced many to abjure allegiance to the United States...and whereas he now works his subtle influence to poison the minds of those who are truly loyal...whereas, he is by virtue of his position as pretended chief...he is exercising an influence adverse to the wishes and interests of all loyal Indians...whereas, we believe him still at heart an enemy of the United States...we the undersigned Commissioners...refuse in any way or manner to recognize said Ross as chief of the Cherokee nation."

In the following silence, Ross rose from his chair, cheeks reddened in Scottish indignation and eyes flashing anger. "Sir, I deny the charges asserted against me. I defy any person to come forward and prove these charges against me, who will state truth. I have been forty odd years Chief of the Cherokee, elected time after time. I came late to this meeting after burying my wife and burying my son, James. I had three sons, James, George, and Silas, who served in the Union Army, also three grandsons and three nephews. We had two regiments that served in the Union cause. No one can call us disloyal.

"I have never been charged with being an enemy of the United States. I resisted to the last the policy of disunion. I have a character, which is more sacred to me than my life. I have borne a reputation, that I have maintained up to the present time, sir, which is worth more to me than is my life." Ross paused then calmly concluded. "I thank you for the privilege you have given me to respond to these charges."

Cooley made no effort to reply.

The next day E.C. Boudinot, son of the slain Elias Boudinot, presented the credentials of the Southern Cherokee delegates, which included Stand Watie. Boudinot then produced a document which stated their objections to some of Cooley's proposals. Soon he digressed and launched into a bitter denunciation of Chief Ross. "I will show the deep duplicity and falsity that have followed him from his childhood to the present day. When the winters of sixty-five or seventy years have silvered his head with sin, what can you expect of him now..."

Cooley swung his gavel. "I'm sorry, Mr. Boudinot, I refuse to let this session become one of personal abuse. Your factional and domestic troubles will have to be settled outside this council."

When the council was ready for business the following Monday, the Watie faction signed the treaty drawn up by Cooley, with two exceptions. Disgusted with the council's proceedings, and stung by the rejection of their chief, the Ross faction had gone home.

The Southern delegation urged Cooley to divide the nation if no reconciliation could be made with the loyal Cherokees. Cooley declined, stating that he had no authority to do so. Ill and discouraged, he adjourned the council on September 21 and declared that definitive treaties would be made next year in Washington.

Ross collapsed after the council. Suffering from a malarial fever, he was confined to a bed at the Murrell house for over a week. A doctor was summoned and sat beside the ailing seventy-five year old chief night and day until he showed signs of improvement. Ross was also suffering from heartbreak and sorrow and the doctor knew no remedy for that.

*   *   *   *

When he was strong enough to ride, Ross and Hanks borrowed two horses and rode to Park Hill. Hunched against a cold drizzle, Ross surveyed the rubble and ashes of Rose Cottage. What remained were a battered chicken house, a ruined carriage house, an old dun horse, and a few surviving peach trees. In a halting voice he spoke as tears trickled down his weathered cheeks. "Here I brought my young Quaker bride; here she bore a daughter and a son. Those were the happiest years of my life. Now she is gone. Thank God she never saw this. How fleeting is happiness; how strong the memories."

At the end of October, in a feeble state of health, Ross delivered a short message to the annual meeting of the National Council.

When he had finished, Smith Christie addressed the Council. "It is to our shame and our sorrow that we acknowledge that some of the worst enemies of the Cherokee tribe are in our own camp. To counter the Southern Waite party, which would cleave our nation in half, it is my opinion, and my motion, that we send a delegation to Washington, headed by Chief Ross. I would further charge the delegation not to proceed with negotiations until the rank and prestige has been restored to our stalwart defender. Degradation of his character, as espoused at the Council at Fort Smith, will not be accepted by loyal Cherokee people. If Ross is counted as an enemy, then the United States has no friend. If he is a rebel, then there are none loyal. We rely upon the United States to do full justice to John Ross."

On a chilly day, November 11, Hanks, with a wagon and team of horses, took Ross from Park Hill to Van Buren, Arkansas. As the old chief boarded the steamer, American, on the afternoon of the twelfth, Hanks had a premonition that he would never see his friend again.

Ross traveled down the Arkansas River, up the Mississippi and Ohio Rivers to Cincinnati. Taken sick again, he boarded the cars and arrived at 708 South Washington Square in Philadelphia on the 20th of November in a debilitated state of health.

Nursed back to health by his daughter, Annie, the old warrior was back in Washington by early January, 1866. He and his delegates took rooms at Joy's Corner on 8th Street and Pennsylvania Avenue, along with fifty other boarders, including some members of Congress.

On January 15th Secretary of Interior, James Harlan, accompanied Ross and his party to the White House for an interview with President Johnson.

"Ah! Chief Ross," said the President as he extended his hand. "It's good to see you again. Please introduce your companions."

Ross did so. After shaking hands all around, the delegates took seats. Captain James McDonald, one of the delegates, rose. "Mr. President," he said, "I would like to speak of the agitated and dangerous situation in which the Cherokees were placed after Albert Pike, on behalf of the rebellious states, had entered into treaties with all the tribes surrounding us. We were also facing a large rebel army which placed our lives and property in jeopardy. Only then was Chief Ross compelled to face the inevitable. In August of '61 he told us: 'We are in the situation of a man standing alone upon a low naked spot of ground, with the water rising rapidly all around him. He sees the danger, but does not know what to do. If he remains where he is, his only alternative is to be swept away and perish. The tide carries by him, in its mad course, a drifting log. It perchance comes within reach of him. By refusing he is a doomed man. By seizing hold of it he has a chance for his life. He can but perish in the effort, and may be able to keep his head above water until rescued or drift to where he can help himself.'

"Mr. President, the Cherokee people saw and adopted the only means within their reach for self-preservation and an alliance was formed under duress with the rebellious states. A division of our nation was avoided. We drifted along in hardships, dangers, and death, in support of the Union cause until we reached the shore to stand upon the ground of our original rights. The is no case for charging Chief Ross with disloyalty or demanding that he be deposed as was done at the Fort Smith council."

Cooley, who had joined the group, rose in dispute. "I have never used the word depose in regards to Mr. Ross. We did not have the power to depose him. I only said that I would not recognize him as chief of the Cherokee."

"You certainly did use the word depose," Ross cut in, "the word can be found in your published reports." Turning to Johnson, he added. "Mr. President, due to Mr. Cooley's commitment to the rebel Cherokees and his unjust prejudices toward me, I would ask that our further negotiations be conducted with Mr. Harlan."

"That would be most satisfactory to me, Mr. President," Harlan quickly agreed. His interests in acquiring millions of acres of Indian lands along rights-of-way for railroads that would link the midwest with Texas, and his intense interest in building a railroad to the Pacific via the southern route, must not be sabotaged by a contrary Cooley! He would secure his objectives either through Ross or the Watie delegation.

On March 15 Ross submitted a draft of a treaty to Harlan. Ross would cede no lands and would give no rights-of-way for railroads. Instead, he insisted that the treaties with the United States be enforced. Harlan totally rejected the proposal.

The Watie party had no objection to granting all the lands and rights-of-way to railroads, as Harlan requested. They were willing to cede land as reparations for the rebellion. In exchange for their compliance, they wanted the government to divide Cherokee lands into two nations. Cooley supported their request.

On Sunday, March 25, Ross was taken down with pains in his chest. Doctor J.C. Hall found that the chief was bilious. A mustard plaster was applied to his chest and his legs were bathed with hot water. Although confined to bed, he demanded to know from his delegates what had transpired in each negotiation session.

Feigning compassion, Cooley visited Ross in his humble hotel in April. He knew that Ross would do anything to keep his people united. "I learn, Mr. Ross, that you are seventy-five years of age and have served your nation over fifty," observed Cooley.

Drawing himself up in bed with as much dignity as possible, the gray haired Ross replied. "Yes, Sir. I am an old man and have served my people a long time. My people have kept me in the harness, not of my own seeking, but of their own free choice. I have never deceived them. I have done the best I could, and today, upon this bed of sickness, my heart approves all I have done."

On June 13 Cooley concluded negotiations with the Watie faction and sent the proposed treaty to President Johnson. The rebel Cherokees were elated. Ross had relapsed and was expected to die. After an interview with the president, they were in high spirits. Their elation did not last long. Johnson refused to sign their document.

On July 11 a weary Ross signed his last will and testament. At one time a wealthy man, in his will he bequeathed to his relatives a dozen silver spoons, a dress, a gold pencil, a few gifts of fifty dollars each, and his wife's breast pin.

Eventually, the Cherokee delegates and the United States officials came to an agreement. Though not thoroughly satisfactory in its terms to either of the discordant Cherokee factions, on July 19, 1866 a treaty was signed. In the end Ross agreed to permit rights-of-way for two railroad tracks, accepted a lower price for the Neutral Land, and granted equal citizenship to freedmen.

$$* \qquad * \qquad * \qquad *$$

With daughter, Annie, guiding a tremulous hand, Ross signed the treaty from his bed on July 27, 1866.

Early Wednesday evening, August 1, with Annie by his bedside, his questions came weak and halting. "All my life I have tried to serve my people, my country, and my God. Have I failed? Has it all been for naught?"

"Shush, father. You have fought the good fight; you have not failed. The United States government recognizes you as the Principle Chief of the Cherokee and your ultimate lifelong goal has been achieved...the Cherokees remain one nation!"

With that, the old warrior breathed his last.

*   *   *   *

The first funeral service was held at Jay's Hotel in Washington. The following Sunday services were held at the Grace Methodist Episcopal Church in Wilmington. With loyal Cherokee delegates serving as pall bearers, Ross's body was laid to rest in the Stapler family plot near his beloved Mary.

The Cherokee National Council, at its next session, decreed that Ross's body should be returned to Park Hill. On that solemn occasion, William P. Ross, said of his uncle. "We claim not for John Ross exemption from error and imperfection, but believe that he enjoyed in an eminent degree a power of intellect and endurance, a tenacity of purpose and an earnestness of soul which belong only to great men, qualities which impress themselves upon the character of the day, in which their possessors live, and send an influence far down the stream of time."

In early May of 1967 William P. Ross, Jesse Bushyhead, and Riley Keys returned the chief's coffin to Tahlequah where it lay in state at the male seminary until June 1. On a small rise, a short distance from where Rose Cottage once stood, Ross's body was interred. E.J. Mock, a Moravian minister, conducted the last rites. Before the casket of his uncle, William P. Ross delivered his final reflections. "It is proper, that here, should his dust mingle with kindred dust, and that a suitable memorial should rise, to mark the spot where repose the bones of our greatest chieftain. It will keep alive within our bosoms a spirit of patriotism. It will impart strength and hope in the hour of adversity. It will teach us to beware of domestic strife and division. It will serve to unite us more closely in peace, in concord, and in devotion to the common welfare. It will soften our asperities and excite the thoughtful youth of our land to patience, to perseverance, to success, and to renown."

EPILOGUE

Lesser men would have quit. Opposed by a president who commanded the public will; exploited by politicians, whose avarice exceeded principles and who regarded treaties with Indians as nothing; and betrayed by a brother and life-long friends, lesser men would have buckled in spirit. Defeat followed defeat but John Ross never faltered in striving for what he believed to be right. He never lost sight of the welfare of his people and he never sacrificed the interests of his nation to expediency. His works are inseparable from the history of the Cherokee people.

Stand Watie signed a surrender document on June 25, 1865. He was the last Confederate general to give up. He lived a full and active life after the war. He died on September 9, 1871 and was buried in Polson's Cemetery in Delaware County, Oklahoma.

Sam Houston died on Sunday, 26 July 1863 after a distinguished career as general, governor of Tennessee and Texas and the first United States Senator from the state of Texas. He was buried at Oakwood Cemetery in Huntsville, Texas.

Elias Cornelius Boudinot died 27 September 1890.

978-0-595-39588
0-595-39588-0

Printed in the United States
54582LVS00005B/100-117